PRAISE FOR LEE MA

"I guarantee you'll want to devour *The Desire Card* series in one glorious, heart-pounding sitting."

LAURA BENEDICT, EDGAR NOMINATED
AUTHOR OF *THE STRANGER INSIDE*

"A compulsively addicting thriller series."

INDIEREADER

ALL SINS FULFILLED

THE DESIRE CARD BOOK THREE

LEE MATTHEW GOLDBERG

ROUGH
EDGES
PRESS

All Sins Fulfilled
Paperback Edition
Copyright © 2022 (as revised) Lee Matthew Goldberg

Rough Edges Press
An Imprint of Wolfpack Publishing
5130 S. Fort Apache Rd. 215-380
Las Vegas, NV 89148

roughedgespress.com

This book is a work of fiction. Any references to historical events, real people or real places are used fictitiously. Other names, characters, places and events are products of the author's imagination, and any resemblance to actual events, places or persons, living or dead, is entirely coincidental.

All rights reserved. No part of this book may be reproduced by any means without the prior written consent of the publisher, other than brief quotes for reviews.

Paperback ISBN 978-1-68549-129-1
eBook ISBN 978-1-68549-128-4

ALL SINS FULFILLED

"It is hard to contend against one's heart's desire; for whatever it wishes to have it buys at the cost of soul."

— **Heraclitus**

PROLOGUE

HARRISON STUMBLED INTO CENTRAL PARK clutching the silver briefcase, his body shaking from being hunted. Clouds clogged the sky. The trees seemed like towering creatures. He turned around to see the man in the Humphrey Bogart mask running toward the entrance, a gun bulging from the guy's inside pocket. The man's cold eyes scanned the park, then zeroed in. Harrison took off down a dirt path until he was alone with only the wind ringing in his ears.

He wanted to collapse; he begged himself to just give in. Nature would destroy him soon anyway, and his shins were starting to feel like they'd been repeatedly stabbed. He coughed up an excess of blood and mucus that spilled down a rock. Now he'd gone so far down the trail that he couldn't see where he entered. The sound of footsteps came from all directions. A distorted laugh caused all the nearby pigeons to shoot toward the sky. The laugh was followed by an eerie whistle that became louder and louder as he spun around, expecting to see his pursuer.

A shadow passed behind a tree, bigger than any animal. He propped himself up against a rock, too exhausted to move any farther, closing his eyes and waiting to die. He could see tomorrow's headlines declaring his death as a mugging gone wrong.

"Gracie," he cried, trembling. "Brent, my boy...oh God."

He had pissed himself now, the urine hot and sticky as it trickled down his pants leg. He still held the silver briefcase close to his chest, resolving not to let it go without a fight.

The man in the Bogart mask emerged from behind a tree holding a gun.

"Just hand it over, Mr. Stockton," the man said. The voice box attached to his mouth made him sound robotic, weirdly calm. "You don't want this to get any more complicated than it already has."

The man made a grab for the briefcase, but Harrison held on tight.

"You'll kill me anyway," Harrison yelled, spooking any pigeons that hadn't already flown away.

"Only if you force me to do so."

The man kicked Harrison in the shin, causing him to nearly buckle over. Harrison was thrown to the ground, the man pinning him down. He still managed to hold onto the briefcase as if it was fused to his hand.

"The boss doesn't know about what you've done yet," the man said, hitting Harrison's head against the hard dirt. "Do you understand what that means? That means you can still live. And he'll never find out as long as we get what we're owed."

"Why would you do that for me?" he asked, seeing four masked men spinning around.

The man stepped back and pointed the gun between Harrison's eyes.

"The boss doesn't like when things don't go according to plan. I could be in as much trouble as you for letting this slip-up happen. So let's make this easy for both of us."

Harrison got on one elbow and hoisted himself up.

"Do I have your word?"

The man nodded.

"And my family? My wife...my kids? I wouldn't have to worry about them being hurt?"

"As much as you might think that you are our sole concern, we have an entire organization to run beyond your pitiful life. Now I will count to ten and if you don't hand over the briefcase, I'll put a bullet between your eyes."

Harrison thought about what his life had really amounted to. All the hours he'd slaved at Sanford & Co., making rich people boatloads richer. Getting into the office before dawn and often heading home in the middle of the night. Sacrificing his family, his youth, his sanity. How it had made him into a drinker, a serial gorger of all vices, just so he could forget about what he was losing. After all of that, what did he have left to show?

"...eight...nine...ten," the man said, about to pull the trigger.

"All right, all right."

Harrison handed over the briefcase. The man opened it up and appeared to be satisfied, a smirk visible through his mask.

"I'll leave you with this nugget of wisdom," he said, without putting the gun away. "If what you did manages to compromise us in any way, if there are any ripples, be prepared to come across the boss. He's known to wear a Clark Gable mask." The man's smirk had disappeared. "He only appears when he's ready to bloody his hands. Good day, Mr. Stockton."

"Who are you people? Under the masks, who are you really?"

The man raised the gun over Harrison's head.

"I doubt you'll ever find out," he said, and struck Harrison on the forehead with the handle.

A trickle of blood spilled down Harrison's nose and felt cold on his tongue. He slunk down and rested his cheek against the dirt, watching the man in the mask take off through the trees, the silver briefcase shining like a beam of light snaking through the leaves. And then the man finally disappeared—as if he was nothing more than a nightmare brought to life and extinguished once the fitful dreamer finally woke.

Harrison pressed against his rib cage and felt for his engorged liver. Cursed at it. Wanted to tear it from his stomach. He'd been poisoned from within for too long, his unending punishment for all of his crimes. Blood zigzagged into his eyes as the wound on his forehead opened up even more. With his other hand he reached into his pocket and removed his wallet. A thin metallic card fell from out of a sleeve and sat in a puddle of blood that had collected in the dirt.

THE DESIRE CARD
Any wish fulfilled for the right price.
PRESS below to inquire.

He crumpled it up in his fist since it was responsible for letting these psychopaths into his life. He knew he'd never feel completely settled again, always worried that they might come after him and his family. The Desire Card had caused him to seek out gruesome and despicable wishes. From the instant this devil's temptation had been placed in his hands, his moral compass never stood a chance. So he chucked it into the air and watched it sail over the rocks for some other fool to find.

"I'm sorry, Helene," he mumbled to the wind. He knew he'd have to come clean about everything. His head throbbed, and he recalled a memory from twenty-five years ago. Spying her in the quad at Chilton College drinking a cherry Coke, tan and shapely from field hockey, the entire campus becoming muted except for her. He took a chance by flirting miserably and changing the course of their lives.

She would've been better off if they had never met. In such a short amount of time, he'd fallen so far. Now because of him, people had been sliced up, left for dead, and soon he'd follow them to his own grave. As he drifted off into unconsciousness, he remembered that it all began to spiral out of control on his last day at Sanford & Co. over a month ago, this treacherous path he embarked on, his dark and dried-up destiny.

PART ONE

1

HARRISON SAT OUTSIDE THE OFFICE OF THE Managing Director awaiting his fate. The end of the month meant slash-and-burn time, but he had successfully avoided the axe for twelve months now. Something told him this wasn't going to be lucky number thirteen. After almost twenty years of dedication, he swore he wouldn't beg, wouldn't give that fucker Thom Bartlett any satisfaction in letting him go. Thom, with his faux British accent even though he lived in the US since he was two, his nose up the CEO's ass at every chance, his chastising of Harrison's "extracurricular activities," even though Thom was guilty of similar vices. Harrison stared at this fucker's door, as if by monitoring he could will it to stay closed and ensure that he'd forever remain a part of Sanford & Co.'s Mergers and Acquisitions team.

A sharp pain in his abdomen caused him to pitch forward. His stomach churned as a flood of bile crept up his throat. Thom's door now appeared so out of focus that for a second Harrison forgot where he was.

"Bad lunch?" his buddy Whit whispered, from a nearby seat.

Thom's ancient secretary glanced up at them from her fury of typing and went back to punishing the keys.

Harrison clutched his stomach and let out a stifled belch. The air now smelled like he'd been dining on garbage. His chronic halitosis had only been getting worse. He could barely recall the last time he'd kissed Helene like when they were young with an appetite to devour. At most he received a peck while she held her breath. It's not like her body hadn't also changed, and yet he still found her a knockout: whip-smart and sophisticated, alluring whenever she was in deep thought and chewed on the earpiece of her reading glasses. Only once had he participated in a particular "extracurricular activity" outside of their marriage. It was something he instantly regretted—but she had been treating him like a pariah in the bedroom for almost a year, and he found himself in the arms of another. So now he let her give those little digs about his hygiene, one of the small pleasures she seemed to have during the scant few hours a day when he was home.

Whit seemed to inch his chair away from Harrison's death burp and occupied himself with the new Breitling hanging from his wrist. Here the two were about to be sliced up and gutted and Whit had spent last weekend dropping ten K on a watch. Sure Harrison indulged in more luxuries than most and hated his old Tag enough to go splurging, but unlike Whit, he had two kids in uptown private schools to worry about.

"Drinks at Mobeley's later tonight?" Whit asked, placing his hand on Harrison's shoulder. "Whatever the outcome of this summons might be?"

Harrison nodded with tired eyes.

"You're a VP here, Harry. Higher up on the rung than me. You've got a better chance of surviving."

Whit's hand still massaged Harrison's shoulder, but his encouragement was not convincing. He had probably expected a similar consoling reply, except the room was spinning too much for Harrison to care.

"You're not looking well," Whit said. Thom's secretary seemed to glance up from her typing again to nod in agreement. The two of them caught each other's eye, as if they were conspiring against him. Well, we couldn't all look like Whit. Just a few years younger but still with a full head of thick black hair only slightly graying at the temples, something that made him appear even more distinguished. Pecs and abs that he never shut up about. A terror on the racquetball courts who slaughtered Harrison every time. The son of a well-known surgeon at NYU Medical with a hot Japanese wife barely out of her twenties whose goal in life was to be at his beck and call. Whit had been made an associate two years earlier than Harrison and was able to maintain a rapport with the higher ups that Harrison could never manage: calling the CEO Dougie to his face instead of Mr. Sanford and still having a job the next day.

The secretary picked up the phone on her desk while still typing away.

"Certainly, Mr. Bartlett," she chirped into the receiver, then turned her disapproving gaze to Harrison. "Mr. Bartlett will see you now, Mr. Stockton."

Harrison gathered up his briefcase and overcoat. He had to hold onto the seat as he stood, his feet pivoting and almost sending him to the ground.

"Gotta watch those martini lunches," Whit said, slapping Harrison on the back and pushing him toward his doom.

Harrison put one foot in front of the other slowly, avoiding Thom's inevitable decision for as long as possible.

Even if he wound up being let go today, an outsider looking in might assume that his life was still going well: two decades of marriage, healthy kids, and a fantastic New York apartment, but he felt like he'd been going through the motions for too long. A major chunk had been missing, a spark of excitement, adventure, and meaning. He couldn't put his finger on what it was, just that he desperately longed for it to exist.

As he put his hand on the doorknob and turned, he tried to think of what would make him happy, something he wanted more than anything that would cause him to shoot out of bed every morning with a smile.

He squeezed his eyes shut, willing this desired vision to appear, but all he saw was darkness.

———

Who in their right mind didn't covet Thom Bartlett's office? High floor with downtown skyline views, fluffy clouds outside of the windows, a wet bar that Harrison eyed. Some good Scotch had already been opened. Harrison had forced himself to keep sober during a gobbled lunch of an Italian sub without his trusty flask to chase it down. Now his hands trembled at the thought of that Scotch burning his throat.

"Can I offer you something?" Thom asked, indicating the bar with a grand sweep of his arm, as if to say,

Yes, I have a bar in my office, which you, dear sir, never had here and regrettably never will.

"I might as well," Harrison coughed, scooting over and pouring two shots' worth into a glass. He sat across from Thom and put the comforting drink to his lips.

Thom fiddled with a stack of papers in a folder on his desk. He looked up at Harrison through the thick frames he kept low on his sloping nose, almost touching his top lip.

"So Sanford & Co. has become swollen lately. We're too big for our own good right now and need to restructure—"

"Just spit it out," Harrison said, knocking back half the glass of Scotch.

"I'm sorry, Harrison. We're going to have to let you go, effective today."

Thom delivered this news while fixing his Windsor knot, which Harrison figured had taken him numerous tries that morning to perfect. Harrison wanted to grab him by that knot and choke his tiny little bird head until it popped off.

"I've given practically twenty years to this firm," he said, running his hands through his thinning hair. "I sleep here, I eat here. I barely exist at home anymore."

"It's the same for all of us, mate."

"I'm not your fucking mate," Harrison said, finishing the rest of the Scotch and starting to sway.

"Old boy, I am not the villain here. Every firm on the Street has been feeling this strain since the economy collapsed. Now we're offering you a solid severance package, which I think is more than generous. I'll also save you the spectacle of having security escort you out."

"What was Sanford's reason?" Harrison asked quietly, not wanting to hear the answer but knowing he'd be unable to leave without one.

Thom had already started pushing the folder across the desk, shutting Harrison up, getting this over with. His face looked exhausted from delivering executions.

"We've heard from some clients," he said, taking off his glasses and pinching the bridge of his nose.

"Heard what...?"

"Have you looked at yourself in the mirror lately, huh, Harry?" he asked, his voice rising to the level of an uncomfortable squeal. "Your skin, mate...sorry, but you're looking rather yellow, and your eyes, well there's this permanent creaminess to them...I'm just using the client's words—"

"Which client?"

"Which one hasn't mentioned this is more like it."

Harrison went to respond but now Thom was on a roll.

"As a VP, this is a face-to-face business. I go for manicures, mate, you think I like it—it's a requirement. Maybe if you cut back on the drink...."

"I've advised some huge mergers here over the years." Harrison pointed at Thom with his empty glass. "I didn't realize this was only a pretty boy's game."

"You've let some messy pitchbooks slide through recently, as well."

"Shouldn't the analysts be blamed for creating them?"

"Don't think they haven't been dealt with, too."

"So maybe I've gotten lax with a couple of pitchbooks for smaller clients, but never any of the big ones."

"When was the last time you've been to a doctor, Harry?"

"Doctors," Harrison said, brushing them all away with a flick of his wrist. He had always believed that no matter what, doctors tried to find something wrong with you so you'd give them more business. And yeah, his skin had developed a yellowish hue as of late and sometimes his gut felt like it was rotting. Varicose veins had multiplied along his thighs and there were moments when he'd lose balance and have to dry heave in an empty stall once no one else was around, but he was a professional drinker like his dad had been, and that son of a bitch had put back a liter of gin and a pack of smokes a day up until the ripe old age of eighty-eight. Hell, who needed to live longer than that anyway? Life could be brutal, and if some booze, smokes, and pills provided a relief from the banality of it all, then screw any doctor who'd tell him otherwise.

Thom tapped on the folder to indicate it was time to wrap this up.

"I have to make sure that you understand what's in the package," he said, pushing it closer to Harrison until it practically fell off the desk.

Harrison opened it up and flipped through: six months' pay, benefits as well, blah, blah, blah. He closed it and went to throw it in his briefcase.

"Tut," Thom said, wagging his finger. "There's something you missed that Mr. Sanford wanted to make sure you saw."

Harrison reopened the folder and spied a card clipped to the first page.

THE DESIRE CARD

Any wish fulfilled for the right price.
PRESS below to inquire.

"What the hell is a Desire Card?"

Thom reached over and unclipped the card.

"You have been a valued employee here. Mr. Sanford wanted to make sure you understood that we're not parting on bad terms. This is what's best for everyone."

Thom handed him the card. Harrison turned it over and over with his stubby fingers.

"It's like...a phone or something too?"

"Of sorts, just to keep their network as secure and exclusive as possible. We didn't include this in everyone's package, so you know. This is an organization that Mr. Sanford has a long history with, very hush-hush obviously, very elite. If you want something, *anything*, they have the power to make it happen."

"Can they get me my job back?"

"Cute, Harrison, don't ever lose that charm."

Thom reached over to take the empty glass away.

"So tonight, Harry, instead of drowning your sorrows in a bottle, give the card a try and have them ring you up a girl I guarantee you'll enjoy. Or whatever else you wish. We promise we'll give a glowing report to any future job prospects so consider this the start of a paid vacation."

Thom stuck out his hand to shake, the nails manicured, no rogue cuticles to speak of; but the hand was delicate and unassuming, not someone with the power to hold Harrison's life in his palm, a meager messenger. Harrison slipped the Desire Card in his pocket and shook Thom's hand, squeezing hard as Thom grimaced.

"And see a doctor," Thom replied, giddy now that this ordeal was over.

"Watch out, you'll be gutted next," Harrison said, rising and feeling his legs give out. He collapsed back into the chair as Thom let out a spurt of a laugh.

"You all right there, mate?"

"Piss on England."

Harrison gave standing up another try. He gripped Thom's desk for support. Thom looked worried that Harrison might take the whole desk down with him, but Harrison was doing his best to maintain even though it felt like he was viewing Thom through the wrong end of a telescope.

"You can go ahead and send Mr. Carmichael in," Thom said, fixing his Windsor knot again that had become slightly askew. "Best to Helene and the children."

Harrison slung his coat over his arm and gripped his briefcase as he headed for the door. After a few steps, his vision became cloudier and he could feel the creamy tears falling from his eyes. They stung his cheeks as he grappled with the doorknob and lurched into the hallway.

In the front office, Whit was leaning over the secretary's desk; the two engaged in hushed words that stopped once Harrison emerged. Harrison ran his finger from one side of his neck to the other. Whit gave him a solemn nod back, but Harrison couldn't hold it in any longer and puked up the barely digested Scotch.

"Oh my!" he heard the secretary say.

He stared at his sickness bubbling on the floor, a mix of half-chewed capicola and salami in an amber soup with specks of dark red blood throughout, the clots of blood so dark they looked like tar. He wiped his mouth and trudged past all the onlookers toward the elevators outside, glad that a part of him would remain embedded in Sanford & Co.'s carpet.

As the elevator arrived and he stepped inside, he wished for the undoing of everyone involved in his termination, knowing that only their collective downfall could get him to shoot out of bed with a smile.

CHAUNCEY, THE FAMILY'S GROSSLY OVERWEIGHT cat, greeted Harrison with a wheeze when he returned home. He had spoiled the cat ever since they'd gotten him as a kitten before Gracie and Brenton were born. Chauncey ate all of Harrison's leftovers, ranging from filet mignon, to *foie gras*, to heaps and heaps of ice cream, and now the cat's belly had distended and swept against the floor as he prowled over and curled around Harrison's leg. Helene often chided him on the excessive feeding that she deemed animal cruelty.

"Chaunce," he said, bending down and feeling his knees crack as he tickled the cat's neck. Chauncey purred in response and then dragged himself away, moaning with each brutal step. Harrison could sympathize with the cat's plight.

He put down his briefcase and stared down the foyer toward the row of windows that offered views of Central Park. The apartment was on Fifth Avenue but not on a high floor and didn't have the luxury of anonymity. Below, a fire truck roared down the street, its spinning red lights beaming into the living room.

Last year Helene had talked about upgrading, since a four-bedroom had become available fifteen floors higher. That way she could have a home office, a respite from working in the bedroom. He'd asked what she could possibly need a home office for, especially since she didn't work and only donated her time to charity, to which she replied that "charity is work, something far more important than the buying and selling of others like *you* do." Always with the sharp tongue, his Helene, but his tongue could be sharper. "Well, if your *work* at UNESCO can pay for the exorbitant increase in maintenance then by all means let's go ahead and call the moving vans."

As if Helene had sensed that he'd been thinking maliciously about her, she sauntered past the foyer with a fistful of envelopes and did a double take upon seeing him at the door.

"Why it's barely five o'clock," she said, narrowing her eyes. The earliest he ever returned home was usually ten or eleven and that was on an exceptionally light day at the office. "Are you picking something up?"

The two made a hesitant dance toward each other as he leaned in for a kiss and she gave him her cheek.

"No, I'm home."

She tilted her head and cleared her throat in suspicion.

"I have an auction to get ready for tonight so we'll be eating early. I picked up a selection from Citarella."

"Sounds lovely," he said, his tongue forming the words: "I was fired," but he couldn't tell her yet since he wasn't ready to admit it to himself.

He staggered closer to her again, putting his arm around her waist and wanting a never-ending hug. She recoiled, unused to his affections, as he tucked his chin into the nape of her neck and let out a deep exhale. The peachy scent from her shampoo became engulfed by his fetid odor, and she waved her hand in front of her nose.

"Your breath these last few weeks," she said, slipping out of his grasp. She shoved the envelopes under her arm and scuttled away. "I left that mouthwash my dentist had recommended in the medicine cabinet."

A soccer ball flew from one side of the living room to the other.

"Brenton!" she said, clutching her neck. "What have I told you about balls in this apartment?"

Not too long ago, Helene would have been unfazed by a soccer ball flying past her nose. She used to have a sense of humor, but ever since she started at UNESCO, she began to speak only in terms like "sustainable development," or "the observance of human rights," or "the alleviation of poverty." What had happened to important things like a good long lay at the end of a hard day, or a stupid mindless comedy on TV that once brought tears to her eyes? When had life become so serious for the two of them?

She'd been his party girl back when they met at Chilton, a field hockey star who pounded beers better than any of his frat brothers. She pulled him away from his economic textbooks, alluring as always in her oversized sweatshirts and the Umbro athletic shorts she wore everywhere. She had taken him back to her parents in Greenwich for Thanksgiving after a few great hookups, and he thought her home looked like the White House. Her father had even re-created a grand staircase right out of a plantation mansion. He was the CEO of some international corporation, and Helene always spoke of him shuttling off to exotic locales. She gushed with delight at the kind of power her father yielded and the fact she was the only one able to melt his gruff exterior.

When they sat down to dinner, Harrison was in awe that a cook prepared their meals and everyone had napkins made of cloth with a silver ring to keep them in place. Each family member had a nickname like "Chip" or "Vi" and dressed like the royal family was joining. And then there was Helene, already drunk off of some Bartles & Jaymes wine coolers, wearing flip-flops with her hair in a ponytail, and her father beaming at her like she could do no wrong. When her father glanced over at Harrison, the look he gave was one of disbelief. How could his perfectly lovely daughter possibly bring home such a poor, bumbling creature?

All through dinner, he thought of his parents back in New Haven spending Thanksgiving in front of a football game on their tiny TV, eating yams with Fluffernutter on paper plates with cans of beers in a cooler. The entire room filled with cigarette smoke until a fight would start about who drank the last beer and someone would wind up with a busted lip by the end of the night. Helene would teach him about a life beyond clipped coupons, but never make him feel inferior.

That night after the Howells' golden turkey was finished, the two crammed into Helene's single bed. She wailed theatrically at each of his thrusts and he clamped his hand over her mouth, but she bit his fingers and wailed even louder. He kissed her lopsided smile, her chestnut brown eyes, and the worry line like a dent between her eyebrows. He admitted that he loved her and one day wanted to marry and give her even more than her extraordinarily wealthy parents had: adorn her with big diamonds and take her to tropical islands and make beautiful babies and promise to always make love like this even when they were old and saggy. She kissed him and they devoured each other until the sun rose, wildly planning every detail of their lives together and starting with the name of their first-born child—that it must begin with a "B" after her dying Grandma Bitsy.

As he watched her yell down the hallway after Brenton, he could barely recall the excitement he felt that post-Thanksgiving night. She was no longer that sporty young girl, hopeful of their future. They were adults now who simply put on a show.

"Helene, I was fi—"

Brenton leaped into the room in full soccer gear almost knocking Helene over, his body newly big like a man's and no longer a boy's. Harrison remembered when he'd been fourteen as well and woke up to sore limbs from growing rapidly overnight. Now his son had become the spitting image of his youth, thick and stocky, cheeks always flushed red from a trace of rosacea, but Brenton was more so the clown in the back of the classroom with a farting noise erupting from his armpit.

"Sorry, Mom," the kid called out and gave the same double take that Helene had upon seeing Harrison.

"Dad?" he said, picking up the soccer ball. "What are you doing home while it's still light out?"

Brenton's tone was accusatory, as if his father was a passing stranger in the hallway, an apparition he'd see out of the corner in his eye in the middle of the night when Harrison would return home and sometimes stand at the foot of the bedroom door watching him sleep.

"I decided to come home early today, is that a crime?" Harrison said, managing to make himself laugh, but the laughs hurt as they erupted from his mouth, so he stopped them abruptly.

Brenton gave his father the same glare as Helene, the two of them locked in a symbiotic relationship that Harrison could never dream of possessing. Even as a young boy, Brenton had clung to Helene in an unhealthy way, like he'd crumble every time she was out of sight. The two even shared a gibberish language that Harrison always knew was slander against him, mother and son spouting gobbledygook and pointing at Harrison with grins. Then Gracie had been born, and of course she'd been young enough to pick up that gobbledygook and align with the obvious power—the people who actually lived in their apartment and didn't just use it as a place to sleep between work hours.

"Uh, not a crime, Dad, just that we haven't all had dinner together in like a decade."

A scathing remark, but sadly, true. Dinner was never a daily Stockton tradition, at least not with him present. Though he didn't like to admit it, he was jealous of Helene's relationship with the kids, mostly because parenting came naturally for her while he always felt like an understudy substituting for the children's real father. It was simpler when they were tiny, make a funny face and they loved you for hours. But since his own parents had only alternated between abuse, neglect, and worst of all, indifference, he found the concept of an evolving family strange. And now since he'd established his role as a provider who occasionally expressed fatherly concern, it was easier to back away from trying to be anything more and save himself the embarrassment.

"No balls in this house," he said, snatching the soccer ball away from Brenton and resting it against his stomach that groaned like it was being attacked from within.

"I gotta practice like every second. Rufus Laynor at Dalton has been gunning for me. He did this today."

Brenton lifted up his shirt to reveal what looked like an awful rug burn down the side of his chest.

"Another boy did this to you?" Helene asked.

Brenton rolled his eyes. "Yeah, I was heading straight for the goal when he knocked me down like he always tries to do."

Harrison was about to speak up to give his son advice, but Helene interrupted. She was the star athlete, the physical one in the family. Harrison had always been the uncoordinated one—his college years spent attacking pizza pies rather than anyone on the field. She used to say he had a football player's build and should try out for the team; now he had rounded into his forties still refusing to ever work out, his body starting to look like a melting candle.

"Back at Chilton," Helene began, "there was this girl at Connecticut College, this real bitch who had it out for me."

Helene stuck out her leg and pointed to a comma-shaped scar on her right calf.

"She did this with her field hockey stick."

"I know this story, Mom," Brenton said, but his tone

wasn't annoyed. He smiled at his mother like he always did.

"So before our divisional game, I went up to her and said that if she ever hit me with her stick again, I would do everything in my power to destroy her because I knew the terrible secret she was hiding."

Harrison had also heard this story before but couldn't remember the outcome.

"What was the secret?" he asked.

Brenton and Helene both looked at him like they had forgotten he was in the room and murmured some gobbledygook under their breaths.

"Duh, Dad, Mom didn't know any secret, she figured that the girl had something she didn't want anyone to know."

"Everyone has secrets, Brenton," Helene said, petting his messy hair. "Even boys, even men."

She glanced over at Harrison as if she knew he'd been fired. The room slanted as he leaned against the wall for support. He blinked wildly, his heart thumping at the thought of his wife's mind-reading abilities. He knew he had other secrets that Helene could be referring to. He watched mother and son locked together in a loving moment: the kid's head on her shoulder, condescending smiles on their faces.

"Let's wash up and eat, today's a regular holiday with your father home for once." Helene kissed Brenton on his sweaty head before the two swiveled around toward the kitchen, arm in arm.

The two glasses of Scotch that Harrison had gulped at a bar on the way back rumbled in his belly, his stomach seeming to condemn him for treating it so cruelly; but this time he managed to keep the creeping vomit down.

———

Harrison wasn't hungry at all when they sat down to dinner. Normally he was the type prone to eating anything unhealthy in sight, but the thought of digesting the chicken Française and crab cakes that Helene had picked up made his stomach churn so violently that it felt like an alien trying to push through his navel.

Gracie had joined them at the dining room table still in her pink tutu from ballet practice earlier that afternoon. She sat poised with her back straight against the chair, slicing each bite of chicken with precision and chewing with her mouth closed, the opposite of Brenton who was shoving each crab cake whole into his mouth.

"Dad, you're not eating anything," she said, as he swam his fork around the plate. When had she stopped calling him Daddy? She used to force herself to stay awake till he came home at night, so excited when he walked through the door. Back then he occasionally returned before midnight. It seemed like yesterday, but he knew it had been years. She'd only been about three, barely a personality yet, but even at that age she was a dancer, leaping across the room and landing on her toes, never crying when she fell. She loved to latch onto his neck so he could swing her around like the monkeys did in the Central Park Zoo. The top of her head always smelled like freshly cut flowers. Now he stared at her, realizing that he hadn't truly looked at her in a long time. She had put her hair up in the kind of bun an old librarian would have. Her neck was so long and thin that the bones along her spine showed. A very determined child, much like he had been at that age.

"I had a big lunch," Harrison replied. "So how are things going with ballet?"

Helene caught his eye, telling him not to bring it up. Gracie sank into her plate of food.

"I think Ms. Elliot will make me chorus again."

"Well, have you been practicing hard?"

"Yes, Dad!" She looked up toward the ceiling as her eyes became teary. "But Becca Danshore is just...she always gets the lead."

"Honey, every part is an important one," Helene said. "There will be plenty of lead roles in your future."

Helene reached out to touch her daughter's hand. Gracie sighed and placed another small bite of chicken between her lips.

"Your mother is right, Gracie—"

"Oh, Dad, whatever. You've never even come to any of my performances."

Helene nodded in agreement.

"Oh, shit." Brenton laughed. "Gracie slammed you, Dad."

"I would come to every one of your recitals if I could, but work..."

Harrison stopped himself. This would be the perfect time to tell them all the truth about being fired, to turn their accusations into sympathy. He pictured his family dwarfing him with hugs and support, he pictured himself at one of Gracie's recitals as he clapped foolishly at her curtain call, he pictured being under the covers with Helene later on after what felt like eons apart. She would say that she didn't care anymore about his high six-figure salary, or about maintaining their status, or even about what her father might say if the family downgraded to—God forbid—an outer borough. She never married him for his money and would swear that nothing had changed in her mind.

"I was fired today," he said, looking into his wife's chestnut brown eyes, his body going cold as he waited for a response.

Everyone at the table started talking at once, and it was hard to take in what each person was trying to say. Harrison parsed out that Gracie was concerned about being able to continue at her school, Chapin, knowing that she didn't have "any other friends with *both* parents not working." Helene had responded to Gracie's complaints by stating that she "*does* work, and works very hard," then proceeded to launch into a speech about the role of charity in today's selfish society. Brenton, as always, took the news as a joke and formed his hand into the shape of gun.

"Pow! Fired!" Brenton said, while Helene grabbed at his pretend gun with one hand and put a finger to her lips with the other to silence Gracie.

"Is this because of how you've let yourself go?" she asked Harrison, nodding at his yellowing skin and bloated cheeks, his belly straining his belt.

"I need to use the bathroom," he said, feeling an overwhelming urge to urinate, and flew into the bathroom off the living room. He stood over the toilet, pissing for what felt like hours, dizzy and supporting himself by holding onto the sink. He hated to admit that even his urine smelled worse than usual, his whole body deciding to turn against him. He flushed the toilet, put down the lid, and sat. He wanted to cry but couldn't. He clenched his fists begging for a release, but nothing happened, his cheeks bone dry. When he opened the door, Helene was in the hallway.

"I made the kids go watch TV," she said, pulling him into the bedroom and shutting the door.

He sat down on the edge of the bed with his head in his hands.

"I'm sorry for what I said about you in front of them. But you don't look well—"

"We're all getting old," he said, but then wished he had responded in a different way. Her fingers darted to her hair, covering up the strands of gray by her left ear.

"You don't seem healthy," she said. "You haven't in a while."

"I was fired today. I really don't want to talk about anything else."

"You're right."

She stepped toward him and put a hesitant hand on his back.

"What does this mean for us? Should I take a leave from UNESCO? I could dig out my old résumé and look for something in publishing like I did before we had Brenton. Or I could talk to my father. Let me at least ask for his advice—"

"No," he said, swatting her hand away. "I refuse to have anything change. We have a ton in investments, and they gave me six months' severance including medical for all of us. That means six months to find another job."

"Maybe you should think of something other than finance? Bill Apton's son was laid off over a year ago and can't get an interview—"

"Bill Apton's son is just a kid. I have twenty years of experience."

"Well, if you need to take a pay cut or a demotion, don't let your pride get in the way."

She had opened up the closet and selected a dress still in its dry cleaning bag.

"What are you doing?"

She removed the blouse she was wearing and slid down her pants.

"I'm getting ready," she said, taking a navy blue dress out of the dry cleaning bag and slipping it over her head.

"You're going to that auction?"

"Harrison, I cannot be a no-show. Caroline Hendrest is waiting for me to slip-up to she can tell the members of the board that my work is unnecessary and a waste of time and resources. That witch of a woman has actually used those words before."

"Stay here with me tonight," he said, rising on shaky legs and helping her zip up her dress. He took in another great whiff of her peach shampoo.

"We'll have plenty of time to discuss things tomorrow if you're not going to work."

She dashed over to the bureau, picked up a vial of perfume, and sprayed it into the air. He walked into the spray of her perfume, hoping it would mask his scent. He pulled her close to him, wanting her as much as he used to back when they were dumb college kids looking for an isolated spot in the library to screw.

"Harrison, really," she said, trying to laugh while removing herself from his grasp, but he was holding on too tight. "Harrison!"

She pushed him until he finally released her.

"I just want to...*be* with you. Is that so wrong?"

She stood in front of the mirror trying on a necklace made of diamonds and then ran a brush through her hair.

"Were there any other reasons they gave for firing you?" she asked, brushing her hair more vigorously now and eyeing him through the mirror.

"The same things they probably told everyone."

"You've worked pretty much until midnight every night since you started there, how could they possibly base it on job performance?"

"Thom Bartlett said that I'd been getting lax with the pitchbooks."

She turned around, holding the brush as if she was about to throw it at him.

"Were you always at the office when you said you were working late?"

He felt his legs give out. She had to have known about all his vices over the years: the boozing, the Adderall/Ritalin cocktails, that night he cheated on her six months ago. He'd been out with Whit and Thom Bartlett after brokering a huge merger and one bottle of Cristal led to five. He usually played wingman to Whit's carousing, hung back and watched his friend play out fantasies with girls whose eyes sparkled at the exaggerated mention of a bottomless black card. He knew that one slip up, one chance affair, might lead to an addiction, so he was content to live vicariously through a scoundrel like Whit; but that night, a group of girls had come over to their table and one of them wound up in Harrison's lap. She was so young, her future limitless. Deep down he felt his own had an endpoint, which might come sooner than he expected.

Her skin was smooth and her nose crinkled when she laughed at everything he said. He was amazed that someone so lovely would even show interest. She whispered in his ear about getting a hotel room. All he desired was to feel wanted, if for a moment, and Whit and Thom weren't helping out by egging him on. So he did. The worst of part of it was that he barely remembered a thing, the girl a blur grinding on top of him. In the morning, she had disappeared from his hotel suite once daylight revealed her inebriated decision, and he had to pop whatever pills he had on him to make it through another sixteen-hour workday.

"Of course I was always at the office," he said to Helene, not wanting to think about that night. "I gave my life to Sanford & Co."

"I know," she said, holding up her hand to calm him down since she could see he was getting upset. She put down the brush and picked up some diamond earrings off of the dresser.

"I bought those for you from Tiffany's for our anniversary," he said.

She nodded as she put each one on.

"Each was about a week's salary, I believe."

"Spending like that has to stop for now," she said. "Understand?"

His hands were trembling, and his left side went numb. He figured he was having a stroke, but then the sensation passed. He just needed a drink.

"I'm going to grab a beer with Whit if you're still headed to the auction. He got the axe today, too."

"I didn't expect you home so Brenton was already set to watch Gracie," she said, and walked into the bathroom.

"Helene?"

She popped her head out of the bathroom with a mascara brush in her hand. He wanted to throw her down on the bed, to find comfort in the thrill of a quivering pause from reality. He couldn't help but imagine his time with her was slipping away. Would she dare leave him? She certainly had her father's financial backing if she ever so desired—he imagined Jay would be thrilled to swoop in with a chance to provide for his darling "Helly" again. The kids would also be old enough to handle the news. But he knew he'd never find someone like her again. Women in Manhattan liked security. They didn't like to hear about some mid-forties guy who was in-between jobs, his money all tied up in divorce lawyers, living out of some studio in a Yorkville walk-up because it was all his accountant advised he could afford.

"What is it, Harrison?" she asked, growing impatient.

"If you come home early tonight, we could be...intimate."

She tapped her fingers against the doorframe, as if considering, but she was really stalling.

"I'm going to be exhausted after dealing with Caroline at the auction. I'll see you in the morning."

What if he charged into the bathroom, threw her up on the sink, and ripped off that navy dress? Would she fight him off, or even worse, resent him even more after he came from a few pitiful thrusts? Their anniversary had been the last time they even had sex. She'd been tipsy from a ridiculously expensive bottle of Château D'Yquem at Le Perigord. She *loved* the Tiffany earrings, possibly even loved him again that night since he always took off work on their anniversary. She lost him at Christmases, during birthdays, even at funerals she stood alone, but never their anniversary. She had come home and gotten into her oversized Chilton sweatshirt, put her hair in a side ponytail like she was twenty all over again, and welcomed him into bed still wearing the diamonds.

That had been almost ten months ago.

———

After Helene left, Harrison got out a tumbler of rye before calling Whit. Thinking about the night of his anniversary had gotten him all riled up, but he knew that being with Helene in that way was no more than a wish right now. And while he usually only played wingman to Whit, after a day like today he vowed to let himself go wild again, pop bottles of Cristal until a girl might wind up in his lap and he could feel something... anything again. It was better than being alone with a medicine cabinet fill of uppers, downers, and other ones to make him go sideways.

He sipped the rye as Whit's phone rang and rang. Just as he thought it would go to voicemail, Whit picked up.

"Harry," he said. "Look, I can't really talk right now."

Harrison eyed the tumbler that was a lot less full than when he'd taken it from the liquor cabinet.

"It's time for some commiserating, man. We can call for a car to drive us around. Maybe even talk to some girls to, ya know forget our sorrows. C'mon, what do you say?"

The line went silent. Harrison thought that Whit had hung up.

"Yeah, about that, buddy. So it turns out I wasn't let go."

"How come that fucker Bartlett wanted to see you then?"

The line went silent again.

"Uh...I might as well tell you since you're bound to hear it through the grapevine."

Harrison gripped the phone tightly, fearing the response.

"They gave me a promotion."

"Son of a—"

"Listen, Harry, I didn't know this was going to happen."

"What's the promotion?"

"I was literally floored when Bartlett gave me the news."

"What's the promotion, you shady fuck?"

"Whoa, slow down there. Okay, yeah, so they made me VP."

"They gave you my position, didn't they?"

"Buddy, I can't tell you how bad I feel...."

Harrison threw the phone to the floor. When it didn't break, he went over to Helene's dresser and launched a vial of her perfume at the wall. He could still hear Whit talking on the other end so he picked up the phone and ended the call. Whit had probably been angling for Harrison's job all along. Their nights spent drinking out of tumblers until dawn, to the times Whit listened to complaints about Helene and the kids, even inviting Harrison to racquetball and slaughtering him in front of Sanford, all had been designed to accelerate

Whit's own career and leave a declining star like Harrison in his dust. Whit had to have been the one to tell Thom Bartlett about any upset clients. The notion that any of those clients had ever spoken up about Harrison's appearance must've all been fabrications.

Harrison felt his throat closing up and downed some more rye until he swayed and swayed. He'd go out anyway and have the night of his life, even without a wingman. He grabbed his suit jacket and fumbled in his pockets looking for his keys, but he found the Desire Card in his front pocket instead. He stared at it, completely having forgotten about its existence, and then pressed the button at the bottom on a whim.

"Hello," said a deep voice after three rings.

"I was given this card..." he started to say.

"What do you desire?" the deep voice asked.

The hairs on the back of his neck rose. He realized that the voice had been digitally altered like on television shows when someone with a blurred face was being interviewed. He almost ended the call out of fear, but he did desire an uninhibited night away from his mind, from his life, from his plummeting decay.

"A girl," Harrison gulped.

He was a gawky teenager the last time he gotten a girl from an escort service. She liked to come to his dorm room so they could do it in his bunk bed. She instructed him well since he had no idea what he was doing. Sometimes she let him hold her afterwards while she painted her toenails. He was able to hold onto her for as long as it took them to dry. He had no clue what a real relationship was so he liked to imagine that she was actually his girl. At the time, the feelings he had toward her seemed like enough to make a man truly happy.

On the other end of the phone he could hear whispering, but he couldn't make out what was being said.

"Any preferences?" the voice asked.

"I'd like to be...surprised."

He heard more whispering coming from the other end.

"She'll be at the London Hotel in room 12G, price is a thousand an hour, five thousand for the night."

Harrison thought of the obnoxious Breitling dangling from Whit's wrist, obviously a reward the guy had given himself last weekend to celebrate his promotion to VP. Well, he figured he deserved a reward too. Either that or someone better hide all the knives in the apartment because he was afraid he'd charge right over to Whit's place and go gutting.

"I can pay by check," he said, taking another swallow of the rye.

"Then it is done," said the voice on the other line before hanging up.

3

IN THE CAB ON HIS WAY OVER TO THE LONDON Hotel, Harrison thought of his freshmen-year roommate at college, Nagesh Patel, and the first time Nagesh had gotten that escort girl for him. This had been during the pre-Helene era. As a teenager at a New Haven public high school, Harrison had been too uncomfortable in his rapidly growing body to make any moves on the tough girls who carried razorblades in their big hair. Therefore, he had come to Chilton a star-struck virgin. Nagesh had a very different early upbringing in Bombay, but like Harrison, he'd spent high school in the States and had also never touched a boob. Skinny and light-skinned, Nagesh smiled constantly like a car salesman and had eyes that always looked surprised. Besides a slight accent, he was as American as they came. The boys' dorm room was an explosion of New England Patriots paraphernalia, Van Halen posters, and a giant eagle taped to their front door to assure anyone who entered that patriotic citizens lived there.

Nagesh's parents had already decided during his

conception that their child would become a doctor. The purpose of them moving to the States had been solely to accelerate their only son's medical career. His father drove a livery cab and his mother cleaned motel rooms; every cent was saved toward good schooling for Nagesh. He and Harrison had bonded instantly even though they looked like polar opposites while walking around campus. Stocky Harrison lumbering along and tripping over his big feet, and tiny Nagesh who was one hundred thirty pounds soaking wet and looked twelve. Two out-of-water fish on scholarships at a place where the other kids spoke of summer homes at the Cape, the boats they owned, and how many different color Lacoste shirts they had.

From the start, both boys found it tough to fit in and never got invited to any of the good parties. They had heard rumors about girls in frat houses dancing on tables to Madonna, fucking whoever was left standing by the end of the night, but rushing a frat proved disastrous since neither fit the physical ideal. So the two friends stuck their noses in textbooks and became content with fantasizing about how they could possibly get laid.

Nagesh had a job waiting tables at a shithole in Hartford with a fitting name of The Beast, and it was there that he met a girl named Staci who spelled her name as if she was already prepping for a career in porn and even turned some tricks on the side. For the price of a day's tips, she had taken Nagesh into the bar's back alley, pushed him against a chain-link fence, slipped her high heels into the grooves, and rode him for the five minutes it took for him to come. By the time Nagesh returned back to their dorm room, he had already mapped out a plan to start up his own *Risky Business*.

Harrison, with his burgeoning econ degree, was coerced into becoming the financial advisor, and Staci would be Nagesh's number-one pro. Then they'd bring in some local girls and Nagesh would pimp them out to other desperate boys who couldn't get into any frats. Nagesh took fifteen percent of the girls' take-home pay as commission and never once treated any of them poorly. He grew some fuzz on his upper lip, which made him appear fourteen now, and referred to himself as "Pimp Daddy." On the celebratory night the boys had amassed a thousand dollars in profits, he insisted on having Staci break-in Harrison.

Harrison could recall how plastered he'd been off of cheap vodka when he saw Staci waiting for him in his bottom bunk wearing a bra with an acid-washed jeans skirt and pointy white boots. She had on enough pink lipstick to bomb him with kisses, and he put two condoms on out of fear that he'd ejaculate the second she'd sit on his dick. After that first romp where she rode him like a cowgirl, he became immediately hooked and began forgoing his financial fees for more.

Of course with Chilton being such a small school, the administration found out about Nagesh's call girl ring and shut it down fast. To Harrison's surprise, Nagesh was solely blamed for the operation and wound up being suspended for the first semester of sophomore year. Harrison never offered to ease his buddy's punishment by telling the administration of his own involvement. By the time Nagesh returned later in the year, Staci had already moved out to Hollywood to try and make it as an actress. A devastated Harrison decided to sweep up the broken pieces of his heart and try to pledge a frat again. He was accepted immediately since the president was luckily a former client, and Harrison wound up spending his time at parties with girls on tables dancing to Madonna. Soon he'd meet Helene, and the two friends would inevitably drift apart.

In the years after college, Harrison kept in touch with Nagesh occasionally, using him as a way to get some prescription meds here and there while Nagesh sometimes called with financial questions. After five years at Chilton, Nagesh had graduated, went on to med school, and had become an internist with his own private clinic in Hartford. Shortly after 9/11, Harrison offered him some financial advice when Nagesh had to shut down his clinic and declare bankruptcy after some terrible investments. The last time Harrison heard from him had been a few years ago when Nagesh sent an email one freezing winter day to say that he'd moved back to what was now Mumbai to open another clinic, certainly not a place he desired to be, but at least it was hot and he could get a decent girl for a few rupees! Ha, ha, ha. Harrison responded by saying that since this had been the worst winter ever in the States, maybe Nagesh should contact old Staci and convince her to join him in Mumbai to make some money on the side. The last email he'd gotten from his friend was a lone smiley face.

As his cab pulled up to The London, Harrison let himself linger on those early days at Chilton—times spent slipping under the covers with Staci after an econ class, her pink lipstick creating a ring around his head from one of her Hoover blowjobs, and then watching her paint her toenails post coitus. One time she told him he was a whiz with numbers and that guys like him usually got a sought-after job at some investment firm in New York City after graduating. She talked about apartments with a maid's quarter and a limo service to drive you around, the finest liquors and five-star dinners billed to the company. So he envisioned this brilliant future and all of its mighty glory, and after graduation he chased it full throttle until he had it in his grasp.

Now as he entered The London's lobby, he had tears in his eyes from coughing up a glob of phlegm that he had to swallow back down, and he shook his head at the thought of how young, dumb, and blissfully innocent he used to be.

Stepping into the elevator, he pushed the button for the twelfth floor and downed two chugs of rye from the large flask he had filled up before leaving home. The rye made him feel settled as he wiped away his tears and got ready for the kind of romp he hadn't had in a long time, something he sorely needed.

———

The door to room 12G was ajar when Harrison reached the hallway. He knocked as he opened it farther and heard the splashing of water coming from the bathroom. From inside, a woman was singing a song in Spanish. She hadn't noticed him yet so he stood in the shadows outside of the doorframe. She lay in a bathtub full of bubbles with one succulent brown leg hanging off the edge of the tub, her toenails painted dark red. She had closed her eyes, invested only in singing her song, and he thought she had a beautiful voice. He imagined being greeted by her birdsong every day when he'd come home. He wanted to stay and watch her for hours, but the phlegm that he had swallowed before was now on its way back up, and he coughed loudly enough to stir her from her trance.

"Close the door," she said, completely unfazed that he'd been watching her. She had a slight accent, a rolling of her R's. He took a few steps back and shut the front door. The room was now only filled with the light from the traffic outside.

She stepped out of the bathtub and let him see her whole body. He liked how dark her skin was, darker than most Hispanic girls. He'd never been with a woman who wasn't white. Her nipples caught his attention, large and brown, and he had the urge to put one in his mouth. Helene's were light pink, no bigger than a quarter. She never liked when he played with them, complaining of their sensitivity.

The woman grabbed a towel and proceeded to put on a show while she wiped away every last rogue bubble. She seemed to be in her late twenties or early thirties, although he wondered if she was even younger and had a tough life. She wasn't beautiful due to a long chin that made her mouth look too big, and her hair had become crinkled and messed from being in the bathtub, but she had a sensuality that made Harrison feel like an electric charge connected the two of them.

"Let's get comfortable in the other room," she said, patting him on the cheek as she whisked past.

He fumbled in his inner pocket for the flask of rye and took another long gulp before exiting the bathroom.

She stood naked by the window in the darkened room, her large ass creating a very voluptuous silhouette. He got out his wallet and took out the check for five thousand dollars.

"This is for the night," he said, resting it on the dresser.

"Oh, daddy, you wanna get started right away," she said, pursing her lips.

"No, I didn't mean it like that."

He rocked from one foot to the other, distributing his weight and trying not to appear as drunk as he was. That last swig of rye had proved to be all too fatal.

"Just so you know, I'm open to doing anything that isn't violent. If you wanted that, you should have specified because they would've gotten you someone different."

"I'd never hurt you," he hiccupped.

She spread out on the bed, her lips shivering from the air-conditioned room. Her bush had been left unkempt like Staci's used to be. He wondered how many times this woman had met other guys in hotel rooms, and if she'd forget him the moment he was out the door.

"Let's get you out of these clothes," she said, rolling over on her side and working at his belt. He sucked in his stomach as his pants slid to the floor. He stepped out of them and kicked his shoes to the side before stumbling onto the bed with her. She went to take off his suit jacket and found the flask in the inner pocket.

"*Coño!* Someone's already had a party." She unscrewed the cap and took a swig. "Gross," she said, handing it back to him.

He drained the rest of the flask in a few gulps.

"Someone's thirsty, too."

"I'm able to buy someone like you," he said to her, as he lay down and stared up at the spinning room. "But what makes you...worth that kind of money?"

"Yes, daddy, you bought me. You're a fat cat, and I promise you I'm worth every last zero."

She ran her hand up and down his big belly showing off her long fingernails with silver star decals.

"I'm a fat cat," he said, proud of himself for the first time that day. This woman still thought of him as either an integral part of Sanford & Co. or some elite suit that had been given the Desire Card. Life could be worse for him. At least he didn't have to sleep with overweight businessmen in hotel rooms for what probably amounted to a small cut.

"So do you want to fuck already, fat cat, or talk some more because you could've went to a psychiatrist for a lot cheaper?"

He pulled her close. The taste of her tongue had a hint of cherry candy like she'd been sucking on a lollipop. He became immediately aware of his rank breath and pulled away.

"I'm sorry," he said, yanking off his tie. He was burning up even though the room had air conditioning.

"Don't be sorry," she said, rubbing his belly again. "You kiss nice."

"My breath is awful."

"It's okay. I can't smell. I fell off a bike and hit my head bad on the concrete when I was a little girl. You can kiss me all you want."

She initiated the kiss this time with his face in her hands. He figured she was lying and had a story on reserve for whatever ailment a client of hers had to make them feel better. Either she was kind or good at making sure she got her money at the end without any complaints.

"I'm Harrison," he said, once she pulled her lips away from his.

"No, baby, tonight's a fantasy. You can be whoever you want."

"Who are you going to be then?"

"You can call me Candy. Do I taste sweet?"

"Yes."

"Well, I taste even sweeter downtown, baby."

She spread her legs and directed him toward her bush. Back in the early days of his marriage, cunnilingus had been the surefire way to get Helene off. He ran through his mind all of the precise steps that it took to please Helene and plunged into Candy with a kind of vigor that he hadn't possessed in years. She squirmed and screamed, overdoing it, but when he looked up at her face, her eyes had rolled to the back of her skull and he realized she wasn't faking.

"All right, all right," she said, grabbing tufts of his hair. "We got all night. You don't wanna make me come yet, do you?"

He shook his head and it felt like his brain was being knocked around.

"You the star, baby." She smiled. "You the king."

She pushed him onto his back and yanked down his underpants. His penis looked almost hidden by his hanging stomach, but she dove in like a pro and deep throated him until his body felt warmed and all of his worries evaporated.

The night passed in a drunken, dreamless haze for Harrison. The power of flesh was all that mattered. He did Candy from behind and then she tasted all of him, something Helene never did, and spit him out into the garbage bin with a toothy grin. While the moonlight still shone into the hotel room, he recalled nestling into her armpit and finally closing his eyes as she stroked his hair: the tang of her honey-like sweat circling into his nostrils. Lust and love became intertwined, and he had the sensation of being on a roller coaster, a sure sign he had fallen for this seductive stranger. Maybe she could be the start of that happy spark he'd been waiting for? One of his hands latched onto her tit, as if holding on for dear life while the bed suddenly seemed to be picked up and tossed around by a tornado. As he closed his eyes, he sensed his stomach doing flips and turns from every foul thing he'd ingested before a rush of bile crept up his esophagus and he opened his mouth for a sweet release.

———

From a far-off land, someone screamed, shattered the night with their crying. He went to open his eyes, but they'd been glued shut. As he tried to flex every muscle to no avail, he became aware of a stabbing pain in his gut, something sticky on his legs, and the smell of vomit, shit, and piss. Through globs of eye crust, he managed to open one eye and saw Candy, or whatever her real name was, hovering over him and draped in a white comforter covered in blood. She had a bloody handprint across her left breast as well and blood with chunks in it dripping down her arms. Next to him on the bed was a pool of blood filled with what looked like bits of rotted flesh.

His ears finally unclogged and her screams became louder, punishing his eardrums for the mutilation that had occurred. He wanted to speak but couldn't. He tried to reach out to her and saw his own hands were covered in blood too. What had he done to this woman —this purveyor of pure gratification, this goddess of desire, that he had turned against for reasons out of his control?

She had the phone by her ear and was screaming for the police, ordering them to come as fast as they could, her eyes darting from side to side, frightened. He lay back as his insides felt like his organs were at war. Slipping into unconsciousness again, he could no longer see the room clearly anymore. Reality fizzled into the air vents and the kiss of a dream beckoned to remove him from the situation. He became a little boy in his parents' front yard spinning around on the grass and pretending like he was a helicopter about to lift off because his father was working overtime, or out drunk until late, or his mom's cancer began attacking her brain and she came at him with a broom because she thought he was an intruder, or the electricity had been shut off because of overdue bills and he was bored and lonely and wished he was somewhere else. He'd been afraid to stop spinning because he knew he'd be sick once he did, so he kept on going, laughing like a maniac as the world passed by in a blur and he spread out his arms, longing to take flight.

Then, like magic, the wind picked up and launched him into the sky. As he soared past the clouds, he swore that since he'd found the secret to escaping, he'd never come back down.

4

HARRISON WOKE UP AND REALIZED HE WAS attached by tubes to a bunch of machines. A steady beeping noise cut through the silence. Frantic, he moved to sit up but the pain in his stomach was too great, and he slid back into a reclining position. Through half-closed eyes, he looked around and surmised that he'd been taken to a hospital. An emaciated old man looked dead in the bed next to him. He raised his arms and saw he hadn't been handcuffed to the bedrails, so maybe he hadn't hurt Candy after all. He was relieved that the blood all over her could've been his, but then he started worrying about what had happened.

"Nurse," he said, his voice stifled in his throat. "Nurse!" he called out again, yelling as loud as he could, but at most it sounded like a whisper.

Feeling claustrophobic, he began ripping off the tubes. A nurse walking past his room rushed inside and held him down.

"Sir, you can't do that," she said, pinning his shoulders and making him unable to move.

"What's...going on?"

"You were admitted early this morning. We had to pump your stomach."

He tried to wiggle out of her grasp, but the nurse was too strong.

"The doctors are running tests now. I'm going to need you to calm down or I'll have to get a sedative."

He gave in and became stiff, missing her touch once she finally let go. Tears formed in his eyes.

"How long have I been out for? Was I in a coma?" he asked, imagining months, years slipping away. He pictured his grown children walking in and being dumbfounded. He had already missed so many of their firsts, he couldn't bear to think that he would miss any more: Brenton graduating high school and Gracie starting to date before he could scare off any overly handsy boys. "Oh God, Helene!" He trembled at the thought of her visiting with a new man in her life, someone more attuned to her needs who cared about the world and making it a better place. He had no chance up against some philanthropist she'd meet at UNESCO. They'd shuffle into his hospital room already holding hands. The guy would have a trim build and all of his hair and she'd appear as if she were ten years younger, the gray strip around her left ear dyed brown, her ankles thin from daily power walks with the new beau.

"You weren't in a coma, just sleeping," the nurse said, shifting him while she made sure he was still attached to all the necessary tubes. "You were admitted about five hours ago."

"What kind of tests?" he asked, taking her hand, relieved at the feeling of human contact after his ordeal. The nurse was old, in sensible shoes with no makeup and her white hair in a short ponytail. She'd been hardened by her choice of careers and refused to give him a reassuring smile.

"Your stomach was pumped because of excessive alcohol consumption, but you show multiple signs of possible liver disease: jaundice, and your legs are heavily bruised and some of the varicose veins have burst. That was the cause for the blood you may have seen before passing out. When was your last physical?"

"About five years ago, maybe more."

"Five years?" she gasped, then let go of his hand like she was ashamed. "Sir, you have not been to the doctor in that long?"

"I've been...busy."

He reached for her hand again. It may have been as coarse as paper to touch, but it was the only thing keeping him from not freaking out. She stuck him with a needle instead.

"What the hell was that?"

"Just a slight sedative."

She finished up and shot him a look, clearly warning him not to mess with her.

"The medical insurance card in your wallet didn't list your primary care physician, and your wife didn't seem to know either."

"My wife is here?"

"The doctor who saw you is in surgery right now, but he will come by after the test results are back. Your wife is waiting outside. I can get her."

He chewed his lip. What if he pretended to still be

asleep? Helene would have a thousand questions he didn't feel like answering, the worst being an explanation about the woman who brought him here. He imagined her armed with divorce papers, forcing a pen into his weak grip.

The nurse left the room and he turned on his side to stare at the old man in the bed next to him. The man was sleeping with his mouth wide open and his eyes fluttered from having an intense dream. A slight moan escaped from his lips, an indication of being fed up with life already, waiting to go gently into the good night. Harrison clenched his fists at the thought of having liver disease and turning into a shriveled-up entity like this old man, but he knew he'd be the type to fight for his survival, that he wouldn't give in to nature's inevitable assault.

"Hello," he heard a voice say from above, and wrestled with the notion that it could be God with staunch advice.

He turned onto his back and saw Candy.

"What are you doing here?"

She was framed by the fluorescent lights beaming down, an angel in a faux fur coat and hooker boots that went past her knees. Her eyes were red from crying and her hands shook. She grabbed onto him as if she also needed human contact at that moment.

"*Ay, coño!* I said I was your wife. I'm sorry, I didn't want you to get into no trouble—"

"Thank you."

Her hands were smooth from the moisturizer she used. He could feel himself slipping out of her grasp and started to tear up.

"No, baby, don't do that. You gonna be fine. They

said they had to pump your stomach and are running tests. That you had drunken too much."

She ran her fingers through what was left of his hair.

"I thought I hurt you," he said.

This made her smile and she shook her head.

"No, no. I woke up and you had vomited blood. It was everywhere. I thought you died. I called for the police and the ambulance came right away. I've been waiting here since."

"You didn't have to stay," he said, and then felt bad because it made him sound like he didn't care at all.

"I'm...responsible," she sniffled, as she started to cry. She used the sleeve of her coat to mop up any excess snot. "About a year ago, I had this old guy whose heart gave out while we were doing it. He was smiling so big that I hadn't realized what had happened. He died inside of me."

She yanked a tissue from the box by his bed and sobbed until it turned wet and started to come apart.

"I thought I was jinxed," she said, shrugging.

"Well, I'm still here, Candy," he said, finding it strange that he was the one being reassuring with the threat of an agonizing illness hanging over him. He decided that if he needed a new liver, he would just have to get one. This one had filtered the gallons of alcohol and abused pills over the years, but modern medicine would come through by giving him a fresh organ with minimal miles.

"My name isn't Candy," she said, dabbing the dark tears from her eyes.

"I know. Could you pass me some water?"

She took a plastic cup and filled it up from the sink by the door.

"I'm Naelle," she said, handing him the cup.

His throat felt licked by flames when he took the first sip, the water struggling to go down. Once it reached his stomach, it sloshed around violently.

"I'm sorry that I had asked you last night if you were worth five thousand dollars."

"Oh." She gulped and put her hand over her mouth, "I can't get you that money back. The boss is very tough about getting his money."

"No, I meant that I couldn't imagine five thousand better spent."

She moved her hand from her mouth over to her heart.

"I truly owe you my life, Naelle. I would be dead if not for you."

He held onto her hands again and the two stayed silent for a moment, taking in the gravity of what had happened between them. She looked prettier in the daylight, removed from her nighttime profession. Her dark hair had curled down her back, and she'd put on a nice shade of red lipstick. A pocketbook was slung over her shoulder and rested on her ass like it was a shelf. He remembered how her silhouette looked in the moonlight and how kind she'd been to him in bed: never judgmental, never frowning at his appearance. She even let him kiss her after he hadn't been truly kissed in so long.

As if she knew what he'd been thinking, she bent down and kissed his chapped lips. He closed his eyes and stretched out his mouth for more but he could already hear her boots clomping toward the door.

"Bye, daddy," she waved, while leaning against the doorframe. "If you ever desire me again, you know where to call."

She blew him a kiss and turned to walk away, then bounced on her heels and faced him again.

"Take care of yourself," she said, pointing a long fingernail at him. The silver star decal on her nail glinted from the fluorescent light in the room. "And chill with that alcohol cause Naelle don't want to open up no newspaper and see your face in the obituaries."

"I promise," he said, actually meaning it. At least until he got his new liver.

"And call your wife," she said, looking over at the cell on his bedside table. "I'm sure she'd wanna know that you're okay."

He glanced at his cell. By the time he looked up to respond, Naelle had gone. He could hear the echo of her boots clicking down the hallway. What Fates had led him to this woman when someone else might've left him to choke on his own bloody vomit? In a world full of selfish people, she had penetrated through—his saint in a disguise he least expected.

He reached for his cell and texted to Helene that he had gone back to the office in the middle of the night to pull any files from his computer before the rest of the firm arrived and that he'd be busy all day with potential meetings. He knew she'd take the lies as truth without a second thought, tired from her charity auction and from getting the kids ready for school that morning.

He turned onto his side to rest until the doctor came. The old man in the adjacent bed had opened his eyes and was staring at him. He wanted to dream of Naelle's loving touch, but the old man's gaze wouldn't waver. The old man opened his mouth wide and whispered "welcome," before an evil grin emerged on his wrinkled face.

Harrison shivered from the old man's declaration, as if this dying person saw another withering soul and was welcoming him into his circle of eminent deterioration. Once Harrison finally shut his eyes to block out the old man's piercing stare, he couldn't see Naelle in his imagination anymore, only his own engraved tombstone with no one there to mourn his passing.

——————

It was still light outside when Harrison woke again. The bed next to him was empty and made up with new sheets. A doctor with a trim beard who looked way too young was talking to the nurse that had been there earlier. She nodded at Harrison once she saw that he was awake.

"Mr. Stockton, how are you feeling?" the doctor asked, and lifted up the sheets to poke and prod at his stomach.

"Yeah, that hurts, Doc."

"So I understand from the nurse that you haven't had a physical in over five years?"

"What happened to the old guy in the bed next to me?"

The doctor seemed shocked by this question. He stroked his neat beard and squinted at the empty bed as if trying to remember.

"He passed earlier today."

"What was wrong with him?"

Both the doctor and the nurse nodded sympathetically.

"He had end-stage liver disease," the doctor said. "Anyway, the test results from your blood work have come back. Has your wife already left?"

"My wife? Oh, yes, she's at home."

The doctor put on a grim face as he looked through Harrison's file.

"As the nurse told you, you wound up here this morning from excessive alcohol consumption. While the cause of vomiting blood could be due to a tearing in the esophagus, in your case it showed signs of liver trauma. Coupled with your jaundiced skin, an extended belly, and the bruising all over your limbs, this usually indicates some stage of liver disease."

The doctor spoke in a calm manner and Harrison hated him for his subdued demeanor. He had probably practiced his crushing deliveries into a mirror every morning. This was part of the reason Harrison hadn't seen a doctor in years—their smug superiority, their God complexes. Just a couple of years out of medical school and this guy could already dictate Harrison's fate before he'd head off to a round of golf with his colleagues, feeling fitter than ever because his liver still worked.

"Normally," the doctor continued, "any physician would've noticed some of your symptoms, possibly even some time ago, and with the right medications and diet could have maintained things. As it stands now, we took both an AST and ALT blood test. In a healthy patient, certain liver enzymes reside in the cells of the liver, in your case they've spilled into the bloodstream, which is potentially fatal. We did a coagulation panel test and saw that your blood is not clotting properly. Also your albumin level is below normal and has caused some leaking into your tissues, and you have elevation of the bilirubin, which is reflected in your yellowing skin. As it stands now, I'm going to have you transferred to New York Presbyterian where they'll put you on some medications to manage the various manifestations of liver disease and evaluate you for a transplant."

"Well, if I need a transplant then I'll get a transplant," Harrison said. He'd been clutching the bed sheets tightly while he received this news. He was about to ease his grip and relax, then he noticed the way that the doctor and nurse were eyeing one another—like they pitied his naiveté.

The doctor cleared his throat.

"We recommend as positive an outlook as possible, but you do need to know that the national donor list is a very, very long one. After evaluations you could receive a call in a few weeks, but the average wait is usually a year and can sometimes be more."

"Do I even have a year?" he asked, his knuckles turning white as he clutched the sheets harder.

The doctor and the nurse eyed one another again.

"Stop looking at each other like that!"

"Mr. Stockton, please calm down."

"Don't tell me to calm down. Now, do I have a year?"

"The doctors at New York Presbyterian will be better at giving you specifics than we can at St. Luke's, but in all likelihood...no. Now this can work in your favor—"

"What the fuck are you talking about, you kid?"

"To move you up on the list, Mr. Stockton," the

nurse said, raising her voice and joining in to protect the doctor who seemed hurt by Harrison's name-calling. Harrison guessed that this hadn't been the first time the doctor's age had been called into question.

"I was a vice president at Sanford & Co.," Harrison said, breathing heavily so he wouldn't go crazy and rip out all of the connecting tubes to strangle the doctor and the nurse. Both seemed to shrug at the mention of Sanford & Co. "I have a lot of money."

"As I said, Mr. Stockton, the physicians at New York Presbyterian will answer any questions you have, but money is not a factor in moving you up on the donor list."

"The hell it isn't, how is that possible?" he said, finally releasing the bed sheets. Blood had collected on his palms. He raised them up toward the doctor, begging for answers as the blood dripped to his elbows. The doctor backed away, threatened by his madness.

"Nurse, get some gauze," the doctor said. She had already dashed to the cabinets above the sink. When she came back, she proceeded to clean and wrap up Harrison's hands.

"I'm sorry," the doctor said, and patted Harrison on the shoulder. Harrison recoiled, refusing to alter his opinion of the doctor who he'd forever associate with the day his life ended.

"Leave me alone," he ordered.

The doctor scrunched up his face about to reply, but then slung his stethoscope around his neck and walked out.

"We'll get you all of the info for the other hospital," the nurse said, "but then we're gonna need this bed in an hour." She finished wrapping his hands, clearly not pleased by his abrasive reaction. She stood to go to the door but stopped herself. "This is why we tell people to get a *yearly* physical and monitor their alcohol intake."

She seemed almost delighted by his diagnosis, smug in the fact she'd easily outlive him.

He thought of Naelle blowing a kiss to him in that very same doorframe, a fantasy from when his life seemed hopeful, only hours ago.

———

During his evaluation at New York Presbyterian, he had to consent to a government-mandated HIV test, a chest X-ray to determine if his lungs were healthy, an ultrasound, a CT Scan, an MRI, and ERCP to take X-rays of his bile ducts, a Liver Angiogram, and a Liver Biopsy. Once the results came back, he'd be placed on the national waiting list managed by the United Network for Organ Sharing. Using the MELD system (the model for end stage liver disease), he'd be given a score ranging from 6 to 40 that was based on how accelerated his illness might be.

His attending doctor was a short little man with glasses and an awkward comb-over who acted a little more empathetic than the one at St. Luke's until Harrison tried to mention that he'd pay "*a lot*" of money to move up on the donor list. The doctor became very offended and launched into a speech about how money can't always be the answer to every problem.

"I understand this news is difficult, Mr. Stockton, but your family needs to know what has happened. This is the time to tell them how much you love them and spend every possible moment enjoying their presence."

Harrison had already decided that he wouldn't tell Helene and the kids yet, at least until he figured out a plan to move up on the donor list. Twenty years of working for the richest of the rich at Sanford & Co. had to have some sway. He remembered Whit's father being some big-shot surgeon at NYU; the guy was always in *New York* magazine's list of best doctors. He'd swallow his pride and contact Whit for lunch tomorrow, certain that Whit would feel remorseful enough to make the impossibility of getting a new liver happen.

The doctor finished the evaluation with prescriptions for steroids and cortisone. After the tests came back, he'd call to schedule regular appointments and prescribe any other necessary medications.

"Sometimes the power of family can be the best medicine in trying times," the doctor said. "My wife has lymphoma, it's a pretty forgone conclusion that I'll lose her, but every morning I'll bring her breakfast in bed, or buy her a nice hat because she's lost all her hair, or I'll tell her that I still love her even more than when we first met. And I do. All I want is to ease her pain. My only desire in life is to brighten her troubling days."

Harrison had no response to that. He had already gotten out his cell and was writing his desperate email to Whit, making sure to pour on the guilt so his former friend would have no choice but to act as his savior. He finished his spiel and hit send.

———

By the time Harrison arrived home that night, the apartment was dead quiet. Like always, Chauncey greeted him at the door, emerging from hibernation to prowl against his master's leg. It was almost eleven, and Helene and the kids would be in bed. This last day and a half had been the longest of Harrison's life: getting fired, almost dying in Naelle's arms, learning that he basically had his head in a guillotine. He'd acted remorseful when he first received the news of his illness, then anger had taken over, now he felt determined. He would get a new liver, whatever it took. While working for Sanford & Co., he'd never taken no for an answer. New York was made up of the most tenacious people in the world, and Harrison knew that no one could be more tenacious than him.

His cell beeped and he checked his email to see that Whit had replied. He agreed to meet Harrison for lunch tomorrow at the Palm Downtown. Whit would figure out the best way to approach his father about Harrison's request, since his father was a difficult man who had to be handled in the right way. Whit finished the message by saying that whatever happened between Harrison and him yesterday, he'd still be pulling for his friend.

For the first time that day, Harrison managed to smile. Just a few hours after receiving the most traumatic news of his life, he was already figuring out solutions. That quick thinking was why Sanford & Co. hired him in the first place. His cognitive skills had paid for his family's Fifth Avenue apartment, for his tailored suits, for the diamonds in Helene's jewel box, for the kids' ridiculously pricey educations. And now it would pay for his survival too.

He picked up Chauncey and wandered into the kitchen, his stomach hollow from only eating from an IV that day. In the fridge he found the leftovers from last night's dinner and dove into some cold crab cakes and chicken along with a bottle of Pinot Grigio that had been recorked. Chauncey hopped up onto the island in the middle of the kitchen where Harrison had situated himself and stared at the diminishing plate of food. After shoving a whole crab cake in his mouth, Harrison broke apart a few pieces from the remaining one and fed it to the cat who licked it up greedily. Oh, how he loved his fat cat, his true soul mate. The two had spent countless midnight hours together wolfing down leftovers and snuggling on the couch. Sometimes it seemed as if Chauncey really listened to Harrison's darkest secrets.

Both of them finished devouring what was left of the cold food and sat back like kings, Chauncey looking like a mini T-Rex because of his giant midsection and short front paws.

"I refuse to let this be my end," he told the cat, who blinked as if he understood everything, then hoisted up to settle on Harrison's lap. As Chauncey purred, the warmth of his big stomach against Harrison's thigh was consoling. Harrison reached under the cat's tummy and felt for where Chauncey's liver would be, stroking it gently, thoughtfully, and if he truly admitted it, jealously.

He picked up a knife encrusted with crab crumbs and held it to the cat's belly. Just a few incisions and that liver would be his; it couldn't be too difficult. He chuckled at the thought. A few years back, he'd heard of baboon hearts being harvested for transplants, was a cat that different? He laughed again. Who would want Chauncey's liver anyway? The cat had spent his life gorging on everything in his path. But as Harrison held the shaking knife to the cat's stomach, he was reminded of that urban legend about someone walking out of a nightclub and getting hit over the head. The next thing they knew, they had woken up in a bathtub full of ice with a gaping hole in their chest and a missing organ. He shuddered at the depravity people were capable of in times of desperation. He pushed away the rest of the wine, which he blamed as being the cause of this nightmarish vision. Then he put the knife down, kissed Chauncey on his furry face, and stumbled off to bed.

5

AFTER SLEEPING WELL INTO THE MORNING FOR ONE
of the first times in his adult life, Harrison headed to the
Palm to meet Whit for lunch. By the time he woke,
Helene and the kids had already left for the day. He
thought it was better that he missed them. He'd take
one look at Gracie's sweet face and start thinking he
might never be able to walk her down the aisle. But now
he had to put that out of his mind since he had a
mission to accomplish. He needed to believe he'd be
leaving lunch with the promise of a new liver.

He arrived before Whit and was seated at a table in
the back. The venerable steakhouse was already almost
filled to capacity, even at noon. Since he had no time for
breakfast, a juicy T-bone would have to suffice.

When Whit finally showed up, Harrison stuck out
his hand to shake, but Whit dwarfed him with a hug
instead and kept mumbling how he couldn't believe this
was happening.

"What did your father say?" Harrison asked,
tucking a napkin into his lap once they both sat.

Whit caught the waiter's eye for drinks.

"Oh, should you not be drinking?" Whit asked.

"It's not like things could get any worse at this point."

The two ordered gin martinis and then dealt with an uncomfortable silence as Whit played with his utensils. Harrison was about to ask again about Whit's father when the drinks arrived and Whit held up his glass for a toast.

"To health," he said, cocking his head to the side as a show of compassion. "And to the best vice president at Sanford & Co."

"You're certainly modest," Harrison said, clinking Whit's glass.

"I was referring to you, Harrison. The company is certainly a fool to have let you go."

"Not as much of a fool as whoever decided to put you in charge."

At first Whit thought Harrison was being serious, but then Harrison laughed and Whit joined along.

"How did Reiko take the news of your promotion?" Harrison asked.

"She doesn't know what the fuck it means, her English is so God awful. I could've told her that I'd been made head of Dirty Sanchez & Co. and she'd say she was so proud. What about Helene? How did the kids handle hearing about your illness?"

"I haven't told anyone about that yet. I was hoping to get some good news from you today that might lessen the impact."

Whit brushed his thick hair away from his forehead. He wasn't looking Harrison in the eye.

"About that, Harry—"

"Is there no shot?"

"You know you should check out the black market, like in India or something," Whit said, knocking back half his martini. "Organ harvesting is all over the news lately."

"Why would I do that when your father—"

"Look, I can't ask my father for something like this."

"But you said you would. You owe me."

Whit made a huffing sound. "Your position at Sanford was given to me fair and square—"

"This isn't about that," Harrison said, slamming his fist against the table. Other diners glanced over and then went back to their meals. "This is my life, don't you understand?"

"I have a history of liver disease in my family," Whit said.

"What does that have to do with anything?"

"My father is the type of person who's only going to let you ask for one favor from him..."

Harrison sat back dumbfounded.

"And what if I *needed* a liver or some other organ in the future? Sure, I work out and keep fit, but I've thrown back a lot of alcohol in my days."

"But I need this now," Harrison said, restraining himself from pounding the table again.

"Besides, it's not like my father specializes in liver transplants; he's a heart surgeon. I doubt he'd have enough connections at NYU anyway."

"That's bullshit, and you didn't even ask him so it's not like you know. You are a greedy fuck."

"I didn't invite you to lunch to be bombarded."

"You think you can just take everything around you," Harrison said, going off on a tangent that barely made sense. "You zeroed in on my job a long time ago, and yeah...you fucking owe me for that. I spent last night vomiting blood."

"Really, Harrison, this is not the time or the place," Whit said, putting on a phony smile and nodding toward all the other patrons to ensure them that everything was A-OK at their table.

"I have a good mind to put my fist through that smug face of yours."

"You want to take this outside like a bunch of hooligans?" Whit laughed. "I used to box back at Harvard undergrad."

"Eat my shit," Harrison said, tossing his napkin in Whit's face, then changing his mind and throwing the rest of his martini at him as well. A woman at a nearby table gasped.

"You're pathetic," Whit said under his breath, as he wiped the spilled drink off his tie.

"And your real name is Whitley, that's a fucking girl's name."

"It's Old English—"

"You have no heart," Harrison said, straining to hold back his tears.

"At least another organ of mine works." Whit smirked. "And don't worry, Sanford & Co. will take care of this bill. I know things must be tight at home now."

Harrison decked him. It wasn't the greatest punch, but he made enough contact with Whit's left jaw to almost knock him off his chair. The same woman next to them gasped louder this time, and now the waitstaff was coming over. Whit rubbed his tender chin that was already starting to bruise and swore to everyone at the nearby tables that he was all right.

"This man has an imbalance," he shouted. "I'm fine. He is not. He's never going to be fine again, but I will. You remember that, Harrison."

Whit was still babbling as Harrison weaved around the nearby tables until he pushed through the front doors onto the street. A gust of wind nearly knocked him over. He felt fragile enough to be swept away. When he got his bearings again, he was crying unlike he had ever cried before, howling from deep within, running down the street like a crazy person as the tears clouded his vision and he ducked into a subway station to weep into the sleeve of his coat like a lost, homeless man. He could see the faces of those passing by who regarded him as nothing more.

———

Fifteen minutes later, Harrison got on the subway. Embarrassed by his earlier tears, he forced himself to quit acting like a little bitch and started replaying the scene he had with Whit to reassure himself that he'd been entirely in the right. Just as he remembered the part of the conversation where Whit mentioned getting black market organs from India, Harrison looked across the train car and became enlightened. He didn't see God or reach any spiritual understanding; enlighten- ment came in the form of a skinny Indian kid with a pencil mustache that had sat down. Immediately he thought of his old friend Nagesh again.

It had been about two years since they last emailed, but it was safe to assume that Nagesh still resided in Mumbai. Would it be crazy to ask him if he had any connections to the black-market trade? Harrison knew he certainly had the funds to make it happen and figured it couldn't be too expensive since Mumbai was filled with the poorest of the poor who'd probably give their organs away for next to nothing.

He reached his stop with the urge to kiss the skinny Indian kid for leading him toward this revelation. As he bounded out of the doors, he wondered how to best approach his request through email. He wasn't worried about offending Nagesh, but if Nagesh did have shady connections, it might not be so smart to discuss this over email. He decided it'd be wisest to be vague at first until Nagesh responded.

By the time he reached his apartment, he'd already typed a draft on his cell. Initially he went to use his regular email from his Sanford & Co. account, but it had already been shut down so he was forced to contact Nagesh from his personal account that he opened more than ten years ago.

To: RajaNageshPatel@hotmail.com
From: Bigspenderrr@yahoo.com
Subject: Advice

Pimp Daddy,
    Are you still in Mumbai, and if so, how is the private clinic going? Wish I was contacting you with better news, but I recently found out that I have liver disease. The doctors here have been hopeless, so I wanted to contact a true professional for advice about what to do next. Heard that things in India might be done a little "differently" than in the States w/ more "alternative options". Of course, $$ is no object. Let me know the best way to reach you.

Your old friend,
Harrison

He entered his apartment and stormed past the doorman while hitting send, completely satisfied with what he'd written. By the time he got upstairs and fed Chauncey a can of Fancy Feast, his cell had already beeped with a response from Nagesh.

From: RajaNageshPatel@hotmail.com
To: Bigspenderrr@yahoo.com
Subject: Re: Advice

Harrison!!! Yes, still in Mumbai w/ my own clinic.
SO sorry to hear of your illness. Contact me at my pre-paid cell # immediately – 011917881718179. – N

He went to click on Nagesh's number but then hesitated. It was certainly sketchy that Nagesh had responded so quickly, as if the guy had been waiting by his computer for a black-market request so he could pounce on it. At the same time, Nagesh could just be acting like a good friend after hearing about Harrison's diagnosis and wanted to reach out in any way possible. Harrison rationalized that calling Nagesh didn't mean he'd be locked into any fixed agreement. It was simply two friends reconnecting and also discussing some of Harrison's options—no harm in that.

He closed the door to the kitchen in case Helene or the kids came home and then dialed Nagesh's number.

"Hello," Nagesh answered after the first ring, sounding out of breath.

"Nagesh. Hi, it's Harrison."

"H-Bomb!" Nagesh said, harking back to one of the many inside names that he had for Harrison their freshmen year. Because of Harrison's gargantuan size (at least from the perspective of Nagesh's small stature), he often "destroyed" everything in his path if he had a few too many.

"Thanks for responding so quickly," Harrison said, putting Chauncey's empty bowl into the sink.

"Think nothing of it. Your email truly saddened me, my friend. Tell me the diagnosis."

Harrison felt his eyes getting misty again.

"Well, they're running tests up at New York Presbyterian, but the doctors seem pretty hopeless."

"This is precisely why I left the States. Too much negativity. I prefer to be hopeful with my patients, but in the US, I'd be an anomaly."

"It's not like I've taken the best care of myself," Harrison said. "But life presents you with vice after vice, how can I pass up alcohol and—"

"You are preaching to the choir, H-Bomb. If I remember correctly, you were the only other eighteen-year-old with an affinity for rye."

The mention of rye made him think of last night. He had swallowed enough to teeter on the precipice of death.

"So since this call ain't cheap, shall we get down to specifics?" Nagesh asked, changing his tone from singsongy to a businessman's pitch.

"A friend mentioned to me about what...goes on in India in terms of..." Harrison began, but got uncomfortable with saying anymore. At first he couldn't believe he had referred to Whit as a friend, but then he had no idea how to put his outlandish request into words.

"Harrison, this is a prepaid phone. It will be in the trash tomorrow. We can speak freely. You called because you want to see if I can get you an organ, yes?"

Harrison had to laugh at the insanity of it all. He thought about his day-to-day existence thus far, nothing had ever come close to reaching the ludicrous level of this conversation. After he'd hang up, he knew he'd erase this foolishness from his memory. He pictured Helene listening on the other line and wondering what kind of monster she'd been sleeping next to all of these years.

"I'm trying to wrap my mind around...I spent almost twenty years in M & A dealing with facts and figures. There are few gray areas with numbers."

"Listen, friend," Nagesh said, his voice rising to singsongy levels again. "You contacted me because you are curious, because no doctor at home has given you another solution. I applaud your tenacity."

Harrison managed to smile at that compliment.

"I'm sure the news in the States is selling the idea of organ trafficking as its latest 'boo hoo' cause. And yes, terrible things are happening around the world. In China, they're executing prisoners for organs. In Mozambique, children are being kidnapped to harvest their organs. Terrible, terrible. But did you know that I've worked with donors who have gladly given a kidney or part of a liver before?"

"Yeah, I don't really know too much about it," Harrison replied, turning his back to Chauncey who seemed to be watching him with the same reproachful glare that he often recognized from Helene.

"I will set the scene for you. A child is dying in the slums of Mumbai. The family has no money for a hospital. The father is willing to give a much-needed kidney. I've done this very transplant in the back room of my clinic."

"My father passed a few years ago."

"That I am sorry to hear. I remember the man. We both loved the Patriots with all of our heart. But I tell you this so you can see that not everything about organ harvesting is bad. And here in Mumbai, a family with no money for food can sell an organ and make enough to put food on the table for years, to even give their children a hope of getting out of the Dharavi or another one of the large slums."

"When you put it that way," Harrison said. Chauncey had leaped up on the counter, but Harrison swiveled around so his back still faced the cat.

"Look, in this world we are unfortunately valued by our assets. This is the sad truth. Some are given everything and some nothing, just as God has made some healthy and some not. For someone who has nothing, health becomes a luxury they can afford to sell."

"And you've done a liver transplant as well?" Harrison whispered, as if their conversation was being monitored. He thought of traces on the phone line, or a nosy neighbor in an adjoining apartment hearing this depraved discussion. He almost hung up out of fear, but his cell had become glued to his ear.

"Yes, I have done this. My clinic is everything to me, but unfortunately due to money issues it is almost as difficult to maintain here as it was in the States. However, here I can skirt what is deemed legal. Here I can maintain a side practice."

"How much does an organ go for?"

"All organs are different prices. Kidneys are most common since we don't necessarily need both to live so they are more affordable. Livers on the other hand are trickier. Ideally it comes from someone recently deceased. That's what you will get from the interminable donor list you'll be put on. What I've done are transplants of livers from someone still alive."

"But how can they survive without a liver?"

"That is the beauty of the liver, it can regenerate in a few weeks. So someone sells about half their liver for the price of a few weeks' bed rest and enough money to save their family from starvation. It's a win-win."

"So how much for a liver from someone who's still alive?"

"One hundred fifty thousand dollars," Nagesh said, slipping back into his businessman's tone.

Immediately Harrison's mind went to his and Helene's bank accounts. One hundred fifty thousand dollars was nothing to sneeze at, but between stocks, bonds, CDs, and saving accounts, they had close to a million. The apartment was also worth about four million, although in this market probably closer to 3.5, then of course Helene's father had set up trusts for Brenton and Gracie—both valued at about five hundred thousand. One hundred fifty thousand would make a dent but nothing that couldn't be buffered eventually, even without a new job on the horizon.

"Are you there, Harry?"

"Yes, just figuring out some finances."

"I'm sure you'd be able to scrape it together. Usually I take a third as my cut, another third goes to the other physicians I'll need for the surgery, and the last fifty thousand goes to the donor. Now keep in mind that fifty thousand is a lot more money than a donor here has ever seen before."

"I don't doubt that."

"I'll need your medical records before I can begin to find a match."

"Yes, the doctor put me through the first round of tests yesterday. Can this truly work, Nagesh?"

"Friend, I would like nothing more than to be the one who eases your suffering. I've done transplants and both parties have gone on to live normal, healthy lives. You Americans—I'm sorry, it's been so long since I've been in the States—but America has created a system of laws without regard for personal cases. What is illegal to one set of ideals does not necessarily mean it is wrong."

"I couldn't tell Helene about this. She doesn't even know that I have liver disease."

"The stress that the patriarch of a family must go through every day is a burden I will never know. No one can judge you for this, Harrison, since you only want to ensure that you can be there to take care of your family. We fight for what we love in this world, all else is superfluous."

"How long does the surgery take?"

"About six to fourteen hours, then a few days in intensive care at my clinic and a few weeks of bed rest. It's usually done in a hospital, but we would work out the particulars."

"I'd have to come up with a good lie to explain why I'd be in India for that long."

"I do not doubt that you will be able to think of

something. You were certainly gifted with intelligence—"

"Thank you, Nagesh."

"I speak the truth."

"No, thank you for...this shred of hope."

"This is more than a shred; it is a likely guarantee."

Harrison shuffled over to the window that looked out on the back alley of their apartment building. Usually very little light filtered through the surrounding buildings, but he glanced outside at the precise moment in the afternoon when a beam like a laser shot through a space between two water towers and filled the kitchen with sunny aplomb. Hope was never something that his logical heart found time to believe in; but at that moment during this personal light show, it was like God himself had reached out with his shimmering finger to bless this house and all who resided in it.

"I need to think about this," Harrison said, after a long exhale.

"Sure, sure."

"Where should I send my medical records once I get them?"

"Let's not involve each other's addresses. Scan anything and send it to SitarFan44@hotmail.com; it's not registered under my real name."

"And this number?"

"My minutes are almost gone. I usually go through a new prepaid phone every week to handle any dealings for my side business. I will email you with my new number."

"I promise I'll get back to you one way or the other."

"Yes, take as long as you need, but the faster we

begin, the faster you will heal. Go ahead and apply for a tourist visa in the meantime since it should take about a week or two should you decide to come. Goodbye for now."

"Nagesh, you are a true friend."

"As are you, H-Bomb. As the Buddha said, 'Even death is not to be feared by one who has lived wisely.' Be wise in this instance, Harrison. I have never known you to be anything but."

The call ended and Harrison removed the sweaty cell from his ear and placed it on the counter. Chauncey leaped up to sniff the cell, and Harrison tickled the cat under his chin. Chauncey looked at his master with absolute love, as if imploring Harrison to remain in this world for as long as possible. The scornful glare that Harrison had thought he'd seen was an illusion.

"Promise not to tell?" he asked the cat, with a finger to his lips.

The water towers outside blocked the beam of sunlight and now the kitchen was draped in shadows. Harrison remained there in the dark for hours, petting Chauncey's coat and meditating on this turning point in his life.

By the time he heard the locks of the front door open and the boisterous sounds of Helene and the kids as they entered, he had already made a decision.

6

THE NEXT COUPLE OF WEEKS PASSED IN A FRENZY. Once the results of the tests came back from the hospital, Harrison had been diagnosed with cirrhosis. If this would've been discovered years ago, he might've had a chance to live with the ailment, but because of his neglect, the damage was too great. His diet had to change immediately. He learned that he could never again eat shellfish, since it contained a bacterium that could cause an infection. Alcohol and any illicit substances had to be avoided as well. The doctor prescribed diuretics to combat edema and ascites, fluids that had developed in his legs and abdomen. He was given beta blockers to lower pressure in his varices and reduce the risk of bleeding again. The first doctor at St. Luke's had been right about his chances for survival, and he was placed on the donor list with a high MELD score, but since he hadn't developed end-stage liver disease yet, he shouldn't expect to move up anytime soon.

Immediately after receiving his diagnosis, he

requested his medical records from New York Presbyterian to email to Nagesh. Since Harrison had the rare blood type AB, Nagesh found a few universal donors with blood type O. The next step was to crossmatch Harrison's white blood cells with that of the donors' to test antigen compatibility. If the white blood cells became attacked and died, then the crossmatch was positive, which meant Harrison had antibodies to the donors' antigens and his immune system would turn on the donated organ. If the crossmatch came out negative, then Nagesh had found a compatible donor. To legally send his blood through the mail, Harrison had to place it in a test tube cushioned by an absorbent cloth and secured in a box with the phrase *Exempt Human Specimen* written in bold lettering. This all was sent to a PO box in the outskirts of Mumbai.

After mailing his blood, the wait to hear back from Nagesh became the most excruciating days of Harrison's life. Nagesh said it'd take over a week to know for certain, but he found himself watching his cell and refreshing his email over and over in the hopes of a response. Luckily Helene had been busy with a fundraising gala for poor third world children that she was hosting later that spring, and he could stay at home all day without her hovering. Sometimes he headed to Central Park, longing to wind through the tree-lined paths while clearing his head, but after a few minutes, he usually became winded and collapsed onto a bench to pass the day, his heart leaping at every beep of his cell that might be Nagesh responding.

Sometimes late at night he'd stare at Helene snoring in bed and found himself wanting to touch her, but she was so far away on their king-size mattress. He longed to tell her all of his deepest sins, beginning with his recent infidelities, his alcohol and pill abuse, and finally the truth of his disease and his plan for survival. But after years of her volunteerism, he knew she'd never understand his desperate plan. She had modeled herself into being a "good person," one that lived for others rather than selfishly and his proclamation would set in motion their final irreversible rift. Since the kids were too young to understand, Chauncey was his only hope for an ear, so he'd slip out of the bedroom to hold onto the cat tightly until the sun rose.

Nagesh's response finally came one chilly mid-April day while Harrison sat on a bench in the Ramble. He'd been observing a band of tourists weaving through a mass of fallen trees, all of them content to become lost in the famous park, when the buzz of his phone cut through the silent splendor. He fumbled in his pockets, dropped the phone in the dirt, and brushed it off to see Nagesh's email with the beautiful subject of: *Success!!!* One of the type O donors had a negative crossmatch with his blood and now the final step was to get him to Mumbai.

"Success!" he shouted, as a flock of startled pigeons chased the sky and the tourists scrunched up their faces at the burly, disheveled man wandering through the Ramble. He punched the air in jubilation and practically skipped back home—except for the few rests he needed to take at benches along the way. Back at the apartment, he celebrated with a glass of Irish on the rocks, and finished up the celebration by draining the bottle and cursing these final moments with his worthless old liver. He pictured himself destroying it with a baseball bat once it was removed from his body.

Already opening a second bottle, he made his way to the computer to book a hotel and flight since Nagesh suggested he come as soon as possible. He decided on five-star treatment all of the way. After the rough couple of weeks he'd been through, he felt like he deserved nothing less. The Taj Mahal Palace that he chose in the heart of Mumbai literally looked like the Taj Mahal and was billed as a blend of old-world elegance and modern facilities including a colossal-sized bathtub and had a personalized butler service all for six hundred dollars a night. He'd book it for three nights from now so he could get his finances in order and come up with a good excuse to give Helene along with enough time to say goodbye to Brenton and Gracie. Booking the trip so close to leaving meant that the hotel for a few nights plus a first-class one-way airfare would run him about ten thousand dollars, but he figured that he wouldn't notice it compared to the one hundred fifty thousand he'd be spending on his new organ. He emailed Nagesh back with all of the details and thanked him again, tears squeezing at the corner of his eyes, the first tears of joy he'd cried in a long time.

When Helene returned home with a bag of groceries in her hands and Gracie pirouetting by her side, he was already tripping over his feet from being so bombed and welcomed his family in the doorframe by grabbing them and attempting an awkward waltz.

"Ow!" Gracie said, and rubbed her foot after Harrison squashed her tiny toes. "I'm only wearing ballet slippers, Dad."

"Sorry," he mumbled, smiling wide.

"Harrison, isn't four in the afternoon a little early

for drinks?" Helene asked, ducking out of his grasp and heading to the kitchen.

"Dad, are you drunk?" Gracie asked, crossing her arms.

"No," he hiccupped. "Well a little, but I have something to celebrate."

"Don't forget, my father is stopping by for dinner after his meeting in town," Helene said.

"Jay's coming?" Harrison said, pivoting from his right to left foot, then deciding to use his right to balance his weight.

"Don't sound so enthralled. Daddy is bound to be lit from a meeting with clients over drinks so at least the two of you will have something in common tonight."

"Does he know about what happened at Sanford?"

"Was it wrong of me to mention?"

Gracie followed Helene toward the kitchen, complaining again about this girl Becca Danshore who'd been given the lead in their upcoming production. Harrison stayed close behind, much to Helene and Gracie's chagrin.

"Darling, if the teacher gave another girl the lead then there's nothing you can do," Helene said, while unloading the groceries onto the counter. Harrison saw that she had bought fresh shrimp and his heart sank, but then he figured eating shellfish should be fine since he wouldn't be using this liver for too much longer.

"Becca's dad donated a ton of money to the ballet studio so that's how she got it," Gracie whimpered, fingering the groceries with disdain. "Gross, I hate shrimp. Roya Abramowitz doesn't eat shrimp because they're bottom feeders and it's not kosher."

"But we aren't Jewish," Helene said, looking over at

Harrison to share in a smirk about their daughter's precocious complaints. "And I highly doubt that your ballet teacher takes bribes."

"Uh, everyone takes bribes if the bribe is high enough," Gracie said.

"She's right," Harrison said, coughing into his sleeve and lingering in the doorframe. He stepped inside and held onto the counter for support. "The world revolves around the dollar sign."

"Today we learned in school about the Chinese yuan," Gracie said. "That's what the world revolves around now. And the Indian rupee. In current events class, Ms. Samner talked about how in twenty years those two countries will be the superpowers and how America may have already seen its peak."

"I'm amazed what they teach you in fifth grade at that school," Harrison said.

"Dad, I'm in fourth."

Helene let out a laugh under her breath.

"Fourth and fifth, it's all the same," Harrison said, and pushed in between his two girls. He took the last groceries out of Helene's hands. "I will make dinner tonight."

"No, Harrison, it's fine."

She went to pick up the shrimp but he took it away from her again.

"I insist."

He held onto to his wife's hand for an extra second until she pulled it away. Her touch had been smooth and he recalled Naelle and the slick moisturizer she had used to make her palms feel so delicate. He gave Helene an awkward smile, but she was already wiping away his own sweaty touch on a dish towel. He thought of the way her hands had felt when he asked her to marry him. He'd been perspiring so much, but she remained cool.

He had proposed during a long, sweaty Memorial Day weekend at her family's house in Greenwich. He was nervous about getting her father's permission, especially since Jay made a point of telling him in private that marriage was the last thing Helene wanted at the time. It was Jay's belief that a girl in her twenties should be testing different suitors rather than feeling like she needed to settle down. When Harrison finally manned up and showed Jay the ring he'd purchased, his soon-to-be father-in-law was silent for once. The man just sipped at his neat Scotch and chewed the hell out of the corner of his lip. Harrison thought that Jay was about to punch him in the face, but then Jay placed a hand on his shoulder instead.

"You've got bigger balls than I thought you did, kid." Jay winked, before knocking back his drink and leaving the room.

Over the rest of the weekend, Harrison wasn't sure if he'd gotten her father's blessing, but then he overheard Jay telling Helene's mother the news, who in turn told her gossipy brother Chip, who then let it slip to Helene, so that by the time he fully got down on one knee she had quickly said "yes" before he could even ask—but he didn't care, he'd been so afraid about her father poisoning his chances. He leaped up on his feet and wouldn't let go of her smooth hands as they kissed in her family's backyard with everyone peeking from behind the curtains in the living room. Any hesitation he had—marrying too young before he had a chance to be reckless and stupid, entering into a daunting family

like the Howells who clearly viewed him as plebeian—
was all erased with her tender kiss and a hint of tongue
like he imagined it would still be when they were in
their nineties crumbling on a park bench together.

"Don't use any cream in the shrimp since Brenton
has become lactose intolerant," Helene said, bringing
him away from twenty-year-old memories and back to
the here and now.

"Since when can't he have dairy?"

"Really, Harrison, try and be present for once in
this family."

She went over to Gracie whose bun had unraveled
and tucked a rogue strand of hair around the girl's ear.

"I'm sorry, honey, I know how much you wanted
the lead," she said, planting a loving kiss on the top of
Gracie's head.

Harrison couldn't remember the last time he'd
kissed Gracie on the top of her head like that and
wondered if it still smelled like freshly cut flowers. He
thought to test it out, but he knew that Gracie would
only think he had gone insane. She had no interest in
being consoled by him. Helene's touch was all she
needed, and Helene lorded that power over him with a
mixture of pride and displeasure.

"It's funny you should mention India, Gracie," he
said, washing off the vegetables in the sink. "Your dad is
headed to Mumbai, that's the news I got today that I
wanted to celebrate."

"What is this for?" Helene asked, holding onto her
neck like she always did when she got nervous.

"A job offer," he said, facing the sink rather
than her.

"In Mumbai?" she asked.

"Dad, are we moving there?" Gracie shrieked. "What about my friends at Chapin?"

"Hold on, hold on," he said, turning off the water and taking a deep breath to face them with the lies he'd practiced. "The company has a sister office out in Mumbai. They want to test me out there but the job would be here in New York."

Helene let go of her neck that had already become red.

"You nearly frightened me to death," she said. "Not that there's anything wrong with India. I would love to travel there, it'd just be an entirely different thing to pack up our lives and move."

"It's a great position and the company is doing really exciting things."

"Which firm is it?" Helene asked, suspicious as always.

"I don't want to say until they make an offer. In fact they asked me to remain silent."

"Daddy, will you buy me a sari while you're there?" Gracie asked, clapping her hands.

He beamed at the fact she called him "Daddy" since it had been so long. She was bouncing on her heels now, eager to hear his response. She showed her love to him again because he'd buy her what she wanted, but that didn't matter. He wiped off his hands and put his arm around her shoulder.

"Of course, Bunny," he said, harking back to a cutesy term that he used to call her. She used to twitch her nose like a bunny, something he found precious. "And what about you, my love?" he asked Helene, on a roll with his terms of endearment. "A sari for you, too?"

"If it's...not too much trouble," Helene said, apparently shaken. It had been a considerable amount of time since either had spoken the word "love" to one another, and her neck had become red once again. He wished he could take it back. "Gracie, why don't you go change and let your father start dinner?"

"No, I want to tell him about the kind of sari I want. I want orange with—"

"You can tell him at dinner, sweetie," Helene said, motioning for Gracie to come away from Harrison and into her own embrace. The girl nodded and sank into her mother's bosom. As the two stepped out of the kitchen, Helene gave Harrison a look that summed up their last twenty-odd years of disintegration—her pupils reflecting all of the lost desires and ultimate disappointments that had thrust them into the present as nothing more than strangers. He wondered if he'd ever hear the word "love" from her again and promised that when he returned from India with his new liver, he'd say it over and over until she finally believed he meant it.

Harrison threw himself into preparing his family's dinner that night. He decided on a shrimp Fra Diavolo with linguini since it didn't require any dairy and crushed up the red pepper flakes on his own rather than using the store-bought. He made sure to cook the pasta al dente and used half a bottle of dry white wine for the sauce. As he brought the food to the dining room, the plates shook in his hands since it had been a long day and he was tired, but once each dish had been placed under his family's noses and he requested that they all take a moment to admire his *art*, he felt a shot of adrenaline course through him like he hadn't experienced in years, if ever. An extra plate of food sat in front of an empty chair, since his father-in-law was taking a conference call in their bedroom.

"What the fuck is this, *you* cooked?" Brenton laughed into his fist.

"Watch that language around your mother, Brent."

"Oh yeah, Dad, like you don't drop F-bombs all the time."

Harrison poured two glasses from the leftover wine and handed one to Helene, ignoring Brenton's accusation.

"Yes, I decided to make dinner," he said, holding the glass up for a toast.

"Shrimp?" Gracie whined, as if she hadn't seen him preparing it earlier.

"Everyone hold up your glasses," Harrison said. Each of them raised theirs slowly. "Now, I want to be serious for a minute. I know that over the years I haven't always been here for all of you."

Helene cocked her head to one side, clearly not expecting this turn of events.

"Brenton and Gracie," he continued, "you're both too young to understand this, but in our society, a man is judged by his work, what he devotes his life to, and I was bitten by the finance bug early on. I've missed recitals and sporting events and even holidays for the lure of Sanford & Co. and my family chugged on without me there. I promise you it will all be different. I promise to love each of you as I should have."

He clinked each of their glasses and basked in the gaze of their stunned faces.

Helene cleared her throat.

"I find it hard to believe that this new firm won't also be slave drivers," she said, and took a sip of her wine.

"Why can't you be optimistic?"

"Not all promises are guarantees."

She traced a finger around the rim of her glass that let out a hum.

"Well, this promise is," he said, jabbing a shrimp with his fork and stuffing it into his mouth. It was just like Helene to destroy a beautiful moment. He had thought out his speech carefully while preparing their dinners and spoke from the heart. He certainly didn't expect a standing ovation, but he figured that at least they'd appreciate the attempt. Regardless, Helene's words seemed to resonate. He thought about how promises were not always guarantees and if Helene had eerily foreshadowed his upcoming trip to Mumbai without realizing. Would he actually be able to come back with a healthy liver? He had to believe that his will and determination to get an organ by any means possible would save him in the end.

Jay entered the dining room grumbling under his breath, mashing the cell phone in his hand that was the cause of his ire. Helene's father had always been an imposing figure; he had a grip that Harrison always tried to match with little success. Jay always said that his youth spent on football fields gave him better training to head up a multimillion-dollar corporation than any flimsy business degree. As a linebacker, he crushed any competitors back then, and as far as he was concerned, nothing had changed. He wore Brioni suits tailored so perfectly they seemed like a second skin, his face was always impeccably shaven as if he'd come from a barber, he had monogrammed silver lighters purely for his Cubans, and he had tough white hair that he slicked back like some relic of a businessman from the 1980s; but the impression he gave off was not of a man past his prime, more like a trailblazer who acted however he pleased and would outlast any trends that had the gall to compromise his style.

"This is dinner?" Jay asked, sliding into his chair and eyeing one especially overcooked piece of shrimp. "I could have us eating at Daniel within the hour."

"A place like Daniel is wasted on the kids," Harrison said. "Besides, I cooked this."

"God save us..." His cell rang and he barked into it before the person on the other end had a chance to speak. "Of course we can make it happen for those kind of zeroes. We're flying out to Macau tomorrow. Now I'm with my grandkids, the next time this cell rings someone better be dead as an explanation."

Helene chewed her food with a delighted smile, slipping back into the role of wide-eyed daddy's girl whenever her father became commanding.

"Hey Granddad, Dad's going to India in two days," Brenton said. "Is Macau near there?"

"It's in China," Jay replied. "Well, an administrative region of China. My company is investing in a casino there. It'll be the tallest in the world."

"Cool, how old do you have to be to gamble there?"

Jay winked at Brent. "I'll make sure you can get in no matter what."

"Sweet."

Jay turned to Harrison. "So you were fired, huh?" he said, spearing a shrimp with his fork and pointing it at Harrison like a weapon.

"Yes, Jay, it seems as if this spiraling economy has made me its next casualty. I'm going to Mumbai for a series of job interviews."

"You're a man of excuses," he said, taking a bite of the shrimp and choosing to leave the rest uneaten. "I don't think a chef should be your next calling."

Brenton laughed and Jay was satisfied with his dig. He untucked his napkin, took out a gleaming cigar case, and puckered his lips.

"Jay, the kids..." Harrison said, indicating the children as if Jay hadn't realized that they were present.

"You're a fine one to talk about immoral things that kids shouldn't be exposed to."

He lit his cigar and puffed a cloud to the ceiling.

"Someday, Brenton, your granddad will show you the pleasure of a fine Cuban."

"Cool, gimme one now," Brenton said, extending his fingers.

"That's not fair," Gracie said, crossing her arms. "What about me?"

"Really...Helene?" Harrison said, gesturing toward Jay.

"Oh, Helly, tell your husband to calm down," Jay said, rising to his feet. "I'll take it to the terrace."

The last thing Harrison wanted to do was get into an argument with Jay that he'd surely lose since his father-in-law was the type to debate all night to prove his opinion. The impending journey to Mumbai had made him excited but rattled as well, and he wished Jay would leave so he could compartmentalize what he was getting himself into.

Jay swept past him as the cigar smoke oozed into Harrison's collar. The son of a bitch held two fingers in the air, beckoning for him to join. Harrison planned on staying firm, but Helene nudged him. He tossed his napkin down and met up with Jay on the terrace.

The night was calm, minimal cars shooting down Fifth Avenue. Jay stood observing the city with disdain, as if the Stocktons' low view of the park wasn't exclusive enough.

"That moral grandstanding bullshit really gets under my skin," Jay sneered, refusing to turn around and look at Harrison.

"There are enough bad habits for Brenton and Gracie to pick up. They don't need to add cigars and gambling to that list."

Jay finally turned around with a big gust of smoke directed at Harrison's face.

"Bad habits?" he said, with a mischievous twinkle in his eye. "You know those all too well, son."

"What are you implying?"

"My Helly deserves a man, not a rube."

"I might not come from stock as well polished as yours, but I've worked hard for the past twenty years—"

"I knew you were fired before Helene told me. Don't forget that Sanford and I rowed for the Bulldogs together in the sixties." He mumbled under his breath. "Between your affinity for young and nubile pussy and your excessive sousing, I'm surprised you made it this long there."

"My affinity for what...? Fuck off," Harrison said, getting close enough to see up Jay's nostrils, thinking how easy it would be to toss him off the ledge.

Jay let out a bark of a laugh and embraced Harrison, his cigar breath flowing into Harrison's ear.

"Now you're going to embrace me and we'll walk

back inside like we're old friends so as not to upset Helly and the kids."

Harrison patted Jay on the back as the two exchanged phony grins.

"You deserve whatever despicable destiny awaits you," Jay said, out of the corner of his mouth and then headed back into the dining room. "You spineless sack of shit."

When Harrison sat back down, he skewered a shrimp with a pout. How much had Jay badmouthed him toward Helene and the kids when he wasn't around? Even now the bastard was chortling under his breath at the way he'd put Harrison in his place.

Trying to focus on anything but Jay, Harrison looked over at Brenton and saw that the boy was still in his soccer uniform.

"Had a good game today, son?" he asked, feeling his skin prickle as a half-chewed shrimp slid down his throat.

"No, we fucking lost—excuse me—freaking lost. It's that Rufus at our rival school, the refs let him get away with murder."

"Well, what are you doing about it?"

"Our coach says to play fair and that he'd rather we lose gracefully than win dishonestly."

"What a fruitcake."

"Harrison—"

"I'm sorry, Helene, but these kids are being taught that defeat is okay." He was looking at Jay, but pointed his knife at Brenton as he continued talking. "Brent, you need to cripple this Rufus if he's standing between you and that win. Do you want to win?"

"Of course I want to win," Brenton said, but from

the tone of his voice it didn't sound like he believed he could.

"How bad?" Harrison asked, slapping the table.

"Real bad," Brenton said, his cheeks burning red.

"You need to take what you want in this life. This is a lesson for you as well, Gracie."

Gracie looked up from her untouched plate.

"If you want the lead in your ballet recital then you need to call out the teacher that's taking those bribes. Blackmail her if necessary." He winked. "You don't roll over for anyone, you hear?"

"That's enough, Harrison," Helene said.

"And if that lady at UNESCO is trying to marginalize you, Helene, then you need to fight to stay." He gulped down the rest of the wine and went to finish the bottle.

"I think you've had more than you need," Helene said, making a grab for the bottle but he was faster.

"This family has become weak. We've let others trample us. And I'm just as guilty—Sanford & Co., my *ex-friend* Whit, even God has tried to destroy me." He eyed Jay again who seemed to be more concerned with a loose cufflink than Harrison's pleas. "This phoenix is gonna rise."

He swallowed the last bit of wine and wobbled in his chair until he got his bearings. Everyone gaped at him.

"Are you done?" Helene asked, shaking her head.

"Baby, I'm just getting started."

He then proceeded to gobble up the rest of the shrimp until his plate was clean.

7

Jay left soon after Harrison's grand show since he had an early flight to Macau in the morning and a car was waiting downstairs to take him back to his home in Greenwich. He had handed Brenton and Gracie a money clip in lieu of hugs, saved the only bit of affection he had for a kiss on his daughter's cheek, and gave Harrison a deigning look when he departed as if he knew what Harrison was traveling to Mumbai for and that his judgmental glare would be something Harrison would have to carry along.

Refusing to let Jay get to him, Harrison cleared the plates with a venomous vigor then sloppily said good night to Brenton and Gracie before meandering into his bedroom. Helene had changed into a nightgown and sat on the edge of their bed rubbing lotion on her legs. The minute she saw him walk in she began rubbing the lotion more dramatically.

"That was a fine display of arrogance tonight," she said, unable to even look at him.

"I was speaking the truth." He burped. "Complacency has become our downfall. I just want to light a fire under those kids."

"Yes, every child should learn blackmail at an early age."

"They better get used to stepping on others to get what they want so they don't get stepped on first."

"When did you become so disillusioned?"

"Why don't you ask your father that? And besides, you're the pessimist. I am going to India to better myself."

"I don't doubt that. You've always put yourself first."

"Everyone puts themselves first."

"No, everyone doesn't."

She threw the bottle of lotion to the ground and stood up. The nightgown hung loosely from her body and he lusted at this new, fiery Helene that he hadn't seen in a long while.

"You think that you can give one pompous speech and erase years of neglect?"

"No—"

"We got married and you vanished, Harrison. And it wasn't necessary. I could've still stayed in publishing and done my charity work on the side. My father could've helped us out; he would've at least paid for the kids' educations. There were different types of financial careers that you could've chosen. You didn't have to disappear into a hole just to eke out another bonus that we'd never even get around to spending."

"Says the woman who's never known what it's like to want."

"I wanted my husband. I wanted my family."

"Well, I came from nothing. From a house where

the lights were turned off because the bills weren't paid, and a mother who died from cancer because she had no medical insurance."

To his surprise, he found himself choking up when mentioning his mother, but he didn't want to lose his train of thought.

"I provided solely for this family, *my* family. Of course there were nights I wanted to be home with you—"

"I know about all of the...*girls*," she said, remaining calm. She sat down on the edge of the bed again and crossed one leg over the other.

"Wait, what girls?" he asked, stalling for time. Technically, he'd been with more than one girl, but besides Naelle, he had only slipped up that one time six months ago when his marriage really started to deteriorate. He always suspected that Helene had found out and wondered if Jay had delighted in exaggerating to her about his philandering ways.

"The ones you...treat," she said.

"Has Jay been in your ear?"

"My father has nothing to do with this," she sighed.

"He's always been too invested in you, you're like his obsession. Of course he'll say anything to make me look bad. He always has."

"Just stop it, Harrison."

"Helene, I have never—"

"Don't try to deny it. Give me some respect at least."

"You've looked at me with revulsion for so long."

"Obviously you're revolted by me, too."

"Never," he said, glancing at her lovely face. When he had spied her for the first time in the quad on an autumn day full of fallen orange leaves, he felt like he couldn't breathe. Time slowed like in some cheesy romantic movie he had always made fun of and all that existed was Helene. Her hair was in a side ponytail and a giant sweatshirt hung lopsided over her left shoulder revealing a pink bra strap. She was laughing loudly with a few girlfriends and he wondered what it'd be like to make her laugh like that all of the time. She played it cool when she noticed him—blinked once in his direction; but it was enough for him to summon the courage to walk over and change the rest of their lives. Now as he stared at her, he saw that her skin wasn't as vibrant as it used to be and her cheeks had puffed out a bit, like she was permanently hoarding traces of food, but she was still a knockout—always refined, always carrying herself as if she was the star attraction. Even while confronting his infidelity, she sat poised and unwavering.

"I'm the disgusting one here," he said, indicating his portly build.

"So go work out," she said, throwing her hands up in the air. "Go to a doctor for once."

"Yes, yes, when I get back from India, I promise to take better care of myself, less drinking, and I can swear to you that I'd never cheat on you again. You hadn't given me affection in so long and it's not like I made a habit out of messing around. It was a slip up—"

"You know, Harrison, I was actually nervous when I took my last STD test. Ridiculous. Here I am married in my forties and biting my nails over whether I have chlamydia. Or whatever's big now. HPV, I don't know!"

"I would never endanger you like that—"

"Really, so you make sure all of your little sluts go through vigorous testing before you fuck them?"

The fact she had cursed caught Harrison off guard. He made a move to try and soothe her, but she turned her back to him.

"I'm not some cad, it was a one-time, well, two-time thing."

"You must think I'm so stupid."

"Never—"

"You obviously do. And don't think I've never had opportunities, but out of respect..." she said, as she began to cry. "God, why am I crying?"

"Because you're disappointed in me?"

"No, because I'm disappointed in *me*."

She got up and grabbed a few Kleenex from a box on the nightstand.

"I should have left you the first time I suspected anything."

He tried stepping closer to her again, wanting to rewind time, but he was scared of her now.

"Do you want a divorce?" he asked, shaking in place.

She blew into the Kleenex and shrugged her shoulders.

"I'll take you for everything you have," she said.

"I don't doubt that."

"The thought of starting over, and dealing with lawyers, and selling the apartment, splitting up the kids between us. My parents would be crushed."

"I didn't know they ever liked me that much."

"They don't, but they hate each other and have stayed married forever. I was always told that you stick it out, you don't divorce. This is the sickness that's been drilled into me."

"What if we discussed this after I get back from India?"

"Right...India."

"I need to go. My livelihood depends on..."

He stopped himself before he revealed anymore. Part of him wanted to finally admit his diagnosis; he could certainly use the sympathy points now, but he shoved a finger into his mouth and chewed on a nail instead.

"You deserve to get what you want, Helene. All I can tell you is how sorry I am, how things can be different."

She nodded, seemingly exhausted from what she'd been holding inside of her all this time and that it had finally come out. She rubbed her red eyes and lay down.

"I want to go to bed."

"I'm leaving the day after tomorrow."

"I still want to go to bed."

"Can we talk about this in the morning?"

She shook her head into the pillow. "I have to get up at six to go over planning for the Faceless Children's Gala with goddamn Caroline Hendrest."

"You do too much."

She didn't respond. He watched the rise and fall of her body, the sweet curve of her backside. His fingers became electrified—the magnetic pull to caress her more overwhelming than ever, but he fought this desire. Touching her now would be deadly; she'd be sure to attack back.

"My flight is at seven in the morning so I'll have to go to bed early tomorrow."

"And?"

"Will I know that you'll at least be here when I get back from Mumbai?"

Her body rose and fell again but she didn't answer. He wondered if she'd already gone to sleep.

"Helene?" he asked, his voice straining. "Helene?" he asked again, but nothing.

He shut off the light and backed out of the door.

In the living room, Chauncey waited to be fed. Harrison scooped up the cat and brought him into the kitchen. Chauncey refused the can of cat food but wolfed down the leftover shrimp. Harrison nuzzled against the cat's body as Chauncey finished eating and allowed the massage.

"At least I know you'll be here," Harrison said, letting the cat lick off the last bit of sauce from his finger.

————

By the time he woke the next morning, Helene and the kids had already left the apartment. After a torturous shower to soothe his aching limbs and a fistful of medications, he headed to the bank to get his finances in order. The deal he made with Nagesh was to send the money once he got to Mumbai. Harrison thought it'd be smarter to have half sent before the surgery and half afterwards if it was a success, but Nagesh said that wouldn't work since the donor and the other physicians would want all of the money up front since they were the ones risking the most. The only tricky part in getting the money was that the majority of his accounts were joint ones with Helene and she'd notice if one hundred fifty thousand had been removed in a lump sum. However, if he set up a personal account by skimming a couple of thousand from a few of their savings accounts and cashing out one large CD, she wouldn't realize anything for a while.

After running around from bank-to-bank all day, he was exhausted by the time he got home and headed straight to bed since he had to get up in a few hours for his flight. He closed his eyes and was asleep instantly. Before he knew it, his alarm went off after what only felt like seconds. He shut it off quickly so he wouldn't disturb Helene. After throwing on some clothes and grabbing his packed suitcases, he decided to peek into his children's rooms. Brenton was splayed on his bed snoring at the ceiling and clutching a soccer ball like a stuffed animal. Pictures of soccer players that Harrison couldn't recognize were taped to the walls and the room smelled like old socks. To be a teenager again. To have minimal cares and your whole life ahead of you. When Harrison had been that age all he wanted to do was grow up. Now he'd kill to be young again. Maybe he'd even do things differently, not get married so young, backpack around Europe and screw a lot before he decided to settle down, maybe then his desire to ever wander would have been squashed. He wondered if a person was ever fully satisfied, or if they were always wishing for what they didn't have.

"Good luck with your next game, son," he whispered, patting the soccer ball by the kid's foot.

Next he went into Gracie's room. The walls were painted light pink and she slept in a canopy bed fit for a princess. She had curled into the fetal position. A small stuffed bunny was propped up against the pillow.

Harrison remembered how she'd been born a little premature, tiny enough to hold in his palm. He'd been negotiating a huge deal for a big client when Helene's water broke and he had to rush to the hospital. But work still remained on his mind since his cell wouldn't stop ringing in the delivery room; Sanford couldn't even give him one night. While holding Gracie for the first time, the phone buzzed in his pocket and he knew that he'd have to put down his little girl soon. But for a few solid minutes he pretended that this new life stirring in his arms was the only thing that mattered. He'd try to make more of an effort to be there for her than he had for Brenton, who was about to start kindergarten at the time and referred to Harrison by his actual name instead of Dad. Looking into Gracie's crusty eyes that had opened for the first time ever, he thought of how fleeting time could be, but he knew that nothing was likely to change: his clients would only become bigger and he'd be forced to see his family even less.

"Goodbye, Bunny," he said, his mind returning to the present.

She turned over in her sleep and he closed her door.

Lastly, he checked in on Helene. She slept with her hands folded over her chest like she was dead. The only sound she made was a wheeze coming from her nose due to a deviated septum. She looked older and more tired than when she was awake. He let go of his bags, crept over to the bed, and planted a kiss on her lips. She didn't stir. She tasted of sweat and a trace of lipstick. When he licked his own lips, he could still taste her. Chauncey ran inside, as if to remind him that his car was waiting, but he took an extra moment to gaze at his wife, his once best friend, the girl who used to make him laugh so hard that he'd feel a pop in his gut, the mother of his children, a figure of hope for all of those poor people in distant countries who she worked tirelessly to help. He had taken this woman for granted, and if she'd be gone when he got home from Mumbai, he had no one else to blame but himself.

Goodbye, my love, he thought, not wanting to take a chance by whispering and possibly waking her. Then he got his bags and headed down the hall.

"Take good care of them all," he told the cat and then left.

———

Before getting on the plane, he stopped at a Starbucks to get a giant cup of iced coffee. As he opened up his wallet to pay the bill, the Desire Card slipped out again.

He paid for the coffee and went to board the plane with the card still in his hand. As he stood in the terminal, he made a mental list of all the things in this world that he desired. At the top of the list was obviously his new liver, but then he thought about what would come second. What wish would he pay any amount to achieve? He thought of his deceased parents and how much he'd pay for a different upbringing. For a father who wouldn't smack him around over something as trivial as spilled milk and for a mother who'd stand up for him instead of pretending like she didn't know what was going on. When they both finally passed after belabored illnesses, their deaths only evoked a shrug in him. He had raised himself and finally severed his old life in New Haven. Since that had been his entire existence for his first eighteen years, he decided he would've paid any amount for someone else's childhood.

Next he thought about Helene and the kids. Would he pay for a different family? Or would he pay for a better relationship with the one he had? In a blink, he'd spent one hundred fifty thousand on a liver, but he didn't know if he'd do the same to mend a family that was clearly broken. Would Helene even miss him if he walked away, or would she be secretly pleased to be free? Would the kids be better off with a more active participant in their lives? But who said that was how it had to be? Once he got a new liver, he could still have half of his life left and make a promise to be more dependable.

Finally his mind went to his career and what he wanted out of that. Did he desire the same grind he'd had for the past twenty years, or had he become a new man since his termination and subsequent diagnosis? On his deathbed, would he ever wish that he had worked more? No, that was ludicrous. But who was he if not a vice president at Sanford & Co.? Stripped of that identity, he cringed to think that he was nothing more than a cipher, eventually becoming like everyone else at some menial job eking out their day-to-day. His clients had been worth billions all put together. He'd made a lot of rich people even richer over the years, and if life was no longer the pursuit of making more money, than what else was there?

The passengers from his flight started boarding the plane. He passed by a garbage bin with the Desire Card between his middle and index finger. As he was about to release it from his grip, he hesitated and slipped it back into his pocket. He wheeled his check-on bag and fell in with the queue: some of them businessmen, some wearing colorful clothing with little children sleeping in their arms, all of them with their own wants and needs, but he bet none had his insatiable appetite. If he'd only been able to control his cravings better he wouldn't be getting on a plane to get an organ off the black market. He wondered how all these people had learned to temper their desires, the ones that tasted so good and punished the worst? How were they able to remain functioning contributors to society, and care for their families properly, and refrain from destroying themselves like he had done?

As he stepped onto the plane, he fingered the Desire Card in his pocket and knew that he'd pay any amount to find out how.

PART TWO

8

DESPITE FORKING OVER SEVEN THOUSAND DOLLARS for a first-class flight, Harrison chose to spend the thirty-five hour trip heavily medicated with sleeping pills. To stay lucid meant thirty-five hours of thinking about the reason he'd come to Mumbai; it was easier to blackout. The layover at Heathrow proved the most difficult since he practically had to be slapped awake by a stewardess so he'd make his connection. After an interminable wait at customs, he got on a rail shuttle to head to a different terminal, his head throbbing, the lure of sleep just a dream. Once he boarded the new plane, he gobbled up the curried prawn dish offered as a main and popped two more sleeping pills until his body felt like it was being carried away in a hot air balloon.

He was awakened hours later as the plane began its descent. A pretty Indian stewardess had her manicured fingers on his shoulder. He couldn't hear what she was saying since his ears hadn't popped yet, but he nodded anyway. The plane didn't land smoothly at Chhatrapati Shivaji International Airport, the sensation akin to

being dropped out of the sky. Bags shifted in the overhead bins. Little children screamed. The wonky
landing jarred the curried pawns he'd ingested. One
especially troublesome piece of shell tickled his uvula.
He grabbed an airsickness bag and breathed in its
papery smell as the plane taxied to its terminal.

Upon exiting with the airsickness bag firmly in his
grasp, he was bombarded by a spicy and fishy aroma
that finally triggered his gag reflex. He peered into the
bag to see the mossy-colored dinner he regurgitated and
then left it all in an overflowing garbage bin. It appeared
as if every other flight in the world had arrived at a
similar time in the middle of the night. He stood at the
luggage belt with other sleepy travelers waiting almost
an hour for his bags to arrive. Men posing as luggage
loaders tried to negotiate rates, but the locals seemed to
be shooing them away. He had only brought one suitcase anyway, figuring he would pick up some throwaway clothes.

After another standstill wait at customs, he exited
onto a slick airport terminal that resembled the inside of
a spaceship to his warped, pill-laden mind. Its newly
built interior was nothing like he had pictured: clean
white floors and walls, concave windows that stretched
out toward a black horizon. He had expected rats
aplenty and people swarming in packs. Stepping closer
to the bubbled windows, he could see the crumbling
shacks and piles of garbage in the neighboring slums.
Lives of turmoil, filth and heartbreak, existences he
couldn't wrap his mind around. Viewing the slums from
the cool of the airport terminals made it seem like he
was watching its wretchedness unfold on television. He
felt himself wanting to change the channel.

At the taxi counter, he foolishly didn't specify for a high-end ride. He was led to a vehicle that seemed to be held together by duct tape. The driver said, "Hello" and dumped his suitcase into a jerry-rigged trunk. Harrison was surprised the guy spoke English. He sat down on upholstery that was caked with dirt and smelled of body odor. There was a hole in the rusted metal floor by his foot. As the taxi sped off, he turned back toward the modern, aesthetically pleasing airport and its bordering slums that resembled apocalyptic wings holding on tight and refusing to let go.

"Have you come to Mumbai for business or pleasure?" the driver asked, glancing at him through the rearview mirror. The driver's face was tanned and dusty and he wore a white turban that almost touched the roof of the taxi.

"Business," Harrison said, uninterested with continuing the conversation.

"Oh, we have many wonderful things to see here as well," the driver said, chipper as ever even though it was early in the morning. "The Gateway to India is a marvelous sight. Right by your hotel."

Harrison gave an exaggerated yawn but the driver kept speaking.

"And the Haji Ali! It is a tomb in the middle of the sea. Tourists all go. And the Chor Bazaar Thieves Market is a must after day of sightseeing. You can test your bargaining skills. My wife has a stall—"

"I don't think I'll have the time."

"I'm not just a taxi driver, but also a tour guide! I will take you wherever you want to go, tell you about the history of Mumbai. For example, the city used to be called Bombay but the government changed the name to honor Mumba Devi, the patron Hindu goddess—"

"I'll be too busy with the business I came here for."

"Yes, yes of course. What kind of business do you do?"

"I'm here to buy something that I can't get back in America."

"Yes, my wife makes saris if you are looking to buy. Very, very, very nice–"

"I'm going to close my eyes for a second."

"Yes, yes, I understand. Long, long flight. You lie back, be comfortable. You will be at your hotel before you know it."

Harrison couldn't keep his eyes shut for long because the driver kept veering to the wrong side of the road and he was afraid his foot would fall through the hole in the floor. They drove down the apparently lawless streets, barely avoiding any speeding cars coming from the other direction. Harrison was almost glad once they reached the heart of the city and were stuck in a traffic jam until the reality of being here became apparent: a symphony of honking horns and barefooted children holding onto infants and tapping at car windows, disfigured men and women hovering with gaping mouths and outstretched palms. He tried to roll up the window, but it was broken and didn't go all the way. One disheveled woman slipped two gnarled fingers inside. She gazed at him, her pupils covered with a white film, never-ending tears the only clean lines on her face. He knocked against the window to scare her away as if she was a nagging pigeon but she persisted, begging for change until he finally slid a dollar between her two probing fingers and she reeled back, bewildered beyond comprehension. Then she clutched the money to her chest with a three-tooth smile directed at the sky. He figured that his measly dollar might feed her for today.

As the taxi inched along, the sun rose and his skin stuck to the leather seats. He asked the driver about air conditioning, but the guy responded by shaking his head.

"No air conditioning in these kinds of taxis, but heat is good for the body!"

"You keep telling yourself that."

The surrounding sights held no interest to him, never being much of a traveler. Any wonders that India might offer were trumped by the illicit reason he came. Taking in any sights could sway his focus. His trips abroad had always been for business anyway, and he preferred weekends in the Hamptons on the few occasions he had time off with his family. The allure of a beach, a cold cocktail—this was the essence of a vacation, not a bustling metropolis crammed with over twenty million people.

After over an hour of stop-and-go traffic, they reached the Colaba neighborhood where the Taj Mahal Palace hotel was located. The area existed on the tip of Mumbai's peninsula and was a small respite from the chaos they had driven through. Bars, restaurants, and a long stretch of street stalls sold everything from clothing to black-market DVDs in front of brand-name stores. As they neared the hotel, the Gateway to India stood watch over the sea with luxury cruise ships docked at its sides. Across the causeway, the Taj Hotel mirrored its namesake in terms of opulence but looked more like a Victorian manor if not for the dome-like spires on the roof that added an Indian flourish.

The driver turned off the motor and scurried around to the trunk to retrieve Harrison's suitcase. He had to bang the trunk a few times until it finally opened and he could wedge the suitcase out.

"There you go, sir," the driver said, wiping his sweaty forehead with a handkerchief. "Door-to-door service, that is my motto! Again if you need a tour—"

"That won't be necessary," Harrison said, and took out his wallet. "Shit, I haven't had a chance to exchange my money from home yet."

"Oh, not so good."

"But it's American dollars?"

The driver scrunched up his face.

"Yes, I do understand, but that is not so good for me with the exchange rate. I am not a beggar so I do not accept everything. So sorry, so sorry."

This was news to Harrison. He hadn't even bothered to look at the exchange rate before he left, since he figured that the American dollar would go very far here.

"You can get Indian rupees from the ATM in your hotel."

When Harrison went inside, he was pleased to see that the hotel was the nicest thing he'd encountered in Mumbai so far. Antique furniture, ornate flower arrangements, and crystalline chandeliers filled up the lobby. The floors were made of marble and the air smelled like turmeric. He had assumed that a five-star hotel in India would likely resemble a three- or four-star one back in the States, but he couldn't have been more wrong. The six hundred dollars a night he'd spent on a room would be well worth it.

He took out some rupees from the ATM and went to pay the driver.

"May your business be fruitful here in Mumbai and may you get everything you came for," the driver said, handing Harrison the card for the taxi company. On the back, he had scribbled: *Buy Saris – Fareeha*, along with a phone number.

"My wife." He smiled. "She make very, very, very nice saris!"

Harrison thought of Gracie. He'd definitely make sure to get her a sari before he went home since she wanted one so badly, but he couldn't worry about it until after he got a new liver.

"Yeah, thanks," he said, waving away the driver who was patting him on the shoulder now. "Goodbye."

The driver folded his palms together and bowed.

"*Namaste.*"

After checking in with the front desk, he headed up to his room. He tipped the bellhop, ordered some dosas from room service, and rested on silky sheets with butterflies along the trim, feminine but soothing. He couldn't help but imagine how much Helene would've appreciated the room's decor.

As he lay back and waited for his dosas, he swore he wouldn't torture himself anymore by thinking of Helene while he was in India. He knew it'd be pointless to analyze the last fight they had, but he couldn't help going back to the moment when she revealed that she knew about his infidelities. If she'd been the unfaithful one, he would've gone ballistic. The thought of another man's hands caressing her, their moans echoing through the walls, unbridled passion that couldn't compare to the rote lovemaking a husband and wife shared—that would be too much for him to handle. He'd want to slaughter any other man she looked at, but if she decided to leave him once he returned, he'd have to accept that he no longer possessed her anymore.

A knock on the door brought in a bellhop with a tray of dosas. Harrison gorged without taking a breath, his stomach hollow. He had plans to meet Nagesh later that day at a place called Café Mondegar, in walking distance. The plan was to catch up and go over the particulars of his surgery. He decided to set his alarm clock and nap for a few hours. He fell asleep the instant he closed his eyes.

He dreamt of a large dim room that looked like part of an abandoned factory. He was lying in a hospital bed, connected to beeping machines. He lifted up his shirt and saw that his stomach had been all sewed up. An Indian man was sleeping on the gurney next to him. The man's body was covered with a sheet and he seemed to be hooked up to even more machines than Harrison.

Harrison heard a door slam at the other end of the room as Nagesh entered wearing doctor's scrubs. He was surprised to see that Nagesh hadn't aged since the two had last seen each other; Nagesh still resembled a gangly kid with greasy, slicked-back hair and a bad teenage mustache. The doctor's scrubs made him look like a child playing dress up.

"So the transplant was a success, H-Bomb," Nagesh smiled. Unlike most people who smiled simply out of politeness, Nagesh's smile could last throughout an entire conversation. Harrison was taken back to his freshman dorm room and countless nights of laughing with Nagesh while getting drunk off rye or smoking some mind-blowing hydro. Days of youth and inno-cence—before life decided to sink its teeth in and draw blood.

He ran his fingers across the stitches on his chest as globs of tears fell.

"I...got a new liver?"

Weeks of living with a death sentence vanished with those beautiful words. He gave into his flooding emotions and let himself rejoice at his revival. He'd been tenacious, even stubborn in his quest; now it had all paid off.

"Yup, you're all sewn up, good as new," Nagesh said, mimicking the motion of stitching a needle.

"And the donor?" he asked, turning to the man on the gurney. He didn't know if there would be retribution for his own success; it seemed too good to be true if both he and the donor survived with long lives ahead. Was it possible that God could behave so strongly in his favor without trying to teach him a lesson?

"Fine, fine, the donor is fine," Nagesh said. "Every-thing is fine. Just the question of money now."

A briefcase appeared at the foot of his hospital bed. Harrison strained to reach the handle, then opened it to show Nagesh the cash. A shimmering gold light beamed from the suitcase once it opened while Nagesh reveled in his new fortune.

"Money well spent," Nagesh said, closing up the briefcase.

"That's about half a year's salary at Sanford & Co. I've worked hard for that money."

"I do not doubt that. So someone is here to see you."

Harrison froze as he saw Helene enter the room.

He couldn't tell from her expression what was going on in her head. Was she relieved that he was all right, or angry that he hadn't told her he was sick and chose to get an organ off the black market? His whole body tensed up as she watched him from afar. He wondered why she wasn't coming closer. Why wasn't her face stained with thankful tears? Was she still upset that he had cheated on her? After twenty-five years together, the surgery he underwent should supersede any lingering resentment.

"Helene?"

His voice croaked, her name barely more than a whisper. Even though he had felt invincible seconds ago, now he needed her approval to avoid plunging into depression.

Tell me that what I've done here is all right.

He looked directly at her, as if she could read his mind, but she remained silent. He'd never been so afraid to look into her chestnut brown eyes.

The donor is doing fine after the surgery. He will have money to feed his family. One could even argue that I'm doing a good thing.

She slowly shook her head.

If I only relied on the donor list, I could be dead before my name came up. You'd be raising our children on your own.

Helene continued shaking her head.

Goddamnit, Helene, this was the only option! Don't guilt me anymore than you already have. I already feel bad for cheating on you, don't....

She shook her head one last time before she turned around to walk away.

Tell me that I'm still a good person. I know that I am

*deep down where it counts. There are those who are truly
evil and then there are people like me that exist in a gray
area. This world is ultimately about survival and that's
all I wish for: to survive, to learn from my mistakes, and
to ultimately become a better person because of them.
You'll see.*

Her high heels clomped against the floor. She
opened the door and slammed it shut behind her.

You'll see.

He faced the sleeping donor. The man's tiny snores
reverberated throughout the large room. From behind
the gurney, Gracie appeared in her ballerina uniform.

"Hi, Daddy," she said, dancing around his hospital
bed.

"Gracie, did you hear that?" Harrison asked. "I'm
going to live. Daddy's not going anywhere."

He spread out his arms and she placed her head on
his chest. He kissed the bun on top of her head.

"I get what I want, Bunny. Do you see that? I wasn't
ready to die."

He could feel her nodding against his chest.

"Daddy?"

She looked up at him with pleading eyes.

"Yes?"

"Did you buy me a sari?"

The machines the donor was hooked up to starting
beeping louder than before. The donor began thrashing
around and clutching onto his heart as if an exorcism
was being performed. Nagesh ran over and tried to
revive the man, but the beeping only became louder
and louder. The donor was screaming now, the room
erupting in chaos. Gracie had disappeared, leaving him
all alone. The donor kept yelling as the stitches on the

man's chest began popping open one by one until his organs erupted.

Harrison closed his eyes as the donor's blood dripped down his face and arms, but he could still hear the beeps of the machine pounding in his mind and the man's cries echoing through the dim room until his own cries began to blend in...

He woke up to a shrill alarm, unsure where he was for a moment. The butterfly sheets brought him to his senses. He shook away any lingering aftereffects of the dream. It was a nightmare, nothing more. Helene hadn't found out what he'd done, he'd get Gracie her sari before he headed home, and the donor would be just fine. He reiterated to himself that he was justified in coming here for a liver and nothing should sway that belief.

When he looked at the clock, he saw he had enough time to shower and change his clothes before meeting Nagesh. He shuffled into the bathroom, waited till the water was steaming and punishing, and stepped into its pummeling massage. Once he emerged, he felt more triumphant than he had in a long time since his new organ was in arm's reach. Unless others had walked in his shoes, they had no right to judge his actions. Let some other morally upright fool die because they were afraid to see their true self in the mirror. Harrison had known who he was for a very long time.

So he put on his gold watch and dressed in some linen pants, a short-sleeve button down, and nice shoes before exiting the room to meet up with Nagesh and begin his unalienable right for a long and fruitful destiny.

9

HARRISON ENTERED CAFÉ MONDEGAR DRENCHED
in sweat from a three-block walk under the hazy, setting
sun. Rings had surfaced around his armpits and gave off
the stench of boiled eggs, a smell he'd grown used to,
but at least in Mumbai his rank scent didn't stand out.
The café was bustling, its walls painted with cartoonish
vignettes of diners. He snagged a table under a depic-
tion of a family eating lobsters, except for one roguish
lobster that had leaped off a plate to pinch the dad on
the nose. He ordered a pitcher of Kingfisher beer and
downed two pints before he spied Nagesh.

Time hadn't been too kind to Nagesh, but not as
cruel as it had been to Harrison. The skinny kid he
befriended twenty-five years ago was still gangly in
parts but now portly in others. Nagesh's arms were thin
without the slightest trace of muscle, and a sad potbelly
poked out from under his shirt that revealed a belly
button hidden by a forest of dark hair. His light skin
had browned from the past decade in Mumbai, the tone
similar to a dulled penny. The peach fuzz that had

dotted his upper lip back at Chilton was now a bushy mustache that wouldn't be out of place in the Wild West. But it was Nagesh's bug eyes that had remained the same, spanning almost a third of his face. They were bloodshot from the polluted air but had retained their wide-eyed innocence like that of a fresh-faced farm girl stepping off the bus in Hollywood. They scanned Café Mondegar before finally seeing Harrison, and a big smile soon followed.

Harrison noticed that Nagesh's smile appeared strained as his old friend made his way over. Weaving in between other diners, Nagesh seemed determined to keep the smile intact despite an obvious shock at Harrison's appearance. It had been over a decade since the friends had last seen one another, a decade for Harrison that consisted of fifty extra pounds, jaundiced skin, and a decaying body.

"H-Bomb!" sang Nagesh, as he mimed a bomb exploding on the table.

"Nagesh, my man." Harrison was already getting misty-eyed as he dwarfed his smaller friend in a bone-cracking embrace.

"Already two steps ahead?"

Nagesh indicated the pitcher of beer as he sat down, his smile straining even more, his accent heavier than Harrison remembered.

"It's good to see you," Harrison said, pouring a glass that spilled over the sides.

"Yes. And you."

The two gulped their beers, avoiding an uncomfortable silence as both of them thought of what to say next. The din of the other diners provided a relief.

"So you've filled out some," Harrison finally said.

"Who me?" Nagesh touched his fat cheeks and rubbed his bowling ball stomach. "Without a wife to cook for me, I've fallen prey to fast food."

"Well, I've had a wife all these years and look at what it has done to me."

The two laughed at that and sipped their beers again, Nagesh's moustache covered in suds.

"And the moustache?"

"Oh yes, it is a big trend in Bollywood these days, especially in Southern Indian films. Trying to stay current, you know?"

"And you like it here in Mumbai? You're happy?"

"Happiness is sometimes overrated. This is where I'm from, where I'm meant to be. Like now I can help you because I'm here, right, H-Bomb?"

A waiter came by and passed them menus.

"The food is so American here," Harrison said, looking around at the even mix of locals and Caucasians. "I guess we're everywhere, right?"

"Yes, this is a heavily touristy area."

They ordered onion rings, chicken wings, and another pitcher of Kingfisher beer.

"How is your hotel?"

"The Taj? Beautiful. Definitely an anomaly from anything else I've seen in this country so far. That cab ride from the airport, I don't look forward to doing that again. No offense or anything."

Nagesh shrugged.

"So, H-Bomb, the wife and the kids, I trust everyone is doing well?"

Harrison clutched his beer and let a sigh pass from his lips.

"Not so much. I mean health-wise everyone is fine,

but Helene and I...things don't look so optimistic there. I still haven't told any of them about my illness."

"They haven't questioned?"

"Is it that obvious?"

"No, no, nothing like that." Nagesh hung his head. "I do not know what I meant."

"I'm aware that I look like death."

"This is but a moment for you, not a lifetime sentence. I will fix you up and make you good as new."

Nagesh's eyes bugged as he frantically looked around the room. "I have not eaten yet today," he confessed, clasping his hands together in prayer. "I apologize if I seem punchy."

"You don't have to apologize for anything. I'm forever indebted. If I were to have another child, I'd name it after you," Harrison said, and then added in a whisper, "Once my new liver takes, of course."

The two laughed quietly at that. The waiter came over with a plate of onion rings and chicken wings. Harrison tore into the food.

"So, this donor...?" Harrison asked in the same low whisper, with red sauce dripping from his lips. "He's one hundred percent on board?"

"My donors are always one hundred percent on board."

"And the liver is in tip-top shape? I would like to meet him before the surgery. Just that I caught a glimpse of the slums here on the taxi ride over. Ghastly business in a place like that. I can't imagine someone from there would have a healthy liver."

"I recently gave him a checkup and his liver couldn't be healthier. But sure, if you want I can introduce you to him if that will ease your worries. In fact, I was going to suggest that for tomorrow. We can visit him and his family."

Harrison made a face. "In the slums?"

"He would not have the means to come to you, nor would he be allowed inside a place like the Taj."

"Of course, of course," Harrison replied, licking off a bone.

"I will set it up for late morning."

Harrison watched as Nagesh picked at his food, one slowly diminishing onion ring being the source of his entire meal while Harrison had left behind a basket of discarded bones.

"I thought you were hungry?" Harrison asked, pointing at the onion ring.

"Oh, yes," Nagesh said, his eyes cast down. "The food is just so hot, hurts my tongue. So, what did you tell your wife about why you're in India?"

"I told her a job interview. I was...fired right before I was diagnosed with liver disease. I said this new company had a sister office out here but wanted me to head up their division in the States. That way she wouldn't get all worried about moving."

"I am so sorry to hear about your job. This was the same firm you've been at all this time?"

Harrison let out a barbequed belch. The chicken wings were rumbling around inside his belly. He didn't want to discuss Sanford & Co., which now seemed like a lifetime ago.

"Yeah, same firm. I gave them blood, but that's not enough these days. New York City is a cesspool of deceit."

Harrison shook his head, drunk now from the beers and the jetlag. He felt himself getting hot with rage.

Thoughts of Whit and Thom Bartlett burned through his mind, the way they had sinisterly aligned to do him in.

"You're lucky you never made the move to New York, Nagesh. That city will wring any goodness left in you and leave you soulless. My soul's been lost for a long time now. I wouldn't even know where to look for it anymore. And maybe that's better since the world spins on greed anyway and I've got to keep up somehow."

Nagesh nodded in response, munching on the same onion ring with mouse-sized bites.

"I've learned that I'm pretty insignificant in a place like Manhattan. I was netting a good six-figure salary, but that's nothing to boast about when you're rubbing shoulders with billionaires."

Nagesh kept nodding, his head snapping back and forth with such a force as if he was trying to break it off.

"But I guess I can see the appeal of a place like India for you," Harrison said, winking. "I know your game."

Nagesh's eyes bugged again as the onion ring crumbled in his fingers. "W-what do you mean?"

"You can live like a king here. A doctor in Mumbai must be royalty. In New York, doctors do well but a lot of them would have a tough time even affording the maintenance in my building plus a mortgage."

"Oh, I see."

"Because why the hell else would you be in a place like this except for the fact that you could get anything you wanted if you waved some dollars around."

"India is a place of burgeoning acceleration right now," Nagesh replied, stiffening in his seat as if he finally started taking offense to Harrison's swipes at his country.

"Yeah, yeah, I know, I know—"

"Sure the rich and poor are greatly divided, but the rich are making more money here than a lot of people back in America. We are not feeling the economic strain like you are."

"And that's why you stay?"

Nagesh leaned in closer and cupped his hand around his mouth.

"Things aren't regulated as much as they are in the States in reference to my side practice. That would be an impossibility back in America, but here I can employ discreet medical professionals to assist the surgeries, and I have trusted contacts who supply me with vital donors from the slums. This is what has afforded me a beautiful house in the suburbs and enough money to retire in the near future. In the States I'd be working like a dog till I dropped."

"Look at me, my friend," Harrison said, shaking his head. "Halfway through life and I've already dropped. But I'm a man who gets what he wants. At least I'll make sure that'll be the case here. And I want to live."

"To life then," Nagesh said, perking up with a smile bigger than the one he gave Harrison when he entered Café Mondegar. He clinked Harrison's glass and finished his last swill of beer.

"To life," Harrison agreed.

"So I was thinking we go out tonight to celebrate. A hot club, girls wearing very little, what do you say?"

"Not much has changed with you, Nagesh."

"There is this place called Tryst in the Lower Parel that I know you will very much like."

Harrison chewed on the last onion ring.

"I might as well have one more night of debauchery before I put my health in your hands."

"That is the H-Bomb I remember," Nagesh said, giving him a thumbs-up. He popped up in his seat and clapped his hands, a frantic ball of energy now. "Take care of the check and I will go get us a taxi."

————

Outside the sun had set, the air dropping slightly in temperature but still with a hot breeze. Nagesh had flagged down a silver-and-blue taxi that was air-conditioned. The trip to Tryst was a short distance into the center of the city. They passed by rows of worn-down, two-story homes and businesses, all of the windows covered with sheets. Clusters of people milled about, walked into traffic as if they had a sixth sense to avoid the speeding taxis, motorbikes, and bicycles. Men varied from wearing casual dress to elders in white robes with frazzled beards long enough to reach their chests. Women were mostly covered from head-to-toe, either dressed in eye-popping colors or with scarves wrapped around their heads. Cripples were everywhere, some walked erect while others were stooped over, their bodies forming the shape of a semi colon. Some were pulled along in crates from old mango boxes with legs as thin as wrists. He could hear yelling through the taxi's closed windows, thumping music as well. Some guy leaped in front of them out of nowhere, almost got hit as if he was seeking a quick death. The guy shook his fist and pounded on the hood. The cab driver gesticulated back. As they continued driving, no one who surrounded them seemed to have an actual destination. The streets were flooded with movement for the sake of moving, anything to avoid stillness, a knife in the face of reality. *Chaos,* Harrison thought, shaking his head. He'd been to places like Tokyo and Hong Kong on business; he was used to cities that made New York seem Podunk in terms of population, but Mumbai appeared otherworldly, haphazard, fraught with back alleys where lives were lost, where people fought each other for an almighty rupee.

Nagesh stared straight ahead like he didn't notice his frenzied city anymore. He nibbled on a fingernail that was almost bitten off entirely. The rest of his nails were the same, chewed up and raw. He slid his hands inside his pockets, as if embarrassed.

"How much farther?" Harrison asked, growing tired.

"Take in my city, H-Bomb. This will be one of your only times for sightseeing."

But Harrison didn't want to look, disgusted with the surrounding clamor. He pictured the soft sheets on his bed at the Taj with butterflies along the trim and sleeping until this ordeal would be over. He was growing nervous and wished he could get his new liver and go home, but this would unfortunately be his home for the next month.

————

Tryst was not how Harrison imagined. Its interior had been set up as a spectacular light show with color-changing LEDs poking out of every corner and bright-green absinthe potions in tall glasses. A DJ pumped house music that assaulted his ears, the flashing lights seizure inducing. Nagesh seemed to know one of the managers so they were given their own private table with a bar and a butler. Harrison figured that Nagesh had probably hooked the manager up with a new organ too.

"Awesome, no?" Nagesh asked, delighted by the cocktail in his hand as he bopped his head to the music. "This is Mumbai at its finest."

"You live in a strange city," Harrison yelled, leaning in close so Nagesh would hear.

"How so?"

"Just that it's so rich in parts and so ridiculously poor in others. You don't find that odd?"

"Mumbai is not a place you'll understand in a day. View it up close and it might seem like a maze of winding dirty streets and alleys, but take a step back to become awed by this vibrant, often beautifully mad place."

"No thanks," Harrison said, becoming lost in his tall drink as he gulped it down. He could tell Nagesh wasn't pleased with his response so he feigned interest. "So then tell me more about Mumbai? What do the people who live here want?"

"I'm not following what you mean."

"Like in New York, people want a stellar career that pays them a lot of money, 2.5 children, prime real estate, a full social calendar, and a weekend house in the Hamptons."

"Here it is more general. The rich want a new, powerful Mumbai, a home of culture and elegance and flashy things that will bring in tourists."

"And the poor?"

Nagesh rubbed his fingers across the endless curl of his mustache. "The poor just want to get out of the slums or build up the shack that they live in. Threats to demolish some of the slums are becoming more real, especially the ones you probably saw by the airport. So those people just want things to stay the same and not get worse. You will see what I am speaking of tomorrow."

Nagesh keyed in another drink order on the LED screen at their private table.

"And here we are spending God knows what for watered down drinks," Harrison laughed. "How much food could feed a family in the slums for the price of our drinks?"

"A good amount I imagine."

"The world is far from balanced, but I can't feel bad for the privilege that I have earned."

"I thought you realized that you were pretty insignificant back in Manhattan?"

"In Manhattan, yes. But it's a whole other ballgame in the rest of the world."

Harrison looked around the club and turned to Nagesh with a sour face. "Didn't you promise that girls would be here? No one seems to be giving me a second glance. They don't like regular white bread, just *naan*, huh?"

The butler for the table arrived with their drinks.

"If you wish I can get you a number for an escort service tonight?"

"Who do you take me for, Nagesh?"

"Probably someone who is lonely, who feels like they have been missing something for some time now.

You said yourself that you and your wife are having problems."

Harrison bit the inside of his cheek, grinding his teeth into the flesh while he stared at his diminishing drink.

"Are the girls even clean? I mean, I wouldn't want some slum whore."

"H-Bomb, what do you take me for? Of course these girls are clean and classy. They do not run cheap either, but that does not seem to be a problem for you."

"Far from it."

"So it is settled," Nagesh said, slipping Harrison a business card with a number: *Nagarvadhus Escorts – "Brides of the Town."*

"Brides of the town?"

"In ancient India, there was a practice of having *Nagarvadhus*, or 'Brides of the Town,' women for all."

"I did say I wanted a night of debauchery before my surgery."

"Ask for Abhilasha, she is *sundar*." He kissed his fingers. "Wet enough to keep you going all night. Sexy enough to question your sanity."

"I've been questioning my sanity for some time now," Harrison replied, almost as if he didn't mean to say it out loud.

Nagesh closed out their bill on the pop-up LED screen.

"I have forgotten my credit card, H-Bomb. All right if the drinks are on you?"

Harrison rolled his eyes as he got out his wallet.

"I'll subtract it from the hundred and fifty thousand I'm about to give you," he said.

Nagesh grabbed Harrison's arm rather forcibly.

"My neck is on the line for you, H-Bomb. I hope you understand that."

"I was just kidding—"

"My practice, my livelihood, everything," he said, his eyes growing wide, fearful. "I am doing this all for you."

"And for your fifty-thousand-dollar cut," Harrison replied, yanking his arm away. "Let's not make ourselves into a martyr."

Harrison was drunk at this point, his thoughts muddled and venomous. Nagesh narrowed his eyes and let out a sly smile.

"Fine then, I am an opportunist. If I remember correctly, you were the same. Back at Chilton, you let me take the fall for our call-girl ring."

"That was twenty-five years ago, we were fucking kids," Harrison said, running his credit card across the LED screen. He put the Nagarvadhus Escorts card inside his wallet. "C'mon, Pimp Daddy, let's get out of here. I'm about ready to go insane."

"I must use the bathroom first," Nagesh said, leaping up from his seat. "I will meet you outside."

Harrison puffed out his cheeks as he strained to stand up. The lights surrounding him flashed in greens and blues and made his head swirl. He felt the effects of the drinks he chugged down pressing against his forehead. Through the crowd of patrons mingling and dancing, he saw a man gazing in his direction from across the club. The man was leaning against a wall, a drink in hand. The flashing lights only let him glimpse the man's face for a moment at a time. All he could really see was that the man was the only other white person at Tryst. Without thinking, he found himself giving a nod of solidarity.

The lights stopped pulsing and bathed the man in an aqua hue. Upon closer inspection, his face was terribly scarred with deep, crisscrossing cuts as if he'd been brutally lashed with a whip. He stared at Harrison before nodding back and heading for the door.

Since Nagesh was nowhere to be found, Harrison followed the scarred man out of Tryst, craving fresh air anyway. Once he got outside, he saw a sleek black car idling in front of the club. One of the windows had been rolled down and a suited elbow hung out. He could make out the silhouette of a person in the back seat.

The scarred man was walking toward the car at a brisk pace. Whoever sat in the back seat rolled up the window as the engine revved. Before stepping into the car, the scarred man gave Harrison one final glance that caused a cold and liquid tingle to shoot down his spine. The person in the back seat gestured for the driver to go and the car sped away.

Swaying a bit, Harrison shuffled over to an alleyway next to the club so he could prop himself against a wall. There wasn't a soul nearby, the quietest it had been since he'd gotten to Mumbai, eerily quiet. He imagined the man with scars getting whipped in the face, the pain unbearable. He knew what that kind of pain was like.

From down the alleyway, six eyes emerged: blinking, examining, coming closer. Before he could even attempt to move, they were upon him. A knife gleamed in the moonlight. The knife nearly sliced his stomach as it cut through the darkness. Now that the six eyes were close enough, he could tell they belonged to three boys, no more than teenagers. One had a harelip, one had long black hair, and the third was tall and thin like a coat rack. They spoke in demanding whispers. The one with long black hair held the knife to Harrison's throat.

"Money. Give now," the thin one said, the leader of the bunch. The other two began arguing in another language. They were pointing toward the street. Harrison could feel the knife pressing against his flesh. One wrong move and he'd be sliced beyond repair.

"I'll give you...whatever...you want."

He was hyperventilating, unable to catch his breath. He needed to sit down, his legs wobbling, his bladder full and punishing his insides. Harelip and Long Hair were still arguing, the tone of their voices getting angrier.

"His watch," the thin one spat, jerking at Harrison's arm and fumbling for Harrison's Tag Heuer.

"*Yaha hamārē li'ē dē,*" Harelip yelled. "*Yaha hamārē li'ē dē!*"

Harelip grabbed Harrison's arm as well, the two of them pulling at him like a rag doll.

"Take it," Harrison said, his whole body starting to convulse. He tried to remove the watch but he was quivering too much to be successful.

"*Yaha hamārē li'ē dē!*" Harelip screamed in his face. His teeth were brown and rotted, his breath smelling like fish left out in the sun. Finally the thin one was able to remove the watch.

"Now the wallet," Thin One said, giving Harrison a shove. Harrison's knees buckled, but he managed to keep his balance.

"Wallet!" Long Hair shouted, waving the knife under Harrison's nose.

Harrison reached into his pocket to take out his wallet. He was crying now, sobbing like a little girl, too wasted and scared to censor himself.

"Please..." he said, as a spit bubble formed on his lips. "Please don't hurt..."

The sound of a door slamming caused them all to perk up. Footsteps were approaching from down the street.

"We go now," Thin One ordered to the other two. He pushed Harrison to the ground. Harrison crumpled up into a shivering ball with his hands at his throat, feeling for how deep he'd been cut.

"You...despicable," Harelip said, spitting in his face.

As he lay back in shock, he heard them scattering away. He stared at the almost full moon hovering in the sky.

"H-Bomb?" he heard. He searched for the voice through the darkness. A slender hand grabbed his own. With much struggle he was pulled out of the alleyway onto his feet. He coughed up some mucus filled with specks of blood.

"What happened to you?"

Nagesh's friendly face came into focus, his bushy mustache twitching.

"There was a car...these teenagers...had a knife... took my watch."

He could barely speak, each word making his stomach burn.

"Yes, pickpocketing is common here." Nagesh hung his head, as if embarrassed. "I regret not coming outside with you." He inspected Harrison's neck. "Looks like the knife just grazed you. Rarely do muggers here cause actual harm."

Harrison gave one final raspy cough and wiped at the tears staining his cheeks.

"They took my watch. It was a Tag."

"How unfortunate," Nagesh said, with a *tut*. "I should have warned you not to wear any flashy jewelry. But you are all right, H-Bomb. You live to fight another day."

Harrison looked down the street to see if the kids were still visible in the distance.

"One of them called me despicable."

"Yes, yes, you have what they desire: nice clothes, expensive watches..."

"Right before it happened, this black car with two people in it drove away. One of their faces was heavily scarred like nothing I've ever seen—"

"You didn't have a car so you were ripe to rob," Nagesh cooed, his hand tracing circles on Harrison's back. "Come now, I get you back to the Taj. You still have the escort card I gave you?"

Harrison looked at him blankly.

"You will call for Abhilasha," Nagesh nodded.

Harrison held out his trembling hand. "I'm still shaking."

"She will soothe you after this ordeal. Come, come. I called for a cab already."

"I can't stop shaking."

"You should drink more at your hotel and then call her to calm you down. You are fine."

Harrison still stared at him blankly.

"Repeat after me, H-Bomb. You...are...fine."

"I am fine," Harrison twitched.

"And let those punks have your watch. You will

have a new liver and a new job soon and even better watches in your future, right?"

A cab pulled up in front of Tryst. Nagesh led Harrison over.

"Do not let this hiccup sway your focus. You are here for the organ. You are here to save yourself. Repeat after me. You are here to save yourself."

"I'm here to save myself."

"Good, good," Nagesh chanted.

Harrison got in the cab and lay back. The moon wasn't as bright as before, partially hidden now by a storm cloud. As the cab took off he saw only dark and alien surroundings, so he closed his eyes until he floated far away and was set down on a beach at the edge of an ocean. He could feel the sand rushing through his toes and the kiss of an island breeze.

"Save myself," he whispered to this paradise, repeating that mantra over and over.

10

HARRISON WAS DROPPED OFF AT THE TAJ HOTEL while Nagesh continued to his home in their taxi. Since Nagesh didn't have enough money on him to cover the ride, Harrison had to hand over the rest of his rupees, but he didn't care. He was glad to be back at the Taj, safe. He stumbled to the ATM in the lobby and took out ten thousand rupees to pay the escort girl. Nagesh had already called the number on the card from his cell so Harrison wouldn't have to wait too long.

Upstairs in his room he swiped two tiny bottles from the mini-bar and glugged, glugged, glugged. He stared into the mirror, satisfied his hands weren't shaking as badly as before.

"Save yourself," he told the mirror. Nagesh was right; nothing should cause him to lose his focus. He was here in India for one reason and that was all that mattered. He'd forget about his ordeal with the street kids. He'd meet with the donor in the slums tomorrow to make sure the guy was healthy. He'd get the operation and begin whatever the next phase of his life would be. He liked to think this pep talk was enough to ease his spirits, but deep down he knew he was impulsive enough to book a ticket back to America and pretend like he never came to this wretched place.

He twisted open another bottle and chugged it down, feeling a sharp prick in the area around his liver as it attempted to soak up the alcohol.

"Fuck you," he said, pointing at his stomach and collapsing on the bed. He laughed at that, but his laughter soon turned into a coughing fit. Once he got himself under control, he stared at the phone on the bedside table. He had always contacted Helene during business trips abroad, if just to say he landed okay. He didn't even remember if he gave her his flight number before he left. Right now it'd be early in the morning back home. She was probably getting the kids ready for school, then dealing with any planning for her Faceless Children's Gala. A call from him would only upset her more, throw off her focus from the tasks of the day. Still her voice might make him feel more settled, even if it'd be tinged with disgust.

Just as he was about to pick up the phone it started ringing.

"Helene?" he mumbled into the receiver.

"Sir, you have a guest to see you," said a voice with a heavy accent, clearly not Helene's.

"Yes, of course," he said. He had momentarily forgotten about the girl from Nagarvadhus Escorts. He slapped at his dick to wake it up. "Please send her up."

He hung up the phone, his stomach rumbling with nerves. He caught himself in the mirror again and patted down a few strands of hair that appeared out of sorts. His skin tone still had a yellowish hue so he dimmed the lights some. He pinched at his gut and made it flap up and down. There was nothing he could do about the rest of his appearance, but he untucked his shirt so his belly wasn't as visible. Standing in front of the mirror, he deemed this makeover as much of a success as possible.

He heard a knock at the door.

When he opened it, a beautiful woman stood in the hallway dressed in a red sari with flowers along the trim. Her nails and lips were painted the same color to match the sari, and she had a gold stud in her nose and big gold earrings hanging from her tiny ears. She had long flowing black hair with red highlights, eyebrows plucked to perfection, and a small, kissable mouth. She seemed more elegant and refined than any call girl he imagined, more like the wife of a well-to-do business-man, or at least his kept mistress.

"Can I come inside?" She smiled, probably already thinking him foolish because he hadn't said anything yet. Her accent was slight, not like the bellhop or the man at the front desk who had just called. Traces of American inflections lingered around her words.

"Yes, yes, of course."

He gestured for her to enter and closed the door. She looked around the room and ran her manicured fingers along the butterfly bedspread.

"Exquisite room," she said, nodding in approval. She gazed out of the window at his view of the Gateway to India and the ink-black waters rocking soundlessly in the distance.

"I didn't expect it to be so nice."

"I've been to the Taj Hotel before," she said. "One

of the nicest in Mumbai, but there are other nice ones as well."

"You were here for other clients?"

She blinked her eyes but didn't respond. He couldn't tell if he had offended her.

"So the price is ten thousand rupees for an hour," she said, losing the smile, her tone purely business.

"Quite expensive."

She shrugged her thin shoulders. "You pay for premium quality, yes?"

"I can't argue with that," he said, taking out his wallet. "But I can only afford one hour."

"That is up to you," she said, with a hand over her mouth to stifle a yawn. "Please leave the money on the dresser where I can see it."

He did as he was told. She counted the rupees with her eyes as he laid the bills in a stack on the dresser. Once satisfied, she began to disrobe. First came her jewelry, which she plucked off with a mechanical nonchalance and placed inside her purse. Watching her undress made him recall the night he spent with Naelle. She'd been the last thing of beauty he'd seen since he was diagnosed with liver cirrhosis, and he was certain that if she was undressing in front of him right now, he wouldn't need alcohol to forget about his nightmarish night. Thinking about her calmed his soul like sticking his toes into warm sand, or ice cream on a summer's day, or the sting of rye dripping down his throat, all the very essence of lovely.

With a hiccup, he was brought back to reality and clamped his hand over one eye since he was starting to see double: two identical, robotic women unraveling their saris. Soon the two women morphed into one body that was folding the sari into a neat little square on a chair.

"Do you want me to dance for you before we go to bed?" the woman asked.

The woman slid out of her shoes and began her dance. She stuck out one foot while twisting her back and bowing her arms into the shape of a heart. She moved ever so slowly, directing him toward her with a curl of her fingers. He bopped his head to silent music, tried to appreciate the swirling of her body, but all he could picture was Naelle. Maybe she was splayed under some overweight businessman while she wondered about all the alternate lives she could have led, or the desires she might never attain, or maybe even of Harrison, the grotesque man who almost died in her arms that she couldn't seem to forget.

"Do you like?" the woman asked, stepping closer and tugging at his collar. Her pretty mouth had rehearsed this sequence a million times before, her eyes mostly glancing at the rupees he laid on the dresser.

"You're beautiful," he said, but he sounded as mechanical and unconvincing as she did. "You seem so refined," he added, scrunching up his face.

Abhilasha nodded as if she had heard it all before and cupped his balls. He resolved to forget about Naelle for the moment and try to get his money's worth. He shook his head back and forth to toss Naelle out of his mind.

"You don't like?" the woman pouted.

"No, it's not that. I didn't expect a girl like you."

She coolly walked over to the bed, sat down, and crossed one leg over the other as if she was being interviewed.

"What did you expect?"

"When I first arrived in Mumbai, I saw the slums that bordered the airport—"

"I do not come from the slums."

The woman crossed her arms, offended. She turned her face, not wanting to look at him anymore.

"No, I didn't think so. Back at home, most who do what you do seem like they would be rough around the edges despite whatever they cost."

"I do not understand this 'rough around edges' term."

"I had met this girl..." He was too drunk to hide his thoughts, a smile exploding across his lips. "She escorted like you. She was sweet to me."

The woman tapped her foot impatiently, obviously realizing this story would take a while.

"I can't help but wonder what she wants out of life," he said. "She can't want to do that forever. What moves her? What does she dream about?"

The woman shrugged again and gave a slight roll of her eyes.

"What is it that you want?" he asked, sitting on the bed next to her. "What do you dream about?"

"Why do you want to know this?"

"I'll tell you what I've wanted. I've had dreams that one day I'll feel excited, truly excited about something, and then it finally happened. I became excited about something again, and that's why I'm here in Mumbai, to replace what's been destroyed."

The woman glanced at the clock beside the bed. "You're already fifteen minutes into the hour."

"That's fine, that's absolutely fine, just answer my question."

"All right," she sighed, "I wanted this profession, even as a younger girl. It is easy. Sometimes I talk to the men for a while like I'm doing with you; sometimes we go right to bed. Either way I make a lot of money."

"What must your parents think?"

Her eyes hardened, as if she was about to tell him to fuck off, but then something clicked inside of her as she stared at the rupees with a Mona Lisa grin.

"I do not care what my parents think. They wanted to marry me off, to pop out babies, to live like people expected me to, to work like a dog as they have for what amounts to very little, but times have changed. We were not poor, but we were not rich either, so then what is the point of breaking your back? This is the most lucrative profession I could choose."

"And this makes you happy?"

"Yes, more than my studies did. I went to university, I always had very good grades; but you talked of dreams. I would dream of all the ways I could please men, the talent I possessed in these fingertips."

She traced his lips with her fingernail.

"For no amount of studying would pay as handsomely as my body. India's new economic affluence has brought an insatiable appetite for the finer things. This is what I want; this is what I have."

She shook a finger in his face. "Now we should go to bed because time keeps ticking down."

"What's your name?" he asked, as she undid his belt.

"Abhilasha."

"Is that your real name?"

"Does it matter?"

He nodded as she took off her bra, her breasts slight

but perky. He sucked on one of her nipples but felt nothing.

"In Hindi, my name has to do with what I can offer. The deities wrote my destiny from the day my parents named me."

She lay back on the bed, slid off her panties. As he went to take off his clothes, she held out her hand in protest.

"Turn off the lights," she ordered. He knew she did not wish to see his body.

He shut off the lights and climbed back into the dark bed. Abhilasha touched the part of his neck where the street kids had left a tiny scar. He flinched but she either didn't notice or didn't care. She ran her fingers down his chest and searched for his penis, shriveled and hiding under his sagging belly. She jerked it with contorted movements that should have brought him pleasure but only made him sad. If this had been Naelle, he was confident he'd be harder than ever and that she'd offer to ease his troubled mind with a soothing Spanish song before they spent the rest of the night making love. But Abhilasha didn't have time to make love. Her jerking had even lost its panache, and now he could feel the frustration oozing from her palms. She had propped herself up on her elbow and yanked and yanked, a condom wrapper already ripped open and hanging from her mouth, a growl emanating from her belly. He twisted her tit in the hopes of some type of spark; he played with her vagina but knew it was futile. He no longer desired a meaningless tryst, a fleeting rise and fall; it might as well have been a sack of potatoes in his bed trying to turn him on. Time crawled by interminably; he lay in a pool of his sweat as Abhilasha tried all of her tricks. Finally a beeping sound blared from her purse and she rolled off the bed.

"Do you want to continue?" she asked. All he could see was a pair of red lips amidst the darkness. "I can wait while you go down to the ATM in the lobby."

He heard her foot tapping nervously and knew from her tone this was the last thing she really wanted.

"No," he said, and groped for his clothes that were scattered across the room.

He turned on the light and saw her wince, either due to the sudden brightness or from the sight of his body.

"I'm sorry about tonight. It wasn't you. I have a lot on my mind."

She began wrapping the sari around her body again, her movements careful and precise.

"I am paid regardless, so..."

"Have you been to America before?"

She squinted as if she couldn't believe he was still trying to make conversation.

"And why do you ask me this?"

"Your accent, I can hear a trace of American."

"I spent a semester there during my studies, not too long ago. Boston, Massachusetts."

"What did you think?"

"This is the last question of yours that I will answer," she sighed, and finished wrapping her sari.

"That's fair," he said, bending down and handing over her purse.

"You have a beautiful country in a lot of ways." She fished for the gold earrings out of her purse. "But you're selfish."

"How so?"

"You think you run the world."

"We do." Harrison nodded.

"No," she said, putting on each earring. "You did."

"What's that supposed to mean?"

"It means that no one stays at the top forever," she said, and snatched the rupees off the dresser. "Everyone falls eventually."

She slunk past him and slipped out of the door.

He sat down on the bed in a pool of his sweat, wet and cold beneath his fingers and shook his head back and forth. Then he picked up the phone to have the front desk connect him to his home phone.

When no one answered, he left a message on the machine telling his family that he had finally arrived in Mumbai and was planning on staying here until he got what he came for.

11

ACCORDING TO NAGESH, THE DHARAVI SLUMS IN
the heart of Mumbai was where the donor's family had
lived for over three generations. In the late nineteenth
century the area had been a mangrove swamp inhabited
by Koli fisherman. When the swamp filled in with
coconut leaves, rotten fish, and human waste, the Koli
became deprived of their fishing grounds, which made
room for others. The Kumbhars came from Gujarat to
create a potters' colony. Tamils came in from the south
and opened tanneries. Thousands traveled from Uttar
Pradesh to work in the thriving textile industry.
Because of this, the Dharavi became one of the most
diverse slums, and the most diverse neighborhood in
Mumbai. To Harrison, it resembled a place of
maddening disorder and overwhelming squalor—like
nothing he'd ever seen before, or ever desired to see
again.

As their taxi headed through the entrance, he saw a
line of cab drivers cajoling their abused Fiats to life.
The leaves on many of the surrounding trees were all

gray. He could hear the morning rhythms of devotional singing and the rush of water as residents opened their hoses to wash the lanes, some of them brushing their teeth in the spray. In the distance toward the potters' neighborhood, black smoke spewed from the kilns. By the filthy industrial canal, the recyclers had already begun their day, since nothing was considered garbage in the Dharavi. Pieces of plastic toys were thrown into large grinders, diced into tiny pieces, melted down into multicolored pellets, and ready to be refashioned into knockoff dolls.

"We will walk from here," Nagesh said, leaving the taxi and continuing down a trash-strewn walkway.

After Harrison paid the driver, the taxi sped away and he became instantly bombarded by the smell of feces, garbage, and decaying animal carcasses. Rats were everywhere, the true kings of the slums, feeding off any waste. He upchucked a little in his mouth before remembering the handkerchief that he had wisely brought, and he covered his nose with its linen delight. He followed Nagesh down a shadowy walkway, passing by rows of tin-roofed shacks, some with only tattered hunks of cloth and tarp to blanket the inhabitants from the rain. The ground was littered with empty water bottles, moldy newspapers, and the skeletons of blown-out umbrellas. Scavengers slept atop garbage bags and guarded them with shifty eyes, as if they feared their bags would be stolen and turned into makeshift beds. Packs of barefooted children crouched around areas of scrub grass and stuffed it into their mouths while muddy pigs, goats, and water buffalos fought with the rest of the dwellers for any remaining space. Even through the handkerchief, Harrison had to keep his lips shut so he wouldn't inhale a mouthful of flies.

"Are a band of kids going to mug me here as well?" Harrison asked, but Nagesh either didn't hear him or chose not to respond.

After about fifteen minutes of winding down the most deplorable conditions he'd ever witnessed, they reached the shack of the donor, which was divided on one side by a sheet and on the other side by a bunch of aluminum scraps. Nearby was a long line for an orange block of concrete toilets. Contents of the public toilets had dumped out on the walkways, and his handkerchief soon became futile. Since he was only able to breathe through his mouth, he wound up swallowing a bunch of tiny flies.

Nagesh knocked on a crumbling door to the shack. Harrison heard yelling coming from inside but no one answered. They pushed open the door that was as light as cardboard. Inside the narrow shack, the walls were green and black with mold, bloated and watermarked from flooding. The place smelled like burnt cooking and a family of almost a dozen who didn't have sufficient water to keep clean. All of the children lay on the floor where they had slept; there were no beds. Some of the smaller ones had swollen rat bites all over their scalps. A ceiling fan and a wooden shrine with a few candles seemed to be the only things that might differentiate this family's abode from the rest of the shacks.

Nagesh started speaking to a one-eyed woman holding a baby in a sling, her eye socket hollow as if the eye had been scooped out. The baby was red-faced and wouldn't stop crying.

"What's wrong with her baby?" Harrison asked.

The one-eyed woman responded with a long speech in Hindi that Nagesh translated as "diarrhea."

Nagesh procured some medicine from his pocket and handed it to the woman.

"I always travel with anti-diarrheal pills," he said to Harrison, as the woman bowed down and began to thank him profusely.

She then gestured to the other side of the hut and started speaking about the man lying on the ground with a rag covering his face.

"She says her husband is trying to combat the heat by sleeping with a wet rag," Nagesh said, and the one-eyed woman nodded in unison.

The woman continued speaking in Hindi to Nagesh who listened patiently. Halfway through her spiel, she broke out in tears until her and the baby had unified into one shrill cry. She pleaded with Harrison now, as if he could understand.

"What is she saying?" he asked Nagesh, his question barely audible over her howling.

"She says that her husband is healthy enough to make you better again. The money her family will receive will change their lives because they can finally get out of this slum and move into a subsidized apartment, the first to do so in three generations."

The donor removed the wet rag from off his face and blinked curiously at the morning. He rose to his feet and weaved around his lounging kids to greet Harrison and Nagesh. Compared to the rest of his family, he looked robust, which Harrison was glad to see. He wasn't emaciated like most of his children and he wasn't fat either—all good signs that might point to a decently healthy liver.

"Chiranjavi," he said, and repeated his name over and over while shaking Harrison's hand. His grip was sturdy, assured. He turned to Nagesh and bowed his head. "*Daaktar*," he said, his eyes overflowing with tears.

Nagesh and the donor began speaking to one another in Hindi. The donor seemed upset but held himself together better than his blubbering wife.

"Ask him how he feels," Harrison said. "His health?"

"I told you that I recently gave him a checkup," Nagesh replied, grinning wide like he always did. "His liver is in great shape."

Harrison wanted to discuss with this donor about what was going to occur. He felt as if he should thank Chiranjavi for the gift of life, but he also wanted the man to realize that his slum family would be receiving the gift of life as well. After the liver would be transplanted, the two of them would be even, neither party indebted to the other. He pictured the donor's children sleeping in actual beds, their hair combed, and their skin free of dirt and grime. He pictured the wife sitting on a couch with her feet up, her baby healthy in a crib, both mother and child crying no more. These thoughts brought the tiniest smile to his face. Nobody should think he was selfish for coming to India to get an organ. Selfish people were guys like Whit, or any of the clones at Sanford & Co. None of them had ever freed an entire family from poverty before.

"Can you tell him that I'm glad we are able to help one another?" Harrison asked Nagesh, who in turn translated and listened to the man's response.

"He says that he has always wanted to donate an

organ to make money for his family, but there hasn't been a match yet. When he heard that you were a match, he thanked the gods over and over."

They heard coughing coming from behind a loosely drawn curtain in the corner. The coughs sounded like phlegm mixed with blood, harsh and unremitting. Harrison figured a bedridden elder burdening the family. As the coughing continued, Chiranjavi and his wife stared at the curtain as if the life had been sucked out of their faces. Harrison saw the pain in their eyes that foretold tiring days and nights, eked-out existences, and cruel gods. His poor upbringing in New Haven could never match their desolation; they'd laugh at what he had deemed a difficult childhood.

Despite the awful smell, he took a deep breath to breathe in their reality, a whiff that allowed him to truly appreciate his own fortune for the first time since his diagnosis.

———

Once the baby in the sling had been given its medicine and finally went to sleep, the wife began serving a dish of lentils, soggy vegetables, and lopsided roti. Harrison didn't want to be rude, but he had no desire to eat the family's food.

"Nagesh, can you tell them that I must fast before my surgery tomorrow?"

Nagesh didn't respond at first, as if he was embarrassed by his friend's elitism. Here the wife had made sure that Harrison's bowl was filled with food while the rest of the family picked at leftover scraps. Finally Nagesh leaned over to the wife and translated Harrison's request. She scooped the food out of Harrison's bowl and parsed it out to her children's plates, happy that they would be able to eat now.

An older son stumbled inside. He was sniffing a white substance from a rag diluted with spit. The wife shook her head as the son walked around the shack dazed, looking for something. She shouted at him in Hindi, but he seemed too out of it to respond. She crossed her arms while continuing to complain to Nagesh.

"She says many of the children here get high off of Eraz-Ex, the Indian equivalent of Wite-Out; it has stolen her son's soul."

The son's nostrils were caked with white flakes that had cracked and settled in his teenage mustache. His eyes were as red as Abhilasha's sari from last night. The wife continued complaining about her "*moorkj*" child, which Harrison assumed meant something along the lines of "foolish."

"They used to have a daughter," Nagesh continued. "She was smart enough to do very well in school and could possibly go onto college or work in one of the luxury hotels, but she was hit by an out-of-control taxi last year and died."

"Please tell her that I am sorry to hear this," Harrison said, not wanting to imagine what it must be like to lose one's child.

Nagesh went to translate but the woman was speaking over him.

"And one of their little girls has TB," Nagesh added, following the woman's desperate exclamations. "She said the gods have sent me to see if I can help, but it may be too late."

Harrison heard coughing again from behind the curtain in the corner, the sound as jarring as if the person was gargling with razor blades. He couldn't believe the sick family member was not an elder but a little girl.

"Have you checked her out before, is she going to be all right?" he asked Nagesh.

For once Nagesh's eyes did not bulge; he gazed at the dirt floor.

"I can already tell from her cough that she is too far gone."

The wife was tugging on Nagesh's arm and then pointing toward the curtain. Harrison figured that part of the deal for Chiranjavi's liver must also include a checkup for his sick little girl.

"Come with me," Nagesh motioned, as Harrison stood and they made their way behind the curtain.

The family had erected a bed made out of sheets to buffer the stone ground. The girl looked to be around the same age as Gracie, her legs the width of large sticks, her cheekbones sharp enough to cut his finger if he were to touch them. Dried blood had crusted around her mouth and onto her chest. The blood no longer had a red color but appeared brown. The girl raised her eyes in his direction, as if looking up required all of her concentration. Harrison nearly vomited at the sight of her decay. He wanted to run out of the shack and away from the slums, forgetting he'd ever stepped foot inside this kind of horror. This was not life; this could only be the devil's fancy.

"*Kyā...āap...dēvatā'ōm...dvārā...bhējā...gayā...hai?*" the little girl asked, fighting for each breath.

"What did she say?" Harrison asked.

"She asked if we were sent by the gods."

"What will you tell her?"

"I will tell her yes since there is no hope for her anyway."

Harrison imagined this girl's life if she lived in New York: going to ballet recitals, having hot chocolate with her friends at Serendipity. This could've been Gracie if fate had decided on a different path for her. How come his daughter wound up in an apartment on Fifth Avenue while this little girl was plagued with a disease that had been cured many years ago, but not for someone as poor as her?

"Why isn't she in a hospital?" he asked Nagesh.

"Too expensive," Nagesh replied, shrugging, his tone devoid of any feeling.

"What about your clinic, can't you help her?"

"She is beyond help, there's nothing that anyone can do at this point."

"That can't be possible."

The little girl coughed up more blood, its color brown again like waste. She closed her eyes, too weary to keep them open any longer.

"So she just dies?" Harrison asked, raising his voice.

"Yes, my friend. She just dies."

Nagesh shut the crudely made curtain around the little girl and put his hand on Harrison's shoulder.

"It is time for us to go. You have met the donor. Now we must head to the bank before it closes, and then you need to rest for the surgery tomorrow."

The entire family had gathered around, awaiting Nagesh's diagnosis. Harrison watched his friend put on a grim doctor's face to explain the bad news. The wife responded in dramatics, flinging her hands to the ceiling with shouts that rocked the shack. Chiranjavi tried to comfort her, but she didn't want his support. Ropes of spit flew from her mouth as she shook her fist and wept at the heavens.

"What is she saying?" Harrison asked.

"She says a ghost had cursed her family a long time ago and that is why all her children are dying off. She knows this is true because a Muslim *fakir* once came to the slums to offer blessings and drive away evil spirits. While performing the *jhaad-phoonk* on her, he beat her with a peacock-feather broom because he sensed diabolical spirits. That was when she knew she'd be cursed."

The woman got in Harrison's face, her one-eye looking him up and down.

"*Ghrinaayogya,*" she shouted, as goosebumps sprang up on his arm. "*ghrinaayogya, ghrinaayogya, ghrinaayogya!*"

"What is she saying?"

"She says you are also cursed, but she is too deep in grief to know what she is talking about."

Nagesh led the woman away from Harrison and tried to ease her suffering by procuring some rupees from his pocket and whispering in her ear. She nodded slowly, sniffing away her tears and stroking the rupees.

"Come," Nagesh said, to Harrison. "It is time for us to go."

Harrison wanted nothing more than to leave, but he felt too spooked to move. The image of the woman screaming in his face had rattled his brain. What if he was cursed? In the span of a month, he'd lost his job, possibly his wife, he'd been mugged, and he'd been told he had incurable liver disease. What terrible fates might be waiting to destroy him next? He felt faint and had to support himself against a rickety wall.

"Harrison?" Nagesh asked, almost as a command.

"I want you to help that little girl."

He looked into the bloodshot eye of the one-eyed woman. If he could save her sick daughter, maybe whatever curse he'd been plagued with would be lifted as well. He turned to Nagesh.

"I want you to do whatever you can for that little girl with TB."

"H-Bomb, there is nothing that can be done."

"If that was my daughter then there is nothing I wouldn't do."

"Look around," Nagesh said, gesturing toward the slum outside. "That little girl is one of many with the same predicament."

"But what about the fifty thousand the family will receive from me, can't that do anything?"

"Like I said, her illness has progressed too far."

"But that's what I was told by the doctors back home, and now here I am willing to do whatever it takes. There's always hope."

"Her family has many other children to worry about. She is only a detriment."

"How can you say that? She is a little girl."

"This isn't America, Harrison. Life does not have the same value in the slums."

"Life is life. Period."

"You are naïve," Nagesh said, getting angry. "You just got here and eventually you will leave. This is not your home; it is mine."

"What if you took her to your clinic and at least allowed her to live her last days in comfort?"

"Listen, I help people with my clinic, I help you, but I cannot help every child in the slum. I need to worry about myself first because that is what everyone else is doing here!"

Harrison had never seen Nagesh become this angry. The entire family watched their conversation as if it was an intense tennis match, their daughter's life lying in the hands of whoever won.

"I am sorry for yelling at you, H-Bomb," Nagesh said, after calming himself down. "But you are a foreigner trying to solve an impossible problem. My clinic is devoted to people who I can save, don't you understand? We are underfunded, understaffed, and hanging on by a thread as it is."

"I didn't know—"

"I applaud your heart," Nagesh said, bowing his hands in prayer. "To think of that child while your life hangs in the balance...that is a testament to who you are. But now we must go so we can reach the bank before it closes, so I can get this family your money as soon as it in my account and then they can begin to start a new life. Don't you see the good that you will be doing?"

Harrison looked around at the shack for one last time and wondered if the family's prosperity would be enough to lift any curse. He decided it would have to be. He did not travel all this way to save one little girl.

"Can you tell the donor that I truly hope the fifty thousand will change his family's life as much as he will have changed mine?" he asked Nagesh, who repeated the words to Chiranjavi.

"Come, friend," Nagesh said, with his hand on Harrison's shoulder as he led him out of the shack.

Stepping out into the walkway, Harrison caught sight of a sick water buffalo snooping through mounds of wet garbage and shitting out the contents onto the family's doorstep. Between the blazing sun and putrid smells, the surroundings started spinning and he found himself stooped over and puking with a velocity he'd never experienced before.

"Are you all right, H-Bomb?"

"Sorry...the smell," he said, wiping his mouth with the handkerchief and then throwing it amongst the trash on the ground.

"We will take care of the money transfer at the bank and then I want you get a good rest. You have a long day tomorrow and shouldn't be too worked up."

They headed down the walkway back toward the main strip where they could get a taxi from the row of old Fiats. Nagesh stayed in step with Harrison, who had slowed due to his sick stomach. They lurched past huts held together by duct tape and rope. People passed by with fungus sprouting from their toes, some faces permanently blackened with soot. A small child sat in the middle of the walkway. She had tilted her head back toward the unrelenting sun that had reached its peak. Her dress was splattered with grime, her body shook either from hunger, disease, or both; but she had closed her eyes and opened her mouth with the slightest smile, as if the sun's rays were carrying her away for one moment. Harrison woke her from her trance by slipping some rupees into her palm. Her eyes grew wide and she looked back up at the sky as if it had answered her prayers and then took off toward her hut.

"I'm sorry for earlier," Harrison said to Nagesh.

"No, no, friend. Do not apologize."

"I'm helping that family," Harrison said, reiterating this to himself.

"Yes, yes, H-Bomb, and you are helping yourself, too. It is win-win."

"Win-win," Harrison repeated.

He watched as the little girl's mother greeted her with open arms once the woman saw the rupees in her daughter's fist.

Soon they reached the Rajendra Prasad Chawl lane and the row of Fiats. They took a cab out of the slum. Harrison observed that the roads became filled with SUVs and chauffeur-driven black sedans, billboards of Indian celebrities advertising fragrances, and the shimmering reflections of luxury hotels: a world of difference inches away from degradation.

"Are you feeling better, H-Bomb?"

For a moment, Harrison had forgotten he was with Nagesh. He turned away from the glitzy flash of Mumbai that they were passing through.

"Those slums were hard to see."

"India is filled with a third of the world's poor. There are many other slums and many who are even worse off than what you saw."

"My mind keeps going back to that sick little girl, how do you not feel guilty?"

Nagesh stroked his mustache and took a moment to answer.

"The sad reality is that miracles are possible in this new India, but not for everyone."

"But they're possible for me?" Harrison asked, feeling terrible to vocalize as selfish a thought as that.

"Yes...a miracle here is possible for you."

Nagesh lowered his eyes, and Harrison saw how

dark his eyelids were, as if he'd put on a touch of eye shadow. Nagesh rubbed those eyes with trembling fingers.

"We are almost at the bank in the center of town," Nagesh continued. "I want to make sure that you are absolutely certain about this before we go through with a money transfer."

"Why would you even question?"

"I am just making sure," Nagesh said, handing over a slip of paper. "Here is the address you will go to tomorrow for the operation."

"We won't go over together?"

"I will be prepping from very early on in the morning. There is no need for you to have to wait around."

"What's the name of your clinic?"

"No name. This is my side practice, remember? It is in the Mumbai outskirts where I don't have to worry about people poking around."

"Right."

"Go to that address. I will be outside to meet you at seven a.m. sharp."

Harrison took out his wallet. His eye quickly caught a glimpse of the Nagarvadhus Escorts card before he crammed the slip of paper in front of it.

Nagesh had placed his hands in his lap and linked his fingers together to stop them from trembling.

"It's a condition," Nagesh said.

"What is?"

"My tremors, sometimes I forget my beta blockers."

"Some doctor you are," Harrison said. "You better not forget them tomorrow when you're slicing me open."

Nagesh blinked his expressive eyes like he'd been

surprised by a camera with a bright flash, but then he replied with his signature grin.

"No, no, H-Bomb, I assure you that everything will run smoothly with your operation."

The taxi finally reached the bank and Nagesh exited quickly, leaving Harrison to take care of the tab again.

Harrison shrugged it off, figuring it'd be the last time in Mumbai he'd have to pay for more than he owed; then he followed Nagesh inside the bank.

12

THROUGHOUT THE NIGHT, THE LITTLE GIRL WITH TB had invaded Harrison's dreams. He dreamt he was being prepped for surgery at Nagesh's clinic while her specter watched. She spoke to him in Hindi, but he could understand every word. She told him that she'd died after he left the Dharavi. Because she was so young she didn't have time to attain good karma and become *moksha*, or one with God. She would now have to repeat the cycle of *samsara* by becoming reincarnated and hoped that her next life would not be as cursed as this one.

"Have you collected good karma?" she asked, as a nurse wheeled her father out on a gurney and placed him beside Harrison.

Nagesh entered the operating room holding a scalpel with a doctor's mask covering his face. He passed right through the ghost of the little girl and stood over Harrison. Blood dripped from the scalpel as Nagesh's hands shook violently. The blood was getting all over Harrison. As Nagesh bent down to make an incision, he took off his doctor's mask and the face of the one-eyed woman appeared in his place.

"*Ghrinaayogya!*" she shouted, as her spittle hit Harrison in the face, the saliva like boiling acid as it dripped down his cheek. "*Ghrinaayogya, ghrinaayogya, ghrinaayogya!*"

Others filled the room now: the three Indian street kids who had mugged him, the man with the scars on his face who had gotten into the sleek black car.

"*Ghrinaayogya, ghrinaayogya, ghrinaayogya!*" they all shouted.

He woke with a start, shrieking at the early morning. The phone was ringing. He picked it up to receive his wake-up call. He clamped his hand over his beating heart, worked to catch his breath, and counted down until he could feel his organs starting to work in tandem again. All but one.

"Soon," he said out loud, the word buzzing on the tip of his tongue. "Soon."

In the bathroom mirror, he strategized. He wouldn't allow himself to be nervous because nothing could go wrong. The only outcome would be a successful one. Nagesh had promised that if there was a problem with the operation, he'd try to find a new donor immediately. Harrison would have to pay for a new organ, but Nagesh would make sure he'd exhaust Mumbai's slum population until they got a liver that would finally take. No matter what, Harrison would be returning to the States a new man.

In the taxi, the driver had to look at the address that Nagesh had given a few times. Harrison tried to remain patient since Mumbai was a huge city and the taxi drivers did not have GPS systems, but the quizzical look on the driver's face was making him anxious. He had planned to leave an hour and a half early to be on the safe side and didn't want his lateness to put a wrench in the day.

"I can ask the hotel for directions," he said, after the fourth time the driver studied the address, but then a sign of recognition sprouted in the driver's eyes and the guy put his foot on the gas.

In the early morning light of the winking sun, Mumbai appeared as empty as it'd ever be, even peaceful. Shops hadn't opened up yet for the day. The beggars still slept since five a.m. wasn't worth their time to try for handouts. Few cars drove past, the roads magically his own. He observed the passing trees and the water to his right as he flirted with meditation, something he never did back at home in New York City. The past hurtled to the forefront of his mind: years of decadence and neglect to his body flipping on by, images of him hunched over at his desk at Sanford & Co. as the night became morning again. He'd destroyed himself from within, he was solely to blame for his alarming health, but he had also worked to be liquid enough to pay for as many donors as it would take to survive.

He meditated more as the present soon replaced the past. The little girl's ghost appeared by his side, a product of the poorest of the poor, her family without the means to save her, the sad reality of a world where money reigned paramount.

As the sun poked up from behind the rushing landscape, the little girl disappeared and his future spread out over the dashboard. He visualized his health, Helene and the kids welcoming him home, the mending of his ruined life, and Chauncey sitting in his lap with a loving purr. No more temptations, just the essence of family, good karma, and a resolve to be a better person each succeeding day.

The taxi soon stopped at an industrial area in the outskirts of Mumbai. Creeping through mangroves and mudflats, the driver searched for the address that Nagesh had given. Smatterings of flamingoes sifted through the gray mud for victuals. In the distance was a hill fraught with chemical factories, refineries, chimneys, and nuclear reactors casting their dystopian shadow.

"Are we close?" Harrison asked, the words tasting bitter on the back of his tongue. His stomach rumbled since the last meal he'd eaten was yesterday afternoon. He hadn't even brushed his teeth that morning, since he didn't want to accidentally swallow any water before his surgery.

The driver kept looking around and then followed his finger across the crumpled address in his hand.

"Trombay," the driver said, showing Harrison what Nagesh had written. He gestured toward the hills.

They soon reached what resembled a shantytown. A fort had been erected, crumbling now due to age. The driver pointed at the fort.

"Here," he said, and waved the slip of paper.

"You must be mistaken," Harrison said. He glanced at his watch and saw that it was ten to seven. It had taken a lot longer to reach the address than he expected.

"Yes, you go," the driver frowned. He showed

Harrison the street that Nagesh had written and then pointed at a street sign with a shrug.

"But there is nothing around here that looks like a clinic."

Sweat broke out on Harrison's forehead and slinked down his temples. Why hadn't he insisted on coming early with Nagesh? Now this buffoon driver had taken him God knows where.

"There must be another street with the same name," Harrison said, but the driver couldn't understand him and chose not to respond.

All the goodwill that Harrison felt on the ride over was seeping out of his pores.

"Are you listening to me?" Harrison said, raising his voice. "There must be a similar street somewhere else."

"Trombay," the driver replied, shaking his head.

"But this isn't where I need to go. I'm having an operation today." He looked at his watch and saw that it was now five to seven. "This is a matter of life and death."

He was yelling at this point and the driver started yelling back until the two were shouting at each other in different languages, neither one understanding what the other was saying.

"This is ludicrous." Harrison kicked at the seat in front of him. "You've taken me to the wrong address. We need to find someone who can give directions."

The driver continued yelling and pointing at the slip of paper.

"No, no, no."

Harrison's heart was racing now, ready to explode. He frantically looked around in all directions.

"Go toward the hill," he told the driver.

The driver didn't budge at first until Harrison took out his wallet.

"I will give you more money," he said, shaking the rupees in the driver's face.

He pointed and pointed at the nearby smokestacks until the driver finally acquiesced. They headed toward the ominous hill. Harrison took out his phone, searching for a signal. Finally he got one and called Nagesh's cell. He heard an automated message that wasn't Nagesh's voice. Even though he couldn't understand exactly what the machine was saying, he figured it had to mean that Nagesh's prepaid cell had been disconnected.

Once they reached the smokestacks atop the hill, Harrison pleaded with the driver not to leave while he searched around for someone. He promised all the money he had on him if the driver waited. The two went back and forth for longer than it should have taken until the driver finally understood. He waved off Harrison as if he wanted nothing to do with him anymore, but then he turned off the taxi's motor and sat there crossing his arms.

By the time Harrison exited the cab it was half past seven. His legs were sore, barely able to support his weight. He wanted to run but became out of breath after a few sprints. The sun was bright and the air started to burn against his face. He nearly puked, but he could only gag. He wound down a street only to turn back in the same direction he came from since he didn't want to lose sight of the taxi. The driver had stepped outside and was smoking a cigarette while complaining to the abandoned landscape.

Finally down one empty street, he saw a man

looking as dazed as him. The man was holding a rag over his face. Harrison flagged him down, begged him to understand, tried whatever charades he could to explain his plight. The man lowered the rag to reveal a nose caked with white paint, the capillaries in his eyes throbbing and seeming as if they were about to burst. Harrison recalled the son that had been sniffing the Wite-Out substance in the Dharavi slums and pushed the drugged man out of his way.

Each street looked even emptier than the one before. In his mind, he repeated over and over that his surgery would still happen and this would all be a misunderstanding. He convinced himself that the more he repeated this mantra, the more likely it would come true. He looked at his watch and saw it was already eight-thirty now. Nagesh would have given up waiting outside, but he wondered why Nagesh hadn't tried to call his cell since he had the number.

He searched for a signal again and rang his hotel, thinking that maybe Nagesh had left a message there, but the front desk said that no one had called for him. He explained that he was lost and searching for an address he couldn't find. He repeated the address as slowly as possible to the man at the front desk. He heard the clicking of keys as the man searched on his computer. He waited to hear about another street in Mumbai with the same name, possibly close by, but the man behind the desk said that this was not the case.

"Are you sure you didn't pass by it?" the man behind the desk asked, as chipper and professional as ever.

"There is nothing here," Harrison yelled.

"Or that you read the address wrong—"

"I'm not a moron," Harrison yelled, even louder. He had an urge to throw the phone to the ground and resisted that impulse. "I'm sorry," he cried, as tears began to form. "I'm over an hour late for a very important meeting."

"Is there a number you can call?"

"It's been disconnected!"

He couldn't see because of the tears blurring his eyes. His whole body was shaking now. He crouched to the ground, too weak to stand. The sun climbed higher in the sky, zeroed in on his distress, causing him to fry. He began to slip into unconsciousness. He felt at the ground to try to get his bearings again. He swallowed a glob of thick saliva as he rose to his feet. The man behind the desk was still talking, but Harrison ended the call.

Since he couldn't see anyone else around, he returned to the taxi. The driver was pacing around and had amassed a pool of butts by his feet. It was almost nine a.m. and Harrison had no choice but to head back to the Taj Hotel. He hoped that Nagesh had been waiting there all along and for whatever reason hadn't thought to leave a message at the front desk.

Heading back in the height of rush hour was a completely different experience from the ride over. It was too hot to keep the windows shut so he was forced to deal with the pulsating insanity of Mumbai again. He tried to shut his eyes to return to the meditative state he'd entered on the way over, but it was useless, the journey felt like a never-ending grueling descent. He was so hungry that he couldn't sit still. His mouth was so dry that his throat became sore. He stuck his head out of the window, willing the traffic to disappear.

When he finally arrived back to the Taj, he paid the grumbling driver everything he had on him and wobbled into the lobby. His vision had become hazy and he could barely keep his balance, but he didn't want to eat on the off chance that he'd see Nagesh waiting on one of the sofas with a logical explanation to justify this horrific day.

He searched through the lobby to no avail, then went to the front desk. His appearance must have looked terrible because the girl at the front desk lowered her eyebrows in concern.

"Sir, are you all right?" she asked, as a vision of four girls finally morphed into one.

He managed to tell her his name and asked if he had any messages, but there were none. He explained that he was supposed to meet his friend at an address in Trombay. When he got there, he realized it was clearly the wrong location.

"Does your friend have a phone?" she asked.

"He uses a prepaid cell and it has been disconnected."

She scrunched up her face and tapped a pen against the desk.

"What about his address?" she smiled, thinking she had reached the solution.

Harrison thought back through all the conversations he'd had with Nagesh. He knew Nagesh had a house in the suburbs, but he didn't know where. The only address he'd been given was the PO box where he sent his blood work.

"I know...his PO box."

He got out his phone and searched through old emails until he found the one where Nagesh had written a PO box number. He showed it to the girl and dashed off an email to Nagesh while the girl looked it up on her computer.

"It's in a post office about fifty kilometers outside of the city. With traffic it should take two hours. Do you want me to call you a taxi?"

He agreed and took out ten thousand rupees from the ATM to pay the driver and for a bribe at the post office. While waiting for the cab, he wolfed down a handful of puffed-rice snacks from the street vendor on the corner. Normally the explosion of onions, tomato, and coriander would've tasted wonderful, but eating the food meant there was no chance for surgery that day, even if he found Nagesh.

He closed his eyes in the taxi, begging his mind to shut off. Luckily, he was able to sleep. When he woke, it was close to noon and he figured he was near the post office. He checked his messages praying that Nagesh had called or had responded to his email, but there was nothing. He surmised that some emergency must've happened to Nagesh after they left the bank yesterday afternoon.

He had the driver stay while he entered the post office. After an endless wait in line, he passed Nagesh's PO box number to the postal employee and said that he needed this man's actual address. The postal employee did not understand, as Harrison expected, but finally someone in the line spoke enough English to help. Harrison explained that he came to India to stay with his friend Nagesh Patel, but had lost his address and only had his PO box number because he'd sent a package there. The man who spoke English listened to the postal employee's response and translated that the post office did not have another address on file. Harrison asked if there was a way to see whether a Nagesh Patel lived in the area, but the translator told him that it was a very common name and there could be over a thousand nearby.

"I don't know what else to do," Harrison said, exiting out of the line with the translator.

The translator squeezed Harrison's shoulder to try and calm him down. Harrison was wheezing at this point. He'd never had a panic attack before, but he could feel the rumblings of one. The crowded post office spun around him as if he was looking through a kaleidoscope.

"You said you had sent your friend a package?"

Harrison had put his head in his hands and was breathing in the grime of a day spent traveling through Mumbai without washing. He managed to nod.

"Why don't we find out if your package even arrived, that way you can know whether you at least had the right PO box number?"

"Of course I had the right PO box number. He told me he got the package!"

"If they can show you what is in his PO box, maybe you will find something that might lead to your friend's whereabouts? For this you will have to bribe the official, but let me take care of it. How much money do you have on you?"

"Enough. Do what you need to do."

They waited on the interminable line for their turn to come up again. The translator mentioned that he deserved some money as well for all of his troubles so Harrison gave him five hundred rupees. When that amount didn't satisfy, Harrison shoved five hundred more rupees into the guy's hand.

When they got to the counter, the translator spoke to a different postal employee. The conversation went on for a while as both talked very intently with many gestures. At first, the other employee didn't seem as if he'd budge, but then the translator indicated for Harrison to show him some money.

"Remove one thousand rupees very carefully so no one sees," the translator whispered. Harrison did as he was told and slid the money into the translator's fist. The translator pretended to write on a form and then hid the money under the form. The postal employee folded up the form with the rupees inside and then walked away from the counter. A few minutes later he returned with a key that he handed to Harrison.

Harrison bid the translator goodbye. He felt slightly miffed that the man had demanded a pay cut as well, but he didn't have time to worry about that now. As he headed to Nagesh's PO box, a thousand scenarios charged through his mind. If Nagesh hadn't picked up mail in a while, there was a chance of finding something that might offer a clue to his address, possibly a letter from a friend that could be contacted, but Harrison figured that with his luck the box would be empty. It was probably stupid to come all the way out here instead of waiting at the hotel, and Harrison doubted that the answer lay in the PO box anyway.

When he reached the PO box, he could see that something was inside. He took a deep breath and removed a package. His hands immediately started trembling. His head began to throb as a dizzy spell took over. The noise of the post office became muffled. He slumped against a counter and stared at the package in disbelief. The words *Exempt Human Specimen* were written in bold lettering, the exact package he had sent with his blood work that Nagesh never picked up.

And then he blacked out.

13

Harrison woke up surrounded by faces peering over him, his body feeling like he was swimming through ice. He was helped to his feet by half a dozen people and given some water. They all spoke over one another but not in English. He couldn't remember why he had collapsed until he noticed the package under his arm that proved Nagesh's deceit. He threw it to the ground and pushed everyone out of his way, stumbling toward the entrance. The icy sensation had melted away and now he felt on fire, a blazing entity, ready to destroy everything in his path. He picked up a rock and hurled it toward the sky. He clenched his fists and screamed until he could scream no more. People entering the post office stepped away, but he didn't care. He cursed and cursed until his anger turned to tears. He began babbling nonsensically before finally embracing his breakdown.

Sitting there under the hot sun, he knew that God must have been laughing. This would be his ultimate punishment for years of sinning. He wondered if anything would've been different had he listened more at Sunday school, or if he'd recited all the Hail Marys the priests had asked him to do during confessions, or even if he paid more attention to the Ten Commandments: honored his parents despite their awfulness, never committed adultery, never lied to Helene. Would he get a new liver then? Or was it all a big ruse? Could he have devoted himself to being a morally upstanding person and still have received the same cruel fate?

After a while of feeling sorry for himself, he found his taxi and headed to the bank in Mumbai where he had transferred the one hundred fifty thousand dollars to Nagesh. During the ride back, he couldn't believe how stupid he'd been. All this time Nagesh had been scheming. The guy probably never even had a clinic in Mumbai, or it had closed down years ago. He could've even been holding a grudge since college because Harrison never admitted his part in their call-girl ring to the administration. Or Nagesh had become so desperate for money that friendship was a luxury he could no longer afford.

After reaching the bank, Harrison waited in another long line. As each minute ticked down, he pictured Nagesh getting farther and farther away. By now Nagesh was probably heading to some island to live out the rest of his life under a shaded umbrella with a cocktail in his hand. Harrison punched his leg in frustration, but the line still wasn't budging. He tried bribing the lady in front of him with a rupee so he could skip ahead, but she looked at him like he was crazy. Finally it was his turn and he stepped up to the window of a teller who was bald except for a few wisps of hair and had a head shaped like a watermelon.

"Do you speak any English?" he asked, and the teller responded with a nod. He wished he could remember the banker that he and Nagesh had dealt with the day before, but it was all a blur now. He began to plead his story. Since he couldn't mention anything about black market organs, he said that he had bought a house from his friend Nagesh Patel and transferred a lot of money into this man's account. Now his friend had disappeared and the house was in disrepair. He said the house would be a vacation home for his family since his wife was Indian but grew up in the States and had always wanted to have a place in India. By the time he finished the tale, he was sweating so much that his clothes stuck to his skin. The teller passed him a tissue through the window.

"Thank you," he said, mopping up the sweat from his forehead.

"I understand what you are saying," the teller replied.

"Good, good, thank you. I just need his address. I had it and now I lost it."

The teller shook his finger.

"I cannot give out anyone's address."

"This man scammed me, don't you see that?" Harrison spat. "He sold me a piece of shit house."

"Sir, your voice," the teller said, eyeing a guard who was loafing by the front doors.

"I'll fucking yell if I want to. Are you protecting your own, is that what this is?" he said, pointing a finger at the window.

"Sir, I do not know what you mean."

"I mean, I'm a foreigner in a strange country and that's the reason you aren't helping me."

"That is not true. It is the bank's policy—"

"Can you at least tell me if he's taken out my money? That way I can know if he's left the country."

The teller debated this request by gumming his thin lips. Finally he nodded and began checking on the computer.

"I'm sorry for what I accused you of doing before," Harrison said.

The teller stopped typing and looked up from the computer.

"The money has been taken out and the account is closed."

"Son of a bitch," Harrison said, slapping the counter in front of him. He motioned for the teller to lean in closer. The teller hesitated but then put his ear against the window.

"This man has taken a hundred and fifty thousand of mine," Harrison pleaded. "If you just give me his address, maybe I could reach him before he leaves, or find some clue as to where he's gone."

He took out some rupees from his wallet and hid them under a form like he'd done at the post office.

"Sir, may I ask what you are doing?"

"No one needs to know," Harrison said, pushing the form and the rupees through the slot in the window. The teller stopped him.

"Take back your money right now, or I will call the police."

"I can give you more—"

"Sir, I will ask you to leave this instant," the teller said, pushing the money back so that it spilled onto the floor. Harrison went to pick up the stray bills and saw that the teller was talking to someone who appeared to be a manager. Realizing that this would bring trouble, he stuffed the rupees in his wallet and dashed out of the front doors.

Next he took his taxi back to the Dharavi slums in the hopes of finding the supposed donor and his family who might have information about Nagesh. He knew Nagesh had definitely left the country by now, but it was worth a shot. He wasn't about to lose that kind of money without trying every option imaginable. When he entered the slums, he remembered the lane with the row of Fiats. He told the taxi driver to stop, but when he stepped outside he couldn't recall which walkway led to the donor's shack. He instructed the driver to wait and covered his mouth with his hand as he began to search around, walking over moldy newspapers and plastic casings that once held toys. He stepped in animal feces, or what he hoped was animal feces. He saw an orange block of toilets that he vaguely remembered from the last time, unless there were multiple blocks of orange toilets throughout the Dharavi. The smell was unbearable, his fat palm unable to stifle the stench. He tried pinching his nose and breathing only through his mouth until he could taste the putrid air on his tongue. Dozens of people waited on the seemingly endless line for a chance at the toilet, everyone squirming. An old woman had given up and was squatting by a sewage lake at the end of a walkway.

"Chiranjavi," he said to the line, recalling the name of the donor. "Chiranjavi?"

The people all looked away in unison.

"Chiranjavi?" he yelled. "Does anyone know a Chiranjavi?"

Had he remembered the right name, or was he pronouncing it wrong? He racked his brain and could feel the name slipping away. Even the face of the donor had started to disappear. He could recall the man's firm shake, but all other defining traits were gone.

"Fuck."

The sun seemed to be at its peak. He looked at his watch and saw it was about three-thirty. His skin started to boil, his mind becoming cooked. He let go of his nose to spit up on the ground as a strong whiff of shit walloped his senses. He gagged but managed to hold in his puke, then turned around to flee as far away from the toilets as he could. He headed back the way he had come, afraid he wouldn't be able to find his taxi if he went too far.

As he stopped to spit up on the ground again, he spied a woman walking with an infant in a sari-sling. Although he couldn't remember exactly what the donor's wife looked like, he hadn't forgotten her one eye.

"Chiranjavi?" he said, as he caught up with her. She turned around spooked and clutched her baby close to her chest. She had one eye as well, although he couldn't recall if the donor's wife had lost the left or the right one. This woman had lost her left eye and the expression she gave Harrison seemed like one of recognition.

"Chiranjavi?" he murmured, touching her shoulder.

The infant woke up and started crying, which angered the woman. She yelled at Harrison in a language he couldn't understand as the infant thrashed around.

She began to shout and beat Harrison with her free hand, the blows like rocks thrown at his face. This was definitely not the donor's wife, and he held up his hands to block her assault. She gave one last whap on the top of his head and stormed off, turning into another woman entirely as she consoled her screaming child with a lilting, "*coo*."

Rubbing his bruises, he hung his head in defeat and walked back toward the taxi. There was no way he'd find the donor in the Dharavi maze. He found himself feeling bad for the donor and his family as well, knowing that Nagesh had probably promised to help heal their sick daughter, then taken off once Harrison had paid. He couldn't blame them for doing whatever they could to save their little girl with TB. All of his anger would stay solely directed at Nagesh.

He knew that his options had all but run out. The only choice that remained was to contact the police and see what they could do. He sank into his taxi looking beaten down, barely human anymore. His stomach rumbled from being so hungry, but he wouldn't stop to eat until after he spoke to the police. He rested against the window as the slums receded from view and Mumbai's city center exploded in his periphery. He wanted to forget that he ever decided to come to India, a land that only yesterday was synonymous with hope and now represented the final nail in his coffin.

After reaching the police station, he sat in a hot office until he could finally speak with an officer. The place was as maddening as the city center he'd driven through. Handcuffed criminals coughed up chunks of phlegm while they waited to be booked. Police officers smoked cigarettes and left the butts in overflowing ashtrays that looked like they hadn't been changed in days. The air was so clogged with smoke that he might as well have been in a hookah bar. Time ticked, ticked, ticked away, as images of Nagesh reclining on some exotic beach flooded his brain. When his turn came up after an hour, he was directed to a poorly lit room where a mustachioed police officer sipped tea even though the room was hotter than it was outside under the baking sun.

"And how I may help you?" the police officer asked, his wary eyes indicating the difficult day he had. He relished each sip of tea as if it was some magic elixir.

Harrison went with the same story he told the bank teller. He had to be very careful not to reveal any illegal actions and decided to keep mentioning the fact his wife was Indian.

"It is impossible for us to search for your friend," the police officer said, straightening the papers on his desk and glancing at the clock on the wall.

"I know that the name Nagesh Patel is common—"

"Yes, very, very common."

"I just need an address."

The officer looked at the clock again, as if to indicate to Harrison his shift was ending and that Harrison was about to become bothersome.

"So many with that name!" the police officer said, slapping a mosquito against the desk and wiping it off his palm. This seemed to anger a swarm of other mosquitoes that flew around their dead comrade.

"Is there a database with a listing of all the Nagesh Patels?" Harrison asked, exhausted. "I'd look through them all myself. I know his age, that would narrow it down, right?"

"Data...base?" the police officer asked, trying to grab at the other mosquitoes.

"Yes, like a listing of names. He lives in the suburbs of Mumbai."

"Many, many suburbs."

"I know. What about a phone book?"

"Phone...book?" the police officer asked, cocking his head to the side. Harrison knew he was being fucked with. He took out his wallet and began to count the rupees he had left. He held out a stack of bills toward the officer.

"Would this change your mind?"

"I do not want your *haram ka paisa*, your dirty money."

Harrison emptied out most of his wallet and handed it to the officer. The officer let out a bellowing laugh as he caught the swarm of mosquitoes in his fist and then slammed his palm against the desk, smearing a bunch of carcasses.

"Okay." He shrugged and counted out the rupees. Harrison wondered how much he'd lost in bribes since he arrived in Mumbai, all for nothing until now. This officer would find Nagesh's address, and even if Nagesh had already left, Harrison would break into his house and search for any kind of clue that could lead him to wherever his former friend had vanished.

With bated breath, he watched as the officer picked up the piece of paper with all of the dead mosquitoes and brushed them off onto Harrison with a grin.

"I will take your dirty money, and as a trade I will

not arrest you for bribing the police. That is all. Thank you."

He wiped off his hands, sat back at his desk, and stuffed the remnants of a greasy dessert into his mouth. Harrison wanted to smash the police officer's face into the desk. He wanted to poke his thumbs into the police officer's eyes until they bled. Once he was finished with the officer, he longed to torture Nagesh for all the trouble he caused. Unfortunately, he knew deep down that this far-fetched desire would never be fulfilled.

The officer pointed to the door as he licked his oily fingers. When Harrison didn't budge at first, the officer yelled: "Get out!" with such force that Harrison bounded from his seat and out of the police station. His taxi still puttered on the sidewalk as he stepped inside its air-conditioned chambers and ordered the driver to take him to his final destination.

He returned to the Taj Hotel numb. Back in his room, he crawled into bed and caressed the butterfly bed sheets. He wasn't angry anymore, he'd drained all of his tears; he felt nothing. He needed to hear Helene's voice, but he couldn't summon up the will to call. What could he possibly tell her? How could she understand what he had been through without admonishing him for trying to get a black-market liver in the first place? The one-eyed woman in the Dharavi had been right, he was *ghrinaayogya*—cursed.

He debated swallowing all the pills he had on him. Death was imminent anyway; at least he'd avoid having to explain himself to Helene and the kids. He got out a bottle of Advil and spilled its contents into a pile on the bed. One by one he began placing the pills in his mouth until they filled up his cheeks. He'd forgotten to pick up any bottled water so he went into the bathroom and turned on the faucet. The water had a creamy tone and smelled of sulfur. The thought of its taste caused him to gag. He spit out the pills all over the sink and turned off the faucet. His stomach was growling. Before he made any rash decisions, he decided to order some room service first.

When the food arrived, he went to hand the hotel employee a tip and saw the Nagarvadhus Escorts card peeking out of his wallet. His eyes widened as a smile spread across his face.

"That's right," he said to the hotel employee, tapping at the card. "That is motherfucking right!"

The employee blinked in response.

"Oh Nagesh, you stupid, stupid son of a bitch," he said, taking out the card and rubbing it between his fingers. "I got you now."

Nagarvadhus Escorts would be Nagesh's one fatal mistake. The entire scam had been set up brilliantly, except that Nagesh had told Harrison to request for Abhilasha, meaning that Nagesh had been with her before, probably more than once. She had to have some shred of information about him, a place that they had met before, anything for Harrison to go on. He tipped the hotel employee some rupees and shoved him out of the door, racing over to the phone with the escort card. Abhilasha certainly liked money, that much was clear from their encounter. She'd come to his room again.

He ground his teeth in delight. Retribution would be his; he could feel it. This would be the undoing of his curse. This would be his greatest success after all the odds had been stacked against him. If everything that had happened so far in Mumbai was a test to prove how tenacious he could be, then this was his final exam.

He'd never been the type to give in to defeat. He was an animal, no longer prey in this wild jungle but a predator now, a bruiser, the last soul remaining in a gladiator's arena, a fighter to the end...far from finished yet.

14

It was late at night when Abhilasha arrived with a knock. He opened the door and saw a displeased expression on her face that quickly turned into a fake smile. She was dressed in a yellow sari this time with red along the fringes and a gold belt to keep it all in place. She sauntered inside as if it was her room, probably thinking he requested her again to prove that he was virile. He had taken out her fee from the ATM in the lobby and left the stack of rupees on the dresser. Her eyes were already on the money.

"Surprised to hear from me?" he asked. He was rocking back and forth a little since he just finished a few small bottles from the mini bar.

"Very little surprises me when I show up to a client."

She began taking off her jewelry in the same robotic fashion as the last time. First came a necklace, then her gold earrings, and finally her bracelets. She placed it all in her purse and set it on the chair.

"Do you want to talk or are you ready for me?" she asked, pushing down her sari to reveal her breast.

"I want to know where he is."

"Where who is?"

She removed her high-heel sandals and began to dance. Just tiny movements: the sway of her hips and pointed toes.

The liquor he drank was sloshing around, seeping into his bloodstream. He thought it might relax him after the day he had, but it only made him want to rage more. He lunged closer, ready to shake the truth out of her. She didn't back away. In her eyes, this was a game, a little bit of sexual danger. She stepped around him and began to massage his shoulders.

"So much tension," she said, with her cool breath in his ear.

She kissed his neck and left lipstick marks around his Adam's apple.

"I don't want sex," he said, attempting to push her away. She kept distracting him with kisses until he pushed her rather forcibly. She almost fell over and eyed him carefully as she regained her balance.

"Nagesh Patel," he continued, pointing a finger at her face. "Tell me everything you know about him."

"I do not know who you speak of..."

"Nagesh Patel. He gave me your card. I need to find him."

She covered up her exposed breast and went for her purse.

"This is not a name that I know. You are a crazy person. *Pāgal*. I am leaving."

She headed toward the door but he grabbed her.

She was thin enough that he could wrap his entire hand around her arm.

"Let go of me."

She struggled but he held on tight. He could sense that she was becoming afraid. This wasn't some sexual game like some other client may have tried.

"Nagesh Patel," he yelled in her ear. "He had to have been a client of yours at some time."

"You can say the name over and over, but I still do not know of him."

He shook her. It wasn't what he meant to do, but he needed to shake something and she was there. Her head whipped back and forth until she managed to slide out of his grasp.

"*Chod dunga,*" she yelled. She slapped him across the face, then seemed to regret it, fearing retaliation. She held up her hands. "Please do not hurt my face, hurt whatever else you want. I need my face to stay perfect."

"I'm sorry...I'm..." He licked the inside of his cheek and felt a bruise. "I didn't mean to do that."

She glanced toward the rupees he left on the dresser, deciding whether to make a grab for them and run. He stood in her way.

"This man owes me a lot of money. I will pay you whatever it takes for some information, your hourly fee plus a whole lot more if you help."

"I've had many clients and names are meaningless to me. Now I suggest you give me my fee and let me leave before my boss pays you a visit you won't like."

"Please, just think if you've ever come across that name before. Nagesh Patel."

"There are thousands with that name in Mumbai.

You will not find him, nor will you get what he 'owes' you. You've come to my Mumbai thinking you can take and take and take. We do not always get everything we want in life, look at me."

"I thought you said you chose this lifestyle."

"This lifestyle chose me. In new Mumbai, I see affluence now and it makes me contemptuous. I will do anything for a taste of it, even this, even you. Otherwise I do not matter here."

She held out her hand for the money.

"My boss is into breaking legs so you know. So unless you want to return to the States as a cripple—"

"I'm already crippled," he mumbled.

Reality was now trickling into the room and strutting around. He would not find Nagesh, not now, not ever. One hundred fifty thousand dollars of his hard-earned money was gone. And there'd be no liver transplant, only a slow, agonizing death.

"Oh God," he said. He went to hug Abhilasha for support but she wasn't having it. He was a trembling mess at this point. He figured he was having a heart attack, a sweet release so he could avoid any forthcoming pain in the long run. He waited to foam at the mouth, to lose control of his bladder, but nothing changed, even Abhilasha's expression. She still held out her hand for the rupees as if she assumed this was some kind of performance.

"I'm sorry," he said, placing the rupees in her palm. He'd expected her to save him, but she was not an angel, she was not Naelle. Oh, sweet Naelle, purveyor of sugary kisses and endless embraces. Her dark, dark skin. Her voluptuous silhouette cast in the moonlight. She didn't care how out of shape he was, or that he had rank breath due to his cirrhosis. She was genuinely concerned for his well-being on the night he almost died. If he dropped dead right now, Abhilasha would step over his body and walk out the door without a second thought.

"Do not call for me a third time," Abhilasha said, as she put the rupees in her purse. "In fact, lose my card."

As Abhilasha went to leave, he caught a final glimpse of her yellow sari billowing from the heavy air conditioning before the door slammed and she was gone. It made him think of Gracie and how he'd be returning without her sari: another disappointment in a string of many.

He opened the wallet he was holding and took out the Nagarvadhus Escort card. It had been his last hope, an evil hoax, so he ripped it to pieces, cursing at the way it teased. Under it was the Desire Card, always popping up when he least expected.

THE DESIRE CARD

Any wish fulfilled for the right price.
PRESS below to inquire.

He felt a surge of adrenaline, a last gasp of fight left in him before he rolled over completely. In his drunken haze he pushed the button.

"Hello," said the same distorted voice as last time after three rings.

"Yes, I've called this number before..."

"What do you desire?"

"I'm looking for someone," he barked into the card. He rubbed his forehead and thought how to best explain the situation. Static crackled from the other end. "This person has stolen a lot of my money and vanished. I want to confront him. I want him to pay for what he's done."

"Where did you see this person last?" the voice asked.

"Mumbai...I'm in Mumbai. Last night...I don't want to waste any more time."

Harrison heard the voice on the other end whispering to someone else.

"The fee for this is twenty thousand, since time is of the essence as you say. What is your credit card number and information?"

Harrison grabbed his Amex with a high spending limit and rattled off the number and his name.

"Please describe the person you are trying to locate."

Harrison gave as much of a detailed description as he could. Nagesh's weird mustache, his potbelly, all the places the guy had lived in the United States, his parents' names, the PO box number, his email address. When he started to talk about Nagesh getting suspended for their call-girl ring at Chilton, the man on the other end cut him off.

"That should suffice, Mr. Stockton. Are you alone right now?"

"Yes, I'm at my hotel, but I don't know how many more days I will be here unless..."

"We will have an answer for you by the morning. That is a guarantee since we have operatives in the area. Good day."

Click.

"Hello?" Harrison said, to a dial tone. He didn't know what else he wanted the voice on the other end to say, but he hadn't expected the call to end so abruptly. In a flash, he'd spent another twenty thousand. He winced at the thought of being so reckless, but he knew he'd pay ten times as much for the satisfaction of finding Nagesh, for a chance to confront the son of a bitch.

He stared at the card waiting for it to ring as his heavy eyes began to close. He couldn't fight it anymore and crawled into bed. Visions of Nagesh assaulted his mind. Nagesh running down some alleyway in the streets of Mumbai and being nabbed by the people of the Desire Card. Someone knocking on Harrison's hotel door as a man stood there with a bag full of his money and stories of a roughed-up Nagesh.

As he drifted off, he embraced these encouraging prophecies, speaking them out loud in the hopes that they'd come true.

———

The wailing Desire Card wrestled him from his sleep. He clawed at the suffocating sheets and reached out to grab it, croaking into the tiny receiver. The room was pitch black, the clock on the nightstand blinking 3:02 in the morning.

"Is this Mr. Stockton?" the voice on the other end asked.

"I...yes."

He turned on a lamp that beamed a tiny pyramid of light.

"We have located the name you gave us," the raspy voice said.

"Nagesh Patel?"

His head was pounding and his mouth was completely dry. He blinked until the room finally came into focus. He reached for a notepad and a pen on the nightstand, his fingers alive and prickling.

"This man is dead."

The pen flew from out of Harrison's grip as he pressed it against the pad. Had he heard right? He asked the voice on the other end to repeat what was said.

"Someone slit his throat," the voice continued. "Apparently a mugging that went bad. He was in a neighborhood he shouldn't have been in. Our operatives in India said he was taken to a hospital, but when he arrived there, he was already dead."

The room spun as Harrison held onto the desk until his surroundings became steady again.

"Are you sure?" he asked. His hands were shaking now, almost causing him to lose grip of the phone.

"I am afraid so. We can send any evidence to your home if you want—"

"No," he snapped into the receiver, then took a long breath as he parsed out what he wanted to say next. "Was there any information about the money he had on him?"

He heard the voice on the line whispering to someone else.

"The body was only found with a driver's license. Everything else had been taken."

"Thank you," he said, hanging up the phone. The room was freezing due to the air conditioning. Little nubs of gooseflesh had sprouted up and down his arms. He felt the gravity of this sudden news in his rumbling stomach and rushed to the bathroom to puke up all the liquids he had ingested. He hugged the cold toilet and couldn't stop thinking ghastly thoughts. Nagesh's throat slit in the shape of smile with flies buzzing around his dead body, feeding on his blood. A thief running away into the night with a hundred fifty thousand of his money.

He flushed the toilet and shuffled back into the bedroom. Seeds of guilt began to fester in his stomach now that it had been emptied. He thought of a moment from decades ago—sharing a blunt with Nagesh and counting the cash from their call-girl ring before it went bust. He should have seen that Nagesh was bad from the start. Nagesh had brought this upon himself; no one forced him to give up his morals so easily. Harrison would mourn the loss of the friend he once knew, but not the con artist he became.

He'd been so naïve at how fucked up the world could be. First he was mugged for his watch and now Nagesh was dead for showboating around with a brief-case full of cash. How many others were being killed over money right now? This cruel planet seemed bent on being as wicked as possible, and he pictured his end too, not cornered in some back alley but hooked up to a bunch of machines a year from now with a feeding tube giving him nourishment. Was that any better?

It'd be easier to end it all right now.

Earlier he had wasted the Advil he brought, but he toyed with finding something else to OD on. He could take a long deep sleep since he was tired, so tired. He puckered his lips as if he was sampling what it'd be like to dictate his own fate instead of his worthless organ calling the shots. He could hope his final dreams would be better than these sagging realities. But he knew he was being dramatic since it wasn't in his DNA to ever quit. He would be strapped to a hospital bed letting those feeding tubes fatten him up, but still angling for a way to get a liver. So instead of searching for another suicidal aid, he decided to let this wicked world slap him around for a little while longer until a miracle occurred or his time naturally came.

———

The next morning, he understood how a zombie must feel. He hadn't slept at all, staying up to find a last-minute flight for a ridiculous amount of money and then chugging all the mini bottles left in the fridge. By the time he had to leave, he was long past being bombed, lucky that the TSA agents even let him fly. Halfway through the flight, he had the woman in the next seat get him some more alcohol once he'd been cut off.

After finishing the last bottle, he felt his eyelids closing. He couldn't stop the visions of death and decay from flipping through his mind. Nagesh on the side of the road, gasping for life as the wound on his throat opened and flies swarmed out. He was trying to tell Harrison something, but only bloody bubbles came out of his mouth. He gestured for Harrison to come closer and Harrison complied. The scent of rotting flesh circled into Harrison's nostrils, as he felt Nagesh's chapped lips against his ear.

"It's a slippery slope, H-Bomb, this thing we call a conscience," Nagesh managed to say. "You and I...we are the same," he continued, before he gurgled a last intake of breath, his eyes wide open in shock.

Harrison stared back at this bullying corpse, frozen. Nagesh was more immoral than he could ever imagine being. So he envisioned himself spitting at Nagesh's body and turning away, afraid to hear any more. Instead he pictured darkness, sweet, engulfing darkness, to tuck him in. His body became weightless as sleep took over. He did not dream, but simply floated through realms of that darkness, places without thought or introspection, exactly where he desired to be—free until New York City's skyline blinked below and the plane landed at JFK with a thud.

———

He returned to his apartment in the middle of the night. Stumbling through the lobby, the doorman needed to help him to the elevator. The few hours of sleep on the plane didn't make him any less drunk. As the elevator climbed to the fifth floor, he dreaded reaching his apartment and facing his family. The kids would be asleep, but he was bound to wake up Helene when he'd get into bed. She'd want to know why he wasn't still in India since he said the trip could take weeks. He decided that he'd say the job wasn't right for him so he came home.

At his front door, he had to try a few keys before one finally fit. He opened the door to a dark living room except for a lamp by the sofa that created a thin band of light. Chauncey was waiting for him like a true best friend, curled into a lump by the front door.

"Chauncey," he said, dropping his bags and getting down on his knees to the pet the cat. Even after the horrific circumstances in Mumbai, one constant in his life remained. He touched Chauncey's soft fur and waited for a purr, but Chauncey didn't respond. Figuring the cat was asleep he nudged it lightly at first. When that didn't work, he used both hands to shake Chauncey out of his slumber, but the cat remained immovable.

"Chauncey?" He gulped.

He scooped the cat up in his arms as its head hung limply to the side. No warmth radiated from its body. He dropped the cat out of fright as tears burned his eyes. He started weeping. He couldn't catch his breath, choking on mucus and the salt streaming down his cheeks. He had never cried like this before, not when his mother or father died, not when he lost his job, or when he'd been diagnosed with liver disease, not even when he found out that Nagesh scammed him, or when he learned that his former friend had been killed. The tears seemed to endlessly flow. Spit and snot hung from his lips as he petted Chauncey's cold body. The curse that the one-eyed woman spoke of had only gotten worse, now it was taking the lives of his family members.

After what felt like hours, he petted Chauncey's face one last time before rising to his feet. He could barely keep his eyes open any longer. He headed through the silent apartment and slipped into his bedroom. The only sound was Helene's light snores. He climbed into bed, still crying from the depths of his soul until Helene finally woke up.

She took off her sleep mask and stared into the darkness.

"Harrison? Is that you?"

He couldn't answer her, his words sounding like

blubbering. He was telling her all that had happened in Mumbai in a language she couldn't understand.

"What are you doing back so soon?" she asked. "What's wrong? Harrison, what's going on?"

"Chauncey's dead."

"What?"

"I'm dying, too," he said, so quietly, a sad whisper of the truth. She didn't hear him because she kept asking about Chauncey, and *why* he was home, and *what* happened in India, but he was in too much shock to answer.

She finally gave up and rolled over on her side, her face mashed into the pillow, clearly deciding to deal with everything in the morning.

All he could do was hold onto her, his anchor after being left out at sea, feeling like he'd lose his sanity for good this time if he let go.

PART THREE

PART THREE

15

HARRISON HAD FALLEN ASLEEP THINKING HE WAS clutching Helene, but in the morning he discovered that a pillow between his legs had replaced her. Salty tears had dried around his lips and tasted like soot and frustration, the flavors of Mumbai. He removed the pillow and wanted to tear out its stuffing, but his insides burned from all the alcohol he'd consumed on the sixteen-hour flight home. With each movement, the pain in his chest only increased. This is how he would die, in this bed if he was lucky, or in some gloomy hospital room if machines became the only way to sustain his life for a little longer.

He closed his eyes as visions of death multiplied. He recalled lying in the hospital a few weeks ago after getting his stomach pumped and the old man in the adjacent bed that had passed away. He remembered the little girl with TB in the Dharavi slums choking on the blood in her mucus. He pictured the repeated image of Nagesh with his throat slit. He thought of Chauncey's bloated body at the front door when he returned home. This last image stayed with him the longest. Chauncey had probably tried to stay alive for as long as possible so he could say goodbye to Harrison, but after a few days the cat had given up and succumbed to death.

Helene had left the curtains open and a harsh sun wasn't letting him waste away the day any longer. After looking at the clock and seeing that it was well into the afternoon, he threw his legs over the side of the bed and attempted to rise. He found his terry-cloth bathrobe draped over a chair and slid into a pair of cold slippers. He brushed his teeth and spit out the grainy textures of India into the sink, then shuffled out of the bedroom.

In the dining room, his family sat at the table eating what appeared to be lunch. He reasoned that it must be the weekend. He crumpled into a chair next to Gracie who was nibbling on a cream cheese and jelly sandwich with the crusts cut off.

"I'm sorry about Chauncey," he said, rubbing her back.

She shrugged, took one last bite of her sandwich, and pushed the plate away.

"It's okay, we're getting a new cat later today."

"What?" he said, then started coughing uncontrollably. "What...did you do with the body?" he asked Helene, once he got his fit under control.

"It was the middle of the night. I left Chauncey outside to be picked up this morning."

"Picked up by whom?"

She put down her coffee and wiped a trace of lipstick off the rim.

"I don't think we need to go into particulars now," she said, nodding at Gracie.

"Mom, I can see you looking at me like that."

Harrison felt the tears build up—remnants of Nagesh's betrayal and his subsequent death, along with his own debilitating deterioration and finally the loss of his true best friend.

"Dad, are you crying?" Brenton asked.

"No, I'm overtired from the jetlag," he managed to say, but it was no use, now he started sniveling.

"Dad, Chauncey was about double the size he should've been. I'm surprised he made it this long."

"We could've had a funeral for him," Harrison said, wiping his sleeve across his eyes. "He deserved a proper burial."

"And where would we bury him?" Helene asked. "It's not like we have a backyard. Sometimes you don't think logically."

"But to replace him this quickly..."

"What did you expect me to do?" she asked, getting up and slamming her chair into the table. She stood with her hands on her hips, never a good sign with Helene. "You were the one who overfed him all of the time."

He winced from her insult. Sure, he had allowed Chauncey to indulge, but what other pleasures did a housecat have besides sleep, a little bit of affection, and food? What other pleasures did most of us have, he wondered?

"Getting a new cat is best for the kids," she said, and then made a gesture that the conversation was over before turning to Brenton and Gracie. "Finish up lunch and go get your coats."

"Daddy, did you get me a sari?" Gracie asked.

He turned to her, almost afraid. "I...didn't have a chance."

She leaped out of her seat and slammed the chair into the table like her mother.

"But I *wanted* one."

"Gracie, I had a very rough trip in Mumbai. The job I went for didn't work out."

"Mom, he promised," she said, and slunk into Helene's arms.

"Harrison, you did say you would get her one."

Helene stroked the child's hair, attempting to soothe. For the loss of a sari, Gracie got consummate consoling. He pitied her naivety, her easy world. Born onto Fifth Avenue with views of Central Park, the girl had never known what it was like to want, to experience true gut-wrenching distress. He felt sorry that she'd simply disintegrate when faced with adversity and knew that he and Helene would be to blame for all of their silver spoon-feeding.

"Sweetie, didn't you say you wanted a calico cat?" Helene asked, after Harrison failed to comfort the child. Gracie nodded with a sigh, as if she was being the bigger person by not making too much of a fuss. "Didn't you tell me you wanted to name it Cinnamon?"

Gracie tucked her face into Helene's chest and murmured a soft "yes."

"I also happen to know an authentic Indian store downtown that has the most beautiful saris."

"Really, Mom? You're the best."

Gracie kissed Helene's cheek and headed toward her room. She gave Harrison a disdainful look as she passed. Brenton went over and squeezed his shoulder.

"Tough break, Dad-O. That'll take years of therapy to undo," he said, before heading toward his own room.

Helene craned her neck to make sure both children were gone.

"We need to have a talk tonight."

Harrison stared down the hallway, lost in thought.

"*Harrison*, did you hear me?"

His body yearned to collapse into hers, to be told that everything would be all right.

"What happened to you in Mumbai? Did you really go all the way there just for a job interview?"

No, he wanted to say. *I needed a liver and spent over a hundred fifty thousand to get it off of the black market, but I was scammed. Fucking Nagesh Patel from college saw what a desperate sucker I am and pounced. Now he's dead and some scavenger is running around with my hard-earned money.*

"Why would you question if I went there for a job?"

"Because I don't know what to believe anymore with you."

"I deserve that."

She looked at him as if she wasn't sure if he was serious or simply placating. He tried to appear as earnest as possible but often found it difficult to be apologetic, associating it as a sign of weakness. She began rifling through her purse.

"I'm having dinner tonight at Bice with Caroline Hendrest. The woman wants a full dissertation on every minute detail for the gala because I'm a volunteer. I swear she'll be looking for the tiniest mistake as an excuse to get rid of me."

She continued digging in her purse. He could tell

she was frustrated because her lips had tightened to the point of nonexistence.

"What are you looking for?"

"I forgot to remind you that representatives of Sanford & Co. will be there. You sold them the tickets before you were fired."

"I was let go."

"Really, Harrison, I'm not in the mood for semantics right now. I had to max out my cards to pay for the sponsors, a band, the caterers, the hall. Of course UNESCO will pay us back for all the charges, but..."

She threw down the purse and let out an exasperated, "Ooooohh." This usually meant a migraine was coming on, the only unfortunate inheritance she'd received from her father Jay. She pinched the bridge of her nose and counted down in her head until she opened her eyes as if she'd awakened from a pleasant nap. He noticed a dot of jelly on the corner of her mouth.

"You have some jelly...." he said, picking up a cloth napkin and attempting to dab the pestering blob off her chin.

"I got it," she said, as he still made a move to do it for her. "Harrison, I got it."

She eyed herself in the hallway mirror, removed the jelly, then tensed up as he hugged her from behind.

"In the Mumbai slums, there was a little girl around Gracie's age with TB."

He parted her shoulder-length hair to the side and exhaled into the back of her neck, a comforting spot that evoked summers in the Hamptons because she always wore her hair up there. The salty aroma of the Atlantic Ocean. Her magnificent cartwheels along a shell-strewn beach. A tranquil present of a Sunday afternoon before he'd have to take the night train to be back at Sanford & Co. by dawn.

"You were in the slums?" she asked, zoning in on the flat black sacs under his eyes. His skin appearing even more yellow than before he left. The rundown face of a man past his prime. He knew this was how she saw him.

"No one could do anything for this girl," he continued, allowing himself to cry even though he wasn't crying for the doomed child, but for his own selfish losses and the secrets he couldn't share. "She was covered in the blood she coughed up. The conditions of the shack were unlivable: scurrying rats and a bucket for the children to bathe in..."

He couldn't say anymore and Helene used the pause in conversation as an excuse to slide out of his grasp. He knew she still wanted to lash out at him but wouldn't have wanted to seem insensitive.

"UNESCO works with a lot of organizations that bring help and hope to the slums in India. I could put you in touch with my contacts there if you're interested."

"Seeing that little girl made me feel all alone," he said, the words spewing from his mouth faster than he could think them. "Like if I was dying on a bed would anyone truly care?"

He went to embrace her again, but she wasn't having it. She pinched the bridge of her nose again.

"Don't be ridiculous. Anyway, I don't have time for a debate about mortality either."

Two doors slammed and they could hear Brenton

and Gracie arguing from down the hallway. Helene threw her purse over her shoulder.

"So I need your credit card to pay for a cat because I can't find my checkbook."

"Right. Sure."

He headed past Brenton and Gracie and retrieved his wallet from the bedroom. As he pulled out his Visa, he spied the Desire Card again. What if he waited for his family to leave and requested Naelle? Not for any sex of course but simply to be held, to confide about his horrific days in Mumbai like he would to a therapist, for her to stroke what was left of his hair and tell him that everyone goes through bad times before a reckoning comes. Tenacity would prevail and a new liver would be waiting for him from the donor list. Then maybe he'd nestle into her and close his eyes to be rocked to sleep like he always desired, even as a lonely child.

When he returned to the living room, Brenton and Gracie were horsing around in the foyer, and Helene was clutching her reddening neck, imploring the kids not to break the vase her father gave her from his trip to Marrakesh last year.

"I'll be back no later than ten for a *talk*," Helene said, taking his credit card and ushering the kids into the outside hallway. "Make sure you'll be here," she added, and closed the front door.

He placed his ear up against the peephole and listened until they had all gotten into the elevator. The talk with Helene later that night would certainly end in a divorce or separation. He already envisioned lugging all of his belongings to a walk-up, which would become his final residence. He had wanted to return from Mumbai as a triumphant new man reclaiming his family and a zeal for life, but now even survival was a pipe dream. He found himself thirsting for life more than ever, disbelieving that he ever tried to swallow too many pills, begging for forty more years on the planet. He shuddered at the idea of being beaten and removed the Desire Card from his wallet.

He longed for Naelle, the last bit of kindness he'd received. He pictured her soapy brown leg hanging off the bathtub and pushed the button.

"Hello," said the same guttural voice he'd gotten used to after three rings.

"Yes, I wanted to call this time about..."

"What is it that you desire?"

He was about to say Naelle's name, but then he remembered that she'd billed herself as Candy. In the mere seconds it took for him to realize this mistake, his brain disconnected from his voice box and the truth came out instead. For even though he wanted Naelle, there was something else he still desired a whole lot more, so he went to whisper this ominous request as beads of sweat made his hands slick and he almost dropped the card.

"A liver," he said, shocked at this claim. He had the urge to hang up, to chide himself for entering into a new shady venture. Hadn't he learned from Nagesh's deceit? But he kept the card to his ear, certain that he couldn't be wronged again.

The distorted voice on the other end was speaking to someone else, sounding like the adults from the Charlie Brown cartoons. He bit into his thumbnail and tore it off. The first voice returned to the line.

"Keep the card nearby. We will call you back."

The line went dead. He shook his head since they

gave no indication of how long he'd have to wait. He didn't want to deal with a call from them once Helene and the kids returned with a new cat, but if he was being truthful, waiting only prolonged the possibility of changing his mind.

He occupied himself in the kitchen, chewing on the remains of a cream cheese and jelly sandwich left on the counter. He reasoned that requesting a liver from the Desire Card was no less amoral than what he'd tried to achieve in India. For the right price, maybe these people had the kind of influence to move him up on the donor list, and then he wouldn't even have to deal with attempting to get another organ off the black market.

The card rang loudly because of the echo in the kitchen. He could feel the anticipation in his salivating glands. His nervous hand picked it up.

"Hello," he said meekly, wishing he had exuded more confidence.

"Because of the nature of your request, we must deal with you in person," the distorted voice said. "If you are serious—"

"I'm very serious," he said, as his heart thumped and thumped.

"Then be at the corner of Barclay and Greenwich at six on the dot tonight. A large van will pull up and open its doors. Do you have any medical records on hand to show us?"

"Yes, yes I do."

"Bring them."

"Should I describe myself so you'll be able to locate me?"

"We know what you look like, Mr. Stockton. You've called us more than once."

Harrison exhaled into the receiver.

"If you do not show up tonight, we will come to you to extract some type of fee."

Harrison was about to ask about how much they charged for the whole operation, but the line went dead, the dial tone beeping away as he lowered the card from his ear.

16

Harrison waited on the corner of Barclay and Greenwich Streets scanning the traffic for a passing van. He'd arrived a few minutes early to be safe and wanted to position himself just right. He chose to lean against the facing building, at first attempting to stand with one foot on the ground and the other flush against the building's exterior, but due to his large size and the shortness of his breath, he couldn't maintain the position for long. He figured it was crucial to appear tough and in control. These people would sense weakness the moment they pulled up, and he didn't want to come off as an easy target to get swindled again.

He tried not to sweat but it was futile. Sopping rings grew around his armpits. He could taste the pools of perspiration on his upper lip, but he worried about his clammy palms the most. He knew he'd have to shake hands once he got in the van and his sweatiness would be a dead giveaway to show how rattled his nerves were. He also had to take a huge piss, but that seemed more like a product of his recent condition rather than due to the state of his fluctuating emotions.

Before he could think any further, a brand-new van pulled up to the corner. The windows had been tinted like he'd expected, but he attempted to peer inside anyway. A side door slid open and he could vaguely make out the shape of three men sitting in the shadows.

"Are you coming?" one of them asked, the voice distorted like it had been on the card.

"Yes, of course," Harrison said, hoisting himself into the van. A gloved hand appeared out of the darkness to help him inside. Before he could even squat on his haunches, the van took off, speeding through the night like it was running from the law. The gloved hand reached over and shut the side door.

His eyes adjusted to the darkness. A thin beam of moonlight cut through the front window. He could see that the driver had on some type of mask, but from where he stood, he couldn't tell what it was. In a semi-circle around him sat the three men, each with gloved hands and dressed in form-fitting black attire. The van took an unexpected left turn, which caused the moon-light to flash across their faces. Each also wore a mask, a familiar visage that took a moment for him to register. To his right, a guy wore a Humphrey Bogart mask, in front of him sat Jimmy Stewart, and at his side, James Dean held up a blindfold.

"So you won't know our location," James Dean said.

The masks the men wore had been unlike any he'd ever seen, each looked as if it'd been made out of real skin. Jimmy Stewart's was laden with wrinkles, more so *Vertigo*-era Jimmy Stewart as opposed to *It's a Wonderful Life*. Humphrey Bogart had been cloned from the greedy prospector in *The Treasure of Sierra Madre*, filmed at the tail end of his career. Their bodies, however, remained youthful and physically fit: all imposing muscles and thick necks. James Dean was the only one of the three whose body matched his young face, which was why Harrison guessed him to be the ringleader. The other two appeared as if they had long passed the prime of their careers, their idol status dimming due to the inevitability of old age, no longer remembered as crushes in little girls' heads. The product of time and circumstances had been etched into each of their deeply rooted wrinkles. Only James Dean forever remained the desire of so many from his own era and would continue to do so throughout time. Even this faux James Dean seemed to twinkle with the knowledge of his immortality, standing upright and imposing while the other two were hunched over.

Harrison could remember watching *East of Eden* with his mother on their VHS player as a child while she smoked her Winstons down to the filter. She had already become loose-lipped and nostalgic because of the fifth of cheap gin she put back. She seemed to glow every time James Dean's bad boy Cal appeared on their small rabbit-eared TV. She'd speak into a brimming ashtray about innocent times before she met his father when she was a young girl in bobby socks and a poodle skirt at the movies and this larger than life man on the big screen made her wet for the first time. Harrison didn't know what being "wet" meant, but he knew that his mother looked at James Dean in a very different way than she looked at his father: like she was in awe, like she wasn't worthy, like she'd chuck her whole sad New Haven life if James Dean would hold out his hand through the TV so the two of them could ride off into the horizon together on his motorcycle.

As Harrison looked more closely at the masks, he could tell that the men's hair were part of the masks as well, making it truly appear as if each movie star had risen from the grave to work for this organization. Only each of their mouths gave away the illusion of true resurrection since a tiny speaker had been installed between each mask's lips, most likely the cause of their distorted voices.

Humphrey Bogart whispered something unintelligible to Jimmy Stewart. James Dean placed the blindfold tightly over Harrison's eyes and murmured a threat to establish his authority. Harrison's teeth chattered, he hoped not audibly.

"Till we get to our headquarters," one of them said, his voice even more robotic than the first.

Harrison opened his eyes to darkness and spent the rest of the trip in silence. All he could tell at one point was that the van had passed over a bridge because a breeze full of salty air had rushed inside and left the taste of spoiled fish on his tongue. If he had to guess, they had probably entered New Jersey.

———

Harrison had always been a poor judge of time so he had no idea how long it was taking to reach their destination. None of the men spoke to him throughout the trip, and at most he was only able to hear a murmur of static whispering. When the van finally stopped, he was helped to his feet and guided outside. Cicadas buzzed in the air. The wind whipped through the trees. He guessed he was far out of the city but could really be anywhere.

He wanted to check his watch, knowing that he had to be home by ten for his "talk" with Helene. The likelihood of making it back by then seemed pretty dim, but he knew there'd be many nights remaining to truly battle it out with her and only one to secure his new liver.

The men led him down a rocky dirt trail, holding him upright each time he'd stumble. Even though they appeared intimidating before, in his blind state they became supportive. They were the heroes when all others had failed to come through with viable options, and he felt able to breathe more steadily.

They finally reached an entrance after slowly descending a hill. He pictured their headquarters tucked between two valleys so it wouldn't be visible from afar. A cool rush of air knocked him in the face as he heard the sound of a giant door opening. The men grabbed him under each arm and walked him inside. Through the blindfold, he could sense bright lights being turned on and that the room they entered was large with high ceilings due to the delayed echo of their footsteps.

When they removed the blindfold, the bright lights stung at first and he saw sunspots. He rubbed his eyes as he took in his surroundings. The room was certainly expansive; the ceiling stretched about twenty feet in the air. The walls looked to be metallic, possibly to remain soundproof. A door on the far side of the room had just been shut. Next to the door was a table with a phone and a chair. Above the table was an array of television screens that seemed to depict other rooms throughout the headquarters. He could make out a room that looked like a hospital and the shape of a body lying on a gurney before the image flickered to a different room. James Dean stepped in front of him, blocking his ability to see anymore.

"We apologize for this protocol, Mr. Stockton, but you must realize our need for ultimate discretion."

Harrison attempted to answer, but his tongue tripped up over the words.

"For desires like yours that come with complications, we must deal with them face-to-face to gauge their seriousness."

"I-I am serious. Very serious as I've said."

James Dean held up his hand to silence Harrison. "An organ is a tricky wish. For if one is blessed with health, why should they take a risk as a donor?"

"Yes, that is the conundrum," Harrison said, bracing himself for another coughing attack that had already started itching at his throat.

"So what avenues have you gone through to obtain a liver?"

Humphrey Bogart and Jimmy Stewart had now bookended James Dean like bodyguards. All three waited for Harrison's response.

"I recently returned from Mumbai where I paid for a liver off the black market."

James Dean stroked his fake chin. "I'm guessing that the outcome of this scheme did not turn out in your favor?"

He thought about explaining the whole story, which culminated with the people of the Desire Card telling him that Nagesh had been killed; but he decided to keep things vague so his two recent calls to them wouldn't seem related.

"I was scammed. By someone I thought was a...friend."

This had been the first time he'd admitted his disappointment out loud since he returned to the States, and it surprised him to find that the most difficult part was referring to Nagesh as a "friend." At one point in his life, he had thought of Nagesh not just as a friend but a best friend. He'd never had a best friend before, and in those early days at Chilton, it felt good to be part of a duo. Sure he and Helene used to speak of one another at the beginning of their marriage as each other's best friend, but that had never been entirely true. For the two of them never had much in common besides their blind infatuations. She found watching sports dull in comparison to playing them. He found all of her grand causes unworthy of his time. And someone like Whit had never been a true friend either, simply a man with an eternal dagger over Harrison's back; but Nagesh had been a confidant, and Harrison would've never guessed there was a duplicitous nature hiding behind those wide eyes.

"There are no friends in the nature of business," James Dean said.

"Yes," Harrison said, lowering his head. "This I've realized."

"So now for the particulars," James Dean said, and leaned in closer to Humphrey Bogart to whisper in his ear. Humphrey Bogart nodded and went over to the other end of the room to make a phone call. "I am guessing in India you had a willing donor?"

"Of course," Harrison said, jarred by this claim. He

couldn't prevent himself from holding in his coughs any longer.

"Get Mr. Stockton some water," James Dean told Jimmy Stewart, the static hiss of his voice straining with frustration. Harrison didn't know if it was directed at him for coughing, or at Jimmy Stewart for not responding quickly enough.

A cooler had been installed into the metallic wall by the front entrance. Jimmy Stewart snatched a bottle of water and handed it to Harrison who took a big gulp.

"My condition," Harrison said, wiping a stream of spittle from his lips.

"No need to apologize," James Dean said.

"In India we supposedly had a willing donor, but again it was all a scam."

"A shame," James Dean said, shaking his head. "The business of conning others is not what our organization is all about. We pride ourselves on granting only the finest wishes to our clients, and there has never been a desire within reason we haven't been able to provide."

"Is mine within reason?"

James Dean seemed to smile from behind his mask.

"You are not the first with this request. For a liver... yes, but for an organ, no."

It amazed Harrison to hear he hadn't been the first to succumb to desperation. How many others had tortured their bodies and called the Desire Card for a quick remedy? He pictured an array of organs to choose from; only the best at his disposal so he could erase any sour memories of what went down in Mumbai.

"And you were able to deliver those organs?" he asked.

James Dean let out a crackling laugh. "Like our card says, any wish fulfilled for the right price."

"And what is the price?"

"First you must realize that there is no chance of finding a willing donor. Sure we could spend a lot of time and resources searching across the country for someone desperate enough to sell part of their liver, but we do not have the time. The point is to get you a new liver. How we do so should be of no interest to you."

"You mean kill someone for it?" Harrison said, as the word "kill" ricocheted off of the metallic walls.

James Dean held up his hand again. "First of all, I will ask you to refrain from putting words in my mouth. Part of the liver will be...borrowed. Our organization stretches across many states and beyond this country. We are connected to a vast network of employees, people whose medical records we have, some of whom we have no use in employing anymore."

The water bottle fell from Harrison's hand. The echo made Humphrey Bogart look up from his phone call in the corner. Harrison felt a terrible rumbling in his stomach. He had finally stopped coughing, but now a creeping nausea slid up his throat instead.

"Please, do not think of us as mercenaries," James Dean said, picking up the bottle and placing it in Harrison's shaking hand. "We think of ourselves as genies, for it is sad for someone's desires to remain as a hope and nothing more. We mean to make your deepest fantasies a reality. Whether that be a bottle of sixty-four-year-old Macallan that runs for almost half a million dollars, or simply a new liver to filter that whiskey well."

"What if I wanted you to find a willing donor? How much would that go for?"

James Dean and Jimmy Stewart exchanged a long glance.

"More than you can afford since we are not willing to waste any man hours on that request."

"And to get a liver from an unwilling participant?"

"Three hundred thousand. Half will be given to us once we've found a match and the other half must be delivered on the day of your surgery. We have hospital facilities at our headquarters and you will spend your recovery in the care of our dedicated medical professionals."

"That's a lot of money," Harrison said, massaging his forehead as a ball of bile-infused saliva tickled the back of his tongue.

"How much is your life worth? If you ask me, three hundred thousand is a bargain."

A dizzy spell seemed to latch onto Harrison's head and give it a good shake. He pivoted from one foot to the other until he got his bearings again.

"Seeing the state that you're in, Mr. Stockton, it appears as if you don't have too much time," James Dean said.

Harrison made his way over to the wall so he could lean against something. The eyes of each of the men followed, but none of them said anything else. His breathing had accelerated, and his heart felt as if it was being squeezed. He swallowed some more water until the bottle was empty.

Three hundred thousand. He imagined that much money. He had guesstimated that these people would've charged as much as Nagesh did, but the extra hundred fifty thousand on top of what he lost in India would destroy his and Helene's savings, especially if a divorce was inevitable and their lawyers would eat up any remaining funds. They'd have to sell their apartment in a market where they'd get well under their asking price, and his exorbitant child support payments were bound to leave him with little else. He thought of dipping into the trust accounts that Helene's father had set up for the kids since he knew Jay had more than enough money to replenish those trusts. Brenton and Gracie couldn't get at the trusts until they were eighteen anyway, so it wouldn't be like he was stealing from anything they'd be using now.

"Mr. Stockton, are you liquid enough to pay?" James Dean asked, his scratchy voice sounding more impatient than it had been before.

"Yes," Harrison replied, peeling himself from off of the metallic wall. He knew that there was no other option. If they had said a million dollars, he'd still have to comply and find a way to come up with the cash.

"We have to be very firm with the payments," James Dean continued. "Like I said, we are not mercenaries... unless we are forced to be."

The way he said the last part of the sentence led Harrison to believe that they'd been put in that uncompromising position before.

"Yes, of course. You do not have to worry about being paid."

Humphrey Bogart returned from his phone call at the other end of the room and removed a card from his pocket. He handed it to Harrison.

"This is a new Desire Card," James Dean said. "Do not contact us with the other one. We will contact you."

Harrison nodded and stuffed the card in his pocket.

The door at the other end of the room opened and a

large man with a Cary Grant mask entered the room with a syringe in his hand.

"Did you bring your medical records?"

"Oh...yes," Harrison said, handing them over.

"We will take your blood and start searching for a match right away."

Cary Grant motioned for Harrison to roll up his sleeve and tapped at Harrison's arm to find a vein. He took some blood and placed the filled syringe in a sealed plastic bag.

"We assure you that we will find a match, Mr. Stockton," James Dean said.

"What will happen to the donor?" Harrison asked, rolling down his sleeve. He didn't want to hear the answer, but he knew that his conscience wouldn't let him remain oblivious.

"We have state-of-the-art facilities. The...donor will be monitored by us and given a handsome sum after the surgery for their troubles. They will be kept separate from you and blindfolded for the entire span of their recovery. When it is over, the ordeal will have been a nightmare for them, but I assure you, the money they will receive will help heal any wounds."

"I wouldn't want someone's death on my hands," Harrison said. His voice cracked at this request, as a nugget of guilt began to fester.

"Then you and I think alike, Mr. Stockton," James Dean replied. "Do you have any more questions?"

Harrison tried to think of anything else, but his mind had become clouded. He'd been repeating to himself over and over that anyone else in his position would be doing the same thing.

"No other questions," he said to James Dean, shrugging his shoulders.

"Good, then it is time for us to take you home."

Jimmy Stewart got out the blindfold again and tied it around Harrison's eyes. With only the surrounding darkness, Harrison's mind travelled to thoughts of who'd be the unlucky donor. He could never know their face or anything about them. He'd request for them to be covered by a sheet during the entire surgery so they'd never have to become real.

He knew one glimpse and he'd always see their face in his punishing dreams.

———

The ride home felt shorter than the one going to the headquarters. His fear had been replaced by a billion questions of morality, thoughts he felt he needed to have to justify such a deplorable descent. Others would've balked the instant they found out that the donor would be an unwilling one. Others didn't have sketchy enough scruples to call the Desire Card in the first place, or wouldn't have gone to Mumbai on a whim and even behaved like he had for the last forty-four years. These moralistic people ate their artery-clogging foods in moderation; they didn't drink to blackout, or pop too many pills. They loved their spouses unconditionally and never acted on bringing anyone else into their beds. But he never had it in him to be a model for society. From his first memory, he'd been a being who wanted, who desired more than he had, someone who'd never been fully satisfied but was always looking past the here and now, always wondering what else existed out there for him. *But no more*, he reasoned, as the van ran into stop-and-go traffic and he could tell he was back in the city. Receiving a new liver meant a responsibility to change the kind of person he was: to be generous now to others, thoughtfully unselfish, a giver as opposed to consummate taker, someone who could hit the pillow at the end of the day knowing he'd spread only good tidings. Then he could be justified for all of his sins.

The van stopped and the side door opened. His blindfold was removed as he stepped out at Barclay and Greenwich Street. When he looked back, the van had already sped away as if it had never existed, the card in his pocket remaining as the only evidence of this wild night.

He looked at his watch and saw it was close to midnight. Normally Helene would've given up and gone to bed, but not tonight. She'd be waiting for him, ready to strike with over twenty years of pent-up hostility.

He put his finger in the air to hail a cab. Listening to her vent would be his first step in becoming a giver, the first of many.

17

By the time Harrison returned home, the lights had all been shut off. A peculiar stillness infiltrated the apartment, the sound of solitude: no fire trucks roaring through the night, no buzz or chatter along the sidewalks, an unconscious city. For once he craved clamor, chaos, anything to distance himself from his nagging conscience.

He turned on a lamp expecting to see Chauncey waiting by the front door, but then he remembered that Chauncey was dead. In his place, a tiny calico kitten pawed at the area rug. The cat looked up and hissed at Harrison before darting into the shadows by the living room. This had once been Harrison's home, but no longer. That was becoming clearer.

He headed down the hallway and saw a thin light spooling from his bedroom. Like he suspected, Helene had waited up for him. He pushed open the door and saw her sitting on the bay window seat in a nightgown with a glass of wine. She'd been transfixed by a lone star in the foggy night sky. He shut the door to break her from her trance.

"I'm sorry for being late," he said.

She drained the last few sips in the wine glass and shook her head.

"I'm tired of that word...sorry."

"I'm s—"

Her eyes cut right through him. "How was *she*?"

"No, I was...just out...walking through the park."

She let out a gulp of a laugh, anything to prevent herself from crying. He knew that sad laugh well, having been the cause of it for so long.

"What terrible things did I ever do to you?" she said, fingering the wine glass.

"Nothing. I'm the one at fault."

She threw the glass at him. It missed and crashed into pieces against the wall.

"Helene, the kids."

"Let them hear," she said, standing up. Her teeth were stained wine-dark, her face flush. He wanted to take her in his arms but knew it'd be a mistake.

"I really was walking in the park and thinking of what I wanted to say to you," he said, crumpling onto the edge of the bed.

"So? Speak. Come on."

She pushed his shoulder causing him to slump over on his side.

"I'm sick," he said, as a piece of spittle hung from his lips.

"You're goddamn right you're sick."

It felt cathartic for him to confess about his illness, even if she interpreted that he was sick in the mind.

"I married an enigma," she said. "You exist entirely

in your head. Maybe to others you don't, your former colleagues possibly, but I've slept next to a ghost for over twenty years."

"I know. I'm so sick."

"This has been boiling inside of me for some time, but we've lived separate lives and there was never a chance to say anything since you were always gone. I played the role of an obedient spouse the best I could."

"Yes, you did. More than I could ask for."

She slapped him across the face. The brunt of the force caused her hair to stand on end. She went to slap him again, but he put up his hands to block.

"You took advantage of my inability to speak up. You have wrecked me, Harrison. I put on a good face but inside I'm hollow, just hollow."

She sat down in tears. For an instant, he saw the girl he fell in love with at college who cried once because she got mono and didn't want him to think she'd been sleeping around. She had Frenched some guy at a keg party and swore she hadn't done anything more. That guy had been the only other man she'd ever touched in their twenty-five-year relationship, and this made Harrison sad; for she deserved to be desired. At nineteen, she'd been so vibrant, so curiously sexual and fun. He'd kill for one night with Helene née Howell, the regal creature that he slow-danced with to Foreigner's "Waiting for a Girl Like You," the one whose breast he felt at the back of a movie theater in downtown Hartford instead of watching *The Breakfast Club*, and when they returned to the local theater a week later, she had pounced on him during the coming attractions and they missed the entire movie again. The girl he rocked to sleep when her Grammy Bitsy died, the one he'd watch at field hockey games and felt all squirmy inside if she missed a goal, who won the hot dog eating contest at her Kappa Gamma sorority and then puked all over her dress at a formal later that night and swore to him that she had the best day ever as he got her into a toilet stall and held back her hair. Collegiate Helene and Harrison didn't have children to worry about, or bills that had to be paid, or two decades of built-up resentment. She found him cute because of his sloppy, sad sack gait, and he loved that she called him "dahling," as if they were an old married WASPy couple. He liked that she wore pearls to brunch even if she was wickedly hungover, and that her sense of humor always veered toward the offensive. They never fought back then, which was probably their first mistake, both never spoke up about each other's annoying traits. She always bristled at his poor grammar, but never attempted to correct his less-than-stellar enunciations. He couldn't stand her field hockey friends, a bunch of vulgar girls, but he partied with them and laughed at their lame jokes. Then graduation came along so fast. Most of his frat brothers were moving to Boston, but he and Helene had always discussed New York as the place of their dreams, so it was natural to move in together while he went for his MBA and she edited non-fiction books about horticulture and gardening at a swanky Midtown publishing house. They lived in a tiny studio on Great Jones Street because she refused her father's offer of purchasing a co-op. Every day Harrison hiked up four flights of stairs to a hallway that smelled of their Greek neighbor's terrible cooking, and they slept on a futon in the corner of the studio and got drunk off of terrible wine and listened to the Smiths on their boom box and made love like clockwork each night, as if to prove to one another that after three years they were still hotter than ever for one another. And then business school ended, and he proposed and her father Jay had gotten him an interview as an analyst at Sanford & Co. where he worked terrible hours but promised that it wouldn't be forever, that only bottom-feeder analysts were treated like slaves, but then he was promoted and it only got worse. He got her pregnant to keep her occupied and they moved into the Fifth Avenue apartment. She quit her editing job and became consumed with motherhood. And once Brenton went on to kindergarten, she had Gracie to fill the void. And once Gracie went to school, Helene threw herself into charity work until Harrison became no more than a passing thought, a once-in-a-while blot on her otherwise perfect life. She had children she adored. She was fulfilled by all the charity work she did. She had doting parents and a wide array of friends. In a place like Manhattan, she had convinced herself that she was busy enough to overlook the fact she missed being loved, and held, and wanted, and needed.

For all of this, he knew she cried until there were no more tears left.

"I want you to leave," she said, looking exhausted enough to go into hibernation. A chill wafted inside, and she buttoned the nightgown up to her neck.

"You want a divorce?"

She nodded but then shook her head. "I don't know. I don't want you in this house right now."

She removed a wadded tissue from her sleeve to wipe her leaking nose.

"So you want to separate?"

"Must you *label* everything?"

He kicked at a dust ball by his toe. "I'm just trying to follow what you want."

"That's rich. Now you're suddenly attuned to my needs?"

"What will we tell the kids?"

"It's up to you. This gala has sucked the life out of me. So after it's finished and I have a moment to get my bearings, we can decide what happens next. But for now, I can't look at you anymore."

"You want me to leave tonight?" he said, turning his attention to his sweet bed with pillows soft like clouds. After the kind of night he had, he swore he could sleep for days.

"No," Helene said, reaching for the wine bottle she hid behind the divan. "We'll tell Brent and Gracie in the morning and then you can stay at a hotel."

"How long have you been thinking about this?"

"Do you really want to know?"

He shook his head.

"Let's just say for too long."

She filled up her glass with what was left in the bottle.

"This is that thousand-dollar 1997 Dom Romanee Conti that you won at that shitshow auction Sanford & Co. had last year. By the way, the charity they raised money for was completely fabricated. I looked them up."

"How's the wine?"

"It tastes like spicy berries. It's all right."

"I've so mistreated you."

She threw her head back in annoyance. "Harrison, I

don't want to talk anymore tonight. I told you to be home over two hours ago."

"I want to know when it ended for us."

"You're going to get angry if I tell you," she said. "I want to go to bed; I want you sleep on the couch."

"I will. I promise. Just tell me. I know I'm an asshole. Was I always?"

The corner of her mouth wrinkled into a smile.

"That was one of the reasons you fell in love with me, Helene. I was shocking. I was rough around the edges. You had lived in a bubble. A great bubble, but still a bubble. You had the Tooth Fairy and my dad once knocked one of my teeth out."

She took a gulp of wine and closed her eyes. Her lips moved as if she was counting.

"So are you saying that we never had a chance?" she said, opening her eyes again. "Our worlds were just too different? That's your entire excuse?"

"Yeah," he said, getting in her face. "Because I grew up thinking I had to do whatever it takes to survive. I was always on guard. Because I got it bad from him and from her sometimes. You didn't have to go through things like that."

"I've been telling you for years to go to therapy."

"That doesn't work for everybody. We can't all have a relationship like you and Dr. Samuels do."

"I've been seeing Dr. Samuels since I was fourteen years old."

"Don't you think that's a little strange?"

"It was about thirteen years ago," she said, putting down the wine glass and folding her arms.

"I think you've been seeing Dr. Samuels for longer than that."

"No, it's been thirteen years since I realized we had problems."

His throat closed up. He wanted to choke but couldn't. She walked past him, made her way to the bathroom. She was done talking and closing the bathroom door would end the conversation for good. He let out a hacking cough and staggered after her.

"Wait, wait, wait. Thirteen years?"

"When I first had Brenton," she began. "I can't believe I'm telling you this. I probably should've said something a long time ago. I think it might've helped."

"What are you talking about?"

"I was completely overwhelmed at first, but I didn't feel exhausted or that Brenton was a burden. I was overwhelmed because I loved him so much it would scare me at times."

"I know you had anxiety."

"This has nothing to do with that." She shook her head. "God, you always try to redirect the blame from yourself." She leaned against the wall and composed herself. "Finally, when you were home long enough for me to talk to you about how I was feeling, I expected that you'd say the same thing, but you gave me this rant about *love* instead. You'd had a miserable day at the office, and I probably shouldn't have started something with you, but I really wanted to start something with you because you deserved it. You said that 'love can be a distraction if you don't get it under control,' and I knew you felt that way, that work was paramount and everything else secondary. But more and more I thought about what you said, and one day I realized what Brenton and me would ultimately mean to you in the grand scheme of your life. You would always keep your distance. You would never let yourself get too close."

"I don't think that's true. That wasn't what I meant. And with Gracie, you can't think that I don't love—"

"I didn't say you didn't ever *love* any of us, you just never gave us your all."

"Because people can show love in different ways," he said, raising his voice. "Maybe I didn't say it out loud enough, but I've told you things like that were never said to me."

"You can't keep hiding behind your parents' neglect."

She took another step, but he grabbed her arm.

"Let me go to bed," she said, her eyes dead. Fat purple sacs weighed down the rest of her face. She sniffled again and wiped at her nose.

"I'm capable of love."

"Harrison, it doesn't make you a bad person, it just makes you...you."

"And you realized all of this from that one thing I said?"

"Of course not, but it was something I could never... forget. What else do you want me to say?"

"I loved you. I did."

He gripped onto her nightgown, the silky fabric slipping through his fingers.

"I know you did. But neither of us do anymore."

She pushed him aside and headed into the bathroom.

"So now you know the truth," she said, and shut the bathroom door so loud that the walls vibrated.

When he went to open the door to go after her, she

had already locked it and turned the water on full blast to drown him out.

———

He woke up on the couch the next morning, twisted and aching. Someone was grinding coffee in the kitchen. He made his way into the shower, washed off the excess of a sleepless night, and stepped out of the bathroom even more tired. He dressed for the day, unconscious of what he was putting on. By then the rest of his family had woken up. Helene sat at the dining room table wearing a cavernous wool sweater, her hair in a clip. She sipped coffee and nodded with her eyes. Gracie flipped through a heavy coffee table book about great ballerinas of the twentieth century. She mumbled "hello" as muffin crumbs dribbled down her chin. Brenton was devouring the last of a muffin with another one ready to go in his hand.

"Kids, we have to talk," Harrison said, pulling up a chair and eyeing Helene to make sure that this was an appropriate time.

"I got soccer practice in—"

"All chorus girls need to be at the studio in a hour to begin a run-through—"

Harrison held up his hand to cease their whines. At their age, he could never remember being booked on a Sunday, a day usually devoted to television. But kids these days were mini adults, the innocence of blissful lazy days existing in a long past era.

"You'll both just have to be late," he said.

"No way, Dad, coach'll bench me."

Brenton slapped the table and crossed his arms in a

huff. Gracie copied. Harrison looked at Helene to help. Finally she put down the cup of coffee to run her hands through Brenton's hair.

"This is important," she said, her nose twitching as if she was about to cry.

When had he lost his authority? As a child, he'd feared his father enough for the man to creep into his nightmares. He swore to never raise a hand to Brenton and Gracie, but their belligerence, their expectations that *everything* revolved around them, was too much. He wondered if this separation might even be good since it would pop their perfect little bubbles and cause them to face some harsh realities.

"Now your mother and I love each other very much."

"Harrison," Helene said, in the singsong tone she exhibited when disagreeing. "Maybe I should take this one?"

"What's going on?" Gracie asked, her fingers picking up stray crumbs and trembling.

"Sweetie, come here."

Helene motioned for the girl to come into her lap. Even though Gracie was almost too big to do so, she climbed up and nuzzled into Helene's chest.

"Why don't you suck your thumb while you're at it?" Brenton joked.

"Shut up, I don't do that anymore."

"Let your mother speak," Harrison said.

"Your father and I have been married a very long time now, almost twenty years."

"Do you want us to throw you an anniversary party?" Gracie asked.

Both Harrison and Helene chose to pretend they didn't hear her sad request.

"Sometimes people need a break from one another," Helene said. "Sweetie, remember when your friend Katie slept over the other weekend, and you two were having a great time?"

Gracie stared at her thumb but resisted the urge to put it in her mouth.

"And then by Sunday, you two got a little sick of each other because you'd spent so much time together."

"Are you getting a divorce?" Brenton asked.

"Let your mother explain," Harrison said, trying not to look at either child so he wouldn't get too choked up.

"It's not a divorce," Helene said. "For now your father and I will be simply living apart."

"But where will *we* live?" Gracie asked. Her head shot up from her mother's chest like a periscope, as if she was taking in a view of her home for the last time.

"Of course, you all will still live here...with your mother. I'll be at a hotel for now."

Gracie played with her hair and sunk back into Helene's chest. "All right," she sighed.

"You guys are gonna get a divorce," Brenton said, shoving the other muffin in his mouth.

"No one said those words, Brent."

"Uh, face it. You guys are dunzo. Everyone's parents just say that they're separating, but they all divorce in the end."

"My parents are still together after almost fifty years of marriage," Helene added, but no one responded.

"Whatever, it's no big deal," Brenton said. "Like, of

course you'd get sick of each other. No offense, but who wouldn't?"

"I'll still see you, Bunny," he said to Gracie because she had gotten really quiet and was in fact sucking her thumb now.

She shrugged her tiny bird-like shoulders.

"Your father will be very busy job hunting, so it will be good for him to have some space," Helene said, as if that was the sole reason for their separation.

"We want you both to know that this has nothing to do with either of you. Your mother and I have been thinking about this for some time."

The room grew silent. Slats of light passed over their faces as the sun climbed higher in the sky. Harrison looked around at the place he once called home. Helene had redone the living room recently, jettisoning the classic mid-Century look she'd favored for a minimalistic aesthetic that an interior designer friend said would get them top dollar if they ever decided to sell. So out went the rows and rows and bookcases full of art books and first-edition classics that had been passed down by Jay, and in their place, a sleek, metallic composition had corrupted the apartment. It reminded him of the Desire Card's headquarters from last night, a glimpse into a future of drab but nouveau decor that evoked little emotion.

The apartment's renovation seemed to have affected the children as well. The news of an impending separation barely elicited a response, as if all feeling had been sucked out of their bodies. He had raised two robots who no longer had the ability to care about anything sprung upon them. They both appeared so weighted down by their lives. Even soccer and ballet, the things they both loved, caused them so much stress that they didn't have time for leftover worries. As awful as his own childhood was, a word like divorce would've sent him into a panic since there had always been a shred of hope that his family could be repaired. That his father would get help for drinking. That his mother would wake up and save him. That they'd win the lotto and never look back.

"Harrison," Helene said, raising her voice and bringing him back from his string of thoughts. "Brenton asked what hotel you'll be staying at?"

"The London," he said, because it was the first hotel that came to mind. Forget that The London would forever remain the place that he almost died until Naelle saved his life.

"So can I get ready for soccer practice now?" Brenton asked, already clearing his plate. Gracie looked up at Helene with imploring eyes as well.

"Can I get ready too?" she whispered.

"Yes, my love," Helene said, and hugged her hard. The girl could tell that her mother needed some more comfort and wrapped her thin arms around Helene's neck. She said something in gibberish and Helene nodded.

"You don't have to put on a brave face," Harrison told Brenton, as the boy whipped by. Brenton stopped to let out one solitary laugh before galloping toward his room.

"I'll try not to be shattered, parental units," he said, disappearing into the hallway. Gracie slithered out of her mother's embrace. For a moment, Harrison thought she'd give him a consuming hug as well, but she had finished doling out affections. Instead she gave Harrison a slight bow, as if they were Japanese businessmen greeting one another.

With the children being born after 9/11, Harrison thought of how much they had been affected by the twenty-four-seven news cycle that had become their norm. Terrorist attacks replaced tsunamis, overdosing celebrities dropped one after the other, wars began over money and oil, and bored youths gunned down elementary school classrooms. The world was constantly changing by the hour and the only way to adapt was to remain unaffected. Because of this, he wondered if they'd actually understand his resolve to get a new liver, even at the expense of some unfortunate soul. In the twenty-first century, someone else's life who you had never met held little weight in comparison to your own, so his kids should agree that self-preservation was paramount, whereas Helene would focus on the ethical complications. But unlike Helene, they'd cheer him on only if he was succeeding, for a dying man was already yesterday's news.

Part of him felt relieved to know that his family would be able to move on if the people behind the Desire Card couldn't find a donor to match, or if the transplant wasn't a success. He figured all three might cry, but true devastation wouldn't occur. People had shorter attention spans now, and the children would easily become distracted. They'd move onto whatever was next in line to grab their interests. They'd find new desires to make their worlds go round. The thought of their father would eventually fade away. This revelation made him sad, for they were even more doomed than he. They'd constantly be on the hunt for whatever was fresh, searching for fleeting relationships and quick and meaningless adorations until their stop-and-start existences began to be exhausting And when they'd finally look back to see if they could figure out when things had started to dissolve, they'd already be old and embittered, too far along to make a change, like he had been.

———

Harrison had mixed emotions as he stepped into the elevator of the London Hotel. He was holding the room key to 12G, the exact room where he almost died. He had chosen it since he figured the odds against almost dying twice in the same room had to be in his favor. Instead of regurgitating the contents of his body like the last time, room 12G would become a place of his rebirth. He'd get the call from the Desire Card with news that they'd found a match.

As he wheeled his suitcase into 12G, he remembered the first time he saw Naelle. She'd been soaping up in the bathtub singing a Spanish melody. He closed his eyes to hear her sweet voice. He pictured her toweling off and stretching out on the bed, flashing her wild and untrimmed bush, rolling over as her large tits knocked into one another, blowing him a kiss and finishing her song. He felt guilty that he wasn't thinking of Helene, but he couldn't help his thoughts. After his operation, he'd make Helene and the kids a priority again if she'd take him back, he'd become a new man; but for now, he'd be selfish for one last time. Once he obtained a new liver, he'd vow to never be selfish again.

His gut hurt like always, but he had learned to manage the pain. After what he saw in India, he knew that people lived with worse ailments. He got a couple of liquor bottles from the mini-fridge, screwed off the tops, and went to town. Three finished bottles later, he found himself lying on the bed, staring at the ceiling and imagining Naelle hovering over him. He got out his wallet and looked at the Desire Card.

"What if I called for you?" he said, out loud.

"I've been waiting," her image said, a floating specter descending into his arms. He tried to kiss her, but only tasted air.

"Oh, Helene," he said, chugging the last drops from a bottle and feeling disoriented until his head found the pillow.

He was still jet lagged from India. What had happened there still pricked and made him restless even though he tried to forget. He fingered the Desire Card and willed it to ring with good news on the other line. He wouldn't be disappointed again. God couldn't be that cruel.

A transparent Naelle snuggled next to him, streams of cool breath emanating from her kissable lips. Lying on her side, her ass was a small mountain he longed to climb. He placed his hand where her butt would be, stroked gently.

"I want you," she whispered, directing his hand inside of her. "Come to me, baby. Forget your troubles. Take a vacation from your life."

"Yes."

"Find what you desire again," she cooed. "It doesn't have to stay lost forever."

"I know. God, how I know."

She brushed the hair away from her eyes and showed him how hazel and absorbing they were.

"You'll find me one day," she said, as he mounted her and she spread her legs to welcome him. They fell into a rhythm, and she whispered in his ear. "Once you get a new organ and are healthy, we'll meet on a beach in the Dominican Republic and run alongside the waves. All your worries will wash into the ocean. You'll remember what it's like to feel love and be loved. I'll crack a coconut, and you'll drink its juice, let passion fill up your soul. I'll be there to kiss away your sadness. Whatever it is you think has dried up inside of you will come alive again. You'll be alive again. And when the day is done, the sun will set into the sandy horizon, and we'll make love in a cabana until we forget what day it is and you'll be young once again. Then you will have found what you lost a long time ago and be free, beautiful and free."

"I want that so bad."

He struggled before he finally came into the sheets he had gathered up to resemble the shape of her body. He collapsed into the warmth of the pillow, clutching its soft allure.

———

The sound of the ringing Card woke him up. He had no idea what time it was, his vision too blurry to read the digital clock on the side table.

"Yes?" he barked into the card, finding it in his wallet, which was in his coat pocket, after the fourth ring.

"Mr. Stockton," said the distorted voice of James Dean.

"Yes, yes, I'm here."

He was out of breath, still attached to the fantasy of being on a tranquil beach with Naelle at his side.

"Do you have any news?" he asked, chewing on a fingernail.

"We have found a match," James Dean said.

Tears streamed down his cheeks.

"Thank you. Thank you so—"

"We will give you two days to get us the first one hundred fifty thousand. Be on the northeast corner of Eleventh Avenue and Fifty-Second Street on Tuesday night at six p.m. sharp with the cash."

He turned on a light, its brightness burning his retinas.

"Is that doable, Mr. Stockton?" James Dean replied, his voice sounding more demanding than before.

"Yes, yes, of course I will be there with the money."

"I must stress how important it is that we receive what is owed to us."

"I promise it will not be an issue."

"There is no going back now," James Dean said, before the line went dead.

At first Harrison kept talking until he realized that James Dean was no longer there. He lowered the phone, shaking, the booze from the mini-fridge sloshing around in his belly. He sat on the edge of the bed to get his breathing under control.

There is no going back now, James Dean had said.

In a few days, an unlucky donor would be sliced open and he'd be committing the ultimate theft. The idea was exhilarating, the impossible finally coming true. Even though he'd been defeated before, this time he'd be triumphant. He went to the mini-fridge to twist open the final bottle that remained, one last indulgence.

The liquor warmed his throat and clouded his brain until he was back on that Punta Cana beach, watching his and Naelle's footprints disappear from the ebbing tide. He picked her up and twirled her around until they were both too dizzy to stand up straight anymore.

Then they fell to the shore, delirious.

But happy...so happy.

Their hearts beating against one another to a Caribbean merengue beat.

Two islands fusing together into one.

Beautiful and free.

18

On the morning of his surgery, Harrison woke before his alarm went off. He got out of bed and parted the curtains of his hotel room. The city was wrapped in a giant fog. The air conditioner created an ominous buzz, a ghost's whisper. He wanted to stare out of the window and not think about anything, but two maids were having an intense conversation outside his door. "*Mi hija,*" one of them cried, "*está herido.*" The other maid responded that she'd pray for the girl's soul.

"Pray for mine, too," he said, his mouth drier than ever.

Propped against the wall was a silver briefcase filled with one hundred fifty thousand in cash. He'd already cleaned out most of his CDs and bonds to get the people of the Desire Card the first hundred fifty K he owed. All of his funds had been set up in joint accounts, but either he or Helene could access those accounts on their own. Since he handled the bulk of their finances, it'd be a while before she suspected any wrongdoings.

The second payment proved more difficult. Since

their mortgage had already been paid off, at first he thought to take out a loan against the apartment, but then he figured that would involve the bank too much. They might ask why he needed such a large chunk of cash, and he wanted to remain as discreet as possible. The option he chose was to take out the money from all of their stocks. These were funds that neither he nor Helene ever touched. Its total had dipped some, but there was still more than they invested in the first place, plenty to cover the hundred fifty K.

His stomach did loops as he dressed. Since he hadn't been able to eat for a whole day, he felt as weak as he did on the morning of his supposed surgery in Mumbai. That day he'd been certain that he'd get a liver, never imagining that he'd be wandering the deserted streets of Mumbai, starving and screaming Nagesh's name, about to realize that he'd been conned. The Desire Card could be as big a scam. He wanted to have faith that this time would be different, but he also knew that nothing was ever certain.

He made sure to call Helene and the kids the night before. Just a quick hello to say that he'd settled into his hotel, one last chance to hear their voices in case the unthinkable happened and he died on the operating table. Gracie's had been the most heartbreaking because she reminded him about her ballet recital in a few weeks that he promised to see. He swore he'd still be there and tried not to think about her looking out into the audience to find him, disappointed as always.

The Desire Card rang.

"Be at the northwest corner of Thirty-Ninth Street and Tenth Avenue in an hour," a distorted voice said, sounding different than James Dean's.

"Yes," he said, hanging up.

He wondered what had happened to James Dean, since that guy was the one who usually made all of the outgoing calls. This change in structure unnerved him. He wanted precision and familiarity. Any wrenches in the plan for the day would be too much to handle. James Dean had outlined exactly how everything would go, but he never said that he wouldn't be present. What if one of the other henchmen decided to steal his money and kick him out of their van on the side of the road? What if the hired doctors had a change of heart and chose to turn them all in? These were not thoughts he should be having, but he couldn't stop his mind from replaying a stream of terrible outcomes. To calm himself, he imagined the beaches along Punta Cana. Waves hitting the shore, a cold Cuba Libre in his hand, and a topless Naelle giving him a show as the sun surrounded them like an atomic explosion.

He grabbed the silver briefcase and left the room.

———

Sure enough, James Dean wasn't there when the van pulled up. The side door opened and Humphrey Bogart reached out to pull Harrison inside. Harrison caught a glimpse of a gun in a holster under Bogart's jacket before Cary Grant wrapped a blindfold around his eyes. The two henchmen began to go over the particulars for the day. They'd been drugging "the donor" since early this morning. They had picked up this "donor" the night before, but the person hadn't been conscious for long enough to realize they'd been abducted. Harrison didn't want to know any of this, but he was too afraid to tell them otherwise.

"I'm going to barf," he said, as bile tickled at his uvula and he had to clamp his hand over his mouth.

"Do not throw up in here," one of the men ordered.

The van pulled over to the side of the road and he was led outside. The sun had come out now, piercing through his blindfold. All he could see was red. Rocks crunched under his feet as cars zoomed past and he vomited. The man who led him outside had a handkerchief ready.

"Thank you," he said, wiping away his spittle.

They brought him back inside the van.

About twenty minutes later, he had to puke again. This time whoever led him outside gripped his arm harder than before. As he doubled over on the side of the road, the most he could do was gag.

"It's 'cause I haven't eaten," he said, but the henchman didn't respond.

Sometime later, the van reached the headquarters. Inside the base, his blindfold was removed. The first person he saw was Jimmy Stewart situated by the door as if on guard. Next to him was a desk with a monitor, a tiny radio, a pair of headphones, and a half-eaten sandwich dripping mayonnaise onto a paper bag. The radio played the Beach Boys' "Kokomo." This was not the same place they'd taken him to before. The last headquarters looked like it existed out of a sci-fi film while this one had the feel of an abandoned warehouse. Mice scuttled beneath the floorboards. A large industrial fan churned by a door at the far end. The walls were warped from peeling paint. Moisture dripped from a rusting ceiling.

"You will leave that here," Jimmy Stewart said, indicating the silver briefcase in Harrison's sweaty hands.

"Uh..."

He looked to Cary Grant and Humphrey Bogart to confirm. Both nodded silently.

He handed over the silver briefcase and watched as Jimmy Stewart placed it in a drawer at the bottom of the desk and locked it up with a key.

"Come," Gary Grant said.

They headed past the whirling fan toward the lone door and stepped into a large operating room where two men in doctor outfits wore Fred Astaire and Marlon Brando masks. Fred Astaire was hefty, Marlon Brando skinny; both of them warped versions of their real selves. Fred Astaire tended to a beeping machine while Marlon Brando thoroughly washed his hands at a giant sink in the corner. Two operating tables had already been set up, their corners touching each other.

"Let's get you prepped for surgery," Humphrey Bogart said, leading Harrison behind a standing curtain.

The floor felt cold against his bare feet as he took off his clothes and put on a hospital gown. He could hear some of the men talking through the curtain. They were bringing in the donor.

"Ready?" one of the men asked him.

"Uh...yes," Harrison replied.

Humphrey Bogart pulled back the curtain. He took Harrison by the arm and led him to the operating table. The floor felt even colder than before. A freezing jolt coursed up his legs, entered his veins, made him quiver like he had palsy.

"Are you all right, Mr. Stockton?" Bogart asked.

A fluorescent overhead light was turned on. He

sensed a headache forming. The faint whisper of "Surfin' USA" escaped from the outer room before it became muted. Bogart's face seemed so far away. Harrison lay down on the operating table, shivering.

"I'm so cold," he said, his lips turning blue.

"Yes, we do keep it cold in here," Bogart replied.

"I'm feeling...a little overwhelmed."

He couldn't catch his breath. Bogart touched his shoulder.

"Breathe, Mr. Stockton. You are in good hands here. We've been successful in fulfilling every desire someone has requested."

"Really?" he asked, gulping at the air until he got his breathing under control.

"We have to go take care of a delivery," Bogart said, nodding at Cary Grant. "But we will see you in the recovery room later today."

Bogart let his hand linger on Harrison's shoulder for one last second of comfort before joining up with Cary Grant and leaving the room. The two doctors wearing the Marlon Brando and Fred Astaire masks surrounded him now.

"Can you make sure the donor's face is covered when they're brought out?" Harrison asked. The doctors looked at one another. "I think it's better if I don't know their identity right now."

"Whatever you desire," Fred Astaire replied.

He heard clanging through the walls and wondered if it was the mice. But then the double doors at the other end of the room swung open and a nurse in a Rita Hayworth mask emerged wheeling a gurney. He'd never seen any of Rita Hayworth's films before, but he remembered that she'd been the object of desire for Tim

Robbins' character in *The Shawshank Redemption*. Her poster became the impetus for him to dig to his freedom. Now whoever it was that wore the mask had brilliant red hair down to her shoulders and a vampy sway to her walk. He quickly closed his eyes before he could see what the donor on the gurney looked like and heard one of the doctors telling the nurse to hide the body with a sheet once they lifted it onto the operating table.

The body thumped next to him like a dropped sandbag. He pictured these people just throwing the poor person onto the table. He was going to be sick again. He started counting down numbers in his head to avoid purging.

"Mr. Stockton, the body is all covered now."

He opened his eyes to see Rita Hayworth giving him a bewitching smile. She administered an IV and began prepping him for surgery. Marlon Brando and Fred Astaire were doing the same to the other body.

"Take good care of the donor," he said, latching onto Rita Hayworth's arm.

"We will do the best we can," her distorted voice said.

"What we're doing—" he started to say. His mouth was moving faster than his brain could keep up. He couldn't help but feel morally spent, as if some puppeteer had controlled his strings up until now and he finally thought to snip free. "Are we monsters?"

"I'm not here to answer questions like that," Rita Hayworth replied.

He wanted to be told that what they were doing was all right and the person behind the sheet would be fine in a matter of weeks. Not only that, but they would be a lifesaver. He resolved to pay the people of Desire Card some more money to find out the donor's identity after this was all done. He'd send the money to them anonymously, maybe once a year, enough to assuage his guilt.

Rita Hayworth pried his fingers from around her arm, a beautiful smile frozen on her face due to the mask. The smile told him that what they were doing was okay; that everything would be okay.

Fred Astaire stepped over to his side. "Mr. Stockton, we'll be removing part of the donor's liver first before taking yours out. Halfway through their surgery, the nurse will administer your anesthetic."

The body had been positioned beside him so the doctors could use its sheet as a buffer so Harrison wouldn't see what was happening. He let the beeps of the donor's heart monitor lull him into a trance. The sound became the baseline of a song playing on a Caribbean beach while he took in the sun on the hot sand, his body pleasantly warm. He'd already received his new liver and life was limitless. But then the tide crept up and licked his toes, a cold and unfamiliar sensation as the sun quickly fizzled into the waters and the dream dissolved.

The donor's heart rate started beeping faster, interrupting him from his tranquil fantasy. The lines on the heart rate monitor began to spike. He saw Fred Astaire holding a scalpel covered in blood that had been used to cut the body open. A red circular stain had formed on the sheet as well. Harrison had no idea how long he'd been daydreaming.

"The donor's waking up," Marlon Brando said to Fred Astaire.

"How much did you give?" Fred Astaire asked Rita Hayworth.

"Enough to put down a horse," Rita Hayworth said, grabbing a fresh syringe from off of a counter.

Harrison heard a moan escape from behind the sheet and saw the outlines of the donor's body as they stirred.

"Hurry up," Fred Astaire said.

The nurse darted over to the donor and jabbed a syringe into their arm. Their body twitched, causing a leg to shoot out from behind the sheet. In the deathly glow from the fluorescent lights, Harrison stared at that leg, the skin tone brown and succulent, the toenails painted a dark red. For a moment, the leg became his only concern. The hideous present and any terrifying consequences melted away and all that existed was his fascination for that leg. It called to him, whispered the chilling secret he needed to know: Who owned this impeccable limb?

His mind went blank except for a vision from the past. He was back in the London Hotel headed to room 12G. The door was ajar and he knocked as he entered. A Spanish song glided through the air. Steam poured out of the bathroom. A succulent brown leg hung off the edge of the bathtub, the toenails painted dark red.

"Save me," a faint voice said from underwater.

"Naelle?"

She lurched up out of the bathtub that was now filled with blood instead of water.

"Save me!" she screamed, as he backed up out of the bathroom to retreat from this devastating nightmare.

In the operating room he found himself ripping off his IV and rolling off the table.

"Mr. Stockton!" Rita Hayworth shrieked, as he crashed to the floor.

"I think...I...know her."

Rita Hayworth tried to grab under his arms, but she wasn't strong enough to lift him up.

"Get off me," he yelled, swinging wildly until he came into contact with her cheek.

He crawled on his elbows over to the other operating table and yanked the sheet off of the donor's body. Time froze as the bloody sheet hovered in the air.

"No, God, no."

Marlon Brando tried to restrain him while Fred Astaire stood spooked with the blood-crusted scalpel in hand. Rita Hayworth was cursing at him as she tried to stand up.

From where he lay, he couldn't see the donor's face yet due to the angle. Despite his exhaustion, he was able to throw Marlon Brando off of him because the guy was half his size.

Blood was dripping from the incision Fred Astaire had made under the donor's ribs. Harrison got it all over his hands as he attempted to rise. Marlon Brando tried once more to subdue him, but Harrison punched him the nose, causing it to break. As he rose on two wobbly feet, he could hear Marlon Brando shouting and Rita Hayworth threatening to contact the people of the Desire Card; but the only thing that mattered was if Naelle lay before him, if her blood was on his hands.

"Please," he whispered, making the sign of the cross that he hadn't done since he'd been a little boy forced to fear God's wrath.

But his prayers were futile.

Bleeding out on that operating table was his once powerful Naelle.

He touched her icy leg, as if to make sure she was real. Blood kept oozing from the incision made on the right side of her ribs that curved up to her chest. One of her eyes fluttered open, the pupil spinning around before floating up into her brain.

"She is losing blood," he heard Rita Hayworth say.

"Make her stop bleeding then."

Neither the doctors nor Rita Hayworth made a move. The syringe had been dropped on the floor between him and Rita Hayworth. She went for it but he was faster. Fred Astaire came toward him now, and Harrison stuck the syringe into his neck.

"What the fuck is wrong with you?" Fred Astaire yelled. He lunged at Harrison and the two fell back onto a table filled with medical supplies. By the time they crashed to the floor, Fred Astaire was already out cold.

Marlon Brando was making his way to a phone by the wall. Even though Harrison had a shooting pain in his back from landing on his tailbone, he summoned all the energy inside of him to charge at Marlon Brando with the syringe. The skinny doctor threw his hands up, but Harrison jabbed the syringe into his leg. Harrison removed it as Marlon Brando cried out and fell to the floor. He tried to grab at Harrison, but then his arms started swinging slower until his head crashed to the floor.

Harrison swiveled around as Rita Hayworth tried to stick him with another syringe. He knocked it out of her hand and switched the half-empty syringe he was holding for the one she tried to stab him with. He seized her by the throat and touched its tip to her neck.

"You are making a grave, grave mistake, Mr. Stockton," Rita Hayworth's warped voice said. The two of them were cheek-to-cheek, her sweat smelling like spoiled milk.

"Bandage her up now," he said, panting. His face felt like it was on fire. He needed to stall for time while he figured out a plan.

The mice scuttled through the walls, sounding like approaching footsteps. He glanced at the door, hoping that Bogart and Cary Grant hadn't heard anything. He'd seen that Bogart had a gun and figured that Cary Grant had one as well.

"Bandages won't do," Rita Hayworth said. "She needs stitches now."

"So go do it."

He pushed her toward the operating table and followed on nervous legs, keeping the syringe at her neck. Even though he wanted to close his eyes and sleep away this nightmare, he knew he had to summon every last bit of energy inside of him. Naelle was still bleeding badly. Rita Hayworth went to work on suturing the wound. A dark pool of blood had already collected on the floor.

"Is she going to be all right?" he asked.

"What is it that you plan on doing?" Rita Hayworth asked.

"This wasn't right," he said. "This was not what I wanted."

"You haven't crossed any line you can't recover from yet," her distorted voice said.

"She needs to go to the hospital."

"This is just as good as a hospital, Mr. Stockton," Rita Hayworth said, more annoyed than before. She continued stitching up Naelle's body.

"No, I need to take away her from here."

"A hospital will only ask questions."

"I don't care."

"The boss will not be pleased," she said, matter-of-factly.

"Is your boss James Dean? Is he here now?"

His eyes searched around the room for a video camera. If someone had been watching all of this, the henchmen would already be deployed to come after him. He figured that it had been about ten minutes since he attacked the two doctors and Rita Hayworth.

"None of us are able to reveal our boss because we've never seen his actual face," she said, her eyes looking up from Naelle's body to the other side of the room.

"What are you looking at? Is that a camera over there in the corner?"

Her smile revealed the answer.

"How long do I have?" he asked.

She continued sewing without responding.

"How long do I have?" he asked, louder this time. He pressed the syringe harder against her neck.

"Not long," she said, stitching up Naelle even slower. "Everything is monitored in a control room, but the feed switches every few minutes."

"Then bandage up the rest," he barked. "Let's go."

"Mr. Stockton, I need to finish the stitching."

He picked up some bandages from off of a side counter and tossed them at her. "You have one minute."

She opened the package of bandages and began covering what was left of Naelle's wound.

"You can still walk away from this," she said carefully, as if she was testing him. "The boss is on location right now. He doesn't have to know. He won't want to go over the feeds unless we give him reason to."

Harrison looked over at Fred Astaire and Marlon Brando, both appearing dead to any outside observer.

"We have your money, that is all that matters to our boss," Rita Hayworth continued.

"And what will happen to her?"

Rita Hayworth finished bandaging Naelle's wound.

"She'll wake up eventually, worse for the wear but... alive. We'll make sure of that."

"Why don't I believe you?"

Through the walls, the mice started scuttling again. He could hear their vicious nails scraping against the plaster as if desperately trying to break through.

Rita Hayworth placed one hand on her hip. The syringe's tip had left a tiny spot of blood on her neck that trickled into her cleavage.

"Leave the girl, Mr. Stockton. You'll only bring trouble upon yourself that you can't handle. We are everywhere. We know where you live, where your family lives."

"James Dean said that you people aren't mercenaries."

"We are whatever we need to be," she said, stroking his arm that wasn't holding the syringe, using her entrancing voluptuousness to overpower. He felt weak in her gaze, destroyed in general from the trauma of the last half hour; but leaving Naelle would be sealing her death. There'd be no way they'd let her go now.

"Wheel her to the door," he said.

"A guard is still outside—"

"I'm not asking you twice."

He got behind her and pointed the syringe at the back of her neck. She pushed the gurney toward the exit and he followed in step. When they reached the door, he couldn't hear any Beach Boys music like before. The sound of the churning fan cancelled out every other sound. He peered outside and saw Jimmy Stewart hunched over the desk wearing headphones connected to the radio.

"Is the briefcase with the money still in that desk?" he asked.

"Don't even think about that."

"I've already paid you people a hundred fifty thousand, I'm not giving you the rest for nothing."

"Isn't getting out with your life enough?"

The rest of the bandages had been left on the gurney with Naelle. He placed the other end of the syringe in his mouth while he tied Rita Hayworth's wrists to the handles so she'd still be able to push. Whatever remained of the bandages he stuffed into her mouth as a muzzle.

He peered through the doorway again. Jimmy Stewart still sat with his back to them wearing headphones. The monitor on his desk depicted the operating room before alternating to another room where Bogart and Cary Grant were packing up boxes. This meant that they hadn't left with the van yet.

He signaled for Rita Hayworth to remain quiet and crept behind Jimmy Stewart. He rushed over and got him in a chokehold with the syringe at his neck.

"What the...?"

Jimmy Stewart spun around causing his chair to topple over. Harrison climbed on top of him and pressed the syringe against the guy's Adam's apple.

"The keys to the van and to the bottom drawer of that desk," Harrison said.

"Have you lost your mind?"

Harrison saw Jimmy Stewart staring at the monitor that showed Fred Astaire and Marlon Brando lying on the floor. The guy's eyes widened; he was scared now and Harrison would make sure he stayed that way.

"The keys to the van and to that bottom drawer," Harrison said, patting the guy down. He came across a ring of keys. He jabbed Jimmy Stewart in the chest with the syringe as a hollow cry echoed throughout the warehouse. Harrison rolled off of him, found the tiniest key, and used it to open up the bottom drawer and take back his briefcase. Jimmy Stewart attempted to get up, but the syringe was still sticking out of his chest, slowing him down.

"You...are...so...dead," he said, before collapsing to the ground.

Harrison took off the guy's boots and put them on. A leather jacket had been slung around the chair that he swiped as well. He positioned the briefcase under one arm, removed the syringe from out of Jimmy Stewart's twitching body and made his way over to Rita Hayworth, who'd been watching the scene unfold.

"Let's go," he said, pushing the gurney along with her until they were outside. The van sat parked at the foot of a long dirt trail that snaked off into the wilderness. Surrounding them were thick trees as far as he could see. "How far to a hospital?"

"I...I don't know."

"Bullshit you don't. How far? Is this New Jersey, are we in fucking New Jersey?"

"Yes," she said.

He stared into her eyes to make sure she was telling the truth, but it didn't matter. He'd figure it out once he drove off.

Naelle made a sound like she was being choked. He knew that at least it meant she was still alive.

"C'mon, faster," he yelled at Rita Hayworth, as they wheeled the gurney over to the van. He tried a few of the keys in the lock at the side door until it finally opened.

"What's in those syringes so I could tell the doctors?"

"Horse tranquilizers."

He put the back end of the syringe in his mouth again and grasped Naelle from under her arms.

"You'll tear the stitches," Rita Hayworth said. "Untie me and I'll help."

He had no choice but to comply. He untied the bandages around her wrists. He grabbed one end of the mattress Naelle lay on and Rita Hayworth took hold of the other as they hoisted the body into the van.

"Leave the briefcase," Rita Hayworth said. The wind had picked up and her red hair blew wildly from the pummeling breeze.

"The extra hundred fifty was for the surgery, the surgery never happened. I don't owe you people for that."

"The boss won't be into semantics," she said, gazing into the far wilderness as if she saw something. He looked over as well, but the trees obscured any view.

"I still need a liver so I still need that money," he said, walking toward her with the syringe in hand.

"What are you doing?"

Her distorted voice sounded strained. She began to back up toward the warehouse. He picked up his pace and overtook her until he had the syringe at her neck again.

"But I helped you," she pleaded. "I did everything you said."

He jabbed the syringe into her neck as she collapsed in his arms.

"I know, thank you." He tossed the syringe into the trees. "But I need to make sure that I have a good head start."

He laid her body on the ground. Her red hair spilled across the dirt. He tried to take off her mask as her breathing slowed.

"No," she said, attempting to stop him.

He grasped at her nose and her chin until her mask ripped at the back and came off in his hand. She attempted to cover her face.

"No, no, please," she said, the last word no more than a gasp. "Please," she said again, sobbing quietly. "I don't like anyone to see my face."

He left the wrinkled mask by her side as she continued to sob, then he turned around and got in the van. Through the rearview mirror, he saw she was still covering her face but had stopped moving now. He tried a few different keys before finding one that fit into the ignition, then slammed his foot on the gas and took off down the snaking dirt trail.

19

THE SUN BEGAN TO SET AS HARRISON WOUND DOWN the narrow trail away from the people of the Desire Card. He looked in the rearview mirror expecting Bogart or Cary Grant to be close behind, but all he could see was Naelle unconscious in the back of the van. Rita Hayworth had wedged the mattress in the corner so Naelle wouldn't be jostled around. So far her bandages had stayed intact, keeping her from bleeding out. Her eyes had stopped fluttering, and she seemed at peace. He needed to find a hospital, but the van had no navigation system and the only phone he had was the new card he'd been given.

Once the sun fizzled into the mountains to his left, it got dark fast. The tiny road turned into a wind tunnel, rattling the van around. Branches of intimidating trees scraped against the windows. He tried to look for a house or a sign of life throughout the wilderness, but the people of the card couldn't have found a more deserted area for their headquarters.

Finally a sign at the end of the trail pointed toward

a turnoff onto Clinton Road. Another sign indicated that Route 23 was ten miles north. He'd get on Route 23 and make sure to drive for a half an hour before exiting. It'd be too risky to go to a hospital so close by, especially since he'd have to leave the conspicuous van at its entrance.

He turned on the brights as he headed down Clinton Road. He'd heard of this road before and then he remembered why. It had gained notoriety over the years as an area rife with legends of paranormal occurrences, gatherings of Satanists, and professional killers who had disposed of bodies in the surrounding woods. Since there were no lights along the road, he needed to slow down to avoid an accident. No other cars passed, and he could only make out a few houses every so often. After a few minutes, he saw chalk writing scrawled over both lanes. The words were in another language. As he crept closer, he could make them out.

Spes Omnes Relinquite, O Vos Intrantes

Under the words, a pentagram had been inscribed. From his days at Chilton, he recalled a linguistics class that required a foundation of Latin. Roughly translated the sentence meant: "Abandon all hope, to those who enter." He knew a pentagram was commonly used as a symbol to ward off evil. He wondered if someone else had fallen prey to the people of the Desire Card and lived to tell the tale. He gunned the van over the ominous warning as the back of his neck prickled with fear.

On Route 23, he eventually joined up with a few other cars. He was in New Jersey, somewhere around

Passaic County, and he slowly recognized the names of a couple of towns. He looked back into the rearview mirror before shooting off onto an exit at the last possible second, in case he'd been followed. He nudged the silver briefcase at his side, knowing that because he'd taken it back, he'd be looking in a rearview mirror for the rest of his life.

A small hospital was situated at the end of a street. It had a large lot in the back so he parked the van there. He hid the silver briefcase under the passenger seat so it couldn't be seen from outside. He got out of the car and left the side door wide open, a thousand thoughts running through his mind about how to explain what had happened to the doctors inside. His first hurdle would be justifying why Naelle was naked, but luckily he spied a wad of clothes in a laundry bag dumped in the back of the van. It seemed to just be workout gear, but it was enough to dress her in baggy warm-up pants and a T-shirt. There was also a pair of sweatpants and a hoodie for him so he could ditch the hospital gown.

He lifted her from the van and managed to shut the side door with his foot. His back ached as he carried her to the hospital. After he took a few steps, he wanted to stop and rest but he pushed forward. When he reached the entrance, the electric doors parted and he stumbled inside with Naelle dangling from his arms like a slain bride.

"Help! She needs help!" he yelled, collapsing to his knees as she spilled to the floor. The hospital was mostly empty, only a few sleepy patients waited on orange scoop chairs. A woman at the desk called for the orderlies.

"What happened, sir?" the woman behind the desk asked. She tapped a pen against a clipboard, her eyes suspiciously looking from him over to Naelle who was being hoisted onto a gurney.

"I...found her this way," Harrison said. He shrugged, unable to explain any more.

"What is her name?"

"Naelle."

"And her last name?"

The tears flowed at just the right time. He broke down, a heaving mess. The woman placed a hesitant hand on his back. He cried for them to save her, no longer caring about his own condition, only for Naelle's survival, only to stop his heart from rotting with guilt.

The woman behind the desk was asking if he needed medical assistance. He shook his head and covered his ears, wanting to be alone, pleading to be young again before life had fucked him royally. He longed to return to a smattering of memories before he realized that fathers could be cruel, and mothers could be cold—to a time when he was a tiny boy taking a nap and staring at the dust motes caught in the sun's rays, feeling its warmth cling to his hand and kiss his eyelids, as it rocked him soundly to sleep.

While the doctors attended to Naelle, the woman behind the desk gave him a few minutes to recover and then required an explanation of how he'd found her. He lied and said that he saw her body on the side of the road. She looked like she'd been really hurt, possibly drugged since she told him something about horse tranquilizers. He had seen this girl before, but he couldn't recall where. She might have served him coffee or something like that. All he could remember was that her name was Naelle. The woman questioned if he knew of any of her immediate family. He didn't know of anyone, but he'd make sure to stay at the hospital until she pulled through.

After a little under an hour, a doctor came out to the waiting room. He shook Harrison's hand and explained that Naelle was stable. She'd lost some blood but would be all right. Someone had evidently cut her open with a scalpel and stitched up half of the wound before covering the rest with bandages. The doctor had no idea why someone would do this. She'd been given a powerful sedative by whoever had done this and would be knocked out through the night. In the morning, they'd be able to question her about what happened.

"I'll wait here until then," Harrison said.

The doctor asked him about his own condition since he looked like dog shit, and he spoke of his liver cirrhosis. The doctor offered to check him out but he declined. He just wanted to close his eyes and go to bed. They suggested a nearby motel, but he climbed into one of the orange scoop chairs instead. Should anything occur with the patient overnight, they'd be sure to wake him. He nodded as he hugged the rim of the plastic chair and was asleep in a matter of seconds.

———

The night in the hospital waiting room passed in fits. Dreams struggled to coalesce, nothing more than flashes of disturbing images. In one, he sat in a small room as thousands of mice crawled through the walls.

In another, Rita Hayworth was cutting into Naelle with a scalpel. Her body had been slit open and pinned to the sides of the gurney, revealing every organ. Rita Hayworth then started scooping the organs out one by one and laying them on a counter with price tags attached. Naelle's liver was the last one she removed. She placed it in his hands and kissed him on the lips. As she pulled her lips away from his, he saw that she was no longer wearing the Rita Hayworth mask; her true self had been revealed as a woman scarred with burns as if she'd been dipped in boiling acid.

"Would you kiss me now?" she asked, and puckered her shriveled lips.

The liver fell from his hands and crawled away like some alien slug.

The mice became louder through the walls until it seemed like they were scraping at his brain.

He awoke with a start. The woman from behind the desk had been tapping him on the shoulder. An orderly had been buffing the floor with a machine that mimicked the scurrying sounds of the mice.

"Sir, the girl you brought in last night is awake."

He wiped the crust from his eyes as she led him down the hallway. Sunlight peeked through a window at the far end. In Naelle's room, a curtain surrounded her bed. He could hear a doctor talking to her from behind the curtain. She responded in one-word answers, nothing more than murmurs. She then asked for a glass of water.

The doctor parted the curtains. Harrison saw it was the same doctor from last night.

"She doesn't remember anything that happened to

her yesterday," he told Harrison. "Maybe you could help?"

The doctor filled up a glass from the sink and handed it to him.

"Make sure she drinks it slowly," he said, then left the room with the woman from behind the desk.

Harrison had the urge to follow the doctor and the woman out of the room. He could get the silver briefcase from the van and take a taxi service back home. He could forget Naelle ever existed. He wondered if that would be easier than facing her now.

"Could I have my water?" she coughed, from behind the curtain. Her voice sounded like she'd be gargling with pieces of broken glass.

He parted the curtains. Without any makeup on, she almost looked like a different woman. Her skin tone had lost its luster and instead of the dark copper tan he remembered from their night together, she appeared washed out and pale. Her hair hadn't been combed and stood up in crinkled spears, her eyes watered out of distress. She hadn't realized who he was yet.

He passed her the water. She took it and winced in pain as she gulped it down.

"Thank you, baby."

She handed the glass back to him and their fingers sparked as they touched. He recognized the silver star decals on her fingernails that had already started to fade.

"You?" she said, propping herself up. She gathered the sheets up to her neck as if she'd been spooked. She peered around the curtain looking for the doctor. "*Ay, coño!* What the fuck happened to me?"

He closed the curtain around them until they were

in their own little world. She was breathing funny, shaking her head, and murmuring "*Ay dios mio,*" over and over. She felt around her neck searching for something.

"My mother's cross," she said, and looked up at him with pleading eyes. "It's gone. I was wearing it and now..."

She cursed in Spanish and he couldn't make out what she was saying. He took her hand in his and tried to soothe her like she'd done for him weeks ago when their roles had been reversed.

"They did this to me," she whispered, staring straight ahead. "*Hijos de la gran puta!*"

She started trembling like she'd emerged from a freezing ocean. She squeezed at his hand until he thought she'd break off his fingers.

"Tell me it was them," she yelled. "Those *pendejos*, those *lambe bolsas.*"

She wrenched her hand from out of his grasp.

"And they sent *you*?" she said. "Why you? What do they want you to do to me now?"

She went to kick him, forgetting her pain, but it was too strong. She put her face in her hands and sobbed.

"No...no, I found you, Naelle. I brought you here."

He peeled her fingers away from her face.

"I was at their headquarters to...deliver them some money. They had you in a room like a hospital. You'd been cut open...I don't know why."

"What do you mean? I don't understand."

"A nurse had stitched you up halfway, and then something must've happened and she left to go get a doctor. I took you. I brought you here."

"But why did they do this to me?" she yelled,

beating the sheets with her fists. He was afraid the doctor or the woman from behind the desk would hear and come running in.

"I don't know why they did this," he said, hugging her so she'd calm down.

Naelle bit her lip until it bled. Her face had turned red from crying so hard.

"They will come to finish what they started," she said. "I am not safe here."

She ripped the IV out of her arms and swung her legs over the side of the hospital bed.

"No, no, you need to rest."

"Fuck rest."

She pushed him aside and attempted to stand before her legs buckled and she fell back on the bed.

"Oh, my chest hurts like the devil."

She gritted her teeth and tried to stand again, using him as support.

"I don't know if the doctor will discharge you."

"I need to go home right now. *Entiende*? You can tell that *pendejo* doctor whatever the fuck you need to, but get me away from here."

She held her chest in pain as she picked up the warm-up pants and T-shirt.

"These aren't my clothes."

"I know. You were naked when I found you."

She shuddered at the thought, but took off her hospital gown, determined to leave. The stitching and bandages covered half of her stomach. She pressed her fingers against the bandage as a tiny clot of blood formed and then she broke down in tears again.

"It's going to be all right, Naelle—"

"You fool," she hissed. "They will cut off my legs

and toss me into the river. And you...I pity what the boss will do to you."

The doctor reentered the room.

"What is she doing up?" he asked Harrison. "Miss, you'll have to get back in bed."

She pursed her lips and put her hand on her hip. "You're gonna have to get out of my way, Doctor."

"I highly recommend that you stay the day for evaluation."

"And I highly recommend that you go jump off of a cliff," she said, and finished putting on the warm-up pants and T-shirt. "This man needs to take me home now."

She took Harrison's hand and kissed his palm to show that they were together.

"You had no ID with you or medical insurance," the doctor said, "but a bill will still have to be paid."

"I'll take care of it," Harrison said.

"I don't advise this, Miss."

"You go and get your bill and let us leave. And get me a cigarette, I need a cigarette."

"There's no smoking in this hospital."

"Excuse me but somebody sliced me the fuck open yesterday. All I want is a drag. So could you please just ask someone for a lucy?"

The doctor left the room shaking his head.

Naelle let go of Harrison's hand.

"So how far are we from the Bronx?" she asked him.

———

After much back-and-forth with the administrative staff, the hospital finally agreed to discharge Naelle.

She had carried on about a sick mother that she needed to go see. Harrison didn't know if she was lying or not, but she made a convincing case. The woman behind the desk provided her with hospital slippers and a Newport Light. Harrison helped her toward the parking lot, but she stopped when she saw the black van.

"Oh, fuck no," she said, and started to turn around. "Those *pendejos* found us."

She broke out in a sprint toward the other end of the lot. Halfway there she slowed down, clutching her chest. Harrison opened the passenger door.

"No, I took their van," he called out. "It's okay."

Like a wounded animal, she hesitated at first before retreating toward the van and climbing in the passenger's side.

"You should get rid of the van," she said, closing the door. "They'll be looking."

Her feet rested on top of the silver briefcase.

"That's mine," he said, as she ran her big toe along the edge.

He put the key in the ignition and gunned it out of the lot.

She opened the window and lit her lone cigarette with the van's lighter. After the first exhale, she seemed to relax a little.

"Thank you," she said, patting his leg. "I'm sorry I yelled at you earlier, I was just scared."

"You don't have to apologize."

She kept her hand on his thigh; he couldn't deny it felt good.

"Where in the Bronx do you live?"

"Hunts Point," she said. "In a walk-up by the train station."

She blew a train of smoke and stared at him through the haze.

"*Angel guardiánte*," she said, nodding.

"What's that?"

"It means 'guardian angel.' That's you."

She ran her fingers through her hair, trying to make herself more presentable.

"No, I'm not."

"Yes, you are. I would be dead if not for you–"

"What do you remember from last night?" he asked. He didn't want to hear her unfounded praises. He wouldn't let himself be idolized.

She sucked at the Newport Light until half of the cigarette had turned into a long coil of ash.

"I was leaving a club. My girlfriends wanted to stay longer, but I had been called last minute to see a client that night. Someone hit me on the back of my head. *Ay coño*, I saw stars and then darkness. That's all I remember."

She took a final drag and tossed the cigarette out of the window.

"I'm so sorry," he said, placing his hand on top of hers. "For everything that happened to you."

"I want to nap," she said, slipping her hand away and curling up against the window.

"Sure," he said, holding back the guilty tears that he'd release once she closed her eyes. "Get some rest. I'll wake you when we reach Hunts Point."

20

NAELLE LIVED IN A DILAPIDATED WALK-UP ON A block with a closed-down bodega, a mural depicting a rat in a cop uniform, and a barefoot druggie on the corner singing a warped version of "Amazing Grace." Harrison made sure to take the silver briefcase with him out of the van. Once they got inside, Naelle had to ring her landlady's bell to get a spare set of keys so Harrison waited in a graffiti-ridden stairwell that smelled of urine, clutching the briefcase to his chest. It was then that he decided he'd help her get away from a life like this. He'd give her the money in the briefcase and wouldn't take no for an answer.

She stepped out of the landlady's apartment with a spare key and they climbed the piss-scented stairs to the top floor. He felt winded when they reached her door since he'd been negligent with his medications over the last few days and it was starting to take a toll.

"Baby, you okay?" she asked, genuinely concerned. "Is it your bad liver?"

They walked into a tiny studio apartment. A dusty

mattress had been dumped in the corner, the sheets in disarray. A small TV with an antenna had been propped up on a stack of yellowing magazines. A lone window with thick bars led out to a fire escape. Crosses adorned the walls along with fading pictures of an older woman and newer ones of a little gap-tooth girl.

"Who are the pictures of?" he asked, but Naelle had vanished. He finally saw her on her knees pulling a large suitcase out of the closet. She began to stuff in as many clothes as possible.

"What are you doing?"

"I'm getting the fuck out of here, that's what."

She crawled over to the mattress and lifted it up to remove a Ziploc bag filled with a few bills.

"Shit," she said, counting the cash.

She stood up and darted to the window looking worried.

"I was making sure that nobody followed us the whole time," he said.

"It doesn't matter, they know where I live."

She removed the crosses and the pictures from the walls and placed them in the suitcase.

"Where will you go?"

"Home," she said, as if it was obvious. "They can't have known my mother's address in the DR. I should've gone back there a long time ago."

She stuffed the Ziploc bag into the waistband of her warm-up pants.

"How much you think a last-minute ticket is?" she asked.

"I don't know. Seven, eight hundred dollars."

She sat on the mattress, her head in her hands.

"Are you sure they'll come after you?" he asked.

"You don't know these kinds of people and how ruthless they can be."

"Why would you work for them?"

"I needed some money for my baby, Yeesica. She's with my mother. Her father ran out on us while I was pregnant. So I came here over a year ago. Started dancing at this club. A girlfriend I met told me she worked for these people. Real *rico* and stuff. She said they paid their girls well. I found the cheapest apartment I could find, any other money I sent back to Yeesica. She started kindergarten this year."

"I have a daughter, too. Gracie. She's nine."

Mentioning Gracie's name brought him back to reality. The last two preposterous days had bordered on the surreal. After all he'd been through, he still didn't have a liver. He'd be able to make it to her ballet recital, but he also understood that he'd have to start figuring out how to say goodbye soon.

Naelle rose and lurched into the bathroom wincing. She came out fumbling with a bottle of Tylenol. Once she opened it, she gulped a few pills and crunched down.

"Does it hurt badly?" he asked.

"That's like asking if a cat chases mice."

He led her over to the silver briefcase. "I need to show you something."

"Listen, I gotta leave right now—"

"Look," he said, opening the briefcase.

She gasped when she saw what was inside. He knew she'd never seen that kind of money before.

"I want you to take it."

She fingered a crisp bill and shook her head.

"This will get you to the DR and could help you and Yeesica start a good life."

"I can't take your money. You have a family, a daughter too..."

"They don't need the money like you do."

"No, no, no. I don't deserve it. This is too much."

He closed the briefcase and thrust it at her.

"You saved my life before," he said. "You need to take it."

She kept shaking her head, trying to give it back.

"You saved my life, too."

"But I didn't." He thrust it at her one last time. "I'm responsible."

In the van while driving her to the Bronx, he had looked over as she slept restlessly. He realized that he'd have to tell her the truth about why she'd been cut open. If he didn't, his selfish actions would gnaw at him, follow him past the grave. He desired only a free conscience now, one bereft from all sins, a soul he could be proud of, despite however gnarly it may have been.

"I don't understand," she said, embracing the brief-case like a small child in her arms. Maybe she was picturing baby Yeesica and how different their life would be if she agreed to his donation.

"It's true that I got you away from those people after they cut you up—"

"I know, that's why I called you my *angel guardiánte*, baby."

"But there's more..."

His tone seemed to unnerve her. She let go of the briefcase like it was made of tarantulas and it crashed to the floor.

"I don't have time for this," she said, grabbing her

own suitcase instead. Harrison couldn't believe that her whole life in America fit into that suitcase. He thought of how many bags he'd need if he decided to flee; but all that truly mattered to Naelle were a few old pictures and crosses. Anything else important existed in the Dominican Republic.

She stepped toward the front door but he stopped her. She was strong and it took everything in his power to hold her steady.

"You need to listen to what I have to tell you."

He'd raised his voice and she shut her eyes because of his shouting, but she gave up trying to weasel out of his grasp. She touched the bandages under her T-shirt as if she knew what he was going to confess.

"Why were you at their place?" she whispered, biting the words. The lovely Naelle he had known was gone. In her place stood a seething woman.

He took a deep breath, stretched out time for one last moment as her Guardian Angel before he'd plummet back to Earth.

"I had called the Desire Card for a liver—"

She cut him off by slapping him across the face. Then she was upon him with fists and a kick to his shin. He curled into a fetal position, blocking his face with his hands. She stopped thrashing him and leaned against the wall holding her chest in agony.

He spit out a tiny wad of blood and struggled to a crawling position. From there he was able to rise.

"I didn't know you'd be the donor."

"Donor," she laughed, but it soon turned to defeated tears. "Like I volunteered for any of this."

He made a move to step closer but she slid past him and picked up her suitcase again.

"The minute I saw it was you, I couldn't let them go any further," he said. "I attacked all the doctors; I stabbed the guard at the front with the syringe they used to drug you."

"So what? If it wasn't for you, I never would've been there in the first place."

"I'm dying. I was desperate."

He stared at his hands, anything but her judgmental face.

"I had a donor in India, but it was all a scam. They took my money, a lot of my money."

She glanced at the silver briefcase. "So you thought you'd use more money to solve your problem. That's all you people do. You have money to burn on girls like me. We meet at fancy hotels where they put mints on the pillow in the morning. You men tell me I'm more exciting and beautiful than your wives, but your wives aren't the kind of people who get knifed like a fish. That kind of outcome only exists for a poor brown girl like me."

She reached into the kitchen off to the side and picked up a pot to throw at him. It missed his head by an inch and sailed to the other end of the apartment. She went for a pan next.

"Naelle, please."

He caught up with her, pulled the pan from her fingers, and dropped it to the floor. She was crying loudly enough for the neighbors to call the police if they cared. He threw his arms around her in a hug and held on tight until she finally stopped fighting.

"Take the money," he whispered in her ear. They were cheek-to-cheek now and flashes of their night together exploded in his brain, but he knew he'd never have her again.

"I do not want your filthy money. Now let go of me."

With much chagrin, he let her go. He stooped over, feeling like an old man with no life left in him.

"At least take enough to get you a ticket back home."

"I said I don't want your filthy money."

He opened the briefcase and took out over a thousand dollars in cash.

"Don't be foolish."

He held out the money. He could see she didn't want to look at it but couldn't help herself.

"You're right," she said, chewing her lip. "I've been foolish for too long."

She snatched the cash and stuffed it inside the Ziploc bag.

"Hold on," he said, and took out a business card from his wallet. He took a pen from the counter and scribbled some writing on the back. "That's my home address. I want to make sure that you're safe. Will you write to me? And if you need more cash..."

She considered the card. For a moment he thought she'd crumple it up in her fist, but then she placed it in the Ziploc bag as well.

"Will you move aside from the door so I can leave now please?"

Her voice was tired, strained beyond any audibility.

"You said I was your guardian angel, but you're wrong, you were mine," he said.

She rolled her eyes and crossed her arms. "I ain't shit to you."

"That night with you before I wound up in the hospital...."

He got too choked up, unable to continue. She tapped her foot angrily, telling him to finish his babbling so she could get out of there.

"I hadn't had a night like that since the early days with Helene...my wife. And it wasn't just the sex. You meant more, so much more because you cared. I know you didn't care about me personally, I'm not delusional, but you cared about making that night truly wonderful for me, for it to be everything I desired."

She had her hand on the doorknob, turned it halfway.

"That's my job." She shrugged.

"No, that's you. That's what an angel does."

She pursed her lips and put her hand on her hip. "Mister, if I'm your angel, then you got fucked in the angel department."

———

Naelle agreed to let Harrison walk her down to get a cab to the airport. He knew it was only because she was still afraid that the people of the Desire Card might've followed them and were waiting downstairs. Once more he tried to give her the rest of the money in the briefcase but she refused. The two of them waited outside of her apartment building as a black livery car pulled up. The driver popped the trunk and she tossed her suitcase inside.

"Don't think of me as evil," he said, like it was an order.

The homeless druggie on the corner started belting out the gospel song "Sinner Please."

"*Sinner, O see the cruel tree,*" he sang over and over.

Naelle opened the back door of the livery car and tapped her long fingernails against the window.

She sighed. "What do you want me to say?"

"Just that I'm not evil," he said, misty eyed.

"*Sinner, O see the cruel tree,*" the druggie yelled to the sky.

"You ain't evil, baby." She sucked at her tongue. "But you ain't completely good neither."

"I know."

He stared down at the filthy sidewalk, but then forced himself to look her in the face because he knew it would be his last chance.

"But who's really good anymore?" She shrugged. "I make men commit adultery; I've used my flesh for money. Yeah, it's for survival, but I could've found other ways. Good don't matter no more in this world. It's just about making it till tomorrow with my baby girl safe. That's all the good I have left in me."

"I'm sorry," he said again, his voice hoarse. He didn't know if he'd spoken loud enough because she got in the back seat and closed the door without responding. He pressed his face against the glass and soaked up one last glimpse. She was telling the driver where to take her. Her buckteeth hung over her bottom lip and she had the faintest smile. She would see her daughter soon. Even after all the trauma of the last two days, the hope of being with her daughter would be enough. He waved goodbye as she looked at him for one last time. She blinked in response, and he knew that would have to be enough. The stoplight had already turned green and the livery car took off down the block.

> "Sinner please don't let this harvest pass
> And die and lose your soul at last."

The druggie had finished his ditty as his last words soared through the gridlocked streets.

Harrison stepped back from the curb, his heart heavy. As he turned around, he spied the henchman in the Humphrey Bogart mask standing between him and the black van. Bogart shook his head with a *tsk* sound coming from his voice box before he took off toward Harrison in a sprint, his gun prominently displayed in the holster at his side.

21

HARRISON HAD LITTLE TIME TO THINK AS THE GUY in the Bogart mask rushed toward him. He remembered Naelle saying that she lived in a walk-up by a station and noticed an entrance for the 6 train on the opposite corner. He took off as fast as he could, glad he'd gotten back the silver briefcase with the cash so he'd be pursued instead of Naelle. Behind him, Bogart followed in close pursuit, his steps heavy against the pavement. Within seconds Harrison felt out of breath, his stomach jiggling up and down and making him want to retch. The subway's entrance called to him, promised his survival should he reach its enticing steps. A car barreled toward him down the street, but he managed to race past it in time. Before he descended into the subway terminal, he looked over and saw Bogart waiting for the car to pass. Even though Bogart was devoid of any expression due to his mask, Harrison could tell he was pissed.

Harrison fumbled with his wallet for a Metro Card while leaping down the stairs two at a time. His face had already become flush with tears and he could barely see, but he wiped them away as he found a Metro Card and reached the bottom of the staircase. He swiveled around a large black lady who held onto a small child in each hand and went through the turnstile.

He looked behind him and saw Bogart's feet coming down the stairs. The black lady had started to climb the same stairs with her two children in tow and created a wall that blocked Bogart. Bogart moved left, she moved left. He moved right and she did the same. Finally he pushed one of her children out of the way and hurtled down the rest of the staircase.

A train hadn't arrived yet but a lot of people were already waiting on the platform so that meant one would be coming soon. Harrison weaved in and out of the crowd saying, "excuse me" with urgency. Behind him Bogart had jumped over the turnstile and was glancing in the opposite direction. While Bogart gazed toward the other end of the tunnel, Harrison tried to hide behind two burly guys, but it was no use. Bogart then turned his head and the two locked eyes. Both froze for a second, anticipating what the other might do. Harrison could try to head back over the turnstile and make his way out of the terminal, or he could run toward the end of the platform. He tossed out the third option of leaping onto the track to try his luck at making it to the uptown side; he'd save that desperate measure for when it'd be his only available choice.

He felt a rumbling in the soles of his feet. Down the dark tunnel, he could make out a faint light. A gust of wind blew the garbage from off the tracks onto the platform. He took his chances that the train would arrive in time and moved toward the other end of the platform. He couldn't run due to the amount of people in his way, but that meant Bogart couldn't either. He looked over his shoulder to see Bogart in pursuit a few yards behind, knocking into people as if they were nothing more than cones in his way.

The lights of the train crept along the rails and the wind became stronger as it rushed through the tunnels. He was almost at the end of the platform as the train whipped into the station, the wind slicing against his face. The crowd lurched toward the doors, creating a blockade. There were too many people to tell how much Bogart had gained on him. The doors finally opened as passengers struggled to get off and others pushed to get on. He thought to trick Bogart into getting on the train while he stayed on the platform, but as the mass of people emptied through the doors, he saw that Bogart had been thinking the same thing. Both waited with one foot inside the train and the other on the platform. The silver briefcase dangled from his hand; he had an idea to throw the briefcase onto the platform since Bogart would be sure to stay behind to retrieve it, but then the doors beeped and he slid into the train car instead.

As the train took off, he looked out onto the platform but couldn't see Bogart, which meant that the guy had made it on the train a few cars away. In his car a rail-thin Hispanic guy had gotten on with his cap extended for a handout. The guy had a Hitler-like mustache and curly hair like he'd stepped out of a 70s film. He spoke loudly about contracting AIDS and needing money for medication. No one even glanced his way.

The beggar started speaking louder now, imploring people to listen since no one responded. He came closer to Harrison stretching out his quivering hand, his eyes on Harrison's briefcase. The train reached the next station at Longwood Avenue. People pushed past him as they made their way out of the doors. Harrison spun around to right himself, grasping onto a pole with one hand while holding the briefcase tightly out of fear that the beggar might try to take it. The train took off again as Bogart's masked face appeared at the door between the cars. Bogart narrowed his eyes looking for Harrison through the sea of people and then thrust open the door once he spied him.

The train shook as it careened through the tunnel, jostling people to the left and the right. Harrison kept close to the beggar who was still trying to convince him "to be so kind and give some change." Bogart stepped through the car doors and glanced out of the window, probably to see how close they were to the next stop. Harrison let out a gasp and looked into the eyes of straphangers around him for help, but no one acknowledged his plight. As Bogart came closer, the beggar spun around, his eyes milky and yellow, his trembling hand reaching out toward Bogart.

The train came to a stop as it reached the next station of East 149th Street. The doors opened but too many people were getting on for Harrison to attempt to get off. Just as the train picked up speed again, he barreled into the beggar, who in turn, fell into Bogart. Coins flew in the air as the beggar let out a cry like he was being tortured. Bogart and the beggar fell back onto a row of seats. Two women who had been sitting close by starting yelling while Harrison stumbled around them all. He opened the door and stepped between the cars, the tunnel air smelling of rotten sewage.

He could hear an argument brewing in the train car he left. Through the window he could see that the beggar and an older woman were locked in a shouting match as Bogart got to his feet and headed toward Harrison. Harrison opened the door to the next car and ran inside. The people in the new train car frowned at the heaving, sweating mess of a man that had entered their universe. This car was even more crowded than the first and there wasn't much room for him to push through. The train reached the next stop at Saint Mary's Street and a few people exited, enough for him to make his way forward.

Once he got to the other end, he heard a door slam open and craned his neck to see that Bogart had entered. Harrison flung open the door in front of him and stepped into a new car as a wave of vertigo rushed over him and nausea sloshed around in his stomach. The people he passed appeared as ghosts, dozens of souls who didn't bother to save him, all of them selfish. His eyes scanned for a cop but there were none in sight as the train reached the next stop at Cypress Avenue and the doors opened.

Bogart had entered the same car now. Both he and Harrison waited at the edge of the open doors to gauge whether the other might leap out onto the platform. Harrison faked throwing the briefcase out of the train car, but Bogart didn't buy into his bluff. The doors closed as the train started up again. Bogart pushed past the straphangers in his way, his gun glinting from the train's fluorescent lights.

"This train is only so long, Mr. Stockton," he yelled over the heads of straphangers.

No one blinked at the oddity of a man in a Bogart mask. Harrison knew that in New York City, only something ridiculously shocking caught people's attention, and this chase did not qualify. He realized that in two more stops the train would reach 125th Street, a large enough station to try and outrun Bogart.

One more station passed by and Harrison prayed that Bogart wouldn't catch up to him. As they came closer to 125th Street, he knew that a massive amount of people would be getting on and off. The two men stood at opposite ends of a train car. As the train slowed to a crawl, he saw a crowd waiting three people deep for the train to arrive. Sure enough the 4 train was pulling in at the same time as well. This would be his chance and he'd have to take it.

He pretended as if he wasn't going anywhere once the train stopped and the doors opened, but then he held the briefcase to his chest and pushed as hard as he could to exit while others were trying to get inside. He didn't look to see if Bogart was doing the same thing. He was too fixated on taking the chance that he could make the other train.

The platform was crowded with people moving in all directions, and he almost knocked over an older man as he pushed toward the 4 train. He heard the train beeping and reached out his silver briefcase, hoping to catch the closing doors in time. The doors slammed against his briefcase and opened again as he weaseled inside and collapsed into a seat to catch his breath. With tears itching at the corner of his eyes, he hugged the briefcase tight, thrilled that he'd gotten away. The train took off and rattled through the tunnel before stopping at 116th Street. He looked from one end of the car to the other but didn't see any sign of Bogart.

His breathing had returned to a normal pace, but the thought of moving again seemed impossible since his legs were really starting to burn. He'd stay on the train to Fifty-Ninth Street and then take the briefcase to his apartment. If Helene were home, he'd have to clue her in on what was happening. Maybe he wouldn't have to tell her everything yet, but the people of the Desire Card knew where he lived, and he had to figure out a way to keep his family out of jeopardy. At least Naelle had gotten far enough away and would be at the airport soon. After he talked to Helene, they could decide together what to do next. Part of him was nervous that she might tell him to sacrifice himself, that the hundred fifty K was more important to the family's livelihood than he was at this point, especially once she'd have to deal with the back-to-back shock of learning about his liver disease and that he'd paid off a strange organization to steal him an organ.

Before he could debate about what he'd do when he saw his wife again, the train began to slow to a crawl at Eighty-Sixth Street. A mass of people huddled in front of him as the door to the adjoining car swung open. His throat closed up when he saw Bogart. Sweat broke out on his forehead and his bowels shook as a thousand scenarios ran through his brain. Finally he grasped the pole to help him rise to his feet and fled out of the train onto the station. He knew that Bogart would've gotten out as well, but he wouldn't let himself look back. He made his way to the staircase, summoning every ounce of adrenaline inside of him to leap up the stairs two at a time. There'd be an entrance to Central Park only a few avenues up, which would be his best chance to lose Bogart. He ran across the street, knowing deep down that this would all end badly. He was too exhausted to run anymore once he reached Park Avenue, but when he saw Bogart on the other side of the street waiting for the light to change, he had no other choice. He picked up his pace all the way to Madison Avenue, huffing and puffing, drool and snot dripping from his face. At the next avenue, he made the stoplight while Bogart got stuck. As the wind blew against him, his chest felt like it had exploded leaving his guts along the sidewalk. At the entrance to Central Park, he came to a halt. He chewed at the air, hoping to get back his breath that he'd left somewhere on Park Avenue.

He stumbled into the park, his body shaking out of fear and from being cold. Clouds clogged the sky. The trees seemed like creatures towering over him. He turned around to see Bogart running toward the entrance like a Terminator machine, his cold eyes scanning the park, then zeroing in. Harrison took off down a dirt path away from the few people mingling at the entrance until he was alone with only the wind ringing in his ears.

He had pissed himself now, the urine hot and sticky as it trickled down his pants leg.

Bogart emerged from behind a tree holding the gun. "You were the one who contacted us for a liver," Bogart said, walking closer. "Remember that. All we did was try to fulfill your desire."

Harrison shook his head, not wanting to hear about his culpability. He was long past crying anymore; his tear ducts had all dried up.

"I never asked for that to happen to her," he said, wanting Bogart to really understand.

Bogart stuck the gun in Harrison's gut.

"Just hand it over, Mr. Stockton. You don't want this to get any more complicated than it already has."

Bogart grabbed at the briefcase, but Harrison managed to hold on tight.

"You'll kill me anyway," Harrison yelled.

"Only if you force me to do so."

Bogart kicked Harrison in the shin, causing him to nearly buckle over. He was thrown to the ground, the man pinning him down. He still managed to hold onto the briefcase, as if it had fused into his hand.

"The boss doesn't know about what you've done yet," Bogart said, shaking him and hitting his head against the hard dirt. "And he never will as long as we get the money we're owed."

"Why would you do that for me?" Harrison asked, seeing four masked men spinning around.

Bogart stepped back to point the gun between Harrison's eyes.

"The boss doesn't like when things don't go according to the plan. I could be in as much trouble as you for letting it happen. So let's make this easy for both of us."

"James Dean is a tough son of a bitch, isn't he?"

"James Dean isn't our boss," Bogart said, shaking his head. "In fact, he's been rather untrustworthy lately and was sent to Marrakesh right now to prove his loyalty."

"Who's your boss then?"

Harrison had to know. He needed a face, the very definition of the devil—cruel enough to slice open an innocent girl for some cash. Someone out there with the capacity to be even more evil than him.

"Fine, will you give me the briefcase if I tell you?" Bogart asked, his voice losing patience.

"Promise me you won't go after the girl."

"I assume she's long gone now already."

"I have no idea where she is."

"I think you're lying, but I do not care. As long as she stays hidden, it's the same as her being dead."

Harrison got on one elbow and hoisted himself up.

"Do I have your word?"

Bogart nodded.

"And my family? My wife, my kids? I wouldn't have to worry about them being hurt?"

"As much you might think that you are our sole concern, we have an organization to run beyond your pitiful life."

"And what about the next guy that calls for an organ?"

Bogart chuckled.

"It's just wrong," Harrison mumbled.

"How can I be judged, Mr. Stockton, when I'm nothing more than a façade? Now I will count to ten and if I don't have the briefcase in my hands by then, you will have a bullet between your eyes...eight...nine...ten," Bogart said, about to pull the trigger.

"All right, all right."

He handed over the briefcase. Bogart opened it up to count the money, a smirk visible through his mask.

"There's a thousand missing," Harrison said.

"Gave it to the girl?"

"Yeah, the girl."

"Well, since your operation never happened, we'll let the missing grand slide."

Harrison leaned against the rock, a shriveled entity.

"I'll leave you with this nugget of wisdom," Bogart said, without putting the gun away. "If what you did manages to compromise our organization in any way, if there are any ripples be prepared to come across the boss. He's known to wear a Clark Gable mask." Bogart's smirk had disappeared, his robotic voice sounding like it was quivering. "He only appears when he's ready to bloody his hands. Good day, Mr. Stockton."

"Who are you people? Under the masks...who are you really?"

Bogart raised the gun over Harrison's head.

"I doubt you'll ever find out," he said, and struck Harrison on the forehead with the handle of the gun.

A trickle of blood spilled down Harrison's nose and felt cold on his tongue. He slunk down and rested his cheek against the dirt, watching Bogart take off through the trees, the silver briefcase shining brilliantly from a beam of light snaking through the leaves. And then Bogart finally disappeared—as if he was nothing more than a nightmare brought to life and extinguished once the fitful dreamer finally woke.

Harrison pressed his hand under his rib cage on the right side of his chest and felt for his engorged liver. Cursed at it. Wanted to tear it from his stomach. He'd been poisoned from within for too long, his eternal punishment for all of his crimes. Blood zigzagged into his eyes as the wound on his forehead opened up even more. With his other hand, he reached into his pocket. The Desire Card fell from his wallet and sat in a puddle of blood that had collected in the dirt. He crumpled it up in his fist since it was responsible for letting these psychopaths into his life. He knew he'd never feel completely settled again, always worried that they could be waiting to hunt him down along with his family even though he handed over the briefcase. It had stolen his soul, caused him to have gruesome, despicable wishes. From the instant this devil's temptation had been placed in his hands, his moral compass never stood a chance. So he chucked it into the air and watched it sail over the rocks for some other fool to find before he drifted off into unconsciousness.

PART FOUR

22

It turned dark while Harrison laid unconscious in the dirt. When he came to, a crescent moon winked in the sky. A line of blood had hardened down his face. He could feel it flaking as he rose to his feet. With each step, he awakened more and more until he emerged from the park. He intended to head home, not to his cold hotel room at The London. He desired nothing else but his real bed and the arms of his soon-to-be ex-wife for one last time before he revealed to her the entire truth, warts and all, of what had become his ridiculous life.

Since it was about eleven at night, the kids were probably already in bed and Helene had either put on her sleep mask or was invested in some trifling book about three divorcees spending a weekend in Nantucket.

When he finally entered his apartment, the new cat that Gracie wanted to name Cinnamon sat poised on the couch, its claws digging into the fine leather. Chauncey had always known his place and never dared to sit on the couch. It had taken months of training to regulate Chauncey to his cat bed, and it exhausted Harrison to think of all the work that would have to go into this new cat that would eventually die and be replaced by another kitten who'd require the same diligent training.

The apartment's smell caught him off guard, the warm familiarity of the overpriced scented candles and the smell of takeout that Helene had warmed up in the oven earlier, a buttery roasted chicken with onions—not home-cooked, but thoroughly less depressing than the room service he'd been getting each night.

He headed down the long hallway toward the bedrooms. There were no lights coming from either of the children's rooms, but a thin band spooled from Helene's. Sure enough when he opened the door, she lay on the bed in a pink nightgown with some book propped on her stomach and a sleep mask covering her eyes. A light snore caused her lips to flap up and down, and a string of drool extended from her mouth to the pillow.

"Helene," he said, clasping her big toe. She tossed back-and-forth until he started shaking her foot.

"What...?"

She hunched up against the headboard.

"Harrison? What are you doing?"

She took off the sleep mask and let it slip from her fingers. She groped for her glasses on the bedside table. Once her eyes adjusted, they bugged at the sight of the dried blood on his face and the clothes he wore that weren't his own. Who was this disheveled half-human that had somehow inhabited the body of her husband?

"Oh my God, were you mugged?" She got to her

feet and touched the scar on his forehead. "I'll get some Bactine."

"Helene..."

She was already in the bathroom before he could stop her. He had practiced the speech he'd deliver to her on the walk over from the park, figuring it was best to begin by evoking sympathy.

"Helene, come and sit down."

She burst out of the bathroom, her fists stuffed with cotton swabs, the Bactine, and Band-Aids.

"You know Deidra Landry's husband Jacob was mugged the other night. Right on the parkside of Fifth Avenue a few blocks away. A couple of teenagers with skateboards. Why do they always have skateboards with them? I didn't even know that teenagers skated so much in this city, seems so suburban."

She dabbed the Bactine against his cut, her touch motherly and welcoming. He thought about saving the truth for tomorrow and possibly rekindling what they had lost tonight. Let her dab his sorrows away while he slid off her nightgown to reveal the flesh he hadn't seen for so long. But he knew it would only make it worse later on if he spent tonight telling her more lies.

"Does it hurt anywhere else?" she asked, placing a Band-Aid over the scar and inspecting the rest of his body.

"Come, Helene, sit down."

He led her over to the bed as she frowned, suspicious now. He clutched her hands with his sausage fingers and looked into the chestnut brown eyes that he once called home.

"Harrison, you're scaring me. Please tell me everything is all right."

His body had slumped over, and he tucked his chin into his chest. Since his tears had dried up, he wouldn't be able to rely on them to score any sympathy.

"Helene, I..." He began to shake, his bowels clenching.

"What? Tell me."

Her voice had changed from soothing to admonishing. He knew she was already thinking that something else must be responsible for his unkempt state other than being mugged by some punk kids.

"I'm sorry," he said, his voice barely above a whisper.

"Sorry for what?"

He shook his head over and over, savoring these last moments of fantasy. She let go of his hands.

"Harrison, sorry for what?"

And then he told her, warts and all.

———

His superwoman Helene: mother, and once his lover extraordinaire. How could she possibly react to this news? Like he assumed, the truth about his liver cirrhosis invoked an angry tirade. She lambasted him for keeping it from his family. Her anger soon turned to blame for neglecting his health all these years. "Everyone sees a doctor periodically!" she exclaimed. Once her anger subsided, a barrage of questions followed. How long did the doctors give him? How could he get on a donor list? What kind of medications was he taking? Did he get a second opinion? How would they tell the kids? Did anyone else know? And what did this have to do with the gash on his forehead?

"There's more," he said, motioning for her to sit back on the bed since she was pacing and making him nervous.

"You know my father might have some pull. I know he donated a lot to Bellevue Hospital recently, or was it New York Presbyterian?"

She had wadded up a few wet tissues and tucked them into the sleeve of her nightgown.

"And you've been living at a hotel this whole time while you're suffering? Harrison, what in God's name is wrong with you?"

"I thought that was best."

"All those steaks and sweets that you've gorged on throughout the years. I've also always denied your alcoholism, but it was bound to catch up with you since it's in your blood." Her eyes widened. "Did Sanford & Co. fire you because of your liver? That is a lawsuit waiting to happen."

"Well, partially. Please sit, Helene, because there's more."

She picked up the phone and started dialing.

"What are you doing?"

"Calling my father."

He took the phone from her and hung it up.

"Will you just sit down for a second?"

She snapped out of the frenzy she had worked herself into and sunk onto the bed, her eyes still staring at the phone.

"To answer one of your earlier questions, I'm far down on the donor list."

"That's why I suggested my father—"

"This is why I went to India."

"India?" she asked, as if she had never heard of that country before.

"Do you remember Nagesh Patel from college?"

"What? Vaguely."

"He said he had a clinic in Mumbai and the ability to get a liver off the black market—"

"The black market?" she gasped, standing up and holding her neck that had turned redder than ever before.

"Let me explain—"

"Is that why you were in the Dharavi slums? Organ hunting?"

She hissed the last words, clearly deeming them wicked.

"Harrison, do you know how many poor children are being trafficked for organs around the world? What do you think one of the things that the Faceless Children's Gala is trying to prevent?"

"It was a scam," he yelled, flush with tears now that had finally started to fall.

"Do not wake up the kids, this is not a conversation I want to have with them tonight."

"I was scammed," he said, lowering his voice. "Nagesh took our money. There was no clinic. He had set the whole thing up."

"How much money did you give him?"

"Helene, please sit down again," he begged, trying to grab her arm but she shook free.

"How much money, Harrison?"

"One hundred fifty thousand dollars."

She wrapped her nightgown tightly around her chest. The window had been left open and a chill permeated through the room. She finally sat down again on the edge of the bed.

"And where is this money now?" she asked, calmer than she'd been since he started revealing all of his secrets, a strange calm that resembled someone who'd been lobotomized.

He was about tell her that Nagesh had been knifed for their cash but decided to remain silent about that twisty turn of events.

"I don't know. I tried to find him after I realized I'd been scammed. But I didn't have his address. He had a throwaway phone. There are a million other fucking Nagesh Patels in Mumbai. And the police there don't give a shit."

"Money is just money. Money can be replaced."

"I'm sorry—"

She cut him off by looking him dead in the eyes. He'd forgotten how much she hated apologies, finding them a simplistic way to express true regret.

"Is there anything else I need to know?"

He took a deep breath. This last confession would be the worst. How could he even begin to explain? She sat on the edge of the bed, pleading for the secrets to end, but he could tell she knew he wasn't finished—for he hadn't explained the gaping wound on his forehead yet.

"Will you stay calm if I tell you?"

She gave a husky laugh, the one he'd fallen in love with, the laugh of a lifetime smoker even though she'd never touched a cigarette before.

"When I was let go from Sanford & Co., they gave me something called a Desire Card."

She shrugged.

"For the right price, the people behind this card aim to fulfill anyone's...desires."

She gasped, already knowing where this was headed.

"Tell me you didn't."

Her words were spaced out, as if by taking her time she could delay the inevitable truth for a moment longer.

He lowered his head.

"Harrison!"

She covered her mouth, shaking her head in denial.

"I was desperate—"

"Goddamnit, I told you my father has a pull at some hospitals. If you would have let me know sooner—"

"Pull doesn't matter for a donor list. They are locked solid until your name comes up. It could be a week, a year, and I don't have a year!"

"So you just asked these...people for a liver, what kind of absurd request is that? And they got one for you?"

"Well...yes. But there was a snag."

"Who are these people? What kind of business is this?"

"I couldn't go through with it. They had found a woman, a young woman...she didn't ask to be a donor. They were going to cut her open."

"Oh, Harrison," she shouted.

"Helene, the kids. Please stay calm. Will you stay calm for me?"

"Are these people the ones who hurt you? Do they know where we live?"

She rose from the bed and stood by the window,

looking to see if anyone was watching them from outside.

"They aren't after us. I promise, you don't have to worry."

"How can you promise that?"

"They've been paid off. Even though I never went through with the operation, I gave them all that I owed. It's true that they hit me on the forehead, but they won't come after me for more."

"I don't even want to ask how much you had to pay them."

"Please, Helene, I want everything out in the open between us."

She shut her eyes, bracing for the worst.

"Is this the last thing you have to tell me?" she asked, clenching her fists.

"Yes, this is it, I promise. You are an amazing woman for being so understanding."

"I am not understanding any of this so you know. I haven't decided how to react yet."

"I know, that's understandable, that's..."

"Harrison, tell me how much before I leap out of this goddamn window."

"Three hundred thousand more."

And that was when Helene finally lost it.

———————

Wisely, Helene had pulled him into the bathroom so the sound of her screams would be buffered from the kids. Harrison imagined a nosy neighbor listening by the grate to her harangues. She was flabbergasted that in the span of a few weeks he had lost almost a half a million dollars, money that could've gone to an upgraded apartment in their building, or even to help begin their new lives if their separation led to a divorce. She labeled him insatiable; he'd always been a self-serving son of a bitch. He'd kept her in the dark about his liaisons throughout their entire marriage, as well as the fatalistic descent of his alcoholism, and to make things worse, he had embarked on an amorally downward spiral with a significant amount of their savings!

"Let's say you had gotten a liver, were you ever going to tell me about any of this?"

She had put down the lid on the toilet and sat while he leaned against the bathtub. His watch said it was well after midnight now. Over an hour of fighting plus the exhausting last few days had worn him out. He could barely keep his eyes open, but he knew he wouldn't be getting any sleep tonight.

"I didn't want to worry you."

"How practical of you, Harrison. And that certainly worked out well, didn't it?"

"I don't expect you to stay with me," he said, fingering the cold grooves of the bathroom's tiles.

"So then I become the abandoner of a dying husband? No thank you."

"I won't spin it that way to any of our friends."

"Oh, I don't care about appearances. But I refuse to let the father of my children waste away on his own."

"What are you saying?"

"What I'm saying is I still want to see if my father could do some finagling at any of the hospitals."

"Thank you."

"And if he doesn't, I will nurse you through this."

He couldn't believe what he was hearing, and his

love for this woman grew exponentially in a matter of seconds. His sweet Helene, his little co-ed with the side ponytail had truly become a woman now capable of an ultimate sacrifice. In the absence of good in this world, in the face of those who conned others out of greed or killed for money, this saint rose above the harsh reality and offered only her unending support.

"I can't ask you to do that for me," he said, because he couldn't think of any other way to respond.

She raised her hand to silence him and pursed her lips together. "Listen, I'm not offering a reconciliation. No. This is for your children, so you can spend as much time with them for as long as you have left. Should my father be able to help with his connections, I will be there for you while you recuperate. If he doesn't, we will pray for the call that your name has moved up on the donor list, and I will stay by your side. But once you are better, I do not want to be in this marriage with you anymore."

Her deal wasn't what he expected, but he knew it could've been worse. He didn't warrant someone like Helene who always put herself last. The yin and yang of their personalities had been cute in college but thrust into real-life scenarios, it had only driven them further apart. She needed someone pure and understanding who would challenge rather than frustrate her, who cared as much about faceless children as she did, who'd tell her how beautiful she was every day and never stray.

"That's more than I deserve," he said.

"And I'm not a martyr, do not think that. I am being selfish as well. I am doing what I need to do in this situation to assuage any guilt."

"Why would you feel guilty?"

"Because two people were in this marriage, Harrison, and I spent the majority of it looking the other way."

"Don't do that to yourself."

She held up her hand again. "You do *not* get to tell me how to react and how to feel."

"You're absolutely right. Thank you, thank you for all—"

"And don't waste your time thanking me either. Put all of your energy into reestablishing your relationship with Brenton and Gracie."

"Yes, yes, of course. What do we tell them?"

"We tell them your diagnosis and that is it. As much as you might advocate bringing a harsh reality into their privileged lives, I refuse to have a debate about organ trafficking with my nine-year-old daughter. I will spare them the pain of knowing who you truly are."

"Do you think I'm evil?" he asked, afraid to hear her response. The bathroom became silent except for a leaky faucet that counted down the seconds with each drip until Helene finally resumed speaking.

"I don't believe you're evil, but you are one of the weakest men I know."

She rose from the toilet seat and headed out of the bathroom.

"I'm turning in now. You'll have to sleep on the couch tonight, but I'll purchase a convertible bed for you tomorrow that we'll keep in the living room."

"Helene...?"

She stood at the doorway, her back to him.

"Yes, Harrison...?"

"I just want to let you know that the first time you

spoke to me at Chilton, I knew I was hooked. You were in the quad drinking a cherry coke, and I tried to flirt and failed miserably, but you told me how if you held your nose while drinking cherry coke you couldn't taste the cherry anymore. I didn't believe it, but when I tried it you were right, and I thought you were so wise. I stared into your eyes and saw our futures together. I saw Brenton and Gracie, and this apartment, and the amazing woman that stands before me now. You are the best thing that has ever happened to me, and if I've made one smart decision in life, then you are it."

He was out of breath when he finished his spiel. She remained in the doorway; not moving an inch until she sighed so loud he could tell it came from deep within.

23

HARRISON WAITED IN THE DOCTOR'S OFFICE AT
New York Presbyterian for his scheduled checkup.
Over the past few weeks, he had made a deal with
Helene that he'd monitor his illness with doctor's
appointments while she pressured her father to see if he
had any pull regarding the national donor list. After
waiting for over half an hour, the doctor finally waddled
in. Harrison promised himself not to get angry for being
kept so long. Another part of the deal with Helene was
to treat people better, a little bit of karma sent out to the
universe that would hopefully come back to him
tenfold.

"I apologize, Mr. Stockton," the doctor said.

Harrison remembered the doctor from the blurry
week when he'd been diagnosed. He chose this doctor
as opposed to any of the others he'd encountered
because the guy seemed to be genuinely concerned
with his well-being.

"How is your wife doing?" Harrison asked, since
the doctor had spoken of a wife with lymphoma.

The doctor rubbed his chubby, liver-spotted hands together. His shoulders slumped forward causing his entire body to seem weighted down.

"Well...not good. Appears to have taken a turn for the worse."

"I'm so sorry to hear that."

"Yes...it's been difficult, but we're preparing for the end now. Just for her to go as peacefully as possible."

The doctor rubbed his eyes under his glasses.

"Thank you for asking, for remembering."

"My thoughts go out to you and your family."

The doctor nodded and got out Harrison's chart, a welcome distraction from his own life for the time being.

"And how are you holding up, Mr. Stockton?"

Had the doctor asked Harrison this three weeks prior, Harrison would've given an entirely different answer. The disappointment in obtaining a liver from the people of the Desire Card and in Mumbai would've been too fresh. Also the lies he'd been keeping from Helene would've still been festering. But now she had accepted his detestable truth and chose to deal with it by focusing on the present rather than any of his troubling past. He had to admit that he expected she'd be petty and use any chance to show her displeasure about his sinking ethics, but her actions proved that he never truly knew how compassionate she could be. She focused solely on his health and in strengthening his relationship with Brenton and Gracie. The very notion of his adultery with Naelle and that other girl, the half a million dollars he had lost, and the depravity of even contacting the Desire Card to steal a liver were never brought up again. He knew she could never forgive him, but he realized she didn't necessarily have to. The most she wished for was an amicable divorce and a healthy ex-spouse to bear the burden of raising the children. To achieve this, she resolved to be his nurse with any free time she had left over from planning her upcoming gala. So she converted the dining room into a bedroom for him by putting the long cherry wood table inherited from her grandfather into storage and getting a convertible bed. She made a thorough Excel chart that covered his array of medications. She forbade all alcohol and any recreational pills. His diet was regulated to fruits, fish, vegetables, and grains, and she began walking with him through Central Park every morning before breakfast.

During these last few weeks, he felt an immense love growing for her, but no longer a sexual desire, greater than anything physical they once had. He loved that his children were lucky enough to have a mother like her: a nurturer, a protector; and he wanted her to find happiness once she was free from him—whether by divorce or his untimely death. Most importantly, he had let go of any anger toward his destroyed liver. He no longer blamed the world for an unjust illness, he blamed himself—for if he would've been more like Helene, if he would have let her influence him with her own stellar morals, he never would've succumbed to a life of hedonism. But he didn't want to focus on regret anymore, only acceptance.

The doctor had been staring at him through coke-bottle glasses, anticipating a response.

"My family has been so supportive," Harrison finally replied. "That's all I could ask for."

"Yes, yes, family is paramount in overcoming difficult times," the doctor agreed, wiping away any newly forming tears.

"Your wife is very lucky to have you, too, Doctor."

The doctor managed a tired grin. "I've been the lucky one all of these years. Now I'm paying her back any way I can."

"To the wives," Harrison said, raising a tiny paper cup full of water.

The doctor filled up his own cup and the two men toasted to their better halves.

———

To foster his relationship with his children, Helene encouraged Harrison to take the kids to school and any afterschool activities. She'd be consumed anyway with the approaching gala and had planned on rehiring their old nanny, Yvette, to chauffeur the kids around town, but handing over the reins to Harrison turned out to be a better plan. While schlepping them around might've seemed too much for a man in his condition, the doctor advocated for him to keep busy as long as he maintained his medications and didn't become overexerted.

Gracie remained cool toward her father since she learned of his diagnosis, but he knew that was just part of her personality. If she was upset, she only showed frustration, mostly in relation to her upcoming ballet recital. Even chorus girls seemed to have a complex choreography to remember. She had such a nervous determination to be perfect in the recital that every-thing else in her life became secondary. Her entire world had become her routine, and if she cried for him, she only allowed herself to feel sadness if it'd help to enhance her performance.

Both he and Helene decided they'd put a positive spin on his chances for survival to make it easier for the kids. Helene figured that the possibility of her father coming through with a donor connection would give them some kind of hope. Brenton even remarked that "Papa Jay can make anything happen," simply because Jay had scored tickets to the World Cup and had gotten two of the most expensive seats available for them plus first-class plane tickets. This god-like buildup of their grandfather seemed to divert the focus away from Harrison's deterioration, so Harrison let them have this hope, even if it proved to be false.

After picking up Brenton every day from soccer practice, Harrison began to get just as excited as Brenton about the last game of the season. The boy's team had been hovering on the precipice of making the playoffs and this final game against their rivals would be the deciding one. Their rivals had already made the playoffs but that certainly didn't mean they'd take it easy on Brenton's team, for the bad blood between the two opponents had become so heated that the coach promised a "battle of biblical proportions" on the field at the end of the week.

The mythical Rufus Laynor, star fullback on the rival team, had had it out for Brenton since the first game of the season when he tripped Brenton for no reason and the referee failed to call a flagrant foul. When Harrison asked the coach why this terrorist of a child had singled out his boy, the coach responded that Brenton was "thought of as weak," since a year prior he'd been kicked in the shin by another member of the rival team and had cried.

While driving down to the final game of the season at a field by the FDR Drive, Harrison was determined to question Brenton about this.

"The coach says that this Rufus has it out for you because you once cried at a match."

"Whatever," Brenton said, rolling down the window and spitting into traffic.

"Weakness is not a good virtue."

The kid fiddled with the radio stations. "What's that mean?"

"It means you can't be weak in this world."

"Were you ever weak, Dad?"

Harrison nodded. "I didn't treat my body as a temple; I fell prey to temptation."

"But how is crying because I'm hurt the same thing?"

"Weakness has still allowed evil to enter into your life in the form of this Rufus Laynor, am I right?"

"I guess," the boy said, fixing his shin guard.

"Be stronger than your old man has been, defeat your enemy."

"He always tries to trip me," Brenton said, crossing his arms as his cheeks reddened. "It's illegal, but I'm gonna try to do the same thing."

"No, be a step ahead of him and don't show him you're afraid. Are you afraid?"

Brenton wouldn't look Harrison in the eye.

"It's okay, your dad is afraid of things, too. I might be facing death, son."

"I know," the boy replied so softly that Harrison could barely hear him.

"Don't sink to his level—that is being weak, that is what your old man was guilty of."

"How so?"

Harrison reached over with his free hand and squeezed the boy's shoulder.

"That's not for you to know right now. Maybe one day once you become a man, but not today."

"I'm a man," the kid said, but his voice hadn't gone through puberty yet.

The car stopped at a red light and Harrison took the opportunity to look his son dead in the eye.

"Then show me you're a man on the field. Outsmart that little fucker. You know his game, you know he's gonna try to trip you. That's his weakness. Do you understand?"

The sunlight poured into the car from the front window and Brenton had to squint to see his father.

"I think so, Dad."

Harrison stepped on the gas as the light changed to green.

"Good. Then you're a better man than I am."

On the field that afternoon, Harrison sat in the bleachers rapt. From the opening whistle the game was a nail-biter. The other team scored an early goal but Brenton's team prevented them from scoring anymore through the half. They were able to tie it up through a fluke of a goal that seemed to enrage the rivals even more. As the game wound down, Harrison put his energy into prayer, not toward God or any higher power, but a prayer for a balance, for the universe to be fair for once. Rufus Laynor had been riding Brenton from the instant the game began, using every available opportunity to trip him when the refs weren't looking and even succeeded three times. One of the times that Brenton fell looked more troubling than the rest when the boy seemed to land poorly on his wrist, but he dusted off any throbbing pain and swore to his coach that he was all right. Then, like poetry in motion, Brenton got passed the ball with only Rufus standing in his way. The two stared each other down, and when Rufus charged at Brenton with the intent to kick the boy in the shin, Brenton anticipated this overused move and lobbed the ball over Rufus' head, a perfect pass to himself that sent Rufus plummeting to the ground and afforded Brenton a clear shot at the goal.

Time seemed to freeze for Harrison, giving him a snapshot of a moment he'd always remember: his son with his leg extended and the goal in his sights. The cheers from the crowd became deafening, a chorus of adulations all for his son, his newly minted little man in a matter of seconds, should he be victorious. So Harrison sent prayers out into the universe from every fiber of his being. Time unfroze as the ball sailed from Brenton's foot and flew past the goalie for a picturesque point. After the moment ended, Harrison watched Brenton receive his team's congratulations, then he flopped back against the bleacher seats holding his throbbing heart, the pain overwhelming. He assumed this would be the moment he'd finally leave the world. The snapshot of his son's success would be his last known thought as Death would welcome him into its bosom; but eventually his heart rate slowed to a normal thump, and he was still alive, truly alive.

A few minutes later the rival team scored again forcing a tie, which meant that Brenton's team would not make the playoffs, but that loss was secondary to the victory on the field that day. Harrison realized that he had not passed down any weakness to his son.

And what more of a salvation could he possibly hope for?

———

The weekend proved to be busy for the Stocktons since Gracie's ballet recital was on Friday and the Faceless Children's Gala was happening the next night. Helene had been planning up until the last minute, forcing her to miss Brenton's match. Caroline Hendrest had the wild idea of having all attendees enter the gala wearing a mask to go along with the theme of Faceless Children, so Helene had to send out a separate note to all attendees that explained this request in further detail. She was, however, able to watch Brenton's triumphant goal on video and swore that she wouldn't miss Gracie's big night no matter what still needed to be done for the gala.

Once Friday night arrived, Harrison demanded that the family show up early to the ballet theater to snag front-row seats. The lights were still up when Gracie's little head poked through the curtains, scanning the audience until her eyes came into contact with Harrison. He gave a goofy wave, but she registered no emotion. He knew she spent the morning nervously puking up her dinner from last night. Afterwards, she forced Helene to watch her practice one final time. Once she finished and Helene started clapping, the girl grilled her mother on any imperfections that might be apparent. Had she gotten the cabriole just right? When Helene couldn't pinpoint any mistakes, Gracie started plucking at her eyebrows, a new form of self-torture Helene insisted she quit. This lead to a screaming match and tears, and when Harrison stepped into the room with an offer of ice cream, it only increased Gracie's disdain for her useless parents.

He attempted another goofy wave and followed it by sticking out his tongue. Gracie strained her facial muscles by trying not to smile, but the hint of a grin poked at her left cheek before she ducked back behind the curtain.

"I spoke to my father today," Helene said, patting Harrison's hand that was resting on their shared armrest.

"Oh?"

While Harrison was certainly grateful that Jay would try to get him moved up on the donor list, he didn't think it was possible. The rich had power, but only to a point. However, if he was being honest, he didn't feel as if he deserved a liver anymore. Even though it was stupid to think this way, he couldn't help it. How many others had sold their souls for a fresh organ? Very few, he surmised. And since he'd finally let go of his fear of dying as well, only a pervading bliss seemed to remain.

"I don't want to get your hopes up but—"

"I know it's a long shot, but please tell Jay that I appreciate all he's done."

"That's just it, my father thinks he might actually have a chance at one of the hospitals. They already have a wing named after him."

"Wow."

Helene kept patting his hand, her touch warming. She enjoyed the power her father had. Jay was never a mortal to his only daughter but some omnipotent and omnipresent being capable of moving mountains with the lightest shove.

"It's just a small wing, though," she said.

"What does your father's company do by the way?"

"What don't they do is the bigger question."

"He's always spoken of it in such vague terms."

"Well, that's just Daddy. Really, it was all a mystery to me growing up. He'd be globetrotting but would always return with a gift for me from Hong Kong, or Monte Carlo, or Antarctica..."

The lights darkened as the ballerinas took place on stage. Harrison nudged Brenton who was playing some portable video game and couldn't care less about his kid sister's recital. Brenton rolled his eyes at his father's warning and slipped the device into his pocket.

The lights came up over the stage and Harrison spied Gracie in the backline. A classical piece played over the speakers as the little girls began twirling around. The lead ballerinas leaped and pirouetted across the stage before giving the backline its turn. In sync, all six girls stood on the tips of their toes before each broke off from the pack with a solo number. As a spotlight hovered across Gracie's allegro, Harrison got choked up. He had cried more in the last few months than in his entire life, but these were his first tears of absolute joy. Time passed in an instant, and when the music ended and the lights darkened, he clapped louder than the rest of the audience. He rose to his feet calling out her name as the lights came on again and all the little girls bowed. She caught his eye from the stage as his thunderous applause dwarfed all the rest, and she let herself smile, enough to wrench his heart from his chest and leave it dangling in front of his face, even though he knew she wasn't smiling because of him.

She had wanted to complete a perfect cabriole more than anything and had achieved the greatest accomplishment of her young life thus far.

———

Gracie was exhausted and slept in his arms as he carried her from the cab up to their apartment. Helene worried that he might strain something, but he was determined to put his daughter to bed since the last time he'd done so she'd been about five years old. Once he undressed her and tucked her in, he made his way to the living room to turn in as well. Helene was pouring herself a drink of vermouth with the cordless phone to her ear. She swiveled around, spilling vermouth everywhere, her hands trembling as she passed him the phone.

All the color appeared to have drained from her face. Two lines of tears snaked down her cheeks. He didn't know if she was elated or in shock.

"That was...that was..." She sniffled, and fell into his arms.

"Helene, what is it?"

She couldn't stop shaking her head and Harrison got nervous. Were the people of the Desire Card trying to harass his family? Maybe the boss had wanted the thousand bucks he'd given to Naelle and was leaving threatening calls now? He searched his mind for any other secrets he may have forgotten to admit.

"It's happened," she said.

Her makeup had started to run now. He tried to wipe away any smudging but it made it worse.

"What happened?"

"They left a message."

"Who left a message?"

He was shaking her by the shoulders. He didn't want to yell but couldn't help it. The people of the Desire Card would never fully leave him alone. He had seen too much of their headquarters. He was foolish to think he was free; he'd always have to rely on a rearview mirror to make sure they weren't close behind.

"My father did it," Helene said.

"Your father?"

"Harrison, that was the hospital!" she said, hugging him tightly.

He looked in her eyes and saw his reflection: tongue-tied and stammering with a haunted blank stare.

"There's a liver waiting for you," she said, as his muscles atrophied and he almost dropped her.

The cordless slipped from her hands as she regained her balance; the pulsing dial tone the only audible sound except for their consuming, dumbfounded silence.

24

HELENE HAD BOOKED THE GRAND BALLROOM AT the Gotham Hall in Midtown for the Faceless Children's Gala. On the night of the event, she and Harrison stepped through the filigree brass doors onto an inlaid marble floor that showcased the best of stylish and sophisticated Manhattan. They passed through the lounge area where guests checked in and cocktails were served. Harrison declined an offer of champagne from the circling waitstaff, but Helene snatched a glass since she was clearly on edge. She handed him her clutch while she sipped the champagne, careful not to smudge her lipstick.

Before she could finish, Caroline Hendrest glommed onto her arm. Caroline's face radiated pure disgust as usual, her appearance similar to a rat with a pointy nose, barely any lips, and faint whiskers she tried to cover up with too much foundation. She smoothed down her short red hair while pecking at Helene.

"There's a problem with the Bollinger champagne we ordered," Caroline said, tugging at Helene's elbow.

Helene raised her eyebrows to respond and took her time to finish the drink.

Caroline yanked at her strapless dress that wouldn't stay up.

"How many cases did you order?" the woman snapped.

"I thought a dozen."

"Well, there aren't a dozen in the kitchen."

"Caroline," Helene began in the tone of a frustrated schoolteacher, "the guests haven't bought their seats because they're expecting Bollinger; we're here for something greater than that."

Caroline grabbed Helene's glass before she could finish.

"Well, at least save what's left for them," the rat woman said. "Now come, you need to meet Ethel Chamberlain of the Reinwald Foundation." Caroline finally turned to Harrison, acknowledging his presence with a wink. "One of the biggest donors that *I've* secured."

"Looks like you'll have to do without me for the rest of the night," Helene said, taking her clutch back from Harrison and rubbing his arm. "I've seated you next to my father. Last I heard, Mother and Chip were attending as well, but you know how hard it is to pin Chip down."

Caroline tugged at Helene again and the two scooted away. As they neared the grand ballroom, Harrison saw both women put on some frou-frou masks with jewels and elaborate feathers. He reached in his pocket and took out the mask that Helene had gotten for him, a standard eye mask that looked like it belonged to an old-time bandit. He put it on and followed them into the ballroom.

Upon entering through the tall brass doors, he gazed at a room built for royalty. His eyes were immediately drawn upward to the astonishing gilded ceiling. In the center of the gold-leaf honeycombed design sat a giant stained-glass skylight. Up at the front was a podium with an enormous photo print of a sickly African child. He'd seen Helene looking through countless photos over the past few weeks to find the right one that would illuminate her cause. Little N'gosi came from a village in Somalia without any water and an evil warlord who had slaughtered his parents. He had two younger brothers who he took care of by giving them any food he was able to find, leaving him malnourished to the point of grotesque. While N'gosi might not have had a recognizable face prior to today, Helene's hope was that enough media showed up to the gala so he wouldn't be faceless anymore, like all the children in need throughout various underdeveloped countries. Harrison couldn't help but think of the sick girl he'd encountered in the Dharavi slums, wondering if she was still alive or had coughed her last bloody cough.

The guests began to enter wearing their masks, most of them choosing ones that simply covered their eyes and not their entire face. No one had sat down at any tables yet and were either mingling by the open bar or munching on the hors d'oeuvres. He kept his eye out for Jay and the rest of Helene's family, but none of them had shown up yet. He sighed at how happy Helene had been after they got the life-changing message from the hospital last night. He didn't feel it was right to tell her that he wasn't planning on accepting a new liver. First of all, she was thoroughly stressed about the gala and his shocking reveal would destroy her spirit, for she simply glowed all of last night once the two of them retreated into her bedroom after catching their breaths. They didn't sleep together in the biblical sense; he might have tried if she was open to it, but he certainly didn't want to push. She had confessed that she only wanted to be held, and he watched her sleep until the sun rose, her face appearing more relaxed than he'd seen in years. How could he tell this sweet woman he had already accepted death's inevitable embrace, that a rogue like him didn't deserve beneficence, only justice, and that justice shouldn't come in the form of a fat cat named Jay Howell with the power to alter the donor list? Harrison wondered whether he'd be honest with Jay tonight, or if he'd quiver in his presence and remain mute.

Before he could ponder anymore over how to handle Jay, he felt a hand on his shoulder and turned around to see his former friend Whit wearing a *Phantom of the Opera* mask with his tiny Japanese wife Reiko hanging from his other arm. Behind them, his former boss Thom Bartlett stood with his wife Laila, a masculine Brit that towered over them all.

"I'm being the bigger person by coming over to you," Whit said, the grin behind his mask more shit-eating than usual.

"Harry," Reiko cooed, and let go of Whit's arm to give Harrison a hug. She was wearing a peacock mask that became tangled with one of Harrison's cufflinks. "Why we no see you anymore?" She giggled.

"Baby," Whit ordered. "Why don't you try all the

treats being passed around at this thing and tell us which ones are the best?"

"Okay!" Reiko clapped.

"Love," Thom said to his wife Laila, as he stood on his toes to kiss her on the cheek. "Why don't you give us a minute too?"

Reiko yanked the tall woman over to a plate of Ahi tuna being offered in the distance.

"So sorry to hear about your illness, mate," Thom said, extending a hand.

"Just another one of life's curveballs," Harrison replied, making sure to squeeze Thom's hand hard as they shook.

"Glad to see your optimism," Thom babbled, but Harrison was staring at Whit, another asshole in a string of former friends who had fucked him over big time. The old Harrison would've wanted to grab a fork and stab it in this fucker's aorta, but not the new serene Harrison, purveyor of benevolence and forgiveness. He figured Whit was too morally bankrupt to even be worth his time.

"In fact," Harrison said, paying little attention to Thom and slapping Whit on the back. "My name just came up on the donor list for a new liver."

"Smashing," Thom cheered. "Some bubbly to celebrate?"

Thom passed a glass of champagne to Harrison and Whit and kept a third for himself.

"That is good news, Harry," Whit said, as they clinked glasses. "You know," he continued, taking out a card from his front pocket, "I couldn't help but feel bad about our little tête-à-tête at the Palm earlier this spring.

It's a shame my father wasn't able to come through with any of his hospital connections."

"Well, you didn't ask," Harrison said, smiling through their entire exchange.

"It's not like it would've mattered."

"Still...you could've tried."

Whit nodded slightly, almost giving Harrison a true apology, then shrugged.

"It appears like it didn't matter anyway since the gods seem to have you in their favor."

He passed Harrison the card from his front pocket. As Harrison turned it over, his heart shot up into his throat and he choked on the last sip of his drink.

In his hand sat the Desire Card.

"Watch it there, old boy," Thom said.

"Thom and I were going to get some top-notch girls for a pretty penny tonight," Whit said. "It's on me, friend."

Harrison thrust the card back at Whit, as if touching it might alert any of the henchmen to this gala.

"I'll take that as a no," Whit said, stuffing the card back into his pocket.

"What about your wives?" Harrison asked.

Whit and Thom gave each other a look through their masks like Harrison was crazy.

"I remember a time a few months ago when you didn't seem to care about your wife." Thom laughed, with his obnoxious British *har, har, har*.

"Sometimes people change," Harrison responded.

"Yeah, try telling me that while I'm balls deep in some snatch," Whit said.

Thom chortled at that remark, but Harrison refused to laugh along.

339 ALL SINS FULFILLED

"All right then, stiff," Whit said. "Mr. Change is getting a new liver and doesn't want to party with his old friends anymore. I was being fucking generous."

"Now, now, Carmichael," Thom added, "we're not here to peer pressure. Harry's enough of a big boy to make his own decisions."

Thom put his arm around Whit to lead him away, but Whit wasn't budging.

"How are those job prospects looking, huh, Har? Any firms ready to bite?"

Thom shook his head, clearly upset that Whit had to go there.

"It's a beast out there, isn't it?" Whit added.

"If I was still looking to stay in finance," Harrison said, and watched as Whit's smile started to falter. "See, Helene kind of woke me up while she was planning her gala."

"So you're looking to save little African children now?" Whit asked, chuckling.

"Maybe it's time to help the poor instead of making the rich even richer," Harrison said, a little bewildered that those words came from his mouth but glad that they did.

"Well, kudos to you that your making this world a better place while I fuck some hot Brazilian chick on the yacht I'll be purchasing this year."

Whit knocked back the rest of his drink and slammed the glass down.

"And good luck with that liver, Mother Theresa," Whit said, and tapped Thom on the chest for the two to take off. "Those little fly-swatting African babies will certainly be counting on your speedy recovery."

Thom nodded goodbye and he and Whit found

their wives, giving the women hugs and kisses with thoughts of the Desire Card probably swimming in their greedy minds.

Harrison was glad to be rid of them for good.

"Harrison?" he heard someone say from behind him, the accent full of a WASP's cadence, riddled from a lifetime of dry martinis and frigid New England winters.

He turned around to see his mother-in-law Vivien and his brother-in-law Chip. Vi always radiated an elegance that Harrison found uncomfortable to be around, as if she was always making a mental note anytime she thought him uncouth. Tonight she wore a sparkling black gown that had the illusion of being covered in shimmering diamonds— knowing Vi it wouldn't have surprised him if they actually were real. She looked her age because she refused to dye her silver hair, but she worked with a personal trainer daily and had the kind of body that most half her age would die for.

Chip, on the other hand, was clearly the black sheep of the family. Despite the black-tie requirement, his suit was peach-colored as if he was channeling *Miami Vice*. He occasionally ran a joke of a PR firm in Greenwich and was usually coked-up to the point of embarrassment. Most of his time was spent seducing barely legal twink boys who gasped at the size of the manor Jay had bought for him. Right now he seemed to be involved in some text war on his cell and gave Harrison a quick hello before darting away.

"Sometimes I think the nurse switched babies," Vi said, "and the real Chip is some responsible forty-year-old raising what should be my grandbabies while I'm straddled with Sunshine over there."

Harrison had heard this jab of hers before. She had a rotating round of about ten overused one-liners when talking about her family.

"You look well, Vi," Harrison said, and the two moved closer for three successive kisses on the cheek.

"Now I can't same the same for you," she pouted, slurping at her martini. "When Helly told me of your illness." She placed her hand over her heart and squinted. "Of course I thought of the children first. Growing up without a father, heavens no. But my husband is truly a miracle worker..."

"We got the call from the hospital yesterday."

"Just splendid," she said, sucking at her teeth. "I know it'll be a lifestyle overhaul. Once you get a new liver the amount of medications you have to take is criminal."

"Is Jay here?" Harrison asked, peering around the grand room.

"He's on his way. Some Moroccan deal of his fell through so he's bound to be a grump. Something about his new casino so do treat him with kid gloves. I did warn him not to put a damper on Helly's big night."

Even though she was speaking to him, Vivien made it apparent that all of her concentration was directed toward her drink.

Before he could respond, Helene stepped up to the podium and called for everyone to take their seats. Vi seized the opportunity to ask a server for "another dry martini, as dry as the Sahara," then followed Harrison over to their table up front.

First Helene thanked everyone for coming. The large room was packed solid. She spoke of the Faceless Children's Gala being a cause dear to her heart for some time now. Two years ago while doing volunteer work for UNESCO, she had visited a small village in Somalia. Warlords had decimated the village, AIDS and hunger ran rampant, and children younger than her own were left parentless. A little boy named N'gosi touched her the most since he took care of two younger brothers and gave them any food he was able to find. N'gosi was a child like many, just trying to make it to tomorrow, and so she spearheaded this gala along with great assistance from the "invaluable Caroline Hendrest" to bring his story to the public. She told the room to think about the money that they spend each day: a ticket for a show or for a new pair of shoes could mean a world of difference for a child like N'gosi. "Remember his face," she cautioned, "for without our help, these children will disappear for good."

Harrison was impressed by her control of the room. People applauded respectfully. The goal was to get all the attendees to donate more than just their thousand-dollar tickets. Helene had hoped for a million dollars total by the night's end, which would mostly come from wealthy organizations like the Reinwald Foundation that a full-time staffer like Caroline secured, but there were always one or two surprise donations in the mix. It would be these surprise donations that should force UNESCO to see Helene's volunteer work as a necessity, despite any resistance from Caroline Hendrest.

As she passed over the microphone to Caroline, Helene gave Harrison a wink, the same one she'd given during meals with her parents at their giant dining room table where it appeared as if she was seated at the other end of the world—a wink to show she cared. It pained him to think of the conversation they'd have about his upcoming liver transplant. He decided not to tell her his decision tomorrow so she could rest before he'd have to break her heart on Monday.

Caroline started speaking at the podium, but he tuned her out. Helene had joined them at their table and received congratulations from all of her close family and friends. She leaned in toward Harrison and planted a kiss on his cheek that was dangerously close to his lips.

"Thank you for coming," she said, as the two held hands briefly.

"You were brilliant as always."

"Have you seen my father yet?" she whispered.

"No, I can't say I have."

He peered around the room looking for Jay. Most of the guests were seated at their tables and there was no sign of his father-in-law. He shook his head as Helene slunk into her chair, a little burned by Jay's absence.

Just as Harrison started digging into the salad that was being served as a first course, he spied a man wearing a Clark Gable mask. He nearly choked on the piece of lettuce in his mouth and dropped his fork to the floor. Instead of picking the fork back up, he stared in fright at Clark Gable. His breathing became shallow as the blood rushed to his face, and he let out the slightest yelp that caught everyone's attention at his table. His teeth chattered as Clark Gable made his way over. The mask the man wore wasn't as refined as the ones Harrison had seen at the Desire Card's headquarters, more like a Halloween mask, but Harrison knew it had to be the main boss. Bogart had warned him that if he ever ran into a man in a Clark Gable mask he had clearly done something wrong. Even though Bogart said they didn't have the time to come after him anymore, he knew that the main boss wasn't the type of man to let anyone fuck with him.

At the podium, Caroline had handed over the reins to some other lady and everyone at the Gala was focusing on the stage. Harrison slumped down in his seat, hoping that Clark Gable didn't notice him, but out of the corner of his eye, he could see Clark Gable coming closer. The two men locked into a dueling stare as Clark Gable picked up his pace until he was inches away. Harrison debated grabbing a steak knife, but everything was happening too fast until Clark Gable was standing right in front of him, his cold hand on Harrison's shoulder.

"Harrison," Clark Gable said. The voice seemed recognizable, but Harrison couldn't place who it was. He thought it might be one of the Desire Card's henchmen, but then he realized that he didn't know how any of them really sounded due to the speaker boxes that altered their voices.

Clark Gable went to take off his mask as a thousand different scenarios of what might happen next flashed through Harrison's mind. He gripped onto the handle of his knife just as the mask was removed.

To Harrison's astonishment, Jay Howell stood before him.

Harrison let go of the knife, speechless. The room started to spin, slowly at first, until he felt stuck on a tilt-a-whirl.

Jay pulled out a chair and sat down. He placed the

Clark Gable mask on the table, inches away from Harrison. He leaned over, his mouth at Harrison's ear.

"Did I miss Helly's speech?" he whispered.

Harrison nodded, gravely. His throat had closed up and he couldn't breathe, worse than ever before.

"Let's you and I have a talk then," Jay said.

With that, Jay scooped up the Clark Gable mask and proceeded toward an exit, not even looking back to see if Harrison was following. Across the table, Helene was watching her father walk away. She glanced at Harrison, as if he could explain.

Harrison imagined a scenario where Jay cornered him into some back room and knifed him in the gut. He wondered if he was being paranoid. The Clark Gable mask could be nothing more than a coincidence, a gag bought at a costume shop. But Jay did fit the profile of who the main boss would be. He was CEO of an organization that he never really specified, the Howells were the kind of rich that had hospital wings named after them, and Jay had even been the one to get Harrison his interview at Sanford & Co., his direct link to the card.

By now Jay was nearing one of the exits and Harrison couldn't just sit there. He'd have to face Jay sooner or later and resolved that it might as well be now. He stood up and carefully slipped the knife into his pocket, certain he would only use it if Jay struck first. It was one thing to accept dying naturally from his liver disease and another thing to die at the hands of Helene's father.

After excusing himself, he followed Jay into a back room being used for storage of extra tables and chairs. The room had no windows and a light that flickered and buzzed once Harrison turned it on. The door slammed shut behind him, any escape futile.

Pushing seventy years young, Jay retained the linebacker physique that had served him well on the football fields of his youth. His hair was blindingly white, thick like buttermilk, and slicked back in an old-fashioned style. He had tiny eyes, two little black marbles, and a presidential nose that boldly announced his presence upon walking into a room. He'd developed a small potbelly over the years, but ran five miles a day and had a lean, windswept face. This face rarely telegraphed any emotions, and even now, Harrison had no idea what the man was thinking.

"So congratulations," Jay said.

"Congratulations?"

Harrison wondered what kind of game Jay was playing.

"The liver I was able to get you?" Jay said. "Better to talk here where we won't be heard."

"Is that what you wanted to talk to me about?" Harrison asked, treading carefully. Jay was tossing the Clark Gable mask from one hand to the other.

"I come through with my promises," Jay said, chewing on the words.

"Yes...thank you. When Helene told me you wanted to try your hospital connections, I didn't think—"

Jay held up his hand, refusing to hear anymore. It was a gesture Harrison had seen Helene do a thousand times when she was frustrated with him.

"You are the father of my only grandchildren, that is why I did it."

"I think we have other things we should discuss first," Harrison said.

"Such as?"

Harrison nodded at the mask in Jay's hands.

"I need to say what's been on my mind," Jay replied, looping his fingers through the eyes of the mask.

"Go ahead."

"I never wanted Helly to marry you. You were beneath her, and I'm not speaking from a class standpoint. I knew you could never fulfill her, and in turn, you would never be fulfilled either. But you both were young and stubborn and saying how I felt would only have driven her away."

"That's probably true."

"You're goddamn right it's true," Jay barked, as tiny pieces of his spittle ricocheted off Harrison's face.

"You have every right to be upset—"

"You bet your ass I do."

"But if you look at it from my side."

"Your side?" Jay laughed. "Why should I look at anything from your side?"

"I think you'd understand why I did what I did."

"I should kill you," Jay sneered, as Harrison clutched the knife in defense, the tip sticking out his pocket. "And here I'm only helping you live. I've had your number since the minute Helly brought you home. A spineless social climber, that's what you are."

Jay's face had turned a nasty red. He pointed a finger at Harrison and poked him in the chest.

"What are you talking about?"

"When you cheated on my Helly."

"Is *that* what this is about?" Harrison asked, completely confused.

"What do you think this is about?" he yelled, shaking the Clark Gable mask and backing Harrison into a corner.

"The...Desire Card?"

"Exactly. You calling up for some whore. That's why I paid those Indian street kids to put the fear in you and teach you a lesson."

"What are you talking about?"

"In Mumbai. Those kids. They messed around with you, took your watch. I knew you weren't in fucking India for a job interview. It was just another excuse to screw around on my daughter!"

Harrison remembered back in Mumbai when he stepped outside of the club and saw a sleek black car and the silhouette of a man in the back seat. The car drove off and two seconds later the street kids jumped him.

"You did that to teach me a lesson? You're insane—"

"My daughter should be put on a pedestal, not treated like sloppy seconds."

"I never thought of her that way. What happened between us was complicated."

"Oh, spare me your excuses."

"Who was the man that got in the car with you that night? The one with the scars all over his face?"

"One of my operatives. I never travel alone."

"Why was he scarred so bad?"

"That's his business. But let's say I collect people like that. I find them more loyal. For I give them what they've always desired, a mask so they don't have to show their true selves anymore."

"What if one of those kids had hurt me by accident?"

"You know, I never should of bit my tongue about you twenty-five years ago."

The men were nose-to-nose now, Jay's breath reeking of alcohol.

"My family took you in and you repaid us with deceit."

Jay poked Harrison in his stomach, harder this time, a quick punch to the core. Harrison slumped over.

"I never once thought to marry Helene for her money—"

"Bullshit," Jay said, making his hand into a fist. "I should pop you right in the nose."

"I'm not taking the new liver," Harrison cried, holding his hands up to his face. "I won't."

Jay finally stepped back, but kept his fist raised.

"What the hell do you mean?"

"I've been doing a lot of thinking. I don't deserve the liver because of the things I've done."

"What kind of nonsense is that?"

"I'm filth," Harrison said. "You of all people know how low I've sunk."

"You stupid fuck, if you think for one minute that you aren't accepting this liver, you are sadly mistaken."

"No, the universe shouldn't work like that."

"The universe? What the fuck are you babbling about? You do not know what I've had to do to replace that piece of shit liver of yours. Goddamn, you have Brenton and Gracie to think about."

"But it's not right," Harrison pleaded. "It's not fair that you have the opportunity to pay for an organ and some poor person just has to accept their fate."

"I don't have time to listen to this horseshit."

"Why should I be able to buy my life, Jay?"

"First of all, *you* didn't *buy* anything. I had to purchase another goddamn wing at that hospital."

"It doesn't matter if you're good or bad," Harrison said, speaking so fast that it all jumbled into one long word. "As long as you're that one percent..."

"I am sick and tired of having to apologize to ninety-nine percent of the world for my good fortune. I work harder than most to maintain my status."

"What you do is despicable," Harrison said, getting angrier. He reached back into his pocket and grasped at the knife.

"Oh, you motherfucker," Jay said, snarling like a pit bull. "You have no idea what I do, and I refuse to continue with this ludicrous conversation. Take the charity I am offering, get better, and then stay the hell away from my family. I paid for this liver so you could be out of my daughter's life for good. Get it?"

"Wouldn't it have been easier to let me die?"

"As much as you may think I don't have a conscience, when it comes to Helly, I'm soft. This was her wish and I am going to grant it. So you can lose sleep over the morality of your actions, but everyone does what they need to do to get by. And if money is what allows me to do this, then you can't tell me that some poor schmuck wouldn't do the same thing if we switched places."

"It's just not right," Harrison said, exhausted.

Jay made a fist again and punched Harrison in the nose. Harrison reeled back as blood gushed from his nostrils. He mopped it up with hands before it leaked to his tux. Jay crouched over him, his knuckles bright white and ready to attack again. Spit flew from his lips.

He grabbed Harrison by his collar and tugged him to a sitting position.

"I know where she is," Jay said.

"Where who is?"

"The girl, you dumb fuck," he said, letting go of Harrison. He stood back, fixed his hair, and straightened his tux before slipping the Clark Gable mask back on.

"That sweet brown pussy is in some condo down in Punta Cana with her mother and the kid," Jay said. "Bávaro Beach, Villas Mar y Sol. We have records on everyone, Harrison. Shit that goes back to before they were even born. You think because you bought her a plane ticket that she's safe?"

"You leave her alone."

"There are plenty more organs we could take," he said, rubbing his hands together. "Maybe a kidney to sell, or even a heart. She won't be able to live without a heart, will she?"

"You son of a bitch."

"Now, now, Harrison. I'm surprised this whore of yours could cause such a stir. You're certainly worrying about her more than my Helene."

"I'd do anything for Helene," he said, rising to his feet and taking out the knife from his pocket.

"You have a knife? Are you going to fucking stab me? That's not gonna save your dark lovely. In fact, I have employees about to head over to Punta Cana. You need me alive to tell them otherwise."

"You're the devil," Harrison blubbered. He was imagining Naelle in a bathtub full of ice as the people of the Desire Card descended upon her with scalpels in hand.

"The devil?" Jay pondered. "That's a new one. As my alias would say, 'Frankly, my dear, I don't give a damn.'"

A disturbing realization came over Harrison, hitting him like a bat to the head. He stumbled around from the imaginary blow.

"Holy shit...Nagesh Patel," he managed to stutter, as Jay scrunched up his face. "Did you...?" It felt like his stomach had been scooped out and left to spoil. "When I called to have him located...and I was so angry at him...and your people said that he'd been..."

A ball of bile lurched up his throat. He squeezed his eyes shut to keep for puking all over his father-in-law.

"What?" Jay barked. "Spit it out, Harrison."

"Did you have him killed?"

A tiny piece of white crust formed at the corner of Jay's lips that he licked away.

"I've never heard that name before."

"I told your people that he had stolen my money and I needed to find him. Just a few hours later they called with the news that his throat had been slit in some back Mumbai alleyway."

"Newsflash, you narcissistic piece of shit," Jay yelled, as a new piece of spittle returned to the corner of his mouth. "Not everything is some giant plot against you. I just lost millions from Moroccan investors dropping out of the casino I'm building in Macau. These are my kinds of problems; you are a flea. You don't even know the scope of what I command, the thousands in my employ, all them fulfilling the elite's wishes upon a star. Calling up for whores, even for a liver, that's the tip of the iceberg, executions happen to be our specialty, the one thing people are guaranteed to pay all they have."

"What about the girl?"

"What *about* her?"

"Did you...did you pick her as the donor to get back at me in some twisted way?"

Jay dabbed the corner of his lip to remove the spittle. Harrison couldn't tell if he was smiling, gloating even.

"Maybe I did, maybe I didn't, but I only *really* took time out of my busy schedule when you decided to change plans with our...donor. Imagine my surprise when my operatives contacted me about that massive fuck up and I heard you were the cause. The mere fact that you're my son-in-law is the only reason you're not dead." He chewed on "son-in-law" as if it was a rancid piece of meat. "No one has ever put *my* organization in jeopardy like that without winding up with cement blocks for shoes."

"What do you want from me then?"

"First, put the knife away. What I want is for you to take the new liver because that's what Helly wants. Be a fucking father to your kids. As much as you might think I'm a monster, I was a damn good father to Helly and Chip. Whatever they desired, I granted."

"I take the liver and you'll leave Naelle alone?"

"That's funny, I've always thought of her as Candy, but I guess the two of you did become close enough to exchange real names."

"How do I know I can trust you?"

"I swear to spare that prostitute of yours. Scout's honor."

Harrison slid the knife back into his pocket.

"But if you don't divorce Helene after your transplant, if you ever cause her the slightest bit of trouble, or if I find out you haven't stepped up to the plate with my grandkids, if you keep behaving like a fucking animal, or if you so much as mention a word of my organization to anyone including my family, so help me God, I will gut that Dominican bitch like the slimy fish she is. I will forever be watching you now. Today. Tomorrow. Till one of us is dead."

Jay smiled through the Clark Gable mask, then turned on his heels and headed for the door.

"Now clean up yourself, Harrison, my daughter's got some faceless children to save."

25

AFTER HIS LIVER TRANSPLANT SURGERY, HARRISON healed at New York Presbyterian for a few days before spending the rest of his convalescence under Helene's care. She watched over him selflessly like a wartime nurse. Of course he never mentioned the conversation he had with her father, or the truth about Jay's organization; anything more than ignorance might put a questioning mind like hers in danger. He figured Jay could absolve himself to her at his deathbed if his conscience so decided. Besides, doing anything that might piss Jay off even more could be hazardous to Harrison's own speedy recovery. The last thing he wanted was a repeat of what happened at the gala.

Brenton and Gracie proved to be invaluable helpers during the month Harrison spent at home. Now that soccer and ballet had finished, school didn't have quite the pull as those obsessions and the two of them had more time to tend to their father. Gracie surprised him the most, letting down the fortress she erected to keep her emotions at bay. Each night she gave him a private ballet dance and a kiss on the forehead before bed. Brenton provided the comic relief. As far as Harrison was concerned, no amount of arm farts could ever be too much.

As for Helene, Harrison couldn't be more awed by her magnanimity. She had raised about a million dollars in donations for the Faceless Children's Gala and decided to take a leave of absence from UNESCO for a month while they considered making her volunteer position into a paying one. With this time off, she devoted herself to establishing a routine for Harrison so he could be on top of all of his medications once he was on his own. Without the medications, his body might reject the new liver so she wanted to make sure that she could trust him to be responsible. He had to take Cyclosporine every twelve hours to prevent any rejection of the new organ. The drug caused hand tremors, tingling of his hands and feet, and night sweats, but the doctor insisted that was common. In addition, he had to take Prednisone once a day, at least until his liver function improved. This caused him to get stomach ulcers so he began popping Zantac as well. Luckily, he avoided any bacterial, fungal, or viral infections.

Soon the month in Helene's care had regretfully ended. Once he moved out, they proceeded with a divorce in the coming weeks. Both agreed to make it as uncomplicated as possible. All savings and assets were split down the middle, including the Fifth Avenue apartment once it sold. Helene would get the kids, but Harrison would retain supervision rights for one night a week. As his health improved, they would discuss bumping it up to two. She didn't want any child support from him, knowing that it could be a while before he went back to work, and Jay was happy to support the family until UNESCO made a decision about the fate of her employment.

She rented a two-bedroom while waiting out negotiations for an apartment that Jay purchased for them on Columbus Ave. Harrison found a one-bedroom rental on the Upper East Side so he could remain close by once they moved. He looked forward to the once-a-week visits from Brenton and Gracie, giving them the bedroom to sleep in while he hunkered down on the couch. He took them to Museum Mile, the Central Park Zoo, the South Street Seaport, and any other touristy things that they had never done before.

He learned from them that Helene had started seeing a man named Peter who was older and had mostly graying hair. Peter volunteered for an organization that worked in tandem with UNESCO. The two had met about a year ago and then recently ran into one another at a function. Brenton and Gracie had only been introduced to him once when he came to pick up Helene. Brenton didn't have an opinion of him, but Gracie said he had nice teeth. Peter had promised to have the kids over to dinner and would show them pictures of his trip to Botswana and of the safari he took.

A few weeks later, Helene invited Harrison to an event Peter spearheaded that combated animal abuse in third world countries. Helene thought it best that the two men should meet as soon as possible. Peter's hair was mostly graying, but he had a rugged handsomeness that Harrison could never dream of possessing. Peter also had a grip that shifted the bones in Harrison's fingers when the two men shook. He did have nice teeth, as per Gracie's observation, and Harrison could see that this new man excited Helene. He hadn't seen her acting excited in a long time. She and Peter already had a few inside jokes after only a month of dating. Harrison promised himself not to be jealous. He was truly happy for her. Peter was the good-natured type of man primed to make the world a better place; the kind of person Helene should've been with from the start. He could already tell that Peter would be the love of her life.

When Peter asked if Harrison was eventually looking to get back into mergers and acquisitions, Harrison was adamant in his refusal to ever work for a blood-sucking firm like Sanford & Co. again. Peter understood this and suggested staying with M & A, but in the emerging nonprofit sector. A former colleague of his had opened his own boutique investment firm called the Richard Davis Institute a few years back. The firm didn't finance or broker major deals like Harrison did at Sanford & Co.; instead they conducted market and industry research and made introductions to organizations looking to engage in strategic partnerships. Since the economic downturn, Peter said that charities needed to examine their financial capacities more and some were looking toward M & A as a way of restructuring their finances in order for their programs and services to continue. Currently, the Richard Davis Institute was one of the few investment banking firms operating in the nonprofit sector, and Peter knew that they were looking to hire and expand.

An interview was set up and Harrison bought a new suit. He'd lost some weight since the surgery and all his old suits proved to be too roomy. Upon entering the offices of the Richard Davis Institute, he was struck by how minimal a setup it was. Richard Davis had one secretary, a smiling lady with a large bowl of butter-scotches on her desk, and only two other people working at cubicles. An empty room sat to the left of Richard Davis' office that Harrison assumed would be his should he accept the job.

Richard Davis was what Harrison would call an aging hippie. His hair was long and stringy, gray as well. Numerous plaques that proved his munificence adorned the walls. He wore sandals and his toes were gnarled. He'd just returned from Lima, Peru where he helped transact a merger between an elementary school and an emerging charity called Rocking the Classroom, which strove to complement required literary curriculums with innovative musical tech-niques. Next on deck was an organization called Book Launch that aimed to provide quality, high-interest books to underdeveloped schools and was looking to be acquired by a larger organization with the financial capabilities and leadership to continue its vision. Currently there was an organization based out of Port-au-Prince, Haiti that wished to focus on the schools in their own troubling country before expanding to the rest of the Caribbean and ultimately the United States.

Harrison discussed his role at Sanford & Co. in great detail, obviously avoiding any of the "perks" he'd been given that might turn off a humble man like Richard. Richard smiled throughout the entire exchange and offered him a butterscotch cupcake that his secretary Rosie had made.

"Why the nonprofit sector, Harrison, if I may ask?"

Richard questioned, licking a blob of frosting from his thumb.

"Not to speak in clichés—"

"Sometimes that's all that suffices."

"I've had a year of personal reflection," Harrison said, allowing himself one bite of the cupcake, a small sugary morsel that wasn't included in his new diet. "I don't know if Peter mentioned my recent liver transplant?"

"Yes, he did," Richard said, as his smile faded. "You look well if I may say so."

"Thank you."

Richard smiled again and took another cupcake.

"Anyway, I certainly learned a lot during my years at Sanford & Co., but my work there had no meaning. I didn't know any better so I never thought twice about it, but in retrospect, my goal was purely to make rich companies even richer. And I had lost myself in the process."

Harrison wondered if he sounded phony, but he was truly speaking from the heart.

"I took a trip to Mumbai a few months back," he said, as Richard raised his brushy eyebrows. "While I was touring the slums, I met a little girl who was younger than my own daughter. She was dying."

"I've done work in many of those slums before," Richard said, putting down the cupcake as his eyes became misty.

"Sometimes one event can change your entire perspective. Here I was moderately well off and had dealt with millions of dollars on a daily basis, but this poor girl would still die. And even if I could save her, how many other little girls would perish from diseases that we have the ability to cure? I had a strong desire to give back in any way I could. Now I know there's always volunteer work, but I'm going through a divorce and need to focus on providing for my family first and foremost."

"Sometimes the plates we've stacked on top of one another are dangerously close to toppling over," Richard said, nodding his head for Harrison to understand.

"I can't see myself going to back into M & A and working for some big corporate firm. I'm so much more than that."

Richard took a bite of the cupcake, considered Harrison's words, and then extended a sugarcoated hand.

"I think you're right. But so you know, you're certainly overqualified for this position and the money will be considerably less than you're used to."

"If money was what I wanted then I'd find another Sanford & Co. clone."

The two men shook hands.

"This is all very inspiring to hear, Harrison. So when can you start?"

———

Harrison threw himself into his work at the Richard Davis Institute. Delighted with Harrison's experience, Richard let him take the lead with the merger of Book Launch and the organization in Port-au-Prince. At the end of the month, Harrison would head down to Haiti to oversee the merger between the two and meet with the administration at the first school in Haiti that would receive the charity.

He had gotten into the routine of taking his meds and seeing his kids on a weekly basis, but other than the time he spent at work, he was thoroughly lonely. The idea of a woman entering his life seemed far-fetched. How could he even begin to go about meeting someone in his state? Since he met Helene so young, he had never learned how to date.

One day he came home exhausted from work to find a postcard in his mailbox that had been forwarded from his old Fifth Avenue apartment. The postcard had no return address, but had a picture on the front of a beautiful Punta Cana beach with the message "*Greetings from Beyond!*" He turned it over to find a short note from Naelle written in flowery, child-like handwriting.

> *Mister –*
>
> *Wanted to send a note to the address you gave and tell you that me and my little girl Yeesica are doing fine in the D.R.*
>
> *I hope you aren't sick no more and got your liver o.k.*
>
> *Thank you for giving me money so I could come back to my home.*
>
> *I'm sorry if I said you weren't good. Your gooder than most.*
>
> *Besos mucho,*
> *Naelle*

He re-read the postcard three times, picturing the sound of Naelle's broken English. He even smelled the card hoping to catch her scent. He still remembered her address in the DR that Jay had told him. What if he showed up at her door? Would she slap him across the face or take him in her arms? Helene had found love again. Didn't he deserve the same? In a few weeks he'd be traveling down to Haiti anyway; it'd be easy to head over to Punta Cana as well. If Naelle rejected him, he'd sadly move on, but at least he'd know that he took a chance. She could very well turn out to be the love of his life.

So he called the airline to extend his trip to Punta Cana for a few extra nights, picturing the lolling waves as his head nestled in Naelle's bosom while she sang her siren song.

———

Since the merger in Port-au-Prince was a lot less stressful than any he'd done at Sanford & Co., he found that he didn't miss having a drink or any pills to function properly. He was too much in the moment. At the school receiving the charity, an assembly was held to introduce him along with the people from Book Launch and the organization in Haiti that fronted the money for the project. The entire auditorium applauded. Afterwards, he helped pass out new books in a classroom of kids around Gracie's age. The kids all sat wide-eyed as he read from an opening chapter of *Harry Potter*, the magic unspooling in their imaginations. After he finished, he got hugs from everyone and couldn't help but think that he'd never been hugged after completing a merger before.

The next morning he took a quick flight on a

rickety ten-seat plane over to Punta Cana. He checked into his hotel at Bávaro Beach to drop off his bags and headed over to Villas Mar y Sol where Naelle lived. Her mother's condo was one of about twelve units, in walking distance from the beach. He headed through a rusted gate and passed a leathery old woman sunning herself in the courtyard. Some lawn furniture had been scattered around an empty pool. The smell of grilling wafted from a window on the second floor. The old woman regarded him with one eye open.

"I'm looking for Naelle," he said to the old woman, who barely blinked at his request. "She lives here with her mother, her *madre*."

The old woman shielded her eyes from the sun and pointed toward the open window where he smelled grilling.

"*Gracias.*"

The woman closed the one eye she had opened and went back to her tan.

He headed up the stairs to the second floor, his knees knocking into one another. He'd been nervous since he woke up that morning, too busy in Haiti to worry about how Naelle might respond, but now the reality of the situation was starting to sink in. He had no idea what he wanted from Naelle. His children lived in Manhattan so it wasn't like he could pick up and move to the DR, and he knew Naelle would never take the risk by heading back to New York. Still, over the next few months, he'd be back in Haiti to assist in more mergers and he wondered if that might be enough for her.

As he stood at her door he nearly chickened out, but

something else beside his brain seemed to take control. He found himself ringing the doorbell.

The door opened and a little girl in pigtails stood there.

"Hi...is your mommy home?"

The girl stared back without responding. From the distance, Naelle shuffled over and hugged the girl close to her chest.

"Sorry, she always likes to open the door," Naelle said, brushing her hair out of her face. It took her a second to recognize who he was.

"Yeesica, *vayas a su abuelita.*"

The girl ducked under her mother's arm and scurried back in the house toward her grandmother who was hunched over the stove grilling plantains with some eggs.

Naelle stuck her head out of the doorframe and looked around the condominium.

"It's just me," Harrison said, throwing his hands up in the air.

"*Coño!*" Naelle said. "I knew I shouldn't of sent you that postcard."

"Can I come in to talk?"

She tapped her foot against the linoleum, shook her head.

"No, I've told my mother about everything you did. She'll come after you with a pan."

"I had to see you," he said, as she crossed her arms. "Can we go down to the beach?"

She looked toward the beach but didn't move.

"The people from your old job aren't after you. I made a deal with their boss."

"You saw the boss?" she asked, afraid. She clamped

her hand over her mouth and began to close the door but he put his foot in the doorjamb.

"I promise, Naelle. We're square with them. You're square. I promise."

"You just said 'promise' twice."

"I promise you a thousand times over. I came all the way here for you."

"Why?" she snapped, rolling her eyes.

"*Tu eres mi angel guardiánte*," he said, unable to control his smile. He'd been practicing that line over and over.

She didn't answer him, just chewed the hell out of a piece of gum and then blew a bubble that popped.

"*Mama!*" she said, calling back into the condo. "*Me voy a la playa.*"

He heard her mother murmur a half-hearted response.

Naelle stepped outside and closed the door. She wasn't wearing any shoes, her soles hardened from a barefooted life in the DR. She had on a bra that could pass as a bikini top and jeans shorts with the buttons opened to let her stomach breathe. She looked good to Harrison. Punta Cana had browned her skin nicely, lightened her hair.

The two of them walked out of the condominium down to the beach. The weather was beautiful, no passing clouds in the sky. Since it was the end of summer, there weren't too many tourists along the beach. Harrison imagined it as their own private paradise. He took off his shoes and socks, rolled up his pants, and sunk his toes into the fine, hot sand.

She kept looking over her shoulder.

"I promise you those people aren't coming here," he said.

"I've gotten used to watching my back."

"You don't have to—"

"Why are you really here?" she asked, pissed off now as if he was wasting her time. "You had asked me to tell you I was okay, so I did. Isn't that enough?"

"How is your scar healing?" he asked, pointing at the fading scar on her chest.

"It's there as a reminder for me not to be stupid again."

"Same with mine," he said, touching the tender area around his own scar. "I'm so sorry, Naelle—"

She cut him off, held up her hand like Helene would, which only made him love her even more.

"I don't want your sorry. What's that gonna do for me? I got myself into that mess. I only have myself to blame."

"I got a new liver through a hospital."

She shrugged her shoulders. "Yeah, I figured someone like you would get what he wanted, I wasn't worried."

"I'm doing work in Haiti. I brought books to some very poor schools."

"Okay, so you got some kids some books, should I make a parade?"

"I had to see you."

She'd been walking faster than him; he had to take double the amount of steps to keep up. Finally they fell in sync and he took hold of her elbow. She reacted by jerking her arm away.

"I don't like to be grabbed—"

"I didn't mean it—"

"After what happened," she said, her eyes welling up.

"I completely understand."

"I should go back to my mother's place. Breakfast will be getting cold."

"Will you sit with me?" He sighed. "Just for a moment? To watch the waves?"

She uncrossed her arms and plopped down. His knees cracked as he did the same.

"Do you believe in fate?" he asked.

"I don't know. Fate? What does that even mean?"

"It means that things happen for a reason."

"Like God's work or something?"

A motored boat took a parasailer out on the water. He and Naelle both watched as the parasail lifted up into the sky.

"Some days I don't believe in God," she said, running her fingers through the sand. "Well, I'm starting to believe a little more again."

"That's good."

Her eyes cut into him, revealed all of her pain.

"Is it?" she said, brushing the sand off her palms. "Where was God when I was being sliced open?"

"You were closed up eventually, weren't you?"

She laughed under her breath.

"So tell me about this God of yours that's so great," she said, her voice losing patience.

"I don't really believe in God. The thought of one being controlling the world with puppet strings...it's too much. But I do believe in something more."

"And this is the 'fate' that you speak of?"

"I've been thinking about this a lot lately. It'd make sense if we have many different fates, many different paths that might lie ahead based on the kind of person we are. If we're cruel to others, or if our lives are purely driven by temptation, then our path will be torturous. Maybe not right away, but eventually."

She scrunched up her face and he could tell he was losing her.

"But if we don't sell our souls, if we strive to be as good as we possibly can be, then our paths will reflect that goodwill and keep that so-called devil at bay."

"So do good and good things will happen to you?"

"Yeah, that's what I believe, what everyone should believe."

"Is that what brought you here, Mister?"

The motorboat slowed down as the parasailer descended into the water.

"Can you call me Harrison? And yes, that's what brought me here. I want to do good things for you. I think we can be good for each other."

He chanced it by taking her hand and letting their fingers become entwined. Her fingernails had been repainted with the silver star decals he remembered. To his surprise, she didn't recoil. She had to have been thinking about him since she returned to Punta Cana. Some crazy magnetic energy existed between them, too confusing to put into words but clearly apparent. The small space between them seemed to magically glow.

"I'll be here for the next couple of nights," he said.

Her lips moved to speak, but there were no words.

"Can I take you to dinner?"

She rested her chin on her shoulder and gazed at the parasailer that dove down into the water to cool off.

"We can start over," he said. "I can show you how good I could be."

She licked her lips that were brimming with sweat. "*Ay, coño*, I don't know—"

"Just dinner. I've read that a typical meal here is called *la bandera*, made with rice, red beans and some type of meat."

"You pronounced it wrong," she said, the corner of her mouth turning upwards. "*La bandera*. There's no accent on the vowels."

The motorboat sped off into the horizon, the beach now empty of sound. The parasailer looked like some blurred phantasm as he swam closer to the shore.

"So is that a yes, Naelle?"

They were still holding hands. He took that as a good sign. She blew a bubble half the size of her head that popped against her face.

"Here," he said, as he reached over with his free hand to wipe away the sticky gum.

Once her mouth was clean, he moved in for a kiss, delicate and without a tongue, a true first kiss more intimate than anything they'd done before. She tasted like watermelon from the gum she chewed. He loved watermelon.

She pulled away after what seemed like hours of delight to him, but it was a matter of seconds. The tropical sun made for an excellent spotlight, its rays divine and shimmering. A perfect postcard picture—"*Greetings from Beyond!*"

She giggled into her shoulder, tossed back her hair. "I told you when I first met you that I tasted sweet."

The parasailer had disappeared now, leaving them isolated in their own paradise. Harrison resigned that he would do whatever he could to make it work with Naelle, even though oceans separated them. He desired her from the depths of his very being, enough to drive him insane if she didn't reciprocate, but he was certain that she would in time.

She relaxed against his shoulder and closed her eyes as the tide licked the shore by their feet. An object was washing up on the sand, some vestige that the parasailer had left behind when he dove down. Harrison strained his eyes to see it more clearly as a wave kicked the object into his lap.

He looked down as the Clark Gable mask stared up him with its empty eyes.

His body ran cold. He thought to fling it off of him as if it was a ticking bomb, but he didn't want to alarm Naelle. Her eyes were closed and she remained blissfully innocent. His stomach turned noisily as he scanned the beach for the parasailer but didn't see anyone.

This new life he desired with Naelle, evocative and roaring in its simplicity, was nothing more than a pipe dream. He wanted it badly enough to believe in its existence, but he needed to accept that he'd always be monitored, the eyes of judgment forever staring back. Jay would never allow him true happiness. His ex-father-in-law had the power and the means to put him at the bottom of a river without ever having it traced back. Sparing Harrison's life was all the charity someone like Jay would be capable of. And if Harrison would ever attempt to live a life filled with excitement and pleasure, or even worse if he'd devolve into a sinner again, he knew the Clark Gable mask would be the last thing he'd ever see before his execution.

He nodded to show that he understood this message, since one of the henchmen from the Desire

Card would certainly be watching. Then he flung the mask back into the ocean to get washed up by the tide before Naelle saw anything.

She was sitting back, her eyes still closed, taking in the hot sun. He wanted to reach out and touch her smooth skin one last time, but it'd be too risky. So with a lump in his throat, he studied the glistening drop of sweat dangling from her eye like a tear. As it dripped to the sand, he stood up quietly, knowing he had no other choice but to walk away, a trail of footprints the only evidence he'd ever been there.

AUTHOR'S NOTE

This tale has had a long journey into print, but that's only allowed the universe of the Desire Card to expand. It began as a stand-alone novel about a pretty terrible guy who works on Wall Street and needs a liver after abusing his own. Right now, I've finished the third book in the series with the second *Prey No More* coming out soon. It'll be five books in total. I could never have imagined the Desire Card would have so many tentacles.

As an organization that prides itself on granting *Any wish fulfilled...for the right price*, the Desire Card represents the genie in a bottle for those rich enough to purchase their fantasies. The book began after the recession and during Occupy Wall Street, a movement against economic inequality. Whether in New York or India, money becomes the source of evil for the characters. For Naelle, who needs it to send to her daughter in the DR and takes a job at the amoral card, or Harrison who believes he has the means to buy a second chance at life, or Jay with the capability to amass enough riches to control whoever he desires. The moral line blurs between what they will do to get what they want.

As for the readers, ask yourself what line you would cross if you were that desperate too?

ACKNOWLEDGMENTS

I'd like to thank Chris McVeigh for being so excited about the series when he read the first book on a flight. To Chris Rhatigan for his precise edits, along with Fiona Davis and everyone at Fahrenheit Press for nurturing the novel so well.

For my agent Sam Hiyate, who always believed that Harrison Stockton could be embraced by readers and never gave up on the manuscript.

For all the readers who offered feedback and guidance throughout its many edits over the years all the way back to 2012. Thank you, Vicky Forsberg, Brooke Lombardy, Erin Conroy, Dani Grammerstorf-French, and Mom. Jackie Saunders for her medical advice. And to all my friends and family who showed support and had encouraging words.

To Dad, who was always my best and first editor. He didn't like the way the novel ended originally so I changed it and made it a ton better. He's not here any longer to see this be published, but I am thankful for his love of books and all he taught me.

And always to Central Park and my tree where a good chunk of a first draft was written during a particularly mild winter. Also to the New York Public Library on 42nd Street where the final drafts were honed.

A THOUGHT-PROVOKING THRILLER WHERE NO ONE IS SAFE IN THIS MENACING WEB OF DECEIT.

When the granddaughter of a rich and powerful CEO is abducted, a vicious ripple effect destroys the lives of everyone connected.

Ex-Army sniper J.D. Storm kidnaps the granddaughter of The Desire Card's head guy-in-charge—his former boss, known only as Clark Gable—in the hopes that he can lure Gable out into the open. But J.D. is quickly reminded that the illusive organization's master schemer won't stand for being toyed with.

As Gable is in the throes of rebuilding his organization, he's threatened by Laurence Olivier—the sociopathic head of the Card's international office, who sees this time of weakness an as opportunity to seize control.

Meanwhile, Detective Monica Bonner, who recently lost her son and watched her marriage disintegrate, is assigned to the kidnapping case. She soon finds herself plunged into the underbelly of The Desire Card, where her obsession for justice will not only endanger her, but her loved ones as well.

As these lives converge...no one is safe.

A pulse-pounding thriller, *Vicious Ripples* follows those indebted to this sinister organization—where the ultimate price is the cost of one's soul.

"Lee Matthew Goldberg's The Desire Card is a

character-driven, enthralling thriller series that introduces readers to a dark underworld powered by an equally mysterious organization loaded with as much menace as promise." —Alex Segura, acclaimed, award-winning author of *Blackout* and *Secret Identity*

AVAILABLE AUGUST 2022

Lee Matthew Goldberg is the author of eight novels including *The Ancestor* and *The Mentor* and the YA series *Runaway Train*. His books are in various stages of development for film and TV off of his original scripts. He has been published in multiple languages and nominated for the Prix du Polar. *Stalker Stalked* will be out in Fall '21. After graduating with an MFA from the New School, his writing has also appeared as a contributor in *Pipeline Artists*, *LitHub*, *The Los Angeles Review of Books*, *The Millions*, *Vol. 1 Brooklyn*, *LitReactor*, *The Big Idea*, *Monkeybicycle*, *Fiction Writers Review*, *Cagibi*, *Necessary Fiction*, *Hypertext*, *If My Book*, *Past Ten*, the anthology *Dirty Boulevard*, *The Montreal Review*, *The Adirondack Review*, *The New Plains Review*, *Maudlin House*, *Underwood Press*, and others. His pilots and screenplays have been finalists in *Script Pipeline*, *Book Pipeline*, *Stage 32*, *We Screenplay*, the *New York Screenplay*, *Screencraft*, and the *Hollywood Screenplay* contests. He is the co-curator of *The Guerrilla Lit Reading Series* and lives in New York City. Follow him at LeeMatthewGoldberg.com.

CPSIA information can be obtained
at www.ICGtesting.com
Printed in the USA
LVHW042356110722
723217LV00015B/549